counting down to you

ALSO BY SARAH J. HARRIS

The Colour of Bee Larkham's Murder

One Ordinary Day at a Time

Meet Me on the Bridge

counting down to you

SARAH J. HARRIS

LAKE UNION
PUBLISHING

This is a work of fiction. Names, characters, organizations, places, events, and incidents are either products of the author's imagination or are used fictitiously. Any resemblance to actual persons, living or dead, or actual events is purely coincidental.

Text copyright © 2025 by Sarah J. Harris
All rights reserved.

No part of this book may be reproduced, or stored in a retrieval system, or transmitted in any form or by any means, electronic, mechanical, photocopying, recording, or otherwise, without express written permission of the publisher.

Published by Lake Union Publishing, Seattle

www.apub.com

Amazon, the Amazon logo, and Lake Union Publishing are trademarks of Amazon.com, Inc., or its affiliates.

EU Product Safety contact:
Amazon Publishing, Amazon Media EU S.à r.l.
38, avenue John F. Kennedy, L-1855 Luxembourg
amazonpublishing-gpsr@amazon.com

ISBN-13: 9781662525278
eISBN: 9781662524929

Cover design by Emma Rogers
Cover image: © Tatgynsy © Evgeniya Khudyakova © Arman Emon © Pacha M Vector © ArtForYou © Piyanat nethaisong © kimman © Panadesign © Artic Concept © Zara's Gallery / Shutterstock

Printed in the United States of America

For Mum and Dad, with much love.

1

SOPHIE

Saturday, 17 December 2016

Numbers are everywhere.

The mud-brown carpet in Joan's sitting room contains 3,095 geometric shapes, the Christmas tree has 71 baubles and 587 flashing lights, and rain pounds against the window at 63 decibels. But the most important figures tonight are 5 hours, 39 minutes and 23 seconds. That's how long I have left to prevent Joan Harding's death. Dotted along the red-tinsel-lined shelf are 6 framed family photos. Her son, Trevor, and grandchildren, Nadia and Mikey, gaze imploringly at me as I perch on the edge of the threadbare sofa. I shiver, and not just from the cold.

Today will be different from all those other times. I won't let my lovely friend die.

Her neighbour's front door slams shut, making the glass ornaments shudder. One falls off the tree, smashing. Has the vibration set off a fatal chain of events elsewhere in the semi? Could something seriously injure Joan while she makes hot drinks? I've secretly removed the sharp knives from her drawer in case she's destined to suffer a freak accident. But she *could* spill boiling water and go into shock if her hand jolts while pouring the kettle . . .

I stand too quickly, steadying myself on the settee arm as blood rushes to my head.

'Joan? Do you need a hand making the tea?'

Panic flutters in my chest when she doesn't reply and I dart into the hall, stopping when her voice echoes from the kitchen. She's chatting to Trevor on the phone.

'It will be fine, love,' she says. 'I'll let you know later what I decide.'

Exhaling deeply, I return to the sitting room and peer out of the rain-spattered window. Wan headlights penetrate the darkness shortly before a car pulls away from outside next-door's house, windscreen wipers flapping. Earlier, I'd spotted Joan's thirty-something neighbour clutching a bunch of red roses. Steve has dark-brown hair, a patchy goatee and a whopping 21,917 days left to live. He might be soaking wet and late for his night out, but he doesn't have anything critical to worry about for another six decades.

Joan isn't as fortunate. I sit down, chewing my nails. The clock on the mantelpiece ticks unbearably loudly. It's 6.24 p.m. I focus on the numbers in Joan's patchwork quilt to distract me from her horribly low digit. She made the cover from Nadia's and Mikey's old babygrows and toddler clothes. It contains 40 tulips – her favourite flower – made from 120 geometric shapes. Her sewing basket has 15 cotton reels and she's made 16 neat stitches on the elbow of her threadbare cardigan.

Despite sounding like a massive maths geek, I gained a D in the subject at GCSE – that was when I used to see the world like everyone else. But ever since my brain injury after prom last summer, I see statistics for every object and person. They appear above them as if on an invisible screen. But even if I could stretch out and touch the digits, my ability doesn't come with an on/off button. When I described the figures to my consultants after the car crash, they claimed meds would clear my 'floaters'. They didn't. The only neurosurgeon who believed I could see things others couldn't said the tissue damage was irreversible. That was medical language for saying I was totally screwed.

'Here we go, love.'

Joan's pale-blue eyes narrow with concentration as she shuffles into the room with the tea tray. I flinch when I see her dismal figure – *1* – even though it's been present all day, along with her hand-knitted Christmas pudding jumper.

'Let me get that for you.'

My hands tremble as I take the tray and place it on the table, making the china clink and a spoon shiver. Joan sits down heavily next to me, pulling the cover over her knees.

'Ooh, it feels good to take the weight off my feet. I'm weary but you've spoilt me rotten today, Sophie. I don't know what I've done to deserve it!'

Shakily, I pour the tea and grab a tissue to mop the spilt liquid in the saucers. I'd saved up from my cleaning and house-sitting jobs to treat Joan to a shopping trip in Plymouth city centre, followed by dinner at Nando's, to disrupt her normal routine. Usually on Saturdays, she walks past a building site on the way to local stores, as well as the homes of a pit bull owner and a drug dealer. I needed her to avoid these hazards since she's in good health and I've ruled out a heart attack or stroke causing her death today, aged 73 years, 2 months and 9 days.

'It's an early Christmas present to say thank you for your friendship. It means a lot to me. I always look forward to our sewing lessons.'

Joan smiles broadly, patting my hand. 'It's a pleasure, dear. I enjoy our chats and it's lovely to share my hobby with someone. My grandchildren have never been interested in quilting, but you have quite the eye for it. Fate must have brought us together that day!'

Did it?

I was crying on a bench in the rain outside the local library, overwhelmed with loneliness and grief, completely on my own after Mum's accident a month earlier. I was still mourning the loss of my best friend, Lily Palmer, last summer and the split from my boyfriend, Adam Bailey, when Mum drowned in Bali.

Joan had stopped and asked if I was okay. My vision was blurry with tears, but her figure was visible – a miserably low 112 days. I stood up to leave, claiming 'boy trouble', but Joan had pulled me in for a hug, saying I looked like I needed one. I'd cried harder then, her embrace reminding me of the 'famous' hugs Adam used to give. *They* came with a '100 per cent guarantee' to make me feel better. That bleak August afternoon, Joan's cuddle had a similar effect – it was the first human touch I'd experienced in months. Afterwards, she'd mopped my tears and suggested we went for a cuppa to talk things through. We've met a couple of times a week ever since and she's taught me how to sew – and laugh again.

Changing her fate is my way of giving something back. Admittedly, nothing I've tried before has altered anyone's digits. I'd pushed a man away from collapsing scaffolding on his last day, but he was struck by a car as he waved to me while crossing the road immediately afterwards. Mrs Berg had employed me to house-sit while visiting relatives in Stockholm with her husband and two young children. I'd hidden their passports because their numbers ran out on the day of their flight. But later, I discovered her husband had driven them to the Swedish Embassy in London to apply for emergency travel documents and they all died in a head-on crash with a lorry. Next, I distracted a drunk homeless man and prevented him from taking a dip at Bovisand beach, only to watch from a distance as he argued with a friend, who killed him with a single punch minutes later. My catalogue of failures goes on and on . . .

Could I have been defeated previously because I didn't know any of these people well?

There was nothing I could do for Lily after the crash and Mum didn't hang around long enough for me to try, but I have a greater understanding of my ability now. Hopefully, being closely involved in Joan's life over the last 3 months and 21 days has given me an advantage. I've researched her habits and made a list of all the potential risks.

Joan takes a gulp of tea and glances at the clock above the fireplace. 'I don't mean to hurry you, love, but it's bingo tonight. I'll need to leave in ten minutes.'

I grip the edge of the sofa as the room swims. The ticking sound is deafening. Aside from her twinkling Christmas lights, which could malfunction and burst into flames, this trip is one of the main hazards. The branch of a large tree on her route to the social club has shifted by 5 degrees in the last month. This, combined with the wind and driving rain, could increase the weight of the wood and bring it crashing on to the pavement.

'No! You mustn't go out in this weather. It's not a good idea.'

'You sound like Trevor!' Joan says with a laugh. 'He wanted me to call a taxi, but I told him a little rain never did me any harm. It'll only take a quarter of an hour to walk.'

'You shouldn't get a cab either. Stay inside where it's safe. *Please.*'

The lines between Joan's eyes deepen. 'What is it, love? You're trembling like a leaf.'

I shake my head.

'You can tell me anything.'

'I know. You've been like a surrogate gran, the only person who's cared about me in a long time.' I take another breath. 'I know this sounds crazy and melodramatic, but I'm worried something terrible will happen tonight and I'll lose you.'

Joan reaches out and takes my hand. 'I'm touched you're trying to protect me, Sophie. I know you've been struggling since your mum's accident, but you mustn't worry. I'm wearing my lucky jumper and have no intention of dying!'

She pulls me in for a hug, the way she did when we met. I bury my head into her jumper and sob over my losses, still so raw it feels as though I was bereaved yesterday. After working out what the dwindling numbers meant, I'd warned Mum last Christmas that she had 7 months to live. Instead of bringing us closer, she turned our house into an Airbnb and left in early March on a one-way plane ticket 'to make the most of seeing the world while she could'. Wrapped in Joan's arms now, I cry for Lily and the life I left behind in south Devon: I can never see Adam, Lily's boyfriend Tom, or her parents again. They were my 'real' family back home in Modbury, but I've lost everyone that mattered.

Pain and grief sever my heart in two. It makes no difference how many numbers I see, I'll never find the right sequence to mend it.

'There, there. Let it out, love. You've had a rough time. But things will get better, I promise.' Joan strokes my hair gently. 'Will it help if I give bingo a miss?'

The knot in my chest loosens and I brush away my tears. 'You'd do that for me?'

'Of course!' She picks up her phone and taps out a message. 'There! I've told Trevor you've talked me into staying in. I'll have an early night.' She leans over and kisses the top of my head. 'Please don't fret. I'm here whenever you need me, including over the holidays. I hate the thought of you being on your own. You must join me and Trevor's family for Christmas lunch.'

'I'd love that, thank you!' The tension dissolves from my shoulders as we embrace tightly.

I've made certain she'll be here on 25 December, haven't I?

My close connection with her *must* have saved her life.

Joan breaks apart first. 'You should get a move on – the roads might flood, and the buses will be bad.'

I hesitate. Ideally, I'd stay until shortly after midnight to make sure she's safe, but I can't ask to sleep here. That might freak her out. I should return to my bedsit.

'I'll listen to the radio in bed and mend clothes – nothing risky,' Joan says, as if reading my mind. 'Why don't you come back next weekend? We'll carry on making Trevor's log cabin quilt – take this section, to practise your stitching. I'm including Chester!'

'Great!' I take the green fabric, which has a printed picture of her son's rough collie in the centre. Yellow and brown strips of material are pinned around it.

I follow her into the hall and pull on my anorak, scooping up my rucksack.

She kisses my cheek. 'Thank you for being such a caring friend.'

'You too!'

Wind blows in a funnel of water as she opens the door, spraying the floor. I step out and wrestle to keep my hood up in the gale.

'Remember to turn off your Christmas tree lights,' I shout before she disappears inside.

I pelt down the path, triggering a security light fixed above next-door's porch. It illuminates a skip on the drive, which contains a sink, kitchen cabinets and an old gas boiler. My socks are sodden within seconds. Further along the flooded pavement, the tree groans in warning, but I don't slow or stop. I try not to worry about how many days *I* have left. Staring in mirrors has never revealed a glimpse of my number; the date of my death is a mystery. I pass beneath the sagging branch and increase my pace. Three seconds later, a loud splintering sound reverberates. I spin around as 152 kilograms of timber smashes on to the pavement.

Yes!

I punch the air with joy. Joan would have been crushed to death if she'd walked beneath it. Our friendship has saved her life. I shove my hands into my pockets, searching for my gloves, and feel something rectangular and stiff. I pull out Joan's bus pass – I've accidentally picked it up. I hurry back to stick it through her letterbox, my heart light.

Suddenly, a huge explosion booms, setting off car alarms. Bricks and debris pelt on to the road with heavy thuds. Someone screams. My ears ring and numbers swirl treacherously in front of me like a swarm of poisonous insects. I run blindly towards the deathly sounds, tripping and stumbling until I reach number 40.

Breath is squeezed from my lungs and my blood turns to ice. Joan's house is no longer standing, and neither is her next-door neighbour's. Both homes are reduced to piles of rubble. Flames lap hungrily over the shells of the buildings, and smoke spirals high into the sky.

People run from nearby houses towards the carnage.

'Someone ring the fire brigade!' a man yells.

I'm frozen to the spot, unable to pull out my phone. I can't tear my gaze from the charcoaled carcass of Joan's house; the wreckage is unsurvivable.

'Crews are on their way,' a woman calls back. 'The operator's asking if anyone could be inside the houses?'

An older female voice pipes up. 'Joan's usually at bingo tonight, but the weather may have kept her indoors.'

'Steve's taking his wife out for dinner to celebrate their anniversary,' a man adds. 'They wanted to get away from the building work – they're having their kitchen refitted.' He pauses. 'Oh God! The force of the explosion . . . Nothing else could bring down two houses like this apart from a ruptured gas pipe.'

My knees give way and I sink to the pavement as I remember the boiler in the neighbour's skip. I hadn't registered the danger lurking in plain sight. I slump on to my side. I don't feel the slick wetness of the concrete against my cheek, or through my clothes; I can't feel anything at all.

'I think she's gone into shock,' someone cries.

'Joan,' I whisper.

'What was that?' A young woman crouches beside me. 'You think Joan's home?'

I nod and close my eyes. I've failed *again*. I'm responsible for the death of my friend and everyone else I've tried to help. Lily's fatal injuries last summer were all my fault.

Blinding lights, smashing glass and ripping metal.

I want to rewind the numbers to the days before that awful prom night and replay them in a new order that saves Lily, Mum, Joan and all those strangers. It will take me back to Adam, to the life we could have had together. But deep down I know I'll never find the magic formula for love and happiness. I don't deserve either.

Emergency sirens whine in the distance.

'*Sorry, sorry, sorry.*'

I repeat the words in between ragged breaths as the fire engines draw closer.

'It's not your fault,' the woman says reassuringly.

I peel open my eyelids and see a concerned face – and another low number. An anguished howl pierces my eardrums. It sounds like someone in unimaginable pain. It takes a few seconds before I realise the cry is coming from my lips. I press the heels of my hands into my eye sockets to try to block out her lonely, single digit.

'I can't do this anymore,' I scream. 'I want it to stop. Please make it stop!'

'Stop what?' she asks.

'The numbers! They won't stop counting down.'

'What numbers? How do you mean?'

I can't help anyone. It's futile. If I try to change the course of things, fate always intervenes and finds a way.

I give up.

I'll never attempt to save another person's life, however much I love them.

2

SOPHIE

8 YEARS, 2 MONTHS AND 23 DAYS LATER

WEDNESDAY, 12 MARCH 2025

'Can we exchange numbers before you leave?'

Stefan leans closer and shouts in my ear as we stand at the cramped bar. I've already made my excuses before everyone moves on to a club, but I've reluctantly promised to have one more drink. I frown, pretending I haven't heard above the babble of voices, which have reached over 100 decibels, and study the side of the counter. There are 113 subway tiles in total, which shine in glossy teal and measure 75 mm by 150 mm.

'I've heard so much about you from Flora!' Stefan roars. 'It's like she's your personal publicist. She gives you great press.'

'She usually introduces me as her friend who doesn't get out much and does her tax returns for free!' I shout back.

I'm only half joking – that's a blunter summary of how she once drunkenly described me to a random stranger on a night out.

'Well, that too. She calls you the Numbers Girl.'

I raise an eyebrow.

'She said you're amazing with figures.'

I will him to continue looking at my face instead of stealing another quick glance at my boobs, and not to clarify what he meant.

'Figures as in maths, rather than your actual figure.' His eyes glint suggestively. 'Which is obviously fantastic.'

I feel my cheeks pinken. He's *definitely* picturing me naked.

'Thanks for clarifying. I was confused for a minute.'

He leans closer, speaking directly into my ear. 'I'd love to get to know you more. We probably have tons in common.'

That's doubtful. We have one mutual connection – my former flatmate, Flora, whose birthday we're celebrating. She's a social butterfly and has invited dozens of people tonight from her start-up events company, university, the gym, and God knows where else.

I force the corners of my mouth to curl into a small smile to avoid Stefan describing me as stand-offish in any post-mortems of our conversation later, but not a large enough one to give him the impression he has any chance.

'How are our drinks coming along?' I ask.

He turns his attention to the bartender, who is vigorously shaking a cocktail for another customer. I need more alcohol to get through the rest of this evening. Stefan is one of Flora's old school friends who's only recently returned to the UK after working in New Zealand. I had the horrible suspicion Flora might be secretly plotting to set me up with him when she messaged earlier, saying: **Wear some lippie and your lovely new red dress!**

I did neither, sensing another disastrous attempt at matchmaking. I also forgot to steam my latest silk creation and sew on a button, which is a feeble excuse when I mend other people's clothes for a living. But I do have on my best jeans, sparkly combat boots and a bright-pink blouse, so I can't be accused of making zero effort.

Stefan produces another smile as he passes me a bottle of Prosecco to take back to our table. I've already had a few glasses, plus a double gin and tonic, but it's not enough to dull all the digits that keep popping up. Sunglasses would make them hazier, but I can't wear them in a dark, crowded pub. I estimate three-quarters of the drinkers will enjoy longish lives. Whether they'll be happy or not is a different story. I never get to discover *those* endings.

'Let's go. Watch your back!'

I follow as he weaves through the crowd, holding the drinks tray above people's heads. My eyes remain fixed on the tall blonde in the corner. Flora and I used to flat-share near Bristol Temple Meads station, but she moved out six months ago to set up home with Libby, her now ex-girlfriend. Rakesh, who works nights as a security guard, took her room *and* most of the shelves in our shared fridge. Flora is 30 today and has almost 26,000 days, or rather 71 years, left to live, which means she'll get a message from the king or queen – if the monarchy hasn't been abolished in the future. She's currently wearing a lopsided party hat and drunkenly embracing a friend. We've reached that stage of the evening when she's tearfully telling everyone she loves them, before dredging up a depressing anecdote about someone's unexpected death. She has absolutely no idea how lucky she is.

A dozen presents are piled on the table. I flick a look at my watch. It's almost 10.30 p.m. and there's no sign of a cake. I'm hoping it appears soon. Once Flora has blown out her candles, I'll make a quick exit. Bernard's arthritic hip plays up first thing, so I have to open the dry cleaners. If I get in early enough, I can finish my bed cover; Bernard's letting me hang it in the window to advertise my new quilting business. Plus, the probability of being hit by a drunk driver or attacked by a stranger rises by 19 per cent after 11 p.m., according to my calculations. While I'll never know my own number, I can try to mitigate the risks of dying young.

'There you are!' Flora cries, as we arrive at base camp. 'I'm gasping for a drink.'

Stefan is temporarily distracted by a guy talking about this weekend's football fixtures. I seize the chance to step away and pour Flora a fresh glass of Prosecco, refilling mine.

'Happy birthday!' I say, clinking my flute against hers. 'Here's to the rest of your life. May it be as happy as it is long.'

She chortles. 'You sound like the inside of a greeting-card my gran would buy!'

'Thanks. I really *am* as old as her, but I have an exceptionally good anti-ageing face cream. People never guess I'm actually eighty-two.'

Flora smiles but her eyes mist over as we each take a sip.

'I hate getting old! It's depressing. Who knows what might happen now I'm 30? A friend of a friend received a cancer diagnosis recently and was dead two weeks later. It was *really* quick!' She attempts to click her fingers and almost jabs herself in the eye.

'You're not allowed to get depressed on your birthday,' I tell her. 'We need more alcohol and cake, and fewer tragic stories.'

'True. *Is* there a cake? I dropped hints to Libby before we broke up.'

Flora looks longingly at her red-headed ex, who has 23,741 days – 65 years – left to live. There's a high probability Flora will forget why she split with Libby and end up in her bed tonight.

'She wasn't right for you long-term, which is why you called it quits,' I remind her. 'You both want different things.'

'What I want right now is carrot cake,' she sniffs tearily.

'Libby might be reluctant to settle down and have kids, but she cares about you. She won't have forgotten your usual fix. Mine too.'

Flora and I met when our train was stuck for hours in a tunnel close to Paddington station. We started chatting and bonded over our mutual obsession with finding the best carrot cake *ever* in a café or shop. It requires the perfect proportion of spicy, light sponge and sweet cream cheese frosting.

Flora takes a large swig and twirls the glass between her fingertips. 'Fingers crossed. I need to soak up the alcohol before I get shit-faced.'

Her gaze drifts to Stefan. She jerks her head at him and not in a discreet way.

'What do you think? I told you he's fit!'

I shrug. 'He seems nice.'

'Stefan is single, hot and doesn't just want flings,' she says, frowning. 'He's looking for a girlfriend, probably marriage and kids. He hit the genetic jackpot and has all the good trimmings – like a turkey with roast potatoes, pigs in blankets and big stuffing balls.'

'Nice image, Flora!'

She roars with laughter; everything she says somehow comes back to food or smut, sometimes both. She's right though – Stefan *is* handsome, with spiky blond hair, a slim, athletic physique and soft brown eyes with long lashes. He's friendly, not tight with money and doesn't appear to be a player. He's received admiring looks from a couple of girls across the bar but didn't surreptitiously glance at them mid-chat. Unfortunately, he has a low number (1,801) and just under 5 years left. Even if I overlook his annoying habit of staring at my chest, he's not a long- or short-term prospect. A few months ago, I created a new set of rules, which includes not hooking up with anyone who has fewer than 3,652 days – 10 years. This avoids the risk of it developing into something serious post coitum.

'What was he doing in New Zealand?' I ask, attempting to distract Flora from mentally choosing her bridesmaid dress and a gift for our imaginary wedding.

'Working as a tour guide, but he's come back to be closer to his family. He's an instructor at that rock-climbing centre in Brentry.'

I nod. His pursuit of dangerous sports might also explain what is doomed to happen.

'He's close by and *available*,' Flora points out.

'So are EasyJet flights from Bristol airport,' I say jokingly.

'Funny.' She takes a breath, going in for the hard sell. 'Stefan's funny, clever and great with children – he teaches loads of junior classes. *And* he's had enough of one-night stands. He wants a serious relationship. I've double-checked.'

'*Whaaat?* He won't do a three-way if one of your other friends is up for it tonight?'

'Oh no, he's agreed to that as a special birthday present. It'll be round at yours later.'

I splutter on my Prosecco. 'Touché.'

'But seriously? Any stirrings? *Anything?*'

Her greyish-blue eyes probe mine for the hint of a spark suggesting I share her keenness. I pick my words carefully, knowing she will forensically examine them.

'Like you say, Stefan seems lovely, but he's not my type.'

'Er, hello? Can you remind me what that is? I can't figure it out. You're gorgeous, *obviously*, but way too picky! Why don't you give him a chance, give *anyone* a chance?'

I can't admit that my goal is to fall in love with a man who has more than 20,000 days – 55 years – left to live. We'll be in our eighties before we're parted for ever. It sounds unrealistic but my relationship rules will avoid future heartbreak. I want marriage, kids and grandchildren playing at our feet. Is that too much to ask after everything I've been through? The prospect of grieving in old age for a soulmate terrifies me far more than being alone.

'You weren't even interested in that hot geek, and he sounded right up your street.' Flora's tone is faintly aggrieved.

The bar is packed, and I'm distracted by all the competing digits. 'Who? Adam?'

His name slips out before I can stop it. Why have I dredged up my first love after all this time? Maybe my subconscious is nudging me to stop making excuses. The truth is that no man, whatever their number, will win me over because they're not *him*.

Flora's brow creases. 'Huh? I meant the IT guy who keeps dropping off fresh shirts at your shop so he can summon up the courage to ask you out. Daz or Gaz? He brings you slices of carrot cake, which sounds promising. He obviously knows the way to a girl's heart.'

I laugh. 'Ah, you mean Maz.' Our regular customer has stunning green eyes and a friendly smile, but he has fewer days left to live than Stefan. I can't see the point in getting to know him better.

'He's well into you.'

I shrug. 'The relationship is doomed – his cakes are always stale.'

'Gotcha!' she slurs. 'But who's Adam? And how come I didn't know you *do* have a secret hot geek on the side?'

Luckily, she's distracted by Libby approaching with a gigantic carrot cake, candles flickering, and I don't have to explain that Adam was my first – and last – serious boyfriend. It's too painful to talk about him to anyone. He was definitely my *type* at school. Even though we were only teenagers, I couldn't imagine a future without him. I thought he felt the same way, but we turned into the tragic high-school cliché: splitting after a row on prom night.

I clutch the glass to my chest, swaying, as a round of 'Happy Birthday' rings out, and Flora tearfully hugs Libby. It's been almost ten years since we broke up, but I can still picture Adam's piercing blue eyes, wavy light-brown hair and wide smile that lit up his face. He wasn't conventionally good-looking – his nose was on the large side and had a small dent from our disastrous first surfing lesson. When I close my eyes, we're all back on our beach in south Devon. The light golden hairs on Adam's arms glint in the sunshine and the air is thick with the scent of my best friend Lily's coconut suntan lotion, strawberry bubble gum and Calvin Klein perfume.

I'm tracing my fingers along the freckles on Adam's back. I can hear his infectious laugh and feel his lips on my neck, making my skin tingle. I shiver. No one has ever made my stomach flutter – or broken my heart – the way he did.

I wonder what he's doing now. He's probably teaching undergraduates in California. Last time I checked LinkedIn, he'd graduated from Stanford with distinction and was completing a fast-track PhD ahead of maths postdoctoral research and gaining tenured professorship. He's probably in a serious relationship with another academic who's as smart as him. I've been afraid to stalk him online in recent years. That's not because of my freakish ability – I can't see how many days someone has left from a photo. But I can't face discovering he's happily married with kids or, worse still, that his numbers have run out prematurely.

I blink repeatedly as my eyes well up; a nagging ache grows in my chest. Regret and unhappiness crush my heart. I'm as bad as Flora after a few drinks – an emotional, nostalgic mess who fixates on a doomed relationship.

He hurt you – you wounded him and everyone else deeply. You've both moved on.

I glance at the door as a group of young drinkers burst in, laughing. They look like they recently turned eighteen. Me, Adam, Lily and Tom were forced to wait for our landmark birthdays before setting foot in The Admiral. The landlady knew *everyone* in the surrounding villages so there was zero chance of blagging our way in and publicly drinking underage. Bottles of cider and alcopops on the beach on Saturday nights were a different matter.

The tallest, loudest girl, with long blonde hair, steps aside. My breath falters as I spot her red-headed, freckled friend with a pink sequinned handbag. Her life should stretch ahead, brimming with promise – university, an apprenticeship or a junior position in a new job, the first rung on the career ladder. She should have flings or fall hopelessly in love with The One. There ought to be romantic dates, hot sex and holidays to look forward to, along with hen nights, and possibly her own wedding day and children.

But this teenager won't enjoy any of these normal milestones because she'll be dead in just over a week.

My throat tightens horribly as another gaggle of teenagers arrives and mingles with them. Two boys make a beeline for the redhead, laughing and hugging her. Her sparkly bag blinks balefully under the light.

All three have the same hateful number: 9.

They share the same fate next Thursday and must be destined to die together. Could there be a car crash? Or a bad batch of drugs at a party?

I take a step closer to utter a warning but stop myself.

You tried many, many times to save people and nothing worked. Your last attempt ended with Joan's death, despite months of careful research. There's nothing you can do.

Tears blind my eyes, and the oxygen is squeezed out of my lungs. The teenagers' numbers spin around like malignant sprites, taunting me. The girl notices me staring and nudges her male friend. They both glare. I turn my back, screwing my eyes tightly shut to block out the figures, but they shine vividly behind my lids. I clutch the edge of a table, almost spilling a glass of wine, as the bar pitches like the deck of an unseaworthy boat.

When I finally feel strong enough to let go, I chug the contents of my glass. Someone in our party has abandoned their gin and tonic, so I neck that too.

That's not enough. I grab the bottle of Prosecco and refill my flute to the top.

I need to drink myself into oblivion – anything to stop myself from thinking about all the countdowns.

3

ADAM

Thursday, 13 March 2025

Wren thunders down the stairs and runs across the hall. She'll throw open the kitchen door in five, four, three, two, one . . .

'Good morning!' I say brightly as the handle clicks. 'It's the countdown to another great day!'

The door bangs against the wall, no doubt creating another scuff. I don't turn around in case Wren interprets my wince as criticism of what she's wearing. My mind whirrs as I continue foraging in the drawer for a pen. What *has* she put on? I can't face checking yet. Her primary school is one of the few in the country with no uniform policy, but the head teacher draws the line at the outlandish. An email dropped on Monday with the accusatory strapline: *Appropriate clothing reminder.* I had the horrible feeling it was aimed at us and avoided opening it. I debated asking the mums on the school run if they had received it. But the last time I chatted to a forty-something mother of twins, she said I'd been voted year 4's DILF – Dad I'd Like to Fuck – and could pick up my medal at her flat after drop-off any day.

I find an old Biro beneath a pile of takeaway menus and grab a scrap of paper. I need to write instructions for our nanny, Anna, who's caught up in rush-hour traffic.

'I'll take you this morning as Anna's running late. So are we, by the way . . . I just have to write her a quick note about your tea. Erm . . . how about chicken nuggets, or would you prefer pasta? Or . . .'

'It's my Show and Tell this morning,' a surly voice interrupts.

'Hmmm?'

'My Show and Tell is today!' Wren bellows.

'No, it isn't!' My voice is high-pitched and squeaky as I scour the calendar on the fridge. Nothing! Empty white boxes stretch ahead until the end of the month. I meant to put aside an hour this week to jot down everything coming up. Better still, to continually update it the way other responsible parents probably do, but I never got round to doing either. Uncertainty grips me.

'Wait . . . is it?'

I grab my phone to search for missed emails and find another text from Mum.

I tried calling again at the weekend. Do you know your plans for Easter yet? I'd love to see you and Wren if you have time! xx

I've been putting off speaking to her for weeks. I need to tell her I've made other arrangements over the break, which also need to go on the calendar. I scroll past dozens of unopened messages and find something from Dr Hunt, my supervisor at Stanford. He's sent another nudge about my dissertation deadline but I ignore it, hunting for a Show and Tell reminder. Wren's school and after-school clubs have fired off multiple missives. She receives so much correspondence, I should have hired a PA rather than a nanny. Before her mum, Carley, died, she made a file about Wren's likes and dislikes, the names of her friends and other useful info, together with her funeral wishes. But she never mentioned the huge volume of admin, let alone the dreaded year group WhatsApp, which I've muted for eternity. Perhaps she feared it would put me off taking over her parenting reins.

'Mummy would *never* have forgotten it was today.'

Wren's carefully aimed barb finds my heart and slowly pierces it. She's only eight years old but knows how to wound; her torture methods wouldn't be out of place in the Spanish Inquisition.

I steel myself and turn around. I'd left cleanish navy leggings and a non-holey white top on her bed, something nice and plain to make her blend in with the other kids, which won't potentially generate another school email.

Aagh!

She's raided her mum's old clothes again. A mauve and blue tie-dye T-shirt hangs past her knees, twinned with bright pink leggings, a too-large sequin belt that's looped over twice and a huge green cardigan. She's rolled up the sleeves, but her hands remain hidden. I'd emptied Carley's wardrobe into boxes when I packed up their flat last summer; I thought we could go through everything together at a later point. I've been storing the containers in the loft, but Wren made me bring them down a few weeks ago.

My former girlfriend was always a flash of colour on campus when everyone else lived in oversized university-branded sweatshirts and jeans, but she clearly became way more hippyish after graduating from Stanford. My gaze rests on the strings of Carley's purple beads around Wren's neck. The school's 'no jewellery' rule flashes into my mind in letters as large as the Hollywood sign in LA, followed by the words 'not clean' as I spot a juice stain on her top.

My daughter crosses her arms tightly and glares back, challenging me to tell her to take off her mum's necklaces or the dirty T-shirt. Of course, I don't. I could add a whole new chapter to Carley's file about my top ten avoidance techniques; I'll be able to teach a class on the subject at Stanford when I eventually return.

I finally find the Show and Tell email. It's been clicked open, but I don't remember reading the contents.

'I'm sorry, Wren. I have no idea how it slipped my mind.'

'I do! Because it's not *there*.'

She jabs her finger accusingly at the calendar, and my heart sinks further as I spot the sparkly pink nail polish. That will be another black mark against us.

'Mummy always wrote important stuff on our calendar. Why don't you, *Adam*?'

I try not to flinch at the word. She's refused to call me Dad or Daddy ever since Carley first introduced us eighteen months ago. I'd even settle for the more formal Father, but I guess I should be grateful she doesn't call me Dickhead or Arsehole. I honestly feel those could be her personal preferences.

'I know, I know . . . You're right. I need to get more organised. It's not too late to bring something in.'

The voice inside my head screams it *is* . . . we should have been out of the door five minutes ago. I don't want to do the walk of shame across the reception office twice this week, particularly when *I'm* a teacher, albeit at a different school.

'Let's think of something together. Why don't you take a book? How about . . . a *Horrid Henry*?'

The look she shoots me is pure, icy disdain. 'I stopped reading those *years* ago. They're for little kids.'

I'm racking my brains, trying to remember what Carley wrote in the file about reading. I'm sure *Horrid Henry* was among her favourite books. I rub my throbbing temples. I used to easily memorise rafts of formulae for my A levels and at uni, but now I barely remember if I've shaved. The lack of sleep is killing me. I'm juggling teaching, looking after Wren and trying to finish my dissertation, and failing at all three. In my defence, much of Carley's file has become outdated; Wren no longer listens to the music she stated she loves and refuses to eat her supposedly top-choice meals even when I haven't burned them.

It's hard to keep up with all the changes in her despite regularly scouring Carley's notes and reading parenting manuals, hoping to find useful advice. Becoming a full-time dad seven months ago was akin to sitting my final exams after being given the four-year syllabus just thirty minutes ahead of time, with missing pages. However hard I attempt to cram in all the details about Wren's life before I knew she existed, there's still a vast amount to learn. Clearly, I'm not destined to pass *this* subject with distinction. I'll be lucky to get a D.

'Don't worry, I'll find something while you have a bowl of cereal.' I dart out of the room and run upstairs before she declares I've bought the wrong brand of cornflakes.

Wren's bedroom looks like it's been hit by a tornado. Her dirty clothes are strewn across the carpet, mixed up with Carley's. The cardboard box is on its side, with more of my ex-girlfriend's vibrant blouses, dresses and skirts spilling out. I don't have time to stuff everything back in. Frantically, I scour the shelves for something worthy of discussion . . . her gemstones? Multicoloured toy unicorns? The framed picture of Wren and Carley at Bristol Zoo? My gaze rests on the bedside table. Four more photos of them together face her pillow, squeezing out room for anything else. There's no sign of the selfie I took of the three of us while Carley was having chemo; it's the only one we had framed.

My heart squeezes as I find it face down in her bedside table drawer, buried beneath tissues and lip balms. I pick it up. Perhaps Wren could talk about us? I can almost hear my daughter howling with laughter downstairs. I'm not exactly her favourite topic. Plus, understandably, she doesn't want to remember her mum ill and with a scarf covering her hair loss. I return it to the drawer and rearrange the tissues to conceal my snooping.

I stare at Carley's face in the photos on display. They were taken months before she was diagnosed with breast cancer. Her long auburn hair falls around her shoulders. Her mouth is parted into a wide smile as she hugs Wren, who looks like her doppelgänger, even down to the symmetrical freckles on her nose. Wren is the happiest I've ever seen her; she's certainly never grinned like that at me.

Give her time, Carley had advised after I met Wren for the first time and she refused to look at me or answer my questions. *This will be a huge adjustment for both of you after I've gone.*

I wish I'd asked her how long it might take for my daughter to like me, and how Carley made being a mum look easy and effortless. What was her formula for working *and* being a good parent? I hope I'll discover the solution soon.

The urn on the bookshelf containing her ashes isn't giving up its secrets. It brings comfort to Wren, but the metal's judgemental glare scorches through my shirt and finds bare skin. Buried among the detritus of clothes, abandoned plates and empty orange juice cartons is Carley's old uni sweatshirt. I only remember her wearing it a couple of times, but I grab it and run downstairs. Bursting into the kitchen, I find Wren eating her cereal slowly and mechanically.

'How about this?' I ask, brandishing the cardinal-red top. 'I can tell you about the history of Stanford on the way to school. You could talk about how your mum was a member of the robotics club. That's how we met. She was a senior, so we didn't share any classes.'

This is partially true. I only spotted Carley once at robotics club. But I can't admit we met at a mutual friend's party off campus when we were both plastered. We had a drunken fling, followed by a few weeks of dating before Carley graduated and we parted ways.

'Mum hated being in America and couldn't wait to come home,' Wren replies, mid-mouthful. 'She said she didn't fit in and most of the students were rich, stuck-up losers.'

I swallow a sigh at her deliberate goading.

'Well . . . being abroad by herself was difficult, particularly after her parents died. It was a big wrench for me too. Something terrible happened shortly before I joined Stanford and . . .' I stop myself.

'What happened?' Wren's eyes gleam with curiosity and she pushes her bowl away, spilling milk. 'Why was it so bad?'

She scrambles to her feet and walks over, staring at me expectantly. It's flattering she's showing a rare interest in my life, but I don't want to talk about prom night. And I definitely don't want to discuss Lily's death and losing Sophie, the first girl I ever loved.

'It doesn't matter, Wren. Take the sweatshirt or one of your swimming trophies or . . . something. Whatever you want.'

'Fine, *Adam!*' She lets out an exaggerated huff, turning her back. 'I'll take my *Horrid Henry*.' She rummages in her school bag, revealing the book.

Breathe in and out. Stay calm. Write the note for Anna.

My hand shakes as I pick up the pen, running over the meal options in my head. Spag bol? Fish fingers? *With an extra-large side order of arsenic for me, please.*

I write: *Cook whatever Wren wants for tea. Have after-school club. Back @ 6 p.m.*

I'll message her after drop-off about avoiding Wren's room. Anna seems nervous about venturing into that bomb site anyway and claims ignorance about the location of the vacuum, so there's a negligible chance she'll tidy up.

'Right . . . I think we're finally ready. Let's go!'

I look down but Wren's vanished. I head into the hall and find the front door ajar. The wind rustles the growing collection of flyers on the mat. I shoot down the path and spot Wren trudging along the street. She's set off without her coat but *is* wearing her flamingo-pink wellies. Didn't we agree they're only for weekends? I dash back inside and grab her trainers and anorak, along with my rucksack and year 9's test papers. On the way out, I realise I've had another major Dad fail and forgotten to make her lunch box. She'll have to slum it with school dinners again, like me.

I sprint after the little figure, who is drawing further and further away. Some days, the distance between us feels insurmountable; I'll never be able to reach her.

'I hope your Show and Tell goes well. Have a great day!'

Wren stalks through the school gates without replying, her hands shoved into the pockets of the coat I've made her put on, along with the trainers. I linger optimistically, hoping for a wave, but she doesn't look back. Her shoulders sag as a group of girls talk animatedly near her in the playground. Carley and I had agreed that Wren should stay in her school and for me to find somewhere to live here, rather than whipping her back to the US straightaway. Despite this, Wren appears to be completely alone. Perhaps the mates listed in Carley's file haven't arrived yet. I mustn't keep putting off arranging play dates. I should also pay for her class's Science Museum visit and buy something for the cake sale. I'll look up prices for Disneyland Paris over May half term . . . a trip is just what we need to help us grow closer. Or I could save for a blow-out holiday to Orlando in the summer. I should probably write a to-do list instead of trying to remember everything in my head as usual.

I stick in my EarPods, turn up David Bowie, and stride away. I'm calling up Anna's number on my phone to tap out a message about leaving Wren's room when an email with the strapline: PARTY! flashes up. A gasp escapes from my lips as I click on it. It's from my old school, now called Kingsland Academy:

Dear former pupil,

This is a reminder to RSVP for our reunion party at Kingsland golf club on Saturday, 12 April, to celebrate the opening of the school 50 years ago. It's a chance to meet with old friends and raise money to rebuild our crumbling roof and classrooms.

We hope you can make it! Further details below.

Can I? Should I? It would be a welcome night off from being a crap dad. But our prom party was held at the same place, and it will bring back painful memories . . . I've lost touch with everyone from school and it's unlikely Sophie or Tom will go. I dither, checking my watch. Bloody hell! It's 8.20 a.m. already. Clutching my phone, I increase my pace. A teacher late for registration, let alone class, is a bad look, especially for a newly qualified one. I'm supposed to be keen – unlike all the lifers, who appear desperate for parole.

Approaching the kerb, I catch a glimpse of a young woman in a bright-green coat striding briskly along the opposite pavement. Her curly strawberry-blonde hair trails down her back. I gape at her, my jaw slack.

It can't be . . . *Is it?*

My chest feels like it's going to explode with emotion.

'Sophie?' I raise my voice. 'Sophie Leroux!'

I step into the road after her and feel a whoosh of air against my trouser leg. A horn blares loudly as a motorbike courier swerves to avoid me. Breath freezes in my throat. It's happening at high speed yet in slow motion at the same time.

'Watch where you're going!' the motorcyclist yells.

Green Coat Lady turns and stares, along with the gaggle of mums and dads chatting outside the school gates. It's not Sophie, of course . . . the school email caught me off guard, reminding me of her. My heart beats thunderously loud and my cheeks are branded scarlet as I bend down to pick up my phone, which has skittered across the yellow hazard markings. The screen's cracked. Ditto my nerves. One more step into the road and I'd be dead.

Who would look after your daughter then, you idiot?

This is my wake-up call. I have to do better, not only at crossing the road. I must find a way to get through to Wren, but the awful truth is, I barely know her. I can't claw back those missing years and, in all honesty, I don't have a clue what to do with her in the ones stretching ahead.

Taking a deep breath, I try to calm my racing heart. The last thing I need is a full-blown panic attack in front of the other parents.

I must stop beating myself up. Carley would remind me that I can't learn everything in seven months, while simultaneously trying not to mess up my temporary new career.

It's not too late to build a relationship with Wren.

I have plenty of time.

4

SOPHIE

Thursday, 13 March 2025

There's zero time to sort out the mascara streaked down my face or hunt for my missing pink bra. It's buried deep within this strange bed with the faded red duvet. I've hurriedly dressed in the en suite without turning on the light and noisy extractor fan and am now tiptoeing across a navy-blue trellis rug, which contains 36 geometric shapes.

'Are you sneaking out without saying goodbye?'

Shit!

The muffled male voice rings out from beneath the cover. I freeze, shoes in hand, a foot trapped inside one of the 7-sided outlines on the mat and within touching distance of the door.

'No, of course not!'

I'd vowed to go straight home after that slice of disappointingly dry birthday cake, washed down with yet more Prosecco. I'd also planned to discourage Stefan, but he was funny and attentive, briefly helping me to forget my misery. We ended up in that awful club with the bad music and expensive drinks with the rest of Flora's birthday gang. Wincing, I remember suggesting coming back here. I'm trying hard to block out what happened next. Two things are certain: Flora will be ecstatic, and Stefan no longer has to imagine what my boobs look like.

My head is pounding, and my throat is horribly dry. I desperately need a glass of water. I could step over three more shapes on the floor, turn the handle and bolt, but Flora will go ballistic when she WhatsApps later, begging for an update.

'What time is it?' Stefan asks groggily.

Slowly, I turn around, attempting to look pleasant rather than horrified that I've a) been busted and b) broken my new rule about casual relationships.

'Just after six. I need a shower before work. I didn't want to wake you.'

He sits up, bare-chested, and gropes for his watch on the bedside table. 'Jeez! I need to get up.'

Despite his impressive pecs, he looks rough around the edges – his eyes are bloodshot and gritty. I *know* I look far worse. My hair is matted; I can't rule out that something might be nesting in the knots. I edge closer to the door.

'It was fun last night, Sophs. I don't mean in bed, which of course it was.' His face reddens. 'I mean chatting. I thought we had a real connection.'

Did we? And when did he start calling me Sophs?

More memories from the club return. We'd discussed my new quilting venture and how an old friend, Joan, had sparked my interest years ago. I'd explained that my website, Instagram page and Etsy business were only recently up and running. Stefan didn't join in laughing when one of Flora's friends asked, 'Isn't quilting something old people do?' He'd asked about commissioning a bedspread for his nan. But he also begged me to try a bouldering class as an intro to free soloing. The old me would have been there in a heartbeat – I used to love outdoor sports, the riskier the better. But I've calculated there's a 1 in 5 chance that a beginner like me could end up badly injured. Not knowing when I'm going to die means it could happen any day. Who knows? Rock climbing without ropes could be destined to kill *me* before Stefan.

'I need to scarper, sorry. I'll be late opening.'

'Do you fancy grabbing a drink sometime, just the two of us?'

Unfortunately, Stefan's digit is down to 1,800. He's grown on me since the bar but not enough to break my dating rules for a second time. I rack my befuddled brain for a way of blowing him off without admitting my soulmate goal or relying on the worst cliché, 'It's not you, it's me.'

He notices my hesitation and frowns. 'Ah, I get it. This was a one-off. Message received loud and clear. No worries! It's all good.'

I open the door, smiling gratefully. 'Bye, Stefan. I guess I'll see you around.'

'Sure. Wait, you forgot something!'

Dammit. He *does* want a better explanation, and he'll probably report back to Flora.

'It's not personal,' I tell him. 'I'm not looking for *any* relationship at the moment.'

The second-worst cliché ever!

'I meant you left this.' My bra sails over from his bed in a perfect 45-degree arc.

I catch it one-handed and vow to stick to a new rule: no hook-ups with anyone who has less than 1,825 days, or 5 years. Preferably, no one-night stands at all. I need to focus on finding a soulmate with more than 20,000 days. He must be out there, somewhere.

'Good luck with everything!' Stefan adds. 'I hope you smash it with your quilts. I'll email for a quote if that's okay?'

'Sure, thank you!' Heat crawls up my neck.

Stefan *is* a nice guy and Flora's fond of him. While I can't personally prevent his death, I can plant a seed of doubt in his head about his hazardous job and hobby.

'Would you listen if I told you it's way too dangerous to climb without a rope and gear? Would you stop taking unnecessary risks?'

'Nah. Part of the thrill of free soloing is the rush of adrenaline, knowing that one wrong footing and you could be dead.'

I shake my head. 'You could *definitely* end up that way if you keep doing it. Why take the chance?'

'Because I want to live for today instead of worrying about tomorrow. I don't want to regret not seizing chances.' He hesitates, rubbing his jaw. 'Last night you talked about being safety conscious . . . Don't take this the wrong way, Sophs, because I think you're a great girl. But why don't you try taking a few risks? It could be the best thing you've ever done.'

I avert my gaze as he climbs out of bed and gropes for his boxers on the carpet.

'How about sometime between now and never? I might have tried scaling a cliff face without ropes when I was a teenager, but it doesn't appeal anymore!'

'I don't necessarily mean rock climbing,' he replies. 'Obviously, that's not for everyone, but you only live once. You might surprise yourself if you face your fears. You should do something that scares you and see where it leads.'

Back home, I briefly mull over Stefan's parting advice in the shower, discarding it along with my damp towel. I get how he's hooked on the buzz of danger. I was once. But taking one too many risks changed my life forever. That's how I've ended up where I am. I'm never rolling the dice and taking a chance again – the cost to myself and others is too high.

In my bedroom, I feel beneath my wet hair for the long, raised scar that trails down the right-hand side of my scalp before grabbing the hairdryer. I blow-dry my corkscrews in front of the mirror, rearranging the tendrils to disguise the small bald patch. I'd hated my curls growing up because kids called me Goldilocks, but they were a blessing after the brain surgery. Most people don't notice this lasting reminder from the accident, but it's all I see when I look in the mirror. It never lets me forget what I did, the harm I caused to others, almost a decade ago.

I ignore my reflection and pull on jeans and a sea-foam-coloured sweatshirt, before searching for painkillers in the kitchen. My can of Red Bull has vanished from the fridge, but a stack of post has appeared on the table: Rakesh must have accidentally scooped up mine along with his yesterday. I resist the urge to stick another passive aggressive Post-it on the fridge, reminding him not to touch my stuff, and open the envelopes. They're mainly bills, as well as the written offer on Mum's house that I've rejected. I had to stop Airbnbing it due to the leaky roof and damp problem. A property developer's put in a cash bid below the asking price, but I'm pushing my estate agent to ask for more so I can buy a bigger flat in Bristol. I'm also delaying sorting through the boxes Mum left sealed in the loft.

My gaze rests on another envelope, which has been forwarded from south Devon. I pull out the crisp white paper with the heading *Kingsland Academy*. My childhood address must appear on an alumni list – my old school is holding a fundraising 50-year reunion at the same venue as our old prom party. I throw the invite into the bin on the way out and run down the stairs instead of waiting for the lift.

Nothing on earth could persuade me to return to the horrors of my past.

By the time I step off the bus in Clifton Village, the painkillers and Red Bull I bought on the way have kicked in and I feel more human.

Hardly anyone else is around. I take off my sunglasses and lift my face to the pale-blue sky, enjoying watching the drifting candyfloss clouds and listening to the cawing seagulls. This neighbourhood is similar to Modbury with its boutiques, cafés and elegant Georgian townhouses. I walk over the grass to the suspension bridge – my regular haunt before work. I can't resist the pull of water, even if it's the River Avon rather than the Kingsbridge Estuary.

The 'Samaritans' signs are plastered to the brickwork. They've been effective, together with the barriers – no one has died at this spot since I moved here nine months ago. I stare at the long iron poles stretching above my head. They look static but I read online they're always in motion; the bridge was designed to move in the wind. At the halfway point, I line up buildings in the distance with the safety rail, waiting for my vision to adjust. I shiver with pleasure as the angles of the roofs appear to shift, creating shimmering triangles.

'I prefer to close my eyes and feel it.'

I jump, glancing over my shoulder. A familiar thin, elderly man in his usual pork-pie hat and grey raincoat smiles back, his walking stick propped against the railing. Walter holds on with one gnarled hand, the lead of his small, scruffy white dog, Chico, in the other. Walter's one of Bernard's old customers. He's a retired engineer and while he doesn't drop off many clothes anymore, he still pops in to chat to Bernard and says hello whenever I see him around in Clifton.

'You mean the vibrations?'

'Exactly! It's a fraction of lateral movement, almost imperceptible to the human eye. I can sense it – probably because my old bones are sensitive. Luckily, Chico doesn't have this problem.' He peers affectionately at the border terrier by his ankles. 'He's six today!'

'Happy birthday, Chico!'

I force myself to smile back, noticing his ripped lapel. Walter's number is 24: he has a little over three weeks to enjoy the pet he loves so much. My phone conveniently pings with a message inside my handbag. I fish it out and hold it up.

'I have to fly, sorry! Next time you pop into the shop, I'll fix your coat. It's not a problem – consider it a freebie in honour of Chico's birthday.'

Walter tips his hat as I stride away, pretending my WhatsApp is urgent and needs an immediate response. Predictably, it's Flora.

Hey Numbers Girl! Was 69 your lucky number?! Are you and Stefan an item now?

He's a nice guy, I type quickly. But we've agreed we're better off as friends, sorry.

Shame! Was he at least a decent shag? Quick – tell me before this meeting starts.

I reply with a zipped-mouth emoji and shove on my sunglasses, keeping my gaze fixed on the pavement until I reach the shop. I unlock the shutters, switch on the lights and turn on the coffee machine – I'll need a large mug to help me wade through Bernard's chaotic accounting. He always randomly stuffs customers' numbered tags into the old-fashioned till. I put them in 'date of collection' order and tot up yesterday's receipts in my head: £59.90. It's worse than I thought! Bernard admitted takings have dipped as people continue to work from home post-Covid, but I'm hoping this total is one bad day, and not a pattern. I scoop up the notebooks he uses to record transactions longhand and stick them in my bag. I'll create a spreadsheet tonight and study the finances properly, something he avoids like the plague.

I ignore another more explicit, probing WhatsApp from Flora, and make sure my 96 cotton reels are in the correct shade sequence before scanning my list of jobs: high priority is fixing the tear in the hem of a wedding dress and the elbow patches on a well-worn, much-loved sweater. First, I pull out my bedspread from the plastic wrapping. I have 30 minutes to finish a small section and hang it in the window before opening. Bernard has refused to take a cut of potential commissions, but I'll insist he does. Even without deciphering his accounts, I have the horrible feeling he'll need the extra income.

The knots in my shoulders loosen as I hand stitch the final panels. The design is inspired by the triangular roof shapes I see from the suspension bridge. Slotted perfectly together are 900 pieces of fabric. There's a soothing comfort in the rigidity of order: 30 perfectly proportioned triangles in width by 30 in height, encased in a bold emerald border. These are the best numbers – the ones I can transform into something beautiful.

My phone pings with yet another notification. Flora probably won't leave me alone until I sketch her an actual diagram. I grab my mobile, but it's not my former flatmate. It's an email forwarded from my quilting website. I might have my first commission – and not from someone I've slept with. I click it open excitedly.

You have a nerve making memory quilts after what you did! I REMEMBER everything even if you don't. Shame on you! I hope no one buys anything you make.

My stomach drops, and the breath is squeezed out of my lungs. *Who sent this?* My past failures haunt me: the people I couldn't help, like the Berg family and a teenage boy whose heart stopped while he was playing football. But I doubt their relatives or friends ever knew about my attempts to prevent their fate. And despite everything, Lily's parents and her boyfriend, Tom, forgave me for her death. The only person who ever held a grudge was Joan's son, Trevor. That's unsurprising after I told him her death was my fault – I'd convinced her to stay indoors when he'd wanted to arrange a taxi. Trevor swore he'd never forgive me. He banned me from her funeral, pushed accusatory notes through my letterbox and harassed me on Instagram. I had to switch bedsits twice and eventually moved to Torquay, coming off my socials.

He last messaged me three years ago, around the anniversary of her death, so I thought it was safe to return online. Clearly, this was a mistake. It's tempting to reply and say sorry. I could explain how I learned to quilt and mend clothes in memory of his mum, and that I'll always love her. But he's never listened to any of my apologies and angers quickly. It's best not to interact with him.

I force myself to continue stitching, my fingers trembling. I squint at the black, white and grey fabric, my eyes blurry with tears. Everything appears to vibrate and shift as it did on the bridge. The smaller 3-sided shapes rebel and peel off, creating their own patterns. They're desperate to tell their private stories, but I mustn't let them. I must focus on the larger picture, the dominant structure that holds the whole design together.

If I let my guard down, my mind will drift to dark, forbidden places. It'll remind me of the people I've loved and lost, and the strangers I desperately wanted to save.

It will dwell on imminent deaths: the doomed teenage drinkers in the pub last night and Walter.

I stitch faster and concentrate on the triangles.

I want to forget all the tragic numbers.

5

ADAM

Thursday, 13 March 2025

'You are 100 per cent correct . . . numbers are all around us! They're even inside our bodies.'

I beam at my year 9 pupils, ecstatic that Khalid is a) awake and b) interested enough to ask questions, even if they are completely off topic. The gasps from a few other fully conscious students are a bonus: my maths class is a double period at the end of the day, which means it's usually a snooze-fest.

'How is that even possible, sir?' Khalid asks, frowning. 'I can't see anything if I look down my throat in the mirror.'

Someone titters at the back of the classroom.

'Well, the fact you can't see numbers doesn't mean they don't exist. Blood, cells, muscle, bone and tissue must synchronise into the correct ratios for everything to work. More than 50 billion cells die in our bodies each day . . . the volume of blood flowing around the body rises with exercise and Christmas brings additional pounds to our waistlines.'

I wait for laughter, but that's pushing my luck.

'We rely on our phones and other electronic devices to perform complex mathematical algorithms to send messages. We have our own personal totals . . . the number of steps taken, sentences said out loud, and texts sent in a day. Numbers are everywhere!'

Khalid nods enthusiastically. The bell rings, signalling the end of the day, and a large smirk spreads across his face. His classmates scrape back their chairs and pack up. I'm an idiot! Khalid's questions were a perfectly timed ruse to distract me from going through their test papers and setting homework.

'Wait! I mean, hold on, everyone . . . Please research Pascal's triangle as prep for our next lesson.'

I write the mathematical term on the whiteboard. By the time I've turned around, only a few stragglers remain. It's astonishing . . . they take forever to unpack and stop talking at the start of class. But they move unexpectedly fast, like mutant plant zombies in *The Last Of Us*, when alerted to a mass exodus of warm bodies.

'Bye, Mr Bailey.' Khalid waltzes past, smiling victoriously.

I grit my teeth. I wouldn't have been awarded my PGCE if this lesson had been observed during my training. I need to talk in private to Khalid about his disruptive behaviour, but I'll deal with him next time.

'We'll go over your test papers in detail soon,' I say sternly. 'And I'll be asking you to explain Pascal's triangle to the rest of the class.'

'Awesome! Sounds fun.'

The door slams behind him. Khalid is bright but gets bored easily and struggles to understand abstract concepts. He gained the lowest mark in my exam: 3 out of 40. It'll be an uphill battle to explain Pascal's triangle *and* prevent him from distracting his classmates.

I dump my pads and Biros into my rucksack and fish out my phone. At least I remembered to mute it, unlike last week when I threatened to hand out a detention to whoever's mobile was ringing, only to discover it was mine. The screen blinks to life with an alarming number of missed calls from our nanny. My blood pressure rises by about 30 points as my gaze rests on Anna's final message, which contains just two words: I QUIT!!!

I press-gang the unfortunately named Mr Cross into holding my after-school robotics club in return for covering his detention class tomorrow and race home. Whatever has happened between Anna and Wren must be salvageable; I can broker a peace deal, even if it's only fragile.

Anna is waiting by the door as I let myself into our tiny, terraced rented house. Her coat is on, and a scowl is plastered across her face.

'Please don't leave! Let's talk.'

'No! That's it.' She makes a swiping gesture with her hands, her chestnut ponytail swinging jauntily. 'I'm not putting up with this. Wren is horrible to me – *toujours!*'

Ditto.

'I'm sorry! You know things have been rough since her mum died. Carley was her most important person in the world and then she was gone, and everything changed . . . well, fell apart. Obviously, I'm a poor substitute. It isn't easy for Wren, for either of us.'

'I know you're trying your best, but this' – she shakes her head – '*c'est impossible!*'

'I'm attempting to set boundaries—'

'What boundaries? She called me a stupid bitch! She said she hated me. And for what? Cleaning her bedroom. It is a *porcherie*, a pigsty!'

This is more serious than I thought. Wren has tantrums but she's never sworn at Anna or me before.

'I agree, that's unacceptable language,' I say, snapping into school mode, 'and it will not be tolerated in our house. I will make sure she apologises to you in person.'

She shakes her head. 'She doesn't listen to you! She doesn't listen to anyone.'

'I'll make her.' I stride to the bottom of the stairs. 'Wren, come down right now!'

Anna taps her foot, rolling her eyes. My cheeks warm as we watch her point being proven in real time.

'I mean it!' I shout louder. 'I know you can hear me. I want you downstairs *now*.'

Seconds tick by.

'See?' Anna throws open the front door. 'No one can get through to her.'

'I will, I promise. But don't quit. I can't do this alone. *Please.*'

I'm not above begging. I will lie prone at her feet if it stops her from leaving. Anna hesitates.

'I'll make this right,' I say quickly. 'She *will* apologise and it won't happen again. You have my word. Please, Anna. I don't have anyone else to ask for help . . .'

What will swing this? More time off? A one-off bonus?

'I'll give you a pay rise . . . a thousand pounds more.'

She sighs heavily. '*Une dernière chance.*'

One last chance.

'Thank you!' I beam at her, even though my stomach is churning at the cost.

'This is only because I pity you when you are out of your depth, Mr Bailey.'

Ouch!

My grin becomes rictus, but I manage not to let the corners of my mouth droop before I've closed the door. Her wages are already eating away my salary, but it will be far worse to search for a nanny at short notice.

I climb the stairs, two at a time, and rap the bedroom door sharply.

'Wren, it's me. Can I come in?'

She doesn't reply and I enter, bracing myself for battle. Her room is uncharacteristically tidy. Wren is lying face down on her bed, crying, next to the laundry basket, which is piled high with neatly folded clean clothes.

'What is it?' I ask, stepping closer. 'What happened with Anna?'

She doesn't reply, and her shoulders shake harder.

'Why did you call her a bad name? You can't speak to Anna, *anyone*, like that. You have to apologise.'

Wren sniffs but doesn't move, so I continue talking to the back of her head.

'I meant to tell her that you'd tidy up in here yourself, but I got distracted. She was trying to help.'

Wren sits bolt upright. Her face is blotchy and streaked with tears. 'Help? She's ruined everything! So have you!'

'What do you mean?'

She grabs a bright-pink T-shirt from the top of the laundry. The muscles around my mouth tense as I recognise other colourful sweatshirts and blouses.

Wren kicks out at the basket, tipping it over. 'Anna did this! And this!' She scoops up armfuls of clothes and hurls them on to the carpet.

My heart thuds painfully as the realisation hits. I never wrote the WhatsApp to Anna. She's swept up Carley's old outfits into the wash along with Wren's.

'I can't smell Mummy anymore,' she says, in between huge, racking sobs. 'Anna's washed her away. I've lost Mummy forever!'

'I'm sorry. I should have been clearer . . . I should have told her not to touch—'

'Mummy's smell is gone! I can't ever get it back. That's because of you!'

My cheeks sting guiltily. 'We can try . . . Do you know what her favourite perfume was called? Or the washing powder she used?'

'Do *you*?' Her eyes blaze with recrimination.

I perch on the edge of the bed. I have no idea. I reach out to comfort her, but she scrambles away, recoiling from my touch, and crying harder.

'Leave me alone!'

'Wren, please, can we—'

'I hate you! I wish *you* were dead, not Mummy!'

6

ADAM

Thursday, 13 March 2025

'How bad was it exactly, on a scale of one to ten?' Ollie scoops up a can of beer from the side of the armchair and cracks it open. 'Give me a number.'

It had completely slipped my mind we'd arranged to meet tonight, thanks to my dismal calendar skills. I tried to cancel, but Ollie wouldn't take no for an answer. I have form, apparently, for being *a terrible friend* and bailing last minute, repeatedly postponing or forgetting to turn up. He ignored my excuse that it had been the day from hell and brought the pub to me with a box of Beavertown Neck Oil and monster packets of crisps.

'Erm, are we talking linear or the logarithmic scale?' I groan, rubbing my face.

'Preferably something in plain English my last few brain cells will grasp without being fried.'

'In that case, it's a ten on the Richter scale . . . it was city-destroying, earthquake bad. Wren wishes I was dead, and a motorcyclist almost made her dream come true this morning.'

'Wow! The Make-A-Wish Foundation turned dark suddenly.'

I laugh, catching the can he tosses over.

'Oh, and I forgot to add . . . I'm a crap teacher. It's *a lot* harder than I thought.'

'I could have told you that during training and saved you all that time and money. Being a Stanford maths genius is one thing, but dragging everything out of your superhuman brain and explaining it to small, non-cooperative mere mortals is a totally different matter.'

I suppress a sigh and take a swig of beer. Ollie and I met on our PGCE placement and bonded straightaway as we've both come from academia. He'd had enough of his history postgrad at Birmingham uni and wanted to 'make a difference in the real world', whereas this is a stopgap for me.

I *have* to finish my dissertation, even if it kills me. Then I'll finally get my PhD, apply for a postdoc position and return to Stanford with Wren, working my way up to a professorship, as Dad had wanted. That's if I'm not eaten alive first by the kids at my academy or the mums at Wren's school.

'I spend hours writing lesson plans, but the year 9s distract me and everything goes to pot,' I admit.

Ollie frowns. 'Is that someone at the front door?'

'Really? I think it's just Wren going to the loo.' I jump up and open the sitting-room door. I'm about to walk into the hall when I catch the smirk on his freckly face.

'Bastard.'

I throw myself back down on to the sofa as the toilet upstairs flushes. The floorboards creak above our heads.

'I don't think any of the kids respect me,' I admit. 'Wren hates me most of all and I can't blame her . . . I keep messing up. She cried herself to sleep earlier.'

Ollie throws his hands in the air. 'I can't help you with being a dad, I'm afraid. That's beyond my area of expertise. I'd say be yourself, but that's probably a bit much for anyone, let alone an eight-year-old girl.'

'Thanks!'

He stuffs a handful of crisps into his mouth, crunching thoughtfully, as I knock back my drink. My head swims. I'm a notorious lightweight, but my alcohol tolerance has dropped by at least a third since starting full-time work.

'I'm joking, mate.' Ollie shoots me a sympathetic look. 'Give it time. It's early days. You've taken on more than most people our age would ever agree to – and you're on your own. I know I couldn't do it. I wouldn't want to either.'

'Well, I didn't exactly have a choice! Carley and I never had a back-up plan.'

The beer has loosened my inhibitions but guilt claws at my throat.

'I want to do this, *want* Wren,' I clarify quickly. 'It was my decision. I just wish she came with an up-to-date manual. I wouldn't scrape 20 per cent in Dad exams.'

'Except this isn't an exam,' Ollie observes. 'And Wren isn't a car!'

'*Now* you tell me!'

Everything I've said *is* true, but I've explained it clumsily. I couldn't turn down Carley, obviously . . . that option never crossed my mind. Decision-making is never usually my forte, but I knew instantly I had to, *wanted to*, bring up Wren. I'd promised Carley without hesitation, however days like this make me doubt myself even more than usual.

My phone pings with a message.

'Anyone exciting?'

'Hmmm?'

I read Anna's message, heart sinking.

Sorry about washing the clothes. They smelt musty!

It's followed by another: When will I get my £££ rise?

I tap out: **Next month?**

'It's the nanny,' I explain. 'I'm bribing her to stay with us after Wren called her a bitch. And tomorrow, I'm buying Wren a toy, preferably a panda, in a desperate attempt to make the I-hate-Adam-meter dip below 75 per cent for the first time ever.'

I checked Carley's file before Ollie arrived and her notes mentioned that Wren loves anything 'panda related' and a gift shop in Clifton Village in particular. I've been thinking about organising a day out with Wren at the suspension bridge and the downs, but I'll drive over by myself after work and choose a gift.

Ollie raises an eyebrow. 'Ah, I see! It's the classic rich boy "throw money at problems to make them go away" approach.'

'Will *you* leave if I give you a tenner? I have to get on with my paper, pay for a trip to the Science Museum, top up Wren's dinner money and basically everything else I've forgotten to do this week, including finding out how my daughter's Show and Tell went.'

A familiar pressure builds in my chest, squeezing out the air, as I realise I never asked Wren about her talk. I think of the lesson plans I need to check over before trying to make sense of my algebraic geometry notes; it's doubtful anything I've written over the last few weeks is usable in my dissertation. My stomach twists into sharp knots and my pulse quickens.

'It will cost a lot more to bribe me. We haven't got through these yet.' He points at the remaining cans on the carpet.

'I'm absolutely not getting drunk with you. I've got too much to do tonight.'

'Are you trying to get rid of me so you can *do* Claire?'

I frown, checking my phone. Dr Hunt has forwarded his previous email, enquiring about the progress of my paper (snail pace) and when he might see my final draft (sometime between now and eternity). I tap out an optimistically vague reply to hold him off.

'Hmmm? What was that?'

'I said, are you still seeing Claire?'

I'd briefly hooked up with a fellow postgrad student on our PGCE course and had paid Mrs Cook from next door to babysit Wren when we met at her flat after Christmas. She came over here a few times late at night when Wren was fast asleep.

'Erm, no.' I run a hand through my hair. 'That didn't work out. I don't have time for a relationship and it's too soon to introduce a third person into this set-up.'

'You mean, family,' he corrects.

'That's what I said.'

Ollie arches his eyebrow and leans forward in his chair, interviewer-style. 'So it has nothing to do with the fact you repeatedly said another girl's name in your sleep after you had sex with Claire? Bastard!'

My heart sinks. 'You heard about that?'

'Everyone has,' he says, sniggering. 'It's on the group WhatsApp. We've all offered opinions on your post-coital etiquette, or rather lack of it.'

'Great! I've always wanted to be famous.'

'Infamous, more like.'

The PGCE WhatsApp is another group I've muted forever. I pick up a second can, debating whether to throw caution to the wind.

'Who's the lucky girl you were dreaming about?' Ollie asks.

I pull the tab and take a large slurp before sinking back into the sofa.

'Pardon?' I ask, playing for time.

'You heard me. Do you want me to shout out the question for Wren to hear?'

'Sophie,' I say quietly.

'Please tell me she's not one of your year 9s?'

'You're disgusting!' I throw a cushion at him. 'She was my childhood sweetheart . . . the love of my life, really.'

'Aw, that's sweet! You sound like you're in a Hallmark movie. Are you still in touch?'

'No, I messed that up too. She refused to see me again. It was brutal.'

'Teenage break-ups are the worst! It's carnage in my year 12 class – Romeo and Juliet on speed. But you'll be okay. You're the golden boy who always lands on his feet. If you beg for forgiveness, Claire will probably get back with you.'

'There's no point.'

'Why not? She's clever, hot and funny. Plus, she finds maths geeks a massive turn-on for some bizarre reason *and* she's probably open to bribery.'

'But she's not Sophie,' I murmur.

7

SOPHIE

Friday, 14 March 2025

'This is where you've gone wrong – here and here.'

Cynthia, my least favourite customer, stabs a glossy red fingernail at my neat stitching along the seam of her black taffeta evening gown. She's about sixty-five and will pick fault with everything and everyone until her last breath in her nineties. Her hands drip with diamonds and her new handbag is Chanel, yet she haggled over the price of my alteration. She's accusing me of taking in too much fabric at the waist, but my measurements were accurate. It's much more likely she's put on weight since she dropped off her dress a month ago and forgot to collect it.

'I can let it out by another centimetre or two,' I say calmly.

'Fantastic news!' Her voice drips with sarcasm. 'But I'm not prepared to pay extra since this was *your* mistake.'

I'm opening my mouth to argue when Bernard approaches. He smiles warmly while hanging on to the counter to steady himself.

'We'll fix this at no additional cost, Cynthia – just the flat £20 fee.'

I shoot him a look. My study of the accounts last night confirmed they're dismal. Despite his arthritic hip, Bernard will live for another 15 years. His shop, however, might not survive the summer unless trade picks up dramatically. But Cynthia is one of our few regulars, along with Maz, who helps to keep the business afloat. She leaves her husband's shirts for washing and ironing every week and frequently asks me to alter the designer outfits she buys on a whim.

'Thank you! I'll collect first thing on Monday.'

I stifle a sigh. This means staying late tonight to finish my other repairs.

'Before you go, have you seen the quilt in the window?' Bernard says quickly. 'Sophie makes bedspreads from people's old, loved clothing. Perhaps you'd like to take a flyer?'

Cynthia shudders. 'No, thank you. My husband and I prefer White Company bedding.'

She sweeps out of the shop, the bell above the door feebly tinkling.

'Sorry, dear. I think it's lovely.' Bernard nods at my triangular-patterned creation. 'And it is early days.'

'Hopefully, business improves,' I reply. 'Talking of which, we have to take another £400 this month, at least, otherwise we won't cover the overheads.'

'I need a cuppa before we close up and talk numbers!' He rests his hands on the counter, his lined face pinched with pain.

'Sit down and I'll make it.'

I retreat to the tiny kitchen and fill the kettle, checking my emails. No more nasty messages have arrived, thankfully. The bell above the door rings. *Cynthia!* She's probably changed her mind about the seam measurements.

'You're just in time before we close.' Bernard pauses. 'I love your giant panda!'

'Thank you!'

'We usually dry-clean clothes, not toys, but we can make an exception.'

'What? No! I've just bought it. This is going to sound slightly mad, but I want to talk to you . . . well, about Pascal's triangle.'

My hand freezes on the kettle handle. Who is Pascal and why is the man's voice strangely familiar? Water drips into the sink, the sound amplified above the light buzzing from the fridge, but I can't reach out and turn off the tap properly. I'm unable to move.

'S-s-sorry, what?' Bernard stammers.

'The quilt in the window! It's a reproduction of a famous number pattern.'

I turn to face the door, which is open a crack.

'I'm a bit of a maths geek – well, *a lot* of one. I caught a glimpse of the shapes when I came out of the gift shop opposite and had to cross the road. I wanted to ask . . .'

The rest of his sentence blurs into white noise, punctuated by the rhythmic patter of water. My heart hammers loudly against my ribcage as I step towards the voice. It can't be him. It's impossible. The probability of being in the same country, same city, *same shop* as Adam Bailey is around three million to one. This is a random guy.

Heat rises in my cheeks as I try to concentrate on the hum of conversation. Bernard's asking the guy if he wants to take a closer look. The stepladder creaks as the man climbs up to unclip the quilt and jumps down with a thud.

'This is what I mean about the numbers. See, here and here.'

I press my hand against the wood, holding my breath as Bernard mutters something and the man laughs. It sounds like Adam. One push of the door and I'll find out.

'It's amazing!' he exclaims. 'You can find the same pattern in nature with the number of petals in a flower and the way tree branches split.'

'And this is useful? To, erm, mathematicians like yourself?'

Bernard is being polite, but he's struggling to keep up. I have no idea what the man's talking about either. I saw the triangular patterns from the bridge and wanted to get them out of my head and into fabric.

'Yes! Pascal's triangle can be used to solve any probability problem . . . the likelihood of heads or tails in the toss of a coin.'

'Well I never. Who'd have thought a quilt could carry such meaning?'

'I know! This is the perfect example of what we're discussing in my next lesson.'

'Ah, you're a teacher?'

Bernard sounds relieved as they move on to safer ground.

'I teach maths at an 11 to 18 academy close to the city centre.'

I don't know whether to be disappointed or relieved that it's not Adam. He was super ambitious, pushed on by his dad. No way would he abandon his plan to become a professor at Stanford to teach in an inner-city Bristol secondary school.

'I don't suppose this is for sale, or I could hire it?'

My mind is telling me this isn't Adam, but my heart feels differently. Something tugs at my chest, drawing me towards him. *I have to know.* I open the door a fraction wider but panic pinwheels inside me, snatching my breath away.

When I came round after the crash, Mum had 383 days to live.

Lily, 7.

Joan had 112 the day we met.

Everyone I love dies before their time. Nothing can stop the countdowns.

I can't take those six or seven steps closer.

'I'll ask Sophie,' Bernard says. 'She does all my repairs and makes patchwork quilts from people's clothes. They make wonderful presents. She may be prepared to loan you this one for free since it's for a good cause. Here you go. You can read about her sewing here.'

He must have handed over a flyer, which has a photo of my 8-point-star bedspread and contact details.

'Sophie made this?' the man-who-cannot-be-Adam asks breathlessly. 'Sophie Leroux?'

'Yes! Do you know her?'

'Erm, I'm not sure . . . It's an unusual name. I used to know someone called that, but it was a long time ago. She didn't sew or make quilts though. She was outdoorsy and loved to surf.'

'Well, she's about so high,' Bernard says, as if indicating my height. 'Pretty, with hazel eyes and long curly strawberry-blonde hair. See?' He must be pointing to the framed picture on the wall. 'That's her with me, Bernard, and my late wife, Enid.'

The silence feels like it's stretching for millions upon millions of seconds, but I haven't counted past five when the man finally speaks in a low voice.

'Yes, that's her. We were at school together.'

'Oh, how wonderful! Was that here in Bristol?'

'No, south Devon. My parents moved there from Birmingham when I was sixteen.'

The room spins and shadowy dark spots fly before my eyes. Potential numbers flit through my mind. The pressure intensifies in my chest. I can't breathe.

'Well I never! What a wonderful coincidence.' Bernard's footsteps shuffle closer. 'Sophie!' He stops briefly. 'What did you say your name is?'

'Adam. Adam Bailey.'

No, no, no.

'She can't have heard, sorry. I'll fetch her.'

I fumble with the key in the back door and burst out into the alley. It's slippery from an earlier downpour. I trip over an abandoned tyre from next-door's car workshop and fall. Something sharp punctures my fingers, leaving a crimson smear.

That's what I remember most in the seconds after the crash: the brightness of the blood, the drumming of rain through the smashed windscreen and the crackle of flames from the other car.

I run and don't look back.

8

ADAM

Friday, 14 March 2025

Sophie is here in Bristol! She makes mathematically interesting quilts! We're a few metres apart!

Every thought entering my throbbing head is punctuated with a giant exclamation mark. I'm glad Bernard can't see the shock etched across my face. My heart beats uncomfortably fast and sweat beads at the back of my neck as he fetches her. I've often fantasised about meeting Sophie again, but it usually involves a chance encounter on a south Devon beach. I've wondered what I'd say and whether her eyes would light up when she spotted me. But whenever I've imagined our reunion, it's never involved me being horribly hung-over in a dry cleaners, clutching an overpriced furry panda, and a patchwork quilt . . .

I stare at the photo on the wall. Sophie has barely changed since sixth form. She's still the most beautiful girl, *woman*, I've ever laid eyes on. I prop the toy against my shin and check my reflection in the mirror next to the picture as footsteps grow louder. It's worse than I thought! My skin is grey, my eyes are bloodshot, and I haven't shaved for a few days. I probably look 100 but feel like a teenager, calling at her house and waiting for her mum, Jude, to open the door . . . *when* she was in the country. My mouth dries and my palms are clammy. I try to smooth down a few uncooperative tufts of hair.

Bernard limps back alone. I realise I've been holding my breath and exhale slowly.

'Sophie's been unexpectedly called away on urgent business. She didn't hear me call from the back door. Would you care to leave a message?'

He's not hiding his bafflement well. My disappointment swells and bubbles over into exasperation. Un-bloody-believable! Sophie was hiding! And now she's fled out of an emergency exit! I'm using far too many exclamation marks in my head! I glance down at the panda. Its eyes are large and pitying. Even this furry inanimate object is looking at me as if I'm a total loser.

'Hmmm. I should probably go.' I wedge the toy's large head beneath my armpit.

'You could leave a note?' Bernard tears off a piece of paper from a pad and slaps it on the counter along with a Biro.

I stare at the blank page. What should I say?

I'm sorry.

I repeated those words a million times back then, but she refused to take my calls or see me. Nothing has changed over the last decade. Her heart hasn't softened. She blames me for everything. I'm wavering as the bell above the door rings. A guy walks in and places shirts and a small white box on the counter. He has the greenest eyes I've ever seen.

'I need to drop these off. Is Sophie here? I've brought carrot cake.'

I bite the inside of my cheek. This was Sophie's favourite treat. Still is, apparently. We both used to close our eyes whenever we took our first mouthfuls, savouring the taste before awarding marks out of ten.

'She had to leave early, sorry,' Bernard says, examining the shirts. 'Haven't we just cleaned these for you? The tags are on.'

'Yeah, but I need them doing again. Can you tell her the cake's from Maz? I'll swing by tomorrow.' Shirt Guy walks to the door and looks back.

'Nice panda.'

'Thanks.'

He flashes a smile before stepping out on to the street. He's a good-looking guy who knows the way to Sophie's heart. It might explain why she doesn't want to see me. No one wants a blast from the past turning up uninvited when they're dating someone else.

'Shall I give you a moment?' Bernard asks.

'Hmmm.'

I return to staring at the page, my pen hovering. Should I make a light-hearted quip about funny coincidences? But I don't want to make it sound like she's a passing acquaintance. I could be more direct and admit that the mention of her name has left me in pieces. No one else sees me the way she used to, my barriers completely broken down. I've never loved anyone as much or fallen as hard. But how would I explain Wren and Carley? Mum's shock when I told her she was the grandma of a six-year-old? Me leaving Stanford before completing my PhD? Being haunted by my dad's final words on his deathbed, and the promise I broke? How I need to do more with my life . . . *Be* more . . .

How much I've missed Sophie over the years.

There's not enough space or time to express everything. Should I even try? We've both moved on. My life has changed unexpectedly. I have a daughter, a new career and no time for serious relationships. Sophie has started her own quilting business and is probably one slice of carrot cake away from getting serious with Shirt Guy. Perhaps I should be politely formal and distant so she doesn't realise how much she wounded me.

I shove the panda's head back under my armpit as it makes another bid for freedom, scooping up the cuff of my shirt. Staring at the tattoo on my wrist, I realise there's only one possible message I can leave. I replicate the symbol, fold the paper and pass it to Bernard, who places it in an envelope, writing her name on the front in shaky, looped letters.

'I'll make sure she gets this,' he says, as I walk to the door. 'Good luck with your lesson. I hope to see you soon, Adam. Bye, Panda!'

I wave one of the toy's furry paws before stepping on to the pavement. Thankfully, none of my pupils are lurking, ready to capture this moment on their phones for TikTok. I pass an overgrown alleyway and my mortification plunges to new depths. Sophie hurdled over abandoned tyres to escape from me, before I used a panda's limb to say goodbye!

At the pedestrian crossing, I remember to look both ways, but a kamikaze cyclist shoots through the red traffic light, just missing me. *Aagh!* Someone must have taken out a contract on my life . . . possibly the prophetically named Mr Cross because I bailed last minute on covering his detention class.

Back in my car, I realise I'm clutching Sophie's flyer with her details. I hesitate, wondering whether to email her. What's the point? She's made her feelings crystal clear. She has a new life and I'll never be a part of it, not even on the periphery.

I chuck the piece of paper into the passenger seat footwell. It lands among the rest of the rubbish I need to dump in the recycling bin.

Despite the mathematical symbol I drew for Sophie, she belongs firmly in my past.

9

ADAM

Tuesday, 27 August 2013

Sophie scooped her long strawberry-blonde hair into a bun while I dumped my rucksack in the beach hut. My phone vibrated with a succession of messages.

'Do you need to get that before we go in?' A lock escaped from her fingers, tumbling down her cheek.

'Hmmm. Not at . . . I mean, well, no.' I swallowed hard.

I understood abstract algebra, vectors and the rules of integration, but couldn't string together proper sentences around her. She was the most gorgeous girl I'd ever seen. I'd noticed her surfing with friends when we moved here at the start of the holidays and hadn't been able to rip my gaze away. She was fearless and radiant. She looked *free*, as if she didn't have a care in the world apart from the need to catch the next wave. Her boss at the surf school had mentioned she was a pupil at Kingsland comprehensive, and entering the sixth form, like me. This was the perfect opportunity to meet and, hopefully, impress her ahead of term.

I folded my arms, attempting to look decisive. 'It's nothing important.'

My phone buzzed aggressively, as if challenging my statement.

Sophie planted her hands on her slim hips, which were encased in a wetsuit. 'Answer it – I'll wait outside.'

When she left, I discovered four missed calls from Dad. My heart sank. Now Mum was ringing. Reluctantly, I answered.

'There you are! Dad's checked your desk – he says you haven't done any pre-work. Your assignments have to be handed in on the first day of term. He wants you to make a start today – you need to create a good impression at your new sixth form.'

The elation I'd felt at finally plucking up the courage to book private coaching with Sophie drained away. I pictured the A-level textbooks piled high on my desk, the spines waiting to be cracked open, and felt a familiar flutter of panic.

'There's plenty of time. I've signed up for surfing lessons this afternoon.'

'Why? That won't look good on your applications for Stanford or Cambridge. We've all discussed this – you need to concentrate on things you're great at, like tennis, running and debating.'

'Sure . . . I'm *great* at tennis, running and debating.' I parroted her gross exaggeration back at her. 'But I'm guessing everyone around here must surf!'

'Private school pupils will be way ahead—'

I rolled my eyes. 'You're breaking up, sorry. It's bad reception.'

'Adam?'

'Thanks for the heads-up, Mum. Tell Dad I'll do it tonight. Bye!'

I turned off the phone, threw my towel over my shoulder and walked out into the sunshine, misjudging my step. I tripped, staggering towards Sophie.

'Are you throwing yourself at me?'

She raised an eyebrow. I couldn't stop staring at her greenish-brown eyes, which had gold flecks. I'd never seen such an extraordinary colour.

'Erm, yes! I mean no. I'm not usually this clumsy.' I took a breath, attempting to make up lost ground. 'I'm actually quite good at sport.'

'Yes, I've heard you're great at tennis and running,' she said with a poker face. 'But let's not forget your talent for debating.'

Aagh! The tips of my ears and neck burned horribly.

'Sorry!' she said, smiling at my discomfort. 'I'm a terrible eavesdropper! I'm guessing your mum thinks surfing is a waste of time?'

I exhaled heavily. 'You have the same problem with micromanaging parents?'

'The exact opposite. It's just my mum and she's busy running yoga retreats here and abroad. She's not around much.'

Sophie looked down at the ground and spotted an overturned beetle, its legs frantically paddling. She nudged the bug with her foot, righting it, before inspecting the surfboards that were stacked on a wooden rack.

'Oh, so you and your mum . . .'

'Here you go!' She hauled out a board with a turquoise stripe, passing it to me. 'This should suit you.' She picked out another, shorter one for herself, and propped it against her leg.

'Because it matches this?' I pointed at the surf school T-shirt she'd given me to wear over my wetsuit.

The corners of her mouth twitched as she pushed an escaped tendril back into her bun. 'I meant it's the right weight and length for a beginner.'

'I knew that!' I added quickly.

'Sure thing, ten A*s boy. Let's go.'

'W-w-what?' I trailed after her towards the packed beach, my cheeks burning hotter.

'Your mum's telling *everyone* she meets you were in the *Daily Mail* last week because of your top GCSE results,' she said over her shoulder. 'News spreads fast – Adam Bailey is a genius destined for great things.'

'Bloody hell!'

She laughed, but not in a nasty way, and waited for me to catch up.

'Let's see if you get an A* in surfing!'

An hour later, Sophie was close to awarding me an E, after I fell off the board for approximately the hundredth time. The more I attempted to impress, the worse I performed. I couldn't concentrate around her, and my balance was shot.

'Do you want to call it a day?' she shouted. 'It's almost time.'

Water had got behind my contact lenses, stinging my eyes, and my arms ached, but I refused to quit. I *had* to improve; failure wasn't an option. I was good at most things; there was no reason I couldn't get the hang of this.

'What about that one?' I asked, pointing to a wave swelling in the distance.

I'd seen Sophie surf much bigger ones last week with her blonde friend, Lily, who was also an instructor.

'Are you sure?'

'Yep . . . 100 per cent.'

We paddled alongside each other towards the expanse of gathering water. I wanted to reach over and grab her hand for reassurance but managed to resist. The boys she surfed with weren't scared. What was there to be afraid of anyway? Waves were just the displacement of liquid by the moon's gravitational force.

'Remember, pull yourself on, jump to your feet and balance. Are you ready?'

The horizon blurred horribly into a series of grey, undulating lines. I imagined my future towering above me: A levels, university, a PhD, postdoc research and a maths professorship. My life was mapped out, but if I messed up, everything would come crashing down. I'd be a huge disappointment to my parents. Dad most of all. Panic rose in my throat as the long cord attaching me to the board became entangled around my legs. I ripped off the ankle strap, releasing myself, and attempted to turn round and paddle back to shore.

'Stop doing that!' Sophie cried. 'You have to be straight on.'

My throat had seized up. My hands were concrete, my legs even heavier.

'Adam!'

The wave struck me, dragging me down into masses of frothing bubbles. A roaring sound grew louder in my ears as I was tossed around, washing-machine style. Breaking for air, pain erupted across my face. I opened my mouth to cry out but gagged and went under again. The fizzing white foam settled and became clearer the deeper I sank.

This is what it's like to drown, I realised. *It's not scary.*

I felt at peace, as if inside a tunnel that formed a protective shield, keeping out the chaos. I didn't have to try so hard anymore or do anything. I could give up for the first time in my life. *Fail.*

A hand grabbed my shoulder and hauled me upwards. Air burned my nostrils and ripped into my lungs as I broke through the surface. Sophie forced my arms on to the board and pushed me to shore. Reaching the shallows, I fell on my knees, coughing. Blood streamed down my face and dripped into the water.

'Oh God! Are you okay? Lean forward while I fetch your towel.' She returned a few minutes later, gently pressing the fabric against my nose.

'You've probably broken it. I'll fetch ice from the snack kiosk and see if I can find someone to take you to A&E.'

'No.' I caught her hand as she got up. I didn't want to attract more attention; nearby holidaymakers were already staring. 'Please don't go. It'll stop bleeding soon.'

'Let's give it another few minutes.' She knelt beside me. 'What happened out there? Why did you take off the leash?'

My brain scrambled for a plausible excuse. I couldn't tell her the truth . . .

'Sorry, like you said, I'm ten A*s boy and a massive geek,' I blustered. 'I spotted a mathematical spiral shape in the pattern of the wave. It looked like a Möbius strip.'

'What?' She stared hard at me, her eyes narrowing.

'Well, the Möbius strip is a—'

'Stop bullshitting! That had nothing to do with maths.' Her tone softened. 'A boy at school has panic attacks. He completely closes down – glazed eyes, that frozen look, the full works.'

I opened my mouth to deny it.

'You don't need to be embarrassed or ashamed,' she added. 'Things overwhelm me sometimes, and I'm desperate to escape from everything, *everyone.*'

Relief surged over me. Sophie could see through my lies, really see *me*, but she wasn't repelled or judgemental. She wasn't laughing. She looked like she cared. I barely knew her but sensed I could be completely honest.

'You're right . . . it was a panic attack. I wanted to quit. Not carry on anymore. It's stupid, I know . . .'

She gathered me into her arms. 'Don't you dare give up again, Adam Bailey. I won't let you.'

I clung on to her and for those few seconds it felt as though the world had stopped spinning. I didn't want to let go.

As a lifeguard ran towards us, I was certain about two things: Sophie Leroux had saved me.

Also, I was head over heels in love with her.

10

SOPHIE

Friday, 14 March 2025

The wind buffets my body, slapping hair into my face, as I walk briskly across the suspension bridge. I'm trying to stabilise my breathing by counting my steps.

2,001 . . . 2,002 . . . 2,003.

Thousands of paces separate me and Adam, but it needs to be millions more. The temptation to run back and tell him I'm sorry is too strong.

It's been 3,534 days since I last saw him.

84,816 hours.

5,088,960 minutes.

305,337,600 seconds.

We've been apart almost five times longer than we were ever together.

I pick up my pace.

2,043 steps . . . 2,044 . . . 2,045.

I want to tell him he shouldn't blame himself for that night, or the sequence of events that began long before the prom at the golf club. None of this was his fault. It was all mine.

Now I'm running faster and faster.

I don't stop until I'm gasping for breath and the nagging pain in my side is unbearable. I stop, wheezing, outside a huge mansion protected by tall wrought-iron security gates. I stare through the metal bars at all the numbers: anything to take my mind off the weight that presses down on my chest.

The drive contains 3,256,000 gravel chips.

Embedded in the Tudor-style windows are 15,673 tiny diamond shapes.

The nearby birch has 3,240 geometric shapes.

Only two words can have this devastating effect on my heart: Adam Bailey.

When I finally return, Bernard's locked up and gone home. Flyers flutter on the counter from the draught as I let myself in; I'd stuffed the key into my pocket earlier. I flick on the light and lock the door in case Adam's hanging around outside. My face immediately stings from my idiocy. Why on earth would he wait for me? I'm a painful blip in his past. He left dozens of voice and text messages pleading to see me after the accident. I ignored them all.

I fetch my coat and bag from the rack before returning to my worktable, sweeping stray pieces of cotton from the surface and putting the reels into their correct order. My phone sits next to the sewing machine, with a yellow Post-it stuck to the screen.

Please let me know you're safe and sound. Am worried! B x

I pick up my phone and fire off a message:

Sorry. Felt sick and needed fresh air. Better now. Will put on burglar alarm. Sophie x

Bernard starts typing but it takes him ages to compose messages. I pull the dust cover over the sewing machine and tidy up, double-checking he's remembered to put the customers' tickets in the right-hand side of the till. I'll work on Cynthia's ballgown early tomorrow. I'm pulling on my coat when my phone pings.

Glad you're okay. Your old friend, Adam Bailey, left a note. I put it by your sewing machine. See you tomorrow if you're well enough. Maz dropped off carrot cake again, but I ate it, sorry. It was dry. B x

My heart flips when I spot a white envelope at my feet, my name printed in Bernard's spidery handwriting. The breeze from the door must have blown it off the table. I pick it up, my hand trembling. Is Adam's letter recriminatory? I doubt it. He's moved on. He's probably married, possibly with children, which would explain the soft toy. Hopefully, he'll be coldly polite. That's far less dangerous for my heart than sad reminiscences.

I shrug off my coat and sink on to the seat, unpeeling the sewing machine cover. I *will* make a start on Cynthia's dress. Going home is too risky – I'll be tempted to crack open a bottle of wine and pore over the 'before' photos of me, Adam, Lily and Tom. Blood pounds in my ears. I work quicker, but thread catches in the metal foot and snags my neat row. I rip the thread with my teeth and try to unpick the ugly stitches, but my hands are trembling.

Dammit!

I can't put it off any longer. I rip open the envelope, steeling myself for whatever Adam wants to get off his chest. I pull out a scrap of paper torn from Bernard's notebook.

Air escapes from my lungs as I stare at the page.

Adam hasn't written a single word; he's simply drawn a mathematical symbol.

It's a Möbius strip.

Memories of that fateful summer come flooding back.

11

SOPHIE

Friday, 26 June 2015

'It was the perfect wave!' Lily grinned and paddled towards me on her board.

'Tell me about it!' I gasped, attempting to catch my breath.

We'd ridden a six-footer almost to the shore while everyone else fell off. Adrenaline pumped through my body as we caught it, but the feeling was already fading. I wanted another hit.

'Let's go again. It's picking up over there.' I pointed towards the off-limits zone by the rocks, where even bigger waves were swelling. 'By the time the lifeguards warn us, we'll have caught a bomb.'

Lily shook her head. 'We should quit while we're ahead. We can't better that one and our boards could get smashed.'

'Please! Let's do it together. *One last time.*'

Lily wiped a wet strand of hair from her face. 'Sorry, I'm knackered. Anyway, the boys are waiting for us. We should go in.'

She nodded towards the shallows, where Adam and Tom were playing Frisbee. My gaze was drawn across Adam's tight torso to the V-shaped muscle that ran deep into his low-slung shorts. My stomach swooped. He was as sexy as hell.

'You're perving!' Lily said, splashing my face.

'Sorry, not sorry.'

'Me neither!' She laughed as I returned the favour, spraying her back.

My calves and arms ached dully as we hauled our boards out of the sea. Adam and Tom ran to greet us, water flicking from their heels.

'You were both dope!' Tom cried.

'100 per cent!' Adam added. 'I couldn't stand up that long. *Obviously.*'

'That was established a long time ago,' I said teasingly. 'But you should come out with me. I promise I won't charge you.'

The small dent on the side of his nose was a permanent reminder of that disastrous surfing lesson almost two years ago. But it was also a happy memory since we started seeing each other soon afterwards. The four of us became tight in the lower sixth, with Adam and Tom sharing maths and physics classes.

'Stay on dry land, where you're safe,' Lily advised, giggling. 'Sophie will drag you into trouble!'

Tom took the board from her and she elbowed me gently, running ahead.

'As if!' I called after her.

Back at the mats, we peeled off the wetsuits, revealing skimpy bikinis: Lily a classic black and me neon green. It didn't take long to dry off – it was almost 5 p.m. but the sun blazed fiercely. Tom rubbed factor 30 cream into Lily's back before she combed out her long blonde hair. She lay next to him on the towel, popping gum into her mouth. Within seconds, I smelled strawberries as well as coconut suntan lotion and Calvin Klein perfume. This was the scent I always associated with summer.

Adam slung his arm around my bare shoulders and nuzzled my neck, making delicious shivers run up and down my spine.

'I can stay close by if you want to surf,' I said quietly. 'I won't let you get into difficulty.'

'I'll only hold you back. Anyway, I'd prefer to watch *you*.'

His lips found mine, and he kissed me deeply until a paperback bounced off his head.

'Ouch!' he cried as we sprang apart.

'Get a room!' Lily shrieked.

'Talking of which,' Tom said, sitting up, 'I've had a great idea about how to properly celebrate prom night – we duck out of the beach.'

'Really?' Lily's nose wrinkled. 'I'm looking forward to a debauched party!'

It was traditional for sixth-formers to unofficially congregate on this stretch of sand after the school-organised prom in a fortnight.

'Yeah, but we could have even more fun. How about we book a holiday cottage overnight for the four of us? We could go straight back there after the golf club.'

Lily clapped her hands. 'Genius idea. I love it!' She planted a kiss on his lips before arching a delicate eyebrow at us. 'What do you think?'

Adam's hand dropped from my back. 'Hmmm. I'm not sure my parents will go for it . . . Dad in particular.'

'Well, don't tell them,' Tom snorted. 'Just say you're staying over at my house, and Lily is sleeping at Sophie's. I bet they won't bother to check.'

'I guess . . . What do you think?' Adam asked in a low voice, turning towards me.

'I'm in,' I said emphatically.

I'd sneaked into Adam's house a few times this week, returning in the early hours. My mum didn't care that we were sleeping together; she barely registered if I came home at night. But his parents would be livid if they ever caught me. It would be tricky for him to stay out all night – he virtually had to wear an electronic tag, even though our exams were over.

'That's settled then,' Tom announced, before Adam could respond. 'I'll find somewhere close to the golf club that's cheap and clean. All we need are the beds, right?' He winked at us.

Adam gazed out to sea, and I reddened further. He was making *us* sound cheap, but nothing could be further from the truth. Neither of us had felt anything like this before.

Lily dug Tom in the ribs with her elbow.

'Ow! What?'

She shook her head, sighing. 'Boys.'

'Tell me about it,' I said, playing along.

'It *will* make it a night to remember before everything, well, changes,' Adam admitted.

His voice had a note of sadness that made panic course through my veins – we were going our separate ways shortly. Lily was heading to Manchester Met to study psychology, Adam had a maths place at Trinity College, Cambridge, and Tom was Durham bound for economics, if they all got the grades next month. I was the only one staying behind in Devon. I'd applied for a hospitality apprenticeship at the local college and planned to teach surfing off-season. Beyond that, I wanted to travel the world, working in hotels along the way – and see Adam as much as possible. I'd saved for the train fares to Cambridge and was already planning our reunions alongside the River Cam.

'The summer's not over yet,' I said, attempting to sound bright and breezy. 'We have plenty of time.'

'But *do* we?'

There was a strange edge in Tom's voice, which made me look up.

'What do you mean?'

'Maybe time doesn't exist as we know it, and it's been swallowed by a black hole,' he replied. 'In another universe, we've already said goodbye and gone our separate ways.'

'Damn, that's deep,' Lily said, not noticing his sharp tone. 'It's too philosophical for me.'

'What do *you* think?' Tom switched his attention to Adam.

'Why does it matter?' he snapped.

I looked from one to the other. The mood had shifted since they were playing Frisbee; there was a dark undercurrent.

'No particular reason! But you're a bit of a maths geek, Adam – well, a lot of one. I'm interested to hear your theory.'

'Time doesn't matter in the grand scheme of things because it's like a Möbius strip,' he replied.

I shot him a look. Adam had claimed he'd seen that maths symbol in the waves when he was trying to conceal his panic attack during our first ever surfing lesson. He hadn't mentioned it again, despite more anxiety episodes in the run-up to his A levels.

'What's a Moby-Dick or whatever it's called?' Lily asked.

Tom burst out laughing, cutting in. 'The Möbius strip looks like an infinite loop – if an ant crawled on a single-sided surface, it would move along the top and bottom and only reach the end after two circuits. But I reckon it would probably fall off, dizzy, long before then.'

'I still don't get what it looks like,' Lily said, sighing.

'Me neither,' I admitted.

Adam found a red Biro in his rucksack. 'May I?' He took my hand, making me shiver as he drew the shape on the inside of my wrist. 'It's basically a loop with a twist in it.'

'So it's like an infinity symbol!' Lily cried. 'You should both get a tattoo of one before we leave.'

'Maybe.'

I wanted ink but was less keen to have a permanent reminder of being parted from Adam. He was my anchor and protector – all I had to hold on to, and completely reliable, unlike my mum.

'My parents would kill me.' Adam put the pen back and strapped on his watch. 'Getting a tattoo is up there with . . . I don't know . . . riding a motorbike or joining the army.'

And having me as your girlfriend, I thought ruefully.

'What are you both waiting for?' Tom snorted. 'Live for the moment!'

His comment struck a nerve, and I couldn't resist hitting back.

'We're worried it might look as crap as *your* tat,' I said, nodding at his upper arm.

Tom glared back. He'd mistakenly thought his flower tattoo was a lily in honour of my best friend, but it was actually a white tulip.

'No fighting, you two!' Lily cried. 'Let's get a pic. Everyone move closer.'

We dutifully gathered round in front of her phone.

'Smile!' she ordered.

I squinted in the sun as dark specks swirled before my eyes, forming strange patterns. Adam's watch ticked loudly close to my ear. We broke away, and Lily and Tom snuggled up together until he spotted Vinny waving in the distance.

'Back in a sec.'

Tom pulled out a few twenties from his rucksack and jogged over to the most prolific weed dealer in our sixth form, our *former* school. I had to keep reminding myself we'd officially left. Panic prickled in my chest. Huge waves didn't scare me, but the thought of saying goodbye to Lily and Adam, even temporarily, was terrifying. Mum would be in Spain, so I'd have the house to myself for months. Lily's parents had stressed I was 'family' and could stay over whenever I wanted, but lonely weeks stretched ahead.

I stared at my wrist. Water from my hair had dripped on to Adam's drawing, making the ink run in blood-like streaks across my skin.

'What's so important about the Möbius strip?' I asked, running my finger over the shape.

'Hmmm?'

He was miles away, probably worrying about his looming A-level results even though *he* had nothing to fear, unlike the rest of us.

'You've never explained what this means.' I held up my wrist. 'And I'm not talking about the cute marching ants.'

Adam's jaw tensed as he rubbed a tight spot above his shoulder. Something indefinable shifted behind his eyes – it almost resembled sorrow or regret – but passed quickly. He took my hand gently and kissed the pattern.

'The Möbius strip proves that if you travel far enough, you'll end up where you began without even realising it,' he replied. 'It means you can never really be parted from someone because you'll always make your way back to them, however long it takes.'

12

ADAM

Friday, 14 March 2025

It's taken forever to get home after a two-car crash. I tried not to rubberneck when I passed the accident but couldn't help noticing the badly mangled Mini. I parallel park, badly, further down our street, pondering the symbol I left for Sophie. Should I have drawn it? What will she make of it? Hopefully, she'll realise I haven't forgotten *us*, but she may not welcome the reminder. I probably should have stuck to making a joke about coincidences. There's no point worrying about her reaction . . . I didn't leave my number or email for her to get in touch. I turn off the engine, unclip the seat belt and fumble for my vibrating phone, which has slipped beneath the panda. As I pick it up, Anna's name disappears from the cracked screen. She's probably complaining about my lateness. I call up her WhatsApp message.

Are you nearly home? Wren is hurt. She may need to go to hospital.

I abandon the toy and my rucksack and jump out of the car, clutching my phone. Fear crackles in my chest as I run down the street and up our path. I fumble for my key but realise I've left it on the car seat. I hammer frantically on the door.

'Anna! It's me.' I bang louder.

Footsteps tap in the hallway and the door finally opens. Anna's hands and white blouse are smeared with blood. My stomach rolls over and my knees weaken.

'Don't panic, *s'il vous plaît*!' she says quickly. 'This looks far worse than it is.'

'Where is she?'

Anna points behind her and follows as I stagger towards the kitchen. Wren is perched on a stool, white-faced, her hand wrapped in a bloodstained tea towel. I try to embrace her, but she shrinks away as if stung.

'W-w-what happened?'

Wren glances down, her eyes wet with tears. I hover as Anna tightens the fabric around her wrist.

'Well?'

Anna pipes up when my question is met with silence. 'She took the sharp scissors from the kitchen drawer and cut up her *maman*'s clothes. She accidentally stabbed herself. The wound is *très profonde*, very deep. I've kept pressure on it for ten minutes, but it's still bleeding.'

'Why on earth would you do that?' I gasp, staring at Wren.

She shrugs, avoiding my gaze. I spot a bundle of bloodied, ripped clothes next to the washing machine and look away as my stomach lurches.

'Can I see, please?'

Anna lets go. My heart contracts as Wren tentatively stretches out her right hand. I cup it in mine, carefully unwrapping the tea towel, which reveals a large gash. Gloopy redness seeps out. My head swims, pulling me back to the scene of the crash when Tom and I found four bloodied, motionless bodies in the car and the other vehicle ablaze. I steady myself against the counter, battling my light-headedness and the traumatic memories.

'You're right, Anna. I think this means a trip to A&E!'

I'm trying to keep the wobble out of my voice.

Anna sighs. 'I'll find a book for Wren and pack a water bottle and snacks. Your NHS is *très mal* – you'll be there for hours.'

I turn back to Wren to reassure her everything will be all right, but she's slipped off the stool and is already heading out of the door.

Slam!

She's physically incapable of closing it.

'*Je ne sais pas,*' Anna says, lifting her hands despondently.

I have no idea either.

Wren needed four stitches but refused to let me hold her other hand while the doctor injected the area with local anaesthetic. It was our first and, hopefully, last hospital trip. We've driven home in silence, guilt gnawing at me. I couldn't protect her from pain or provide comfort in A&E. What hope do I have of easing her grieving for Carley? The mathematical formula for mending her broken heart is a conundrum . . . unsolvable, at least by me.

I open the front door, juggling her oversized toy and rucksack. Wren kicks off her trainers and runs upstairs.

'Do you want to take Panda with you?' I call after her.

She doesn't reply and I brace for the bang of her bedroom door. I abandon the toy in the hall and retreat to the kitchen, opening the tumble dryer. Anna washed the bloodied bundle before leaving but most of the clothes are damaged beyond repair. Wren can only wear a few things again. I divide the pile into two – salvageable and not – and carry it all upstairs. I knock on the bedroom door and enter, almost tripping over another mound of ripped clothing, which has escaped the bloodstains. I skirt past towards the bed; Wren is buried deep beneath the duvet.

'I'll put your mum's stuff away,' I tell her. 'Unless you want to use one of her cardigans as a blankie? I've read that can help . . .'

Her head shoots out, her bottom lip wobbling.

'No! Take it all away. I don't want to keep anything.'

I stare at her, taken aback. 'You don't mean that.'

'Yes, I do! There's no point. Nothing smells of Mummy.'

'Oh, Wren. I'm sorry . . . If I could rewind time, I would. I'd remember to tell Anna not to wash any of this.' I raise my hands in despair. 'I wish I could make everything better.'

'You can't,' she says brokenly.

'Why don't you keep a few things? You'll be sorry if we throw it all out.'

She shakes her head vigorously.

'Well . . . I don't know . . . I guess if that's what you want?'

I move closer to offer a goodnight kiss, but she dives beneath the duvet again. I perform a U-turn and quickly stuff the clothes into the cardboard box before carrying it to the landing. I return to flick on the night light.

'Goodnight, Wren. I lo—' I stop myself in time.

Dad never used the 'L' word, whatever the time of day. He just said he was proud of what I'd achieved. Wren won't want to hear 'I love you' from me and she's never likely to utter those three words back.

'Sleep well. Hope the bed bugs don't bite!'

I manage to get the words out without choking on them, and leave the door open at precisely eight centimetres wide, per Carley's instructions. I lean against the wall by the bathroom for a few seconds before scooping up the box and heading downstairs.

Questions pound my temples with every step:
Why didn't I remember to tell Anna not to wash the clothes?
When will I learn how to be a better dad?
A better man?

Black dots swirl in front of my eyes and a roaring noise grows in my ears. I drop the container and grab the handrail as air is squeezed from my lungs.

Count backwards and forwards.

5, 4, 3, 2, 1.

1, 2, 3, 4, 5.

I sit on the step, my head between my knees, until my breathing becomes calmer. Panda casts a pitying stare in my direction, the way he did in the dry cleaners when Sophie escaped out of the back door.

Sophie.

Her name is like a lifeline. I can almost hear her voice in my head, talking me through one of my old panic attacks.

You are safe. This will pass. Take it one moment at a time.

I shove on trainers, find my keys and jog down the road to my car, zapping it open. I snatch up the flyer from the passenger seat footwell and return inside. Sitting at the kitchen table, I re-read Sophie's leaflet:

> *Sewing together scraps of a loved one's treasured clothing is a wonderful way to keep their memory alive. A personalised patchwork quilt is a truly unique family heirloom, bringing comfort to those in need. It helps you keep someone close even when they're gone.*
>
> *Please get in touch to discuss sizes of memory quilts and prices.*

Sophie saved me when I was sixteen . . . is there a possibility, however slim, she could come to my rescue again?

Before I can procrastinate, debating all the pros and cons of getting in touch, I tap out an email to the first, and last, girl I ever truly loved.

I take a deep breath and press 'send'.

13

Adam Bailey ABailey235@mail.com
Fri 14/03/2025 22:45
Dear Sophie

I hope this email finds you well after all this time. I'm sorry I missed you earlier today. It would have been good to catch up!! What are the chances we're both living in Bristol?! That's such a bizarre coincidence! Congratulations on your new business!

Bernard gave me your flyer and contact details after I admired the triangular-patterned quilt in the window. I'd like to commission one of your memory quilts if possible. Please can you drop me an email re your rates ASAP?

Warm wishes,

Your old friend, Adam.

P.S. Is it possible to borrow the mathematical quilt to show my pupils?

YourPatchworkMemories <yourpatchworkmemories@mail.com
Sat 15/03/2025 09:33
Dear Adam

I hope this email finds you well too. I was surprised to discover you're here in Bristol.

Unfortunately, I'm run off my feet with orders and have a long waiting list. You could get back in touch in four to six months' time to see if I'm free?

Regards,

Sophie

P.S. Sorry, my quilt isn't available for loan. A customer has reserved it.

Adam Bailey ABailey235@mail.com
Sat 15/03/2025 10:01

Dear Sophie

Thank you for coming back to me so quickly! It's great your quilts are in demand! I'm incredibly happy for you! You deserve every success! I am prepared to offer double what your other customers are paying if you let me jump the queue!

Warm wishes,

Adam

YourPatchworkMemories <yourpatchworkmemories@mail.com
Sun 16/03/2025 18:33

Dear Adam

Unfortunately, I'm unable to alter my booking system. I'm sorry to disappoint on this occasion but wish you luck commissioning a memory quilt elsewhere.

Regards,

Sophie

Adam Bailey ABailey235@mail.com
Sun 16/03/2025 18:51

Dear Sophie

Thanks for the info re your booking system.

I'm willing to offer £700 for a double bed quilt, which is triple the rates I've found online (we have lots of clothes to use!!). What do you think?

Warm wishes,

Adam

Adam Bailey ABailey235@mail.com
Tues 18/03/2025 07:33

Dear Sophie

I haven't heard back from you yet . . . I can go up to £850 max if this can be completed quickly. Please can you let me know what you think? I am free to meet early Thurs or Fri evenings to discuss further.

Warm wishes,

Adam

YourPatchworkMemories <yourpatchworkmemories@mail.com
Weds 19/03/2025 18:33

Adam,

Bernard says you called the shop earlier and discussed commissioning a quilt with him! We've debated your proposal. I can fit you in at short notice for £850 – but only because Bernard needs half this amount for the hire of his in-demand workspace.

Please drop off the fabrics you want me to use and any preferred designs to the shop. We could arrange a Zoom call (the camera doesn't work, sorry) or we can continue to communicate via email?

Regards,

Sophie

Adam Bailey ABailey235@mail.com
Weds 19/03/2025 18:45

Dear Sophie

I'd much prefer to discuss this project face to face.

How about we meet tomorrow at The Friendly Hideout café in Stapleton at 4.30 p.m.? I've attached links to the café website and directions. I think you'll like it!

Warm wishes,

Adam

YourPatchworkMemories <yourpatchworkmemories@mail.com
Weds 19/03/2025 19:15

Dear Adam

I will see you there. Please be on time as I have other appointments.

Regards,

Sophie

14

SOPHIE

Thursday, 20 March 2025

Adam was surprisingly persistent and stubborn, likewise Bernard. My boss argued this could be a great chance to reconnect with a 'lovely' old friend *and* earn extra money. I gave into them both, figuring a short meeting was better than bumping into Adam by chance again in Clifton Village. Splitting the £850 with Bernard will help fill his financial black hole. How bad can this be? I was afraid of seeing Adam's number when caught off guard, but I've had time to prepare. Bernard said he looked 'fit, healthy and handsome'. He claimed Adam's face 'glowed' and his eyes lit up when he gazed at my photo on the wall, but I'm trying not to fixate on that. Adam looked after himself when we were together – he ate healthily, went running and never smoked. He's likely to have at least 24,000 days to his name. He'll probably also have a long-term girlfriend or wife, but I mustn't dwell on that either.

The Friendly Hideout café sounds perfect – it's not close to where I live or work and I can avoid bumping into him if this is his local haunt. It closes at 5 p.m. so our meeting will be purely transactional, with no chance to reminisce about 'us'. Adam has made it clear he's only interested in my professional services. His messages were impersonal, and he used that god-awful phrase 'I hope this email finds you well', which made me want to jump off Avon Gorge. I couldn't resist signing off with a caustic 'regards'. But something niggles. If this is *all* about business, why did Adam draw a Möbius strip? Is he hinting at what the symbol once stood for? Or perhaps he's just being friendly. I've re-read his emails hundreds of times and can't discover any clues hidden beneath the text.

I get off the bus a couple of stops early, clutching my bags. I click on Adam's link to the café website. It serves the usual range of coffee, two varieties of which are spelt wrong. Why does he think I'll like it? It doesn't look anything special – it hasn't created the world's first calorie-free chocolate croissant. It must be close to where he lives. It's only 4.20 p.m. but arriving first gives me a chance to compose myself. By the time I reach the correct street, I realise I haven't noticed anyone's numbers, despite my lack of sunglasses. I check my make-up in my compact outside the gift shop a few doors down and brush my hair. I'm wearing a home-made green silk blouse, emerald jacket and jeans. Hopefully, I look smartly casual and businesslike rather than someone going on a date. Because this definitely isn't one.

You can do this – for Bernard. He needs the money and so do you.

The reunion will be like ripping off a plaster – painful, but over soon. I'll pretend I need to leave in twenty minutes to see another client. I inhale deeply and walk towards the café. Staring through the window, I'm distracted by two large, promising-looking carrot cakes in the glass stands on the counter. Adam was right – this looks exactly like my kind of place, but that can't be why he's picked it. I doubt he remembers my obsession with finding the perfect proportion of spicy, light sponge and cream cheese frosting. I drag my gaze away and scan the bright interior; it's almost empty. A small, freckled girl with auburn hair in bunches is sitting alone at a table, drawing with coloured pencils, and an elderly couple are chatting and sipping from large mugs. My gaze is drawn back to the child – she's wearing a cobalt-blue T-shirt and an oversized orange cardigan, sleeves pushed up, revealing a bandaged right hand.

I've made it before Adam and have time to buy myself a drink and a slice of cake. I'm about to walk in when my phone buzzes in my handbag. I fumble for it quickly. There haven't been any more nasty messages via my website, but I've been on edge all week. Thankfully, it's only a text from Bernard.

Hope it goes well. Say hello to Adam and his panda from me! B x

When I glance up, a tall, good-looking guy with gold-rimmed glasses and tousled light-brown hair has appeared at the back of the café. The sleeves of his blue shirt are rolled up, revealing tanned, muscular arms. My heart races.

Adam.

I reel backwards, blood rushing to my head. His number drills into my forehead, taking my breath away. I steady myself against the doorframe and blink repeatedly, but his digit remains the same. How is this possible? Adam is young – twenty-eight, like me. He looks ridiculously handsome, and not seriously ill. Which means . . .

Bile rises in my throat. Oh God. I wish I'd never let Bernard talk me into coming. I could have carried on with my life without ever knowing this agonising truth. I want to flee before Adam spots me, but I'm unable to move. I can't tear my gaze away as he pulls out the phone from his pocket and answers a call. He was eighteen the last time I saw him and still a boy. He was gorgeous, kind and brilliant at everything – apart from surfing. If I walked into a crowded room and saw him, everyone else melted away as butterflies danced across my stomach. It felt as though time was suspended and it was just the two of us. He's having a similar effect on me now, except I want to cry.

I take in his easy grin, the small mark on the side of his nose and the contours of his face, which I used to know and love, reacquainting myself with him. Adam's frame is more muscular, his jaw fuller, and his hair is slightly lighter, but I notice it still curls up at the ends. I remember raking my hands through it when we kissed deeply. I gulp as my stomach rolls. My gaze travels across his face. He has days-old stubble and dark shadows beneath his eyes – maybe he's become a bad sleeper, like me. The glasses suit him. Back then, he wore contact lenses because he didn't want to look like a 'ten A*s boy'.

Adam must have come straight from work – he's wearing smart tan trousers, but in my memory he's forever frozen in time as a boy in shorts, T-shirts and scruffy trainers. Tears sting my eyes. This detail – which is tiny and silly in the grand scale of things – is extraordinarily painful. I've missed Adam's transformation into the man he's become. Someone else has filled in all those gaps, watching as he matured over the years.

Will they be at his side, holding his hand, when he takes his last breath? Will they comfort him if he's in pain and say it's okay to let go?

Adam puts the phone in his pocket and strides towards the tables. A lopsided smile lights up his face. For a second, my heart leaps because I think he's spotted me. But he's noticed the solemn little girl. Her pigtails quiver as she scribbles. I expect him to veer away, but he walks over to her table, picks up the cookie from her plate and takes a bite.

What the hell? Her mum or dad will go ballistic!

She scowls at him but doesn't cry out to a parent for help. Adam attempts to see her picture, but she protectively curves her arm, shielding it. He ruffles her hair affectionately and sits down opposite her. She pats it down, glaring fiercely, and continues drawing.

My stomach drops, fairground-style. Oh God. I see the resemblance – she shares the same wrinkled brow and look of determination in her eyes he had whenever he stared at mock maths papers. Their face and eye shape are identical.

I fumble for the sunglasses in my handbag and drop the case, almost losing my balance as I bend to pick it up. My hand's shaking as I focus on snapping open the box, keeping my gaze firmly fixed on anything, *anyone*, but Adam.

It doesn't make any difference where I look. I can't stop seeing his digit; can't block out its tragic significance.

It sears through my heart, sharper than a dagger, and causes far deeper damage than any serrated edge.

Adam is a dad and has 24 days left to live.

15

ADAM

Thursday, 20 March 2025

I catch a glimpse of Sophie outside the door, a cloud of long, coppery blonde hair, a heart-shaped face and full lips. My mouth dries and my heart pounds wildly. I stand, almost knocking over my chair, but catch it in time. This is exactly how I remember *us*: her gorgeous and way out of my league, me clumsy, flustered and unable to co-ordinate my limbs.

'Adam?' Wren glances up, her pencil poised mid-air.

'Yep?'

'Why is your smile so goofy? You look silly.'

'Hmmm?'

'Your neck is bright red. Now your cheeks match.'

I lock eyes with Sophie and lift a hand, waving. But instead of reciprocating or pushing open the door, she blanches and shoves on large black sunglasses. Then she runs away.

'Wait!' I bump into the table, almost tipping over Wren's drink. 'Sorry!'

I can't let Sophie leave without speaking to her.

'I'll be right back . . . Stay here and finish your picture. I'll be two minutes.'

Wren shakes her head, sighing, as I streak towards the door. I fumble with the catch before flinging it open and sprinting down the street.

'Sophie! Come back!'

I can't believe we've fallen into old, familiar patterns so quickly. Sophie is fleeing and I'm giving chase, looking and feeling like a total idiot. I need to start exercising again; I haven't been running or gone to the gym since living with Wren.

'Wait! For God's sake! This is ridiculous. Please!'

Sophie stops, giving me a chance to catch my breath. Slowly, she turns around, brushing away something from below the rim of her glasses. But instead of looking straight at me, she stares above my head. I look up and spot a magpie perched on top of the lamp-post I'm leaning against. I open my mouth to speak but am winded further when she takes off her glasses. Her eyes are shiny, that extraordinary mixture of brown and green with gold streaks, and her cheeks are pale porcelain. A hard, painful lump forms in my throat. My fingers automatically reach for my Möbius strip tattoo, brushing against it.

'Sophie?'

I lower my voice and take a hopeful step towards her, but she shrinks back the way Wren does. *Am I that repellent to everyone?* Yes, apparently. She closes her eyes to block me out.

'*Sophie.*'

I repeat the word as a plea to remember we once shared such strong feelings we believed we'd be together forever. It's also a reminder we can surely be within touching distance without tearing each other apart.

'Adam.' She opens her eyes but can't look at me. She's unable to disguise her horror.

'I'm sorry, so sorry,' she murmurs.

'That's all right,' I say, attempting to play down her extreme reaction. 'I've always had this effect on girls . . . they take one look at me and run in the opposite direction!'

She was the exception, of course.

Sophie took me in her arms the first time we met and wouldn't leave my side after I'd described my panic attack. Later, much later, I remember holding her, touching her wrist where I'd drawn a Möbius strip with a Biro, hearing her cry out with pleasure as I kissed every inch of her body. The memory makes me light-headed.

'That's not true, Adam. Lots of girls at school fancied you. You just didn't notice.'

She utters the words softly. Before I can contradict her, she continues talking, louder.

'I'm sorry to do this at short notice, but can we rearrange? I feel unwell.'

Tiny daggers pierce my heart as she keeps her eyes fixed on the pavement. She *really* does want to escape!

'Yes, but look . . . Can't we try to put everything behind us . . . start afresh after all these years?' I'm stumbling over my words. 'I know it's awful how we lost Lily, but we were kids. We'd both make different decisions . . . We're not the same people we were back then.'

I'm stating this to convince me, as well as her, but it doesn't have the reaction I'd hoped for. Sophie darts to the kerbside and bends over, heaving.

Aagh. She *is* poorly! Perhaps I'm not 100 per cent repulsive, just circa 75 per cent. I hesitate before joining her as she retches.

'May I?'

She nods. Gently, I pull back the hair from her face. She hated having it loose when she threw up after a few too many alcopops. Her locks feel like silk between my fingers.

'This is like old times,' I say teasingly.

'Says the world's biggest lightweight!' she retorts, bent double. 'Have you forgotten how you were slayed by a single alcopop? There's a plaque in our school marking the achievement.'

I burst out laughing.

'In my defence, mixing drinks was never a good idea and that sip of your tequila proved lethal. Especially when I finished off the evening with half a lager.'

She smiles as she straightens, meeting my gaze fully. For a fraction of a second, I feel 'it', whatever *it* is. My heartbeat quickens. The world around us slows down and the noise of traffic fades into the background. Nothing else exists except for the two of us in this moment. That's how I always felt when I was with her.

'That was a long time ago and, as you pointed out, we're different people now,' she says stiffly.

'Some things don't change.'

'*Everything*'s changed.'

The moment shatters as quickly as her smile disappears. I hear the roar of an approaching bus and notice a woman pass us on the pavement, holding the hand of a crying toddler.

'Thanks for the hair duties. I must have eaten something dodgy.' She dabs her mouth with a tissue. 'I should go. Can we find another time for the appointment?'

'Sure.' I catch hold of her elbow as she sways. 'But why don't you come back to the café until you feel better? We could have a cup of tea.'

'I don't think so, sorry,' she replies in a small voice.

'Just for a few minutes. You're pale . . . I don't want you to faint.'

She hesitates, looking at my hand. I immediately let go. 'Please? To put my mind at rest?'

Sophie steps back, creating more space between us. 'Okay, I guess.'

Despite her obvious lack of enthusiasm, she hasn't flagged down a taxi or thrown herself in front of a bus to escape, which is progress.

'Erm, can I help carry anything?'

I'm expecting her to brush me off, but she passes two bags, which contain books and albums. Our fingers touch briefly and I'm hoping she doesn't hear the breath catch in my throat.

She coughs. 'Bernard reminded me you're interested in my bedspread in the window. He said you're a big fan of triangles and giant pandas, apparently.'

'What can I say? My hobbies are pretty niche these days.'

She gives a small laugh and fumbles inside the tote she's clutching, revealing triangular-patterned fabric. 'I brought it for you.' She clears her throat. 'For your pupils.'

My eyebrow shoots up. In her email, she'd said someone else had reserved it.

'Thank you, Sophie!' I lick my dry lips. 'This is amazing. I had no idea you were good at sewing when we were . . .'

I catch the look on her face and correct myself.

'But obviously, it must be something you've been doing after . . .' I gulp. 'Since we last saw each other.'

She doesn't offer any information and we fall into step, a large paving-stone-sized distance between us. Unspoken words swirl around that gulf, and I don't know how to find them.

'Thank you for doing this,' I say, breaking the awkward silence. 'For seeing me . . . I'm extremely grateful.'

She shrugs, staring straight ahead. 'Bernard needs the money. Me too. And all this.' She waves at the gap between us, which may as well be Grand Canyon-sized. 'Is all good.'

'100 per cent. Anyway . . .'

She inhales deeply. 'How are you, Adam?'

'Great! Never been better!'

I feel my neck warm from the lie. It's been the week from hell. 'How about you? You look fantastic, by the way!'

Her cheeks flush. 'Thanks, but I meant healthwise. Are you ill?'

'Aagh! Do I look it?' I don't give her a chance to reply. 'You know, it's probably the lack of sleep. I've aged ten years in the last seven months. I'm permanently knackered and stressed and had a monster hangover this week. I had more than one beer . . . a total disaster!'

'Sorry to hear that – apart from the self-inflicted hangover.' She casts a curious sideways look. 'I never pictured you *here* in a million years. I thought you'd still be at Stanford, partying with all the postgrads.'

My mind whirrs. *She's been picturing me?*

'I was at Stanford . . . I mean, I did . . .'

I wonder whether to bring up the past, our shared history. I'm debating what to say when we reach the café. I steel myself for the introductions, but Sophie speaks first.

'Well? Shall we go in?' She stares as I hang back.

'Erm, just to let you know . . . I've brought someone with me today. I hope that's all right?' I take a breath. 'Wren's waiting inside. She's my daughter.'

Sophie pauses for a beat, the corners of her mouth curving into a small smile.

'You're the client – you're paying for my time and can bring whoever you want.'

Client, not even an old or former friend.

Her words feel like a stab to the heart, but it's probably better she's businesslike. I've felt ridiculously nostalgic ever since learning she lives in Bristol. I've wondered what her home looks like and who she shares it with, whether she has a long-term boyfriend, a new lover or even a fiancé or husband. I thought the latter categories were unlikely since Shirt Guy was trying to win her over with carrot cake. Mostly, I've looked through old photos in bed, remembering what we once had. But she doesn't have any residual feelings, which is good to know. Well, obviously it isn't, but it means I must temper my expectations.

'I'm only telling you because the quilt is for Wren,' I clarify. 'That's why I thought the two of you should meet in person. I mean, the three of us.'

'What about your wife? Or partner? Will she be joining you?'

'Carley . . . We're not . . . I mean, well, we weren't married . . .'

Something travels across her eyes. Is it surprise? Pain? Her face hardens as if she's steeling herself for something worse.

'You don't owe me an explanation, Adam. It's *your* life.'

Invisible knives grind deeper into my chest. She's drawn a strict line and doesn't want me to step over it into anything remotely personal. I must follow her lead.

'I agree, but there are a few things you should know before we go any further. Wren's mum . . . Carley died from breast cancer last August.'

'No!'

Her hand flies to her mouth and I notice she's not wearing an engagement or wedding ring. She heaves as if battling more nausea.

'You're a single dad?' She steps closer.

'Can't you tell?'

I point to the bags under my eyes, hoping to make her laugh again, but the corners of her mouth don't twitch.

'I'm so sorry for your loss. And Wren's. It's terrible you're both having to go through this. I wish—' Her voice disappears into the loud hum of traffic.

'Thank you. Carley and I got together at Stanford . . . Anyway, we never . . . I didn't know—'

'Look! The magpie's back.'

The bird flutters overhead, landing on a signpost. It peers down at us curiously. Sophie's right to change the subject . . . this should be a professional, contractual arrangement. I mustn't venture into anything personal if the project is going to work, and it *must*, for Wren's sake. I don't have any other solutions up my sleeve.

'Carley's clothes are . . . well, badly ripped. I didn't want to throw them away and thought a quilt would help comfort Wren. I need you to create something new and beautiful. Things have been . . . bad recently.'

This is the understatement of the year.

'You always were kind and thoughtful.' Her voice trembles. 'Your daughter's lucky to have you.'

'Wren would never say that!' I wince, hating the bitter edge that's crept into my voice.

'Whyever not?' Her forehead crinkles.

'I mean, you choose your friends, not your family. Doesn't every kid want to swap their parents for someone else? We both did at times when we were teenagers!'

I'm trying to sound light-hearted and share common ground, but Sophie quietly studies my face as if she's trying to read my thoughts. I don't want to admit how dysfunctional my relationship is with Wren and lower her opinion of me even further.

'I was sorry to hear about your dad,' she says quietly.

My eyes moisten at the unexpected mention of him. 'Th-th-thank you for the flowers!'

White roses arrived at the church four years ago. The card accompanying the bouquet said *Sorry for your loss* and had a squiggle at the end but no name. The florist had drawn the shape incorrectly, but I instantly knew what the loop meant and who must have sent it. I'd delivered a similarly mathematically coded message and flowers when her mum died at the end of my freshman year. I'd signed it and provided contact details that she never used.

'You care enough about your daughter to reach out to me,' Sophie says gently, interrupting my thoughts. 'Wanting to comfort her when she's grieving and unhappy makes you a good dad. Actually, strike that – *a great dad.*'

I cough to disguise the strangled noise that escapes from my throat. Sophie always knew the right thing to say whenever I was stressing out or, worse still, having a full-on panic attack. Making a memory quilt for Wren is absolutely my main objective, but I could have hired a stranger online: plenty of sewing companies offer similar, cheaper services.

The truth is, I desperately wanted to see her again.

I haven't been able to stop thinking about *us* over the past week.

How can we be in the same city, so close geographically, but not in each other's lives? It's a mathematical impossibility . . . and it's torturing me.

I swing open the café door, inhaling the scent of fresh coffee wafting over from the counter. 'Come and meet Wren. Please? For her sake?'

And mine.

She watches the magpie cawing noisily and flapping its wings, before taking a deep breath and walking inside.

The saying about these birds comes to me as I follow after her.

One for sorrow, two for joy.

The magpie's companion must be lurking about . . .

This chance to spend time with Sophie, even for a few grabbed minutes, fills me with indescribable happiness.

16

SOPHIE

THURSDAY, 20 MARCH 2025

A wave of heat smothers me as I step into the stuffy café. *This is a huge mistake.* I managed to keep a lid on my feelings outside by concentrating on putting one foot in front of the other, but the walls feel like they're pressing in. They're trapping me with Adam's appalling number. I should have fled as soon as I saw that lone magpie: it's definitely a bad omen.

One for sorrow.

I'm consumed by it. Adam overtakes and my fists clench as I follow behind, trying to breathe through my racing heartbeat. I can't hide my emotions behind my sunglasses and instead resort to digging my nails into my palms to prevent tears from welling.

We pass the elderly couple, who are pulling on their coats. They're in their eighties but both have far longer left to live than Adam. So does the fifty-something woman at the till who has deep lines around her lips and carries a pen between her fingers the way she probably holds cigarettes. I'm guessing she's desperate to finish work and have a fag, which might contribute to her death in about fifteen years' time.

Why does she have longer to live than Adam? Why do these pensioners?

More questions race through my head, torturing me.

What will happen to Adam in a little over three weeks? Is he terminally ill? Will his heart suddenly stop? Or is he about to fall victim to an accident or a crime?

Who will look after his orphaned daughter when he's gone?

Why is life so BLOODY unfair? What is the point of having this freakish ability if I can't do anything to help?

Adam hovers by their table, waiting for Wren to make eye contact. She bristles and doesn't look up. I saw Wren's number when I stood outside the café and didn't think anything of it since she's a kid – I'd expect her to have a high digit. But now, her figure is horribly poignant. Wren has more than 29,200 days to live – 80 years – and virtually all of them will be without Adam. Like me, she'll grow up without her dad. Mine was never on the scene, whereas hers will be ripped from her prematurely. Adam will never see her landmark birthdays – her sixteenth, eighteenth and twenty-first – not even her next one, unless it's imminent. He won't drop her off for Freshers' Week at uni or collect her after a night out with friends. He'll never be guest of honour at her engagement party, give a touching, misty-eyed father-of-the-bride speech at her wedding, or kiss his first grandchild.

I grab for a chair as the room tilts. Adam doesn't notice, thankfully – he's trying to gain his daughter's attention. He fake coughs for a second time.

'Wren! This is Sophie Leroux, my old school friend I was telling you about. She's agreed to make the quilt for us.'

His daughter peels her gaze away from the drawing and stares at me with large forget-me-not-blue eyes. They're the exact colour of her dad's. It takes all my strength not to flinch.

Adam has a daughter. He'll be dead in less than a month.

There is absolutely nothing I can do to save him.

I grip the back-rest tighter. I need to stay strong for the next twenty minutes. Then I can walk away and try not to think about either of them again.

'Hello, Wren.' My knees weaken. 'I need to sit down, sorry.'

Adam pulls out another chair for me. 'I'll get you a drink. Tea?'

'That sounds good, thanks. Can I have a glass of tap water too?'

'Coming right up.'

If I closed my eyes, he could be saying those exact words in the old beach café we used to haunt, sharing strawberry milkshakes, slices of carrot cake, kisses and a few furtive gropes in one of the back booths. I bat away the image as he heads to the counter.

'It's lovely to meet you.' I wriggle out of my jacket, nodding at her top. 'We're both fans of bright colours.'

She picks up her pencil and continues drawing without replying, her forehead creased in concentration. That's her dad's 'work' expression. Her bandaged hand rests on the table, steadying the paper. I'm glad she can't see the shock on my face. I'm no expert on kids' ages but Wren must be seven or eight. Despite all those messages Adam left in the aftermath of the accident, he got over our break-up much quicker than me. Did he meet and fall in love with Carley during his first term? They must have been together almost a decade before her death.

Adam arrives and places a glass on the table next to me. I'm conscious of how close he's standing and catch a whiff of his musky citrus aftershave. My stomach tightens. I remember a similar scent when we kissed, and all those times I wept in his arms over Mum's neglect. He'd hug me, making me feel safe and loved – by him, at least.

This is bad, really bad. My body has an automatic reaction to being around him; those feelings never fully went away. They're simmering treacherously near to the surface, however hard I try to keep them bottled up.

'Thanks,' I say, without looking at him.

'Why don't you show Sophie what you're drawing while I get the rest of the drinks?'

Wren shakes her head. I catch a glimpse of storm clouds and a choppy sea before her hand curls protectively around the picture, hiding it.

'She's shy with everyone,' Adam says hastily.

'It's okay.'

Except it's not. Wren is withdrawn and grieving for her mum. Unbeknown to either of them, she's about to be bereaved a second time.

Adam returns to the counter as the waitress turns on a blender, making me jump. Blood-like streaks of red fruit whizz around at speed. I glance away, my nerves becoming more ragged by the minute.

'Shall we look at some designs, Wren?'

She scribbles harder. I pull out the sewing books and lay them on the table, next to the album containing photos of my work, and shuffle the chair closer. The leg catches on a plastic bag. Brightly coloured women's clothes peep out.

These must belong to Adam's dead girlfriend, the mother of his child.

Despite my alarm, I can't tear my gaze away. Carley loved bold prints and vibrant hues, like me. Is that what drew Adam to her? She must have been outgoing and confident, the way I was as a teenager. Were furtive looks exchanged across the lecture hall? Did she walk straight up to him and suggest a coffee after class? Or did he ask her out? Carley was pretty, judging from her daughter's lovely auburn hair and freckles.

I look across at the counter and feel my cheeks warm furiously. Adam is watching me as the lady puts a teapot on his tray. He blushes and rearranges the mugs. I turn my attention back to his daughter.

'How old are you, Wren?'

She ignores me and colours in her clouds vigorously with a black crayon, making a small tear in the paper.

'Seven?'

Her bright-blue eyes fix on my face, burning with fury. She picks up a pencil, turns over the page and draws a large number 8.

'Sorry, eight. You *do* look bigger.'

She carefully writes five letters.

Idiot.

I lick my dry lips. 'Did you know it's the same word in French? You say it differently, like this: id-ee-oh.' I lower my voice. 'But don't tell your dad! I'll get into trouble if he realises I'm *really* here to teach you how to be rude to him in different languages!'

Wren covers her mouth, disguising a snigger.

'Is your birthday soon?' I ask.

She chews her lip and writes 5 Feb, which is 1 month and 15 days ago. It must have been her worst ever birthday – the first after her mum's death.

'I'm sorry, Wren. That must have been tough. I've lost my mum too and my first birthday without her was incredibly hard.'

She stares at me, unblinking, not giving anything away.

'You might not believe this now, but things *will* get better. The pain you feel over losing your mum will always be there, but it becomes less intense, less overwhelming.'

Wren silently flips the paper back to her drawing. She adds lightning to her storm, the yellow pencil carefully etching over the black clouds instead of the previous aggressive strokes. While she works, I process the new information. Adam was in the spring term of his freshman year when she was conceived. He became a dad halfway through his degree! Were he and Carley shocked when they discovered she was pregnant? And how did Adam's parents react? I'm guessing not well. It must have been an accident because Adam's life was mapped out from GCSEs onwards; this was never part of the master plan. Did Adam's mum and dad support them once they'd recovered from the surprise?

I shudder, thinking about how different the month of Wren's birth was for me. I was still mourning Joan's death and being harassed by her son, Trevor. Adam returns to our table, carrying a tray. He puts a smoothie next to Wren and distributes the mugs and plates.

'This is supposed to be the best carrot cake in Bristol,' he tells me. 'I thought you might like to try it?'

He remembered!

My heart aches at the touching gesture. It splits in two when I catch a glimpse of the tattoo on his wrist.

It's a Möbius strip.

17

ADAM

Thursday, 20 March 2025

Our table is deathly silent. I'm trying to sip my tea quietly. Wren is nibbling around the edge of her cookie, the way I used to attack Crunchie bars, biting off the chocolate first. Perhaps it's a hereditary habit. Sophie's watching us, her hand covering her mouth. She looks as though she might burst into tears or vomit again. I chose this café because it supposedly serves amazing carrot cake, but she hasn't picked up her fork.

I'm hunched forward, keeping my right hand on my lap so she doesn't notice my tattoo. It's sweltering in here and I've had to roll my sleeves. Sophie's pale-faced and calm, whereas sweat is beading on my forehead and my heart is racing. I put a forkful of sponge and frosting in my mouth and briefly close my eyes.

'The online reviews are 100 per cent right! This *is* good carrot cake.'

I wipe my mouth with a paper napkin. Sophie used to search for the elusive ten out of ten rating.

'I'd give it seven out of ten for the cake and an eight for the topping, but I'm happy to be corrected!' I say brightly.

She gulps, shifting position. 'I might take a doggy bag, if that's okay?'

'Yes, of course!'

I want to put her at ease, but she looks increasingly uncomfortable. It's probably the shock of discovering I have a daughter . . . and then meeting her seconds later. Sophie hated maths at school, but it doesn't take a genius to work out that Wren was conceived while I was at Stanford. There's no easy way to bring this up, especially not in front of my daughter. I'd thought about dropping Sophie an email last night to explain everything, but put off writing it. I wish I had now.

'I think we should—' she begins.

'I meant to tell—' I say at the same time.

Sophie nods. 'You go first.'

'I was about to say, I should have mentioned my . . . well, personal circumstances before today.'

'Your mum must be thrilled to be a grandma,' she says abruptly, changing the subject.

'Hmmm.'

Wren shifts her attention from the drawing to scrutinising my face. I stuff a large piece of cake into my mouth to avoid answering.

'Will she contribute to the quilt? Or would Wren's other grandparents like to get involved?' Sophie asks. 'You could all pick out the fabrics together as a family?'

'There's no one left on Carley's side, sadly, so it's just my mum.'

'Oh, right. Sorry.' She bites her lip. 'But I guess Mrs B must be a big help? Does she come to Bristol much or are you trekking back to Bigbury regularly?'

The sponge sticks in my dry throat. I take a large gulp of tea, wincing as the hot liquid burns my tongue.

'Here, have this.' She pushes her glass of water closer.

'Thanks!'

I take a swig and focus on my plate until I can speak. 'We haven't seen Mum since Christmas. I've been busy with work, and thought it was important to get Wren settled into a routine at weekends, just the two of us.'

In my peripheral vision, I see Wren cross her arms tightly across her body.

'But you'll go back over the Easter break?' Sophie presses.

'Can we?' Wren chips in. 'I want to see Grandma and play with her dogs.'

'I don't think so, sorry. I've already booked you into the holiday camp you love.'

I smile at Wren, but she scowls back.

'I *hate* sports camp!'

'That's not true.'

'Yes, it is!'

Sophie grabs her glass of water and takes a large gulp.

'We'll probably visit over next half term or in the summer when things have calmed down workwise.'

I tear off small pieces of the napkin. I'm not in a hurry to go back. Mum and I will argue, and I'll feel fresh guilt about how much she and Dad invested in my education only for me to end up as a classroom teacher. How I failed to keep my promise to my dad and let them both down badly. Plus, I want to avoid bringing up Carley's last wishes with Wren: she won't allow me to dust her mum's urn, let alone discuss emptying it on a beach during a storm. Carley was surprisingly specific about the weather aspect.

I push the bits of paper aside. 'About the quilt. Shall we get down to business?' I point at her photo albums on the table.

My words come out sharper than I'd planned.

'Sure,' Sophie replies equally tersely, shoving a book towards me. 'I need to shoot off. Why don't I leave this one with you?

Browse through it together at home. Take your time. There's no hurry.'

'That sounds good. What do you think, Wren?'

She shrugs, which is an improvement compared to her previous death stare. I ram it into my rucksack and pick up the bags of ripped clothes. 'Do you want to take these?'

'No!' Sophie replies vehemently, before softening her tone. 'I'm going straight from here by bus to another client.'

'Of course. I wasn't sure . . . I can take them with us. I brought the car.'

'Great!' Her voice sounds strained, and her knuckles are white as she grips the edge of the table. 'Do you want to make another appointment after looking at the patterns?'

'Great!' I repeat the word back with the same amount of enthusiasm Sophie appears to be mustering for our project. Wren leans over and whispers in my ear that she needs the toilet.

'Shall I come with you?'

She shakes her head and stalks off before I can explain they're on the left, past the kitchen. Sophie's gaze trails after her.

'Actually, can I book something now?'

I tap on my phone's diary app, which is as empty as the calendar in the kitchen. Sophie chews her bottom lip as she scans her phone.

'Erm . . . how about next week?' I prompt when she doesn't fill the silence. 'Thursday and Friday evenings are usually free. Most nights are good, to be honest, including weekends, if you want to pop round. It's not as if I'm out partying. I'm home with Wren.'

God, I sound like a complete loser.

'I mean, I do have a social life, but not, well . . .'

'We could use the shop after hours,' Sophie says, cutting in. 'I'll have my sewing machine and equipment on hand.'

She's right . . . it's far better to meet on neutral territory. That way I don't have to worry about cleaning our house, which consistently resembles a disaster zone even when I can get the vacuum to work.

'The next couple of weeks are busy workwise,' Sophie continues. 'I won't be able to make a start on this straightaway. How about meeting the week beginning the twenty-first of April?'

'In a month's time?' I blurt out.

'Is that a problem?' She doesn't look up and taps at her phone.

'Yes, well, no. But I guess I'd hoped . . .' I rest both arms on the table, before remembering my tattoo. I snatch my hand back, almost knocking over my mug, and rest it on my lap. 'I thought we'd begin sooner.'

My excuse sounds lame, but not seeing Sophie for another four weeks feels unreasonably long and painful, even though this is a fraction of the time we've spent apart.

'I need the quilt to be *made* in the next month,' I stress. 'I can throw in a little extra if that bumps us up the queue?'

I *cannot* afford to go over £850 when I've agreed to increase Anna's pay.

Sophie fixes me with a cool stare. 'This isn't about the money.'

'Sorry. That came out wrong . . . To be honest, I'm desperate. I messed up and need to put things right.' I point at the bags of clothes. 'I have to help my daughter. Carley wanted me—'

'You don't have to explain about Carley, I get it,' she says flatly.

'I mean . . . Wren needs this.'

Sophie closes her eyes briefly as if attempting to block out something horrible. *Me.*

I cough, clearing my throat. 'If you could find an earlier slot, we'd both appreciate it. This could help Wren come to terms with her loss.'

It sounds like emotional blackmail, but it's 100 per cent true. I also have the nagging feeling Sophie is pulling away from me . . .

mentally this time, not physically. I can't let her leave without nailing down the prospect of seeing her again.

'Please, Sophie. I'm not above begging!'

She suppresses a sigh. 'Fine. Let me see if I can juggle a few things and I'll let you know in the next few days.'

Result!

'Thank you. Shall we exchange numbers? I mean . . . so we can keep in touch about the commission? WhatsApp is probably easier than email.'

Sophie looks as though she'd prefer to have all her teeth extracted without anaesthetic but reels off her number as Wren returns. I tap it into my phone and send a message back.

'There, done! Thanks.'

My phone vibrates with a WhatsApp from Anna. I may have to rename our nanny 'Harbinger of Doom' in my contacts.

Smoke coming out of tumble dryer. Have turned off at mains and opened windows to air kitchen. Nothing damaged but you need to call a plumber demain. A.

'Problem?' Sophie asks, standing up.

'The tumble dryer's threatening to burn down our house!'

She breathes in sharply. 'You shouldn't leave it on a cycle while you're out or overnight.'

Sophie is the last person I'd expect to give advice about hazards. She was always the risk-taker who pushed me to try things out of my comfort zone.

'We've aged, haven't we?' I say, laughing. 'Now we're the responsible ones. Well, trying to be anyway!'

Sophie blinks, pushing her chair under the table. 'I should go. It's getting late.'

'Don't forget your cake.'

The cream cheese frosting has melted and slid off into an unappetising pool on her plate, but she heads to the counter while

Wren packs and pulls on her coat. She skirts around her mum's clothes and I attempt to bundle the bags into my arms, along with my rucksack and the shopping.

Sophie returns clutching a small white cardboard box. She doesn't realise she's also potentially holding our future happiness in her hands. She slides the books back into her tote, careful not to bend the pages, and throws on her cardigan and coat.

'Let me help,' she says, watching me unsuccessfully juggle our belongings.

'Thank you!'

After scooping up everything between us, Sophie exits gracefully, but Wren and I bump into each other. She lets out a heavy sigh and dodges past. They both follow me down the street. No one would guess we're together . . . we're walking silently and in single file.

'Here we are!' I say, as we reach Mum's battered Volvo estate.

She barely drives anymore and said it made more sense if I used the car when I returned to the UK. I wish I'd taken Wren's advice before setting off . . . she's written *Clean Me* with her finger in the grime on the boot. I pop it open, pretending I haven't noticed, and arrange the bags inside, delaying the inevitably awkward goodbye.

Should I air-kiss Sophie on the cheek or shake her hand?

'Don't forget this.' Sophie passes the tote containing her triangular-patterned bedspread.

'Thank you! I know one pupil in particular who'll find your quilt helpful.'

'You can keep it if you want? I have lots more at home.'

My mind returns to wondering what her flat or house looks like; has she made all the curtains and cushions? Do patchwork throws cover the sofa and bed? When did she learn to sew? She used to be outdoorsy and wasn't into crafts. Does she make gifts for Shirt Guy? *Are* they an item?

Another more unsettling thought lands. Giving me her creation could mean she fails to fix another appointment.

'No, that's fine, thanks! I'll return it when we meet up next.'

A tremor passes through Sophie. I'm hoping it's not a shudder of dread. She turns to Wren with a faint smile.

'It was lovely meeting you.' Her voice shakes. 'Don't forget to practise your French!'

'I thought you were learning Spanish at school?' I say, frowning.

Wren rolls her eyes and mouths a word at Sophie that looks remarkably like 'idiot' before scrambling into the back seat and shutting the door.

I take a deep breath. 'Can I drop you off at your next appointment? Or . . . somewhere along the way?'

'No, I'm feeling better, thanks. The bus stop is nearby.'

'Soooo . . .'

My head whirrs as I debate the pros and cons of air kiss versus handshake. Sophie steps closer. My heart leaps as she stands on tiptoes and brushes her lips against my cheek. Her hand presses briefly into the small of my back. I catch a whiff of vanilla and white lily. Everything blurs into the distance as I picture the two of us, laughing and dancing in her bedroom.

'Good luck with everything, Adam. Goodbye.'

She steps away, leaving me breathless.

'I . . . erm.'

Wren peers at us through the window, suddenly interested.

'Until we meet to discuss the design . . . next month, if not sooner,' I clarify.

She scrutinises my face as if searching for something. What, exactly? The Adam from her past? *I* barely know him. He's a completely different person. I feel like an actor playing his part and not doing it well. Someone else could perform the role far better.

'Yes, of course, 'til then. Bye.'

I'm trying to hold on to this moment for as long as possible, but she turns and leaves. I catch a glimpse of Wren sighing heavily and sinking into her seat. I'm deflated, but for different reasons.

I watch Sophie walk down the street, becoming smaller and smaller.

Please look at me one last time.

Show me you remember.

You still care.

She turns the corner and disappears without a backward glance.

I touch my cheek. The warmth of her kiss continues to linger, along with the feeling our farewell was final.

I'm 100 per cent certain Sophie has no intention of seeing me again.

18

SOPHIE

Friday, 3 July 2015

'When can we see each other next?' I whispered as I fastened my bra.

I managed to wrestle my T-shirt and hoodie over my head and pulled on my shorts, but Adam still hadn't replied. His arms were flung over his eyes; we both fell back to sleep after the alarm went off on my phone.

'Adam?' I hissed. 'I need to go! We've slept in.'

I'd sneaked in late last night and planned to leave before 5 a.m. as his mum often took their dog for an early walk on the beach. I'd wanted to fit in a surf before waitressing the breakfast shift at the Burgh Island hotel, but it was five forty-five already.

'Hmmm. What?' He removed his hands, rubbing his eyes. 'Sorry. Tomorrow night? No, wait . . . Mum and Dad are taking me out to dinner to celebrate . . .'

'Being a shoo-in for Cambridge.' I finished his sentence, hunting for my socks on the floor. 'You're cracking open the champagne early.'

I felt a small, envious ache in my chest. My mum led an Italian yoga retreat in May and I returned to an empty house after most of my exams. But Adam regularly cycled or drove over to give me one of his 'famous' hugs. He also dropped off carrot cake. *His* parents had supported him throughout his A levels. They didn't need to wait to see his grades next month: his place at Trinity College was practically guaranteed. Adam was never in danger of flunking anything. *Unlike me.*

'I could come over when you're back from dinner? Or any day except Friday – we're having birthday drinks at work.'

'Can I let you know?' Adam said. 'Mum's invited my aunt and uncle to stay and they're bringing their tribe of kids. It'll make overnights and days out trickier.'

'Yeah, sure.'

This was probably a deliberate ploy by his parents to keep him occupied – and away from me – even though his exams were over and I couldn't be accused of distracting him. I looked under the bed – Adam's dumping ground – and snatched up the missing sock, pulling on my trainers.

When I turned around, he was holding out a small black-velvet box. My heart skipped a beat.

'Yes, Adam! Of course I'll marry you. Let's elope to Vegas tonight.'

'What?' His face coloured. 'I mean . . . perhaps, *definitely* sometime . . . in the future, possibly . . .'

'I'm kidding!'

'Ha ha! Open it.'

I flicked open the lid and gazed at a silver necklace with a smooth knot in the centre of the chain.

'It's beautiful. Thank you!'

'Whatever happens after results day, I can't imagine my life without you, Sophie. We're like this Möbius strip: we'll always be together.'

I touched the curved metal, frowning. What did he mean by *whatever happens*? Fear flickered in my heart.

'I had it made specially because the love knots in the jewellery shop weren't mathematically correct,' he continued. 'This is our symbol.'

I pushed down my rising doubts.

'I love it! Help me?'

Lifting my hair, I waited for him to fasten the pendant. The metal felt cool against my skin.

'I meant what I said about *us*, I promise.' He took my hand, placing it on his chest. I could feel his heart beating in time with mine as if we were one body, not two. 'Or I could get a Möbius strip tattoo to prove it?'

'Your parents would murder *me*. I want to live longer than eighteen, thanks!'

He laughed. 'Shall I come downstairs with you? I mean . . . I can thwart any assassination attempts by Mum and Dad.'

'No, go back to sleep.'

I kissed the hollow at the base of his throat, making him shudder, and worked my way up his neck to his lips.

'Come back to bed!' he whispered.

I longed to strip off and curl up beside him, feeling him kiss me tantalisingly slowly and then more passionately, as our urgency increased. I was more experienced than him when we got together. But he grew in confidence and often made me feel like it was *my* first time being naked with a boy. Now, we were equals. We'd learned how to love each other's bodies. I shook my head, fighting off the temptation to have a replay of last night, or to just chat and laugh. We could talk for hours about everything and nothing, and not run out of things to say. Lying wrapped in his arms was where I felt happiest and safest.

'I have to go. Call you later. Love you.'

'Ditto!'

Quietly, I tiptoed down the stairs, past the photographs of Adam picking up awards for the Maths Olympiad and science challenges, and his dad's achievements at various universities, including Cambridge.

Reaching the kitchen, I fumbled with the key in the back door.

'It's stiff. Let me get that for you.'

Holy shit!

I spun around. Adam's mum stood behind me in her white towelling dressing gown, her dark brown bob pushed behind her ears. Pickles, their geriatric terrier, padded into the room, sniffing at his food bowl. The wooden clock above the fridge ticked loudly, the blue tiles behind the sink gleamed brightly.

'I'm leaving,' I told her.

'I know. I heard you come downstairs. I'm a light sleeper. I have been ever since Adam was a child.'

She leaned past me and threw open the door. I attempted to make a quick exit, almost falling over in my hurry to get out.

'I'm sorry, Mrs B.'

'No, wait! Before you go, I wanted to say thank you.'

'W-w-what for?'

This wasn't how I expected her to react. I thought she'd flail my skin off before nailing my bleeding body to the outside wall. Or something less dramatic.

'I misjudged you. I thought you'd try to change Adam's mind and make him stay.'

'We both want him to be happy,' I said, picking my words carefully. 'Being here in Bigbury wouldn't do that, obviously.'

Surprise flickered across her face, followed by another emotion, before she rearranged her features. What was that? Shock? Fear?

'My husband has huge ambitions for Adam, which can be hard to live up to. He's done well not to buckle under the pressure. I think you've helped in that respect, so you have my utmost gratitude for supporting him these last few years. It's meant a lot to him.'

'Adam supports *me*,' I said quietly. 'We love each other. Very much.'

She sighed. 'I see that, but you're both so young.'

'I don't think that makes any difference!'

'Perhaps not now.' She walked over to Pickles and bent down, patting him. 'I understand you want to make the most of being together while you can, but please ask my permission if you want to stay overnight. Adam's dad is old-fashioned about sleeping arrangements. I'll need to raise it ahead of time and talk him around.'

Straightening, she flashed me a surprisingly warm smile. 'Look after yourself, Sophie. I hope things work out for you. You deserve to be happy.'

'Thank you, Mrs B.'

'Goodbye.'

She closed the door behind me with a gentle click. I jumped on my bike and touched Adam's necklace, trying to cling on to his parting words in the bedroom.

But as the distance between us grew, my confidence ebbed away like the tide lapping on the beach below.

I had the overwhelming feeling I was being permanently dismissed from all their lives.

19

SOPHIE

FRIDAY, 21 MARCH 2025

Saying goodbye to Adam for the last time *ever* was one of the hardest things I've had to do in my life. I wanted to memorise his features: the piercing blue eyes, the dimple in his cheeks when he smiles, and the hollow at the base of his throat I used to kiss. I tried to capture every single detail in my mind but felt them slip away as I walked down the street. I hadn't known this grown-up version of Adam long enough to remember all the subtle changes. I don't have an up-to-date photo to study or enough memories from a single encounter. I had to dig my nails into my palms to stop myself from asking for a 'famous' hug. And it took all my willpower not to glance over my shoulder for a final look before I turned the corner.

I roll over in bed, pulling my Bargello-patterned quilt over my head. It's 3 a.m. and half a bottle of vodka hasn't knocked me out or stopped me from dwelling on Adam. His horrifically low number is going round my head on a loop. He is doomed to die and leave his daughter an orphan. Wren faces more trauma on top of losing her mum. Will Mrs B gain custody? She doesn't appear to be closely involved in their lives – they haven't seen each other since Christmas. Have they fallen out? Will he pick up on my hints and visit her during Wren's school holidays? It's doubtful they'll make up in time unless I could . . . Maybe I should . . .

No! I can't change whatever's destined to happen. There's no point trying to discover what he's planning to do on Saturday, 12 April. I have no choice but to let him go for a second time. I trace my fingers over the inside of my wrist. Adam had a Möbius strip tattoo on this exact spot and was trying to hide it from me in the café. When did he get it? And why? It must have been before he met and fell in love with Carley. He might have wanted a reminder of his final school days, or it was just a drunken dare at uni and he's forgotten how it became our secret love language as teenagers. But if that's the case, why did he leave the symbol for me at the dry cleaners?

I let out another muffled cry into my pillow. I'll never learn the truth because I *can't* get involved, I *won't* meet Adam again.

That was the last time I'll ever hear his laugh or watch him run his hand through his hair, become emotional when he talks about Wren or his dad, tear up a napkin while deep in thought and close his eyes when tasting carrot cake. We'll never kiss and cuddle.

I climb out of bed and switch on the light. Sleep is impossible. I pull on jogging bottoms and a sweatshirt and head into the kitchen. The carrot cake from the café is in the bin; I knew I'd probably choke on a single mouthful. Food is spattered on the stove and Rakesh has left his dirty pans and plates before going on shift. I could leave another moany note, but cleaning helps take my mind off things. After scrubbing everything thoroughly and mopping the floor, I grab a glass of water and return to my room to hunt for painkillers.

I tap out a message on my phone for Adam to read when he wakes up, claiming I need to stick to my earliest available appointment date: 21 April. He doesn't realise it will never happen because it's after his numbers run out. My finger hovers over the send button. What if Adam's right and this quilt will help Wren?

I delete the message and sit at my desk. I need to keep busy and distract myself from Adam's countdown. I'll create a large quilt to sell on my website and Etsy that will be intricate and difficult to construct. I sketch out complex variations on a mariner's compass design, but my mind keeps going back to the numbers from my past.

12.

That's how many people I tried and failed to help, culminating in Joan. Their faces haunt me, particularly the children.

Adam could be my thirteenth attempt.

My head is telling me I can't do anything, but my heart refuses to accept the truth. I draw a large 13, double-underline it and add a question mark. The number is considered unlucky in this culture, but isn't the opposite true in China? I'm sure I've read somewhere it's supposed to mean 'definitely vibrant' or 'assured growth'.

I can't shake the feeling it *might* signal promise. I sketch a 13-sided shape, which would be tricky to reproduce in fabric. I increase the size and change the lengths of the sides until I come up with an outline for a cardboard template. If these shapes slot together to form small clusters, I could incorporate them into a complex series of panels in the centre of my design. It would take weeks, *months*, to get the pattern right.

Using a methodical step-by-step approach to crack a problem could help me work out what is doomed to happen to Adam.

The nib of my pen grinds into the paper, ripping it.

What the hell am I doing?

I shove the diagram into my notepad and slam it shut before I descend any further down this rabbit hole of madness.

It's utterly futile.

It doesn't matter what I plan, design or sew.

Adam's number can't be changed.

He will die in just over 3 weeks' time.

20

SOPHIE

Friday, 21 March 2025

My heart sinks as our worst customer breezes in four days late, carrying a Gucci handbag, her phone and a folded local newspaper. Cynthia is the last person I want to deal with today. I've only grabbed a few hours' sleep, and my head is throbbing. It was tempting to call in sick, but Bernard wouldn't cope on his own. He's resting his hip in the back, while I organise the racks of freshly laundered clothes, armed with Red Bull and paracetamol.

'Hello, Cynthia.'

She holds up a finger to shush me as she takes a call, placing her paper and the pink receipt on the counter. I'm glad I didn't attempt to plaster on a smile. I'm about to fetch her newly altered ballgown, which she'd demanded to collect 'first thing' on Monday morning, when I spot the headline:

Three Teenagers Die in Horror Crash

The air escapes from my lungs as I recognise the photos. These are the young people from the pub last week. They shared the number 9. I'd forgotten their digits would run out yesterday. Tears prick my eyes as I take Cynthia's tag and fetch her ball dress.

See? There's nothing you can do to save Adam. This proves his numbers are grimly inevitable.

I rifle through the racks, looking for the right number, my chest heaving with emotion.

'Everything all right?' Bernard asks.

I nod and pull out the correct hanger, returning to the front of the shop. Cynthia's call has finished and she's drumming her long red nails on the counter. I remove the plastic and lay out the taffeta gown.

'I'll run this through the till for you. It should fit perfectly.'

She holds up the garment, frowning. 'It doesn't look right here.' She stabs a finger at the seam.

'This was the only place I could let it out. The stitches aren't noticeable.'

'I beg to differ!' Cynthia scoffs. 'It looks dreadful. My friends warned me I should use a *professional* dressmaker.'

I breathe in, attempting to keep calm. 'You're welcome to find someone else after you've settled your original bill. It's £20. Cash or card?'

'I'm not paying for this when you're incompetent!'

'Madam, you—'

She raises her hand to silence me as her phone rings again.

I grip the edge of the counter, anger rippling through my body. Her number taunts me: 9,100 days. Why does such an appalling woman get to enjoy a long, full life when Adam's will be cut short? He'll be dead in 23 days, leaving behind a devastated little girl. The injustice of it, the cruelty of the situation, makes my head spin.

'I'll take this and find someone else to fix your mistakes,' she says, ending the call without saying goodbye.

I swipe the dress away before she can pick it up. 'Not so fast!'

'Excuse me?'

'We don't work for free, you rude, grasping cow!' The words fly out of my mouth before I can stop them.

Cynthia quivers with fury. 'How dare you talk to me like that?'

Bernard hobbles over, stepping in front of me. 'I'm terribly sorry for the misunderstanding, Cynthia.' He takes the dress from my hands and shimmies it into the wrapping. 'Please accept this with our humble apologies and no fee.'

Spit bubbles at the corner of her mouth. 'I will *never* return to this shop. And I'll be sure to tell all my friends to avoid coming here. You don't deserve *any* business!'

The door slams behind her.

'Oh dear.' Bernard sinks into a chair, resting his head in his hands.

My anger is swiftly replaced with guilt. 'I'm sorry! I couldn't cope with her rudeness. It was too much.'

He sighs deeply. 'I've been thinking the same for a while, and if anything, this past week has helped make up my mind.'

'How do you mean?'

'All this.' He gestures around the shop. 'My arthritis is getting worse, along with the takings. I want to make the most of the years I have left without the daily pain and worry – and the rude customers.'

'You have plenty of time,' I insist.

'Not necessarily. Enid and I dreamed of enjoying cruises together. I owe it to her to squeeze in a few before I pop my clogs.'

I shake my head. 'This is your life, Bernard.'

'It *was*, but I should have retired years ago.'

Panic shoots through me at the thought of losing my job. 'Please don't stop because of me! I'll apologise to Cynthia. I'll do anything to make this up to you.'

'This is about me, not you,' he replies. 'It's time for me to let all this go before it's too late.'

Bernard suggests I take a stroll after breaking his retirement news. He claims my outburst has nothing to do with his decision, but I can't help thinking I lit the fuse – all because I couldn't cope with his customer's healthy digit. Now, I'm screwed. I won't find another mending job that pays as well and lets me quilt on the side. There's no more Airbnb income from Devon, only mounting bills. I need to pay my rent and haven't sold any quilts yet. I'll have to accept the property developer's offer on Mum's house.

A light breeze makes hundreds of thousands of leaves shiver as I pass the row of trees, making a beeline for the suspension bridge. I sink on to an empty bench and let the tears flow for how badly things have turned out. But mainly, I cry over Adam's fate. The wood groans as someone sits down. A small white dog yaps near my feet. It's Walter and Chico. I angle my body away, hoping Walter hasn't recognised me.

'Is there anything we can do to help, Sophie?' He waves a greyish cotton handkerchief under my nose.

'No, thanks. Am just having a bad day.' I quickly wipe the side of my face with my jacket cuff.

Unfortunately, he doesn't take that as his cue to leave. 'So is Chico. Our neighbour bought garden gnomes and Chico's terrified of them! I named him after Einstein's dog because I thought he might be clever but, sadly, that's not the case.'

Despite everything, I manage to laugh.

'That's better. You often look like you're carrying the weight of the world on your shoulders.'

'Sometimes it feels that way,' I admit.

'I'm told I'm a good listener.'

'It's fine.'

'Let me guess, you think an old man with an intellectually challenged dog couldn't possibly understand?'

I give him a wan smile but don't reply. It's a kind offer and he could sympathise over Bernard's decision. But *no one* will comprehend my ability, and the pain it causes. Mum did a runner within months of learning the date of her death. After that, I vowed never to tell anyone for fear of driving them away. The only possible reaction, understandably, is horror. No one wants to know when their number is up.

'In that case, will you humour an old man and let me talk about myself? That's the problem about having long conversations with Chico – he can't *actually* reply.'

'No way! You've shattered all my illusions about dogs.'

'Apologies.' He looks at me. 'What, may I ask, are you grateful for today?'

I swallow a sigh. 'Sorry, but I'm not religious.'

'Me neither, not in the traditional sense. I'll go first.' He takes a breath. 'I'm enjoying feeling the ache lift from my toes as I rest. I'll relish that first sip of a cold pint and the satisfaction from completing a crossword puzzle in the pub. Afterwards, I'll soak up the view from the bridge with Chico. Tonight, I'll eat my favourite macaroni cheese on a tray in front of the TV. When I'm in bed, I'll feel my permanently cold feet tingle because Chico has curled up on top of them. I'll look at the latest videos my son, Harry, and daughter-in-law, Maddy, have WhatsApped over of the grandkids. Matilda's only six months old, but Harry's teaching her older brothers, James and Luke, to surf. I'll look forward to falling asleep because I'll see my late wife, Hellie. Often, in my dreams, we'll be back on our favourite beach in Cornwall, showing our beautiful little boy, Harry, how to stand on a beginners' board and catch a wave.'

I stare at him, surprised. Bernard's never mentioned that his old customer is a widower or a former surfer.

'I'm sorry about your wife,' I say quietly.

'She died eight years, three months and five days ago, but I chat to her every day.' He leans back, flexing his foot. 'My point is that I won't have achieved anything in the grand scheme of things today, Sophie, apart from a series of small wonders and little delights that are meaningless to other people but bring a huge amount of happiness to myself.'

'I get it. I should be grateful for what I have – my health, the people I love, et cetera.'

Closing his eyes, he lifts his face towards the sky. 'Can you feel it, my dear?'

He asked a similar question on the bridge last week. 'Feel what? The sun?'

'No, the joy of being alive.'

I inhale sharply at the thought of what's to come.

'I'm dying,' he continues matter-of-factly.

'H-h-how do you know?' I stutter, stealing another sideways look at him.

His face is impassive. 'Advanced prostate cancer.'

'I'm sorry.'

'Don't be! I've had a happy life. I don't have many regrets, apart from not having Hellie at my side for more of it. I just wish . . .' He looks wistfully into the distance.

'What?'

'That I knew for definite when it was coming. I need to set my affairs in order, make the most of my time left with family and friends. There are things I need to say and do. Plus, I want to make my goodbye as memorable as possible. That needs careful planning.'

'Why can't you arrange to see your family now?' I ask gently.

'Harry and Maddy live in Sydney and have high-powered jobs. They can't drop everything and travel across the world. The doctors say I might have another six to eight months, so I have time for one final trip to Australia. I'll probably book flights to see them in July, during the kids' school holidays, as long as I'm well enough. I don't want to end up a burden in my final weeks.'

'But what if you don't have that long?' I blurt out.

Walter's bushy white eyebrows knot together. 'You mean if I die sooner? Well, my dear, then I'm completely screwed! But I will be reunited with Hellie earlier than expected in some kind of afterlife, hopefully with a beach and great waves.'

I grip the side of the bench. 'If you could find out exactly when you're going to die, would you *really* want to know?'

'Can you look into a crystal ball and tell me?' he says, chuckling.

'What if I could? Would you want me to give you a precise date?'

He frowns hard. 'In all seriousness, yes. I would like to know for certain.'

Only those closest to me – Flora and Bernard – know I'm good at maths, but I would never admit the full extent of my abilities to them or anyone else. However, Walter knows he is living on borrowed time and already understands the pain of losing a loved one. I take a deep breath and describe the car crash and how I suffered a skull fracture and serious brain injury as a teenager, which required emergency surgery.

'When I woke up, I wasn't the same person. I knew the exact angle of the monitors in relation to my bed, the precise gap in the curtain and the height of the ceiling. Everything had a number.'

'That's quite the gift,' he gasps.

'It's a curse! The nurses, doctors, patients, *everyone* had a number. My consultant claimed I was seeing floaters due to the injury and my vision would improve, but it didn't. People's numbers were always there but getting lower and lower.' I lick my dry lips. 'Eventually, I worked out they were counting down to their deaths.'

Walter lapses into silence. His shoulders rise and fall with his natural breathing rhythm.

'I'm sorry for everything you went through, the grief you've suffered,' he says eventually.

'It's not over. I saw Adam, my old boyfriend from school, yesterday and—'

I bend over, my head in my hands. I've revealed my biggest secret, and Walter hasn't got up, horrified, and stalked off. Should I go all the way and explain *everything*? I want to confide in someone.

'There, there, dear. Take your time.' He waits a couple of minutes until I regain my composure and sit up.

'Adam has a small number?' he asks.

'Horribly so. It's only double digits.'

'And you still have feelings for him?'

'I'm not sure they ever went away,' I say truthfully.

'Then you must make the most of this time with him.'

'But I can't!' I shuffle to face him, speaking rapidly. 'I can't stop what's going to happen. I've repeatedly tried to prevent people's deaths. *Nothing works*. Something always goes wrong.'

Walter lifts his face to the sun again. 'Who said anything about intervening? I'm suggesting you savour those tiny joys, the small moments that will create happy memories for the two of you.'

'Even when I know he's going to die?'

He looks at me. 'We're all dying – some of us sooner than others. But you have a unique gift, Sophie. You can help him make the most of his life in the short time he has left. You can't stop death, but you can prevent him from wasting a single minute or having regrets before he passes.'

'I've never thought of it like that.' I bite my lip hard.

Walter pats my hand. 'I can't advise if you should tell Adam how long he has – that is up to you. But you can give him a "good life" in his remaining days. Cherish these moments with him and make sure he hasn't left a phone call unanswered, or a loved one ignored. Whether he realises it or not, you can give him the chance to say goodbye to the people who matter most and create new memories for them. *They* will have the opportunity to tell him he is much loved. It can be a "good death", if there is such a thing.'

I brush a fresh tear from my cheek, thinking about Adam's apparently strained relationships with Wren and his mum.

'I should go.' Walter leans on his walking stick, levering himself up. 'Adam needs your help. I believe *you* need to spend these last few days with him.'

'You're very wise.'

He tips his hat. 'What do you expect when Chico is named after Einstein's dog?'

I smile, my gaze wandering to his ripped lapel. 'I meant what I said – drop by the shop anytime and I'll repair that for free.'

'I will. Shall we exchange numbers, in case you want more pearls of wisdom? Or updates about Chico and his garden gnome nemeses?'

I gladly tap mine into his phone.

'Thank you.' He pauses. 'The truth is, Sophie, I'm not scared of death, but I am terrified of dying alone in my flat, with just Chico for company. I want to know my number.'

'I'm sorry, Walter, but you only have 16 days.'

His eyes widen with shock, and he sways before lifting his chin and readjusting his hat.

'In that case, none of us should dawdle, my dear. You, me and Adam have some living to do!'

21

ADAM

Saturday, 22 March 2025

'Welcome to our home!' I throw open the front door with a huge smile. 'It's great to see you!'

Sophie startles, fumbling with her phone. 'You too, Adam.'

She's a blaze of glorious colour: a turquoise blouse, green coat and red lipstick. Her glossy hair tumbles around her face. I catch the scent of coconut as she flicks it over her shoulders and my abdomen tightens.

I've been counting down to 11 a.m. since I woke up and Sophie is exactly on time. She messaged yesterday, offering to bump us up her schedule after another customer withdrew their order. I misjudged her on Thursday evening. I thought she was on the point of cancelling completely, but her enthusiasm has increased fivefold. She's promised to work flat out on our bedspread over the coming weeks and wants regular appointments.

'Come in!'

She steps into the hallway and looks at the ceiling. I'm hoping she hasn't noticed the spider's web. I didn't have time to get out the vacuum attachments. I've been running round like a madman, tidying and cleaning, since we got back from ballet class an hour ago. I've also managed to shave and not slice my face to bits, which is a bonus.

Sophie puts down her bags and shrugs off her coat. Another faint scent wafts over: vanilla and lily. My stomach lurches.

'Sorry I've interrupted your Saturday at short notice, but I figured you'd want to get cracking?'

'Yes! This is serendipity or . . .' I run a hand through my hair. 'It's perfect timing, for us, at least. We're free all day with ballet out of the way. We can't go swimming this afternoon . . . Wren mustn't get her stitches wet.'

A smile flickers across Sophie's lips. 'It's great you do that together. It must be fun.'

'Oh no!' I say hastily. 'It's a lesson. I watch from the side. Well, I work on my laptop. But you know what I mean . . .'

Why would she? Sophie has no idea what my life is like, and vice versa. But she probably remembers how I babble when nervous . . .

'Go through to the kitchen and I'll get Wren,' I tell her. 'I've left your book on the table.'

Sophie's arm accidentally brushes against mine as she passes, making me jolt.

'Wren!' My voice comes out as a croak as I stand at the bottom of the stairs. I swallow and call louder. 'Can you come down, please? Sophie's here!'

She doesn't reply as usual, but I'm guessing she heard. I head into the kitchen, my heart beating faster with anticipation. Sophie's crouching down close to the sink.

'Have you sorted this yet?' she asks, straightening up.

'What?'

She points to the tumble dryer. 'Your nanny said it needs fixing.'

'Thanks for jogging my memory! I must call a plumber.'

'You shouldn't put off stuff like that, Adam,' she says firmly. 'It could start a fire and you don't have any smoke alarms in the hall or in here.' She jerks her head at the ceiling.

I stare at her, touched by her concern and surprised, again, at her safety advice. Once, she ignored the lifeguard's red flags to surf ten-foot waves during a storm. I bite back another observation about us both being grown-ups. Some days I wonder if I am . . .

'I know, I know! It slipped my mind about the tumble dryer, but I'll get on it. I need to buy new batteries for the alarms before I put them back up. Thank you for that reminder too!' I clear my throat. 'Can I get you a coffee? Or a cold drink? Anything?'

I wipe my damp palms on my jeans. Why am I so nervous? This is a brief chat about a professional service, nothing more. Sophie made that clear in the café, but still . . . hope flickers. I thought she was saying goodbye, *permanently*, yet she's here, isn't she?

'A coffee would be great.' She exhales heavily and hoists her bag on to the table, pulling out albums and books. After stacking them on top of the one she lent us, her gaze lowers to the sacks of Carley's clothes next to a chair. 'I definitely need a caffeine hit,' she adds.

'Late night partying?' I feel a small stab of jealousy. I miss carefree evenings, drinking until late into the night with my colleagues on the PGCE course and my old friends at Stanford. We haunted the EVGR pub on campus or caught a train to San Francisco to tour the bars and clubs.

'Sorry?' Sophie frowns at me.

Was she on a date with Shirt Guy? Do I sound like a possessive stalker? Or a prematurely middle-aged dad who doesn't get out much?

'It's none of my business what you're doing!' I clear my throat. 'Or not doing.'

Aagh! That sounds even worse.

'I'll shut up and make the coffee. I need a caffeine hit too! I haven't had much sleep either.'

The corners of her mouth twitch as she sits down, rearranging her albums. I open the cupboard and pick the two 'best' mugs I haven't chipped yet, relieved she can't see my cheeks reddening.

'I was working late, which is why I look knackered,' she explains.

'You look great!'

I glance over my shoulder, catching her blush, before continuing to spoon the coffee granules into the pot. 'So . . . are you sewing another quilt?'

'No, I've cleared my schedule for you and Wren. I was sketching a new design. I'm trying to come up with something original, and time got away from me.'

'I know the feeling!' I lean against the counter, beaming at her. 'That's exactly what I'm attempting to do with my dissertation.'

Her mouth drops open. 'You're still doing research at Stanford? As well as working as a maths teacher?'

'I haven't stopped completely. I'm juggling both . . . badly, it transpires.'

I place her coffee on the table and realise I've made it white, no sugar, the way she used to like it.

'That's a lot on top of being a dad,' she says, picking up her mug. 'Are you enjoying it?'

'Well, it has its ups and downs, naturally, but being a father is, generally, rewarding.'

Is it? Wren had a quick flick through Sophie's book last night, but she didn't want to discuss patterns and was more interested in finding out how and when Sophie's mum died; they must have had a discussion in the café. It's the first time she's properly spoken to me since Anna's washing debacle. Coming up with the quilting idea has broken the ice, but it's definitely not 100 per cent thawed.

Sophie puts the mug down abruptly, almost spilling her drink. 'I meant workwise – keeping up with your PhD while teaching full time!'

'Oh! It *is* a lot at the moment, but it's not forever. Being here is only a temporary stopgap until I finish my dissertation and . . .' I break off as Wren appears in the doorway, frowning hard.

She's wearing one of Carley's undamaged green T-shirts as a dress with a pink belt. Her hair is suspiciously damp and has created wet patches on her top.

'I told you not to wash your hair on your own!' I'm trying to keep the exasperation out of my voice. 'You're not supposed to get your bandage wet.'

'I did it one-handed with the nozzle.'

'Why didn't you call me? I'd have come up.'

She folds her arms, scowling. 'Because I don't need *your* help.'

'Well, I think you do . . .'

'Hi, Wren.' Sophie scrapes back her chair, smiling warmly. 'It's nice to see you. I love your dress.'

Wren's face softens and she gives a little wave. 'Hello.'

Whether she senses it or not, Sophie is acting as an unofficial intermediary and preventing the outbreak of World War Three.

'Shall we make a start?' she asks. 'Have you had a chance to look through the quilt pictures?'

'Not properly, sorry,' I reply as Wren makes a beeline for the seat next to her.

'That's okay.' Sophie points to the chair opposite. 'Why don't you go there, Wren? Your dad can sit next to you – that way, you can both look through the pages together, side by side.'

We change direction and collide. Sophie watches us closely, sipping her coffee. We manage to sit down without one of us tripping and she flicks open a red album containing photos.

'Let's start with some of my designs. You can pick anything from in here or these books.' She touches her stack. 'I can adapt patterns and create something different, depending on the styles and types of materials. I'm happy to give advice but the decisions are all yours. You need to work as a team on this.'

She looks expectantly at us. I nod but Wren shuffles her chair further to the left and sticks out her elbow, putting more space between us. She places her hand on the table, and I surreptitiously check her dressing isn't wet.

'We can use different shapes like rectangles, squares, triangles, diamonds and hexagons, and in a variety of sizes.' Sophie turns over pages of the album, studying Wren's face for a reaction. But my daughter scans each photo indifferently and doesn't speak.

'When did you . . . do you mind me asking when you learned how to do this?' I ask, filling the silence.

Sophie doesn't lift her gaze from the pages. 'A few days after my nineteenth, Mum went travelling and I moved to Plymouth. I met an old lady by chance in the city centre, and we became friends. Joan made memory quilts from her grandchildren's old clothes and taught me to sew.'

'That's lovely! Are you still in touch?'

A haunted expression creeps into her eyes. 'No, sadly. Joan died months after we met. We didn't know each other long, but she remains my inspiration.'

'I'm sorry.'

Interesting . . . Sophie left Modbury in March 2016, which was my spring quarter. I missed her terribly and continued to call, text and email. Eventually, my mum discovered that Jude had converted their house into an Airbnb. That was the only way I found out she and her mum had moved away, but I had no idea Sophie was in Plymouth.

'You could choose a single block shape that repeats over the entire quilt or use different combinations, like this one.' Sophie points to another photo. 'This pattern contains 999 scraps of material, 200 triangles, 152 hexagons and 303 stars.'

I stare at her in surprise. 'Your sewing is mathematically complex, like the one featuring Pascal's triangle!'

'Who's Pascal?' Wren asks.

Sophie shrugs.

'A famous French mathematician,' I explain. 'A number pattern was named after him.'

'Numbers! Yeuch.' Wren pretends to shiver.

'I hated maths at school,' Sophie admits. 'I wasn't good at anything academically. I just wanted to surf and hang out with my friends.'

Fresh memories return: Sophie's bright-green bikini; playing Frisbee and cricket on the beach; cooking sizzling hot dogs on our disposable barbecue and drinking warm beer from cans after our exams. We huddled together in sweaters as the temperature dropped, our bare legs touching as we kissed passionately.

I shake the recollections out of my head, hoping my face doesn't betray me.

'Maths is hard!' Wren says, pulling a face.

'Only if you don't show your workings the way I've taught you,' I point out.

Predictably, she rolls her eyes. I study Sophie's handwritten notes next to each photo: she's created grids for the total number of squares and their measurements in precise detail. This is definitely another big change, along with her becoming more safety conscious. The girl I used to know hated anything to do with figures. I had to work out her share when we split bills with Lily and Tom in cafés.

'You must be good at maths now.'

I look across the table. A strange expression settles on Sophie's face.

'I am.'

'If you don't mind me asking . . . I mean, well, what's changed?'

I attempt to backtrack as the silence lengthens. 'Sorry . . . That came out badly. I didn't mean to sound patronising or that I'm mansplaining maths to you!'

The ticking of the clock on the wall sounds unnaturally loud. It feels like time is stretching yet contracting.

'The accident,' Sophie says tersely. 'That night altered everything.'

22

SOPHIE

Friday, 10 July 2015

Fifty-nine, fifty-eight, fifty-seven, fifty-six . . .

Adam hugged me as we watched the numbers decrease on the electronic timer hanging on the wall. It was wonky – the golf club only put it up for countdowns to midnight at New Year and, apparently, school proms. Lily and I had been throwing ourselves around to 'Shut Up and Dance'. A bead of sweat trickled down the back of my expensive jade evening gown that I couldn't afford. I'd surreptitiously kept the tag on, hoping to get a refund, but Tom had dropped his glass of punch and red liquid was spattered blood-like on the hem. That wasn't the only crap thing about the evening – Adam was subdued and had refused to dance. We'd played that last song repeatedly before our A levels, flailing around in my bedroom until he felt less stressed. He should have been doing the same tonight, if not more so.

'This is all wrong,' he said, as if reading my thoughts.

'I know, right? What's with you?'

He misheard, checking his watch. 'It's eleven fifty-six, not eleven fifty-seven. We've lost a minute.'

'That's not what I meant!' I touched the twisty shape in my necklace.

I didn't give a toss about the time. My head was pounding from the shots we'd downed before we set off, and the punch here, which Vinny had topped up with vodka. Lily was feeling the effects – Tom was practically holding her upright.

'Two minutes to go!' she shrieked.

'It's actually three,' Adam muttered.

I sighed with exasperation.

'One minute fifty-eight, fifty-seven . . .' Lily let go of Tom. 'Come on, you have to join in, Sophie!'

'It's too soon to start counting,' I protested. 'It needs to be from ten.'

'Boo! One minute and fifty-two.' Lily almost lost her balance, but Tom steadied her. His drink lurched precariously, and I broke free from Adam to avoid being splashed a second time.

'We'll always remember this moment,' Lily slurred. 'Like when we have a school reunion, say in ten years' time. Sophie will be travelling the world, Adam will have cracked a mathematical formula, and I'll be—'

'Sunbathing on the beach,' Tom said, hooting with laughter.

'Possibly! I'll be a psychologist and you'll be—'

'Off his head,' I chipped in. Tom was Vinny's best weed client, after all.

'Funny! I'll be earning a shitload in the City and own a penthouse off the King's Road and a Ferrari. You can borrow it sometime, Sophie.'

I rolled my eyes. 'No thanks! I'll cycle and help save the planet before you and your future Chelsea wanker friends destroy it.'

Tom harrumphed, shaking his head. 'Always the do-gooder.'

'Forever the capitalist,' I hit back.

'Here's hoping!'

'Look!' Lily nodded at the timer. 'It's the proper countdown now, so all of you have to join in. *Ten, nine, eight . . .*' She shot me a reproachful look. 'Sophie! Count with me.'

'Fine,' I said, laughing. 'Seven, six . . .'

I grabbed Adam, throwing my arms around his neck. My grip loosened when I noticed his stricken expression.

'I need to tell you—' he began.

The countdown rolled on to midnight before he could finish his sentence. Someone shouted: 'Happy prom!'

Everyone on the dance floor cheered and hugged.

'Tell me what?' I shouted above the noise.

'I was going to say. . . No, forget it . . . It can wait.' He buried his head into my shoulder, and I staggered beneath his weight. He looked up, his mouth finding mine. We kissed hungrily. My lips felt swollen when we finally parted, my heart pounding.

'I *will* always love you, Sophie, whatever happens next.'

Panic fluttered in my heart as it had that morning in his bedroom. Why did he keep saying things like this? And why did tonight feel like goodbye? He was my anchor, my everything, but it felt as though I was being cut adrift.

Tom dragged Lily on to the dance floor as Queen's 'We Are The Champions' boomed out. They were joined by Vinny, who hugged Tom before they punched the air together. They were all celebrating but suddenly I didn't feel like a winner. Far from it.

'Why are you worrying about uni?' I asked. 'It's not a big deal. I can visit Cambridge at weekends, or you can come back here. Your terms are short.'

Adam gulped, making a tight knot constrict inside my chest.

'I know, but I want to . . . I should—'

'Let's have more punch before we go to the cottage!'

I didn't want to hear the rest of his sentence. I had the horrible feeling he was about to break up with me.

I felt Adam's gaze on my back as I retreated to the drinks table. A few straggling orange pieces bobbed in the plum-coloured liquid at the bottom of the jug. I poured out the remnants and knocked it back, a splash landing on my chest.

'Noooo!' I dabbed at my dress with a napkin, making the stain worse. I definitely wouldn't get my money back now.

Tom lurched over and made a point of tipping the jug upside down.

'All gone. Dammit! But I guess you're drowning your sorrows.'

'Come again?'

'You know, about Adam leaving.'

I tried not to show any emotion. 'It's no biggie.'

'You're not worried about keeping a long-distance relationship going?'

'Are *you?* Manchester to Durham is a pretty long trek.'

Tom's eyes glinted under the light. 'Yeah, but I don't have to fly – those long-haul flights to the US will be pricey.'

My mouth fell open. 'What?'

'Shit, sorry!' He wiped his sweaty brow. 'I thought you knew about Stanford?'

'Adam didn't—' The words dried in my throat. 'They never offered him a place.'

I'd cycled over to his house the day he heard back. I found him lying on his bed, staring at the ceiling. He'd sighed heavily and said it didn't matter – he wanted to go to Cambridge. I'd tried to cheer him up and we'd had commiseration sex. Wait – was that a secret celebratory shag? When I think about it, he hadn't *actually* said he'd been rejected.

'I'm sorry, Sophie. I honestly thought he'd have 'fessed up by now!'

'Tell me.' My voice was barely a whisper.

'Adam had an offer months ago and was weighing it up, along with Cambridge. But his mum told mine last week he's arranged his accommodation on campus. I guess he made up his mind. He must have been waiting for the right time to tell you.'

My fingers flew to my pendant. I remembered what Adam said about the Möbius strip that day on the beach, and when he gave me this necklace. It meant nothing! All this time, he knew our relationship was going to end when he moved to the States. He was putting off telling me until the last possible moment!

Tom stepped closer. 'I'm sorry I had to be the one to break the news. He's a good mate, but he can be really, really shit at times. You deserve to be treated better.'

I couldn't look at him; couldn't speak.

Applause rang out as the last song ended. The heat was stifling and the glistening walls pressed in on me. Nausea rose in my throat. I turned and saw Adam watching us, white-faced, his bow tie unfastened, along with his top buttons.

Like my whole life. It was unravelling fast in front of me.

I could tell from Adam's face that Tom was telling the truth.

'I have to get out of here.'

'I'll fetch Lily. We can all go together.'

'No! I want to be alone.'

I weaved through the hot bodies as Adam strode over. Reaching the foyer, I ran across the black-and-white chequerboard floor, not caring where I put my feet. When we arrived, Lily would only step on the black squares for luck. Rain struck my face as I pushed my way through the revolving doors and stumbled past the waiting taxis. I had to get away from everyone. I ran down the drive, my stilettos crunching on the gravel.

'Sophie!'

Adam chased after me.

'Go away.' I spat out the words over my shoulder.

'Wait! I can explain everything.'

My toe caught on the hem of my dress. It made a ripping sound as I tripped and fell. Sharp stones stabbed my fingers. Blood smeared on my skin, but I didn't feel a thing.

Pulling myself up, I kicked off my sandals and pelted towards the opening to the pitch-black lane.

I had to get away from Adam and his lies.

I wanted the darkness to swallow me whole.

23

ADAM

SATURDAY, 22 MARCH 2025

Memories of that night resurface. My voice was hoarse with fear as I called after Sophie in the lane. Lily blowing Tom a kiss before the car sped away. Minutes later, the sound of glass smashing and metal ripping rang out. Tom and I ran after them and saw . . . I open my eyes, blinking away the harrowing images and sounds.

'Erm . . . how was, *is*, the accident connected to maths?' I ask.

Sophie touches her head, tossing curls to one side. 'I suffered a head injury, and it caused irreversible brain damage.'

'No!' My hand automatically reaches for hers across the table. 'I knew it was serious, but I honestly had no idea . . . I mean, I did try to . . .'

Our fingertips brush briefly before she shifts position. Our hands remain only a few inches apart, but the distance is painful.

'It's okay. It doesn't hurt. I've learned to live with it.'

'Is this the bad thing that happened before you went to university?' Wren fixes me with a laser-like stare.

'Mm-hmm.'

'I still don't understand,' my daughter admits. 'What does that have to do with sums?'

'You don't have to explain, Sophie,' I say hastily.

'I want to.' She inhales deeply before speaking quickly. 'My neurologist said the injury caused damage to an area of the brain that's not usually used. The tear to the tissue must have activated these dormant nerve cells. When I woke up, I discovered I was good at maths, exceptionally so.'

'I think I've read about this . . . well, something similar!' My brain goes into autopilot, digging out the memory while my emotions churn. 'Some people suddenly start speaking Spanish or French after a concussion, even though they weren't fluent before.'

'That sounds cool!' Wren says.

I nod in agreement, attempting to process this info. 'Erm, I guess it must be like developing a new superpower?'

Sophie takes a gulp of coffee. 'Kind of. I started seeing the world mathematically. It means everything comes with a number.'

Wren wrinkles her nose in confusion as Sophie explains how she can see digits all around the room, including in front of her.

'But there's nothing there!' Wren points to the space between us.

'Only I can see them,' Sophie admits. 'Your floor has 121 tiles, this table is 1.3 metres by 2.5 metres and has a height of 75 cm, and you have 97,301 hair follicles on your head.'

'How did you work that out so fast?' Wren gasps.

'It's automatic. People have numbers too – you're 4 foot 3 inches tall. You've grown 0.018th of an inch since I last saw you.'

My daughter's face flushes with pleasure, and I'm trying to stop my jaw from dropping open.

'It's an amazing ability! I wish I had it. I'd finish my dissertation quicker.'

'It has its drawbacks,' Sophie discloses.

'Such as?'

'Nothing looks the same as it did before. I can't turn off the figures when I've had enough. They're permanent.'

'Hmmm.' I frown, trying to imagine what it must be like. 'I guess you don't always want to see them?'

'I'd prefer to see the world like everyone else, but I don't have a choice. I'm bombarded with digits and calculations *all the time* and it can get too much, the way someone with autism might find sounds and colours overwhelming.'

The thought hits me. 'You were wearing sunglasses when you came to the café . . . is that why? To try to turn them off?'

'It dims my vision, but not completely. That's partly why I enjoy making quilts like this.' She taps her finger on a photo of her Pascal's triangle design. 'It gets the figures out of my head.'

'It's incredible how it makes you more creative . . . but I am sorry. I had no idea you were going through this. I wish you'd . . .'

My voice trails off. Why didn't she confide in me after the accident? I'd have hugged her and tried to understand what she was seeing. Was she too embarrassed or fragile to talk about her life-changing injury? It would have been a lot to take in. I much prefer that explanation to thinking she hated me for contributing to Lily's death.

'I don't usually tell people about my injury,' she says, as if reading my thoughts. 'It's too personal.'

I flash her a grateful smile that she's trusted us enough to reveal it now.

'And I've only brought it up so you know I can create mathematical patterns, or we can keep it simple like the log cabin.' She gestures at a picture. 'This was the first design I made on my own. It looks striking with small strips of multicoloured material.'

'Why's it called a log cabin?' Wren asks, rubbing her nose.

'It has a red square in the centre to represent the hearth – the fire in a house. Look, here.' Sophie's curls brush against the table as she traces the colours with her finger. 'Can you see how half the block is light in colour and the other dark?'

Wren leans closer, nodding eagerly.

'That's supposed to show the light in the windows and the rest are the "logs" in the cabin. I prefer to think of it as a person's life. Good and bad things happen; we're all made of the light and dark. Somehow, they manage to co-exist and make us who we are.'

'I like that idea,' Wren says, her eyes bright with interest.

'We could use log cabin blocks around the edges and something different in the middle?' Sophie suggests.

She flicks through the book and a piece of paper falls out. I lean down and scoop it up, placing it on the table. It's a sketch of a polygon, but not like one I've ever seen before.

Wren stares at the shape. 'Ooh, you mean like this? I love how jagged and squiggly it is!'

Sophie's face pales. 'It's just a doodle. I meant to throw it away.'

She reaches for the notelet, but Wren snatches it up and sits back in her seat, examining it closely.

'Mummy drew lots of different shapes whenever she was on the phone. She said it helped her think. I liked her pictures. I wish I'd kept them.'

'I'm sure I came across one the other day, and—' I begin.

'I bet you threw it away,' Wren interrupts.

'I didn't.'

'Well, you never remember where you put anything.' She rolls her eyes.

I'm usually guilty of this, but for once I have a vague recollection. 'I think it fell out of a cookery book when I was looking for a recipe.'

I jump up and yank one from the shelf, flicking through. Searching a second, I spot the tip of a piece of paper. Triumphantly, I pull it out. Carley must have been making an appointment – the notelet is dotted with times, phone numbers and tiny Biro drawings. She's written Wren's name in boxes, capped with triangles on the edges and love hearts.

'Here you go. Da-dah!'

Wren's face lights up with delight as I pass it. She looks far more elated at receiving this compared to when I gave her Panda.

'I can't believe you kept it,' she says gruffly, scouring the page as if studying a precious ancient manuscript. 'Thank you for not throwing it away.' She flashes a rare grin that takes me by surprise.

'You're welcome! I'd never get rid of something that belonged to your mum.'

She nods, her smile growing wider. 'Can we use Mummy's shape *and* the squiggly wiggly one?'

Sophie catches her breath and I have the horrible feeling she's about to say no.

'Erm, that won't be a problem, will it?' I ask, keen to hang on to my daughter's good mood.

Sophie chews her lip. 'We can definitely use the shapes Wren's mum drew, but mine is a silly scribble.'

'I like it, and Mummy would have too!' Wren cries.

'I agree 100 per cent.'

If incorporating strange shapes into our quilt produces more smiles from my daughter, I'm in. I count the edges of Sophie's unusual polygon: it has thirteen sides.

'It might be difficult to stitch, but you said you can create complicated patterns . . . It could look interesting with these shapes.' I point to Carley's squares. 'Could you embroider these triangles and the love hearts?'

'That's what I want!' Wren exclaims. 'Lots of different shapes and a log cabin for Mummy because she's at the centre of everything.'

Sophie's face is chalk white and she grips the edge of the table.

'Erm, are you feeling all right?'

'Yes, sorry. It must be my caffeine hit wearing off.'

'Do you need a refill?'

'Please!'

She rubs her lips, deep in thought as I fetch the coffee pot and milk from the fridge. Perhaps, like me, she's worrying about the huge amount of work that needs to be done in a short period of time. Or, maybe, the numbers she can see have become too much.

'Well . . . what do you think?' I fill her mug.

'Of course. Whatever you both want. This is your quilt.'

Her hand trembles as she picks up a notepad and pencil and begins drawing.

'We could have panels with these shapes in the middle, here, surrounded by log cabin blocks, and squares containing Carley's favourite things in these two corners. That leaves corners for each of you. We could reflect your hobbies, such as ballet or anything you like.'

'I want a panda,' Wren replies. 'And Mummy liked chocolate cupcakes.'

'Also, strawberry ones with vanilla buttercream,' I add.

Wren screws up her face. 'I forgot that. And she *loved* thunder and lightning.'

'The louder the better!'

Wren smiles briefly, then looks serious. 'Mummy wants her pot to be emptied on a beach when there's a storm because the whole sky will light up! But I don't want to do that. It sounds scary.' She rubs her eyes.

'You don't have to,' I tell her. 'I mean, not yet anyway.'

'Her pot?' Sophie frowns.

'The funeral urn.'

'I scattered my mum's ashes on a beach in Bali, which is what she wanted,' Sophie says before I can move the conversation on to safer topics. 'I paddled in the sea and said a few words about her life.' She chews her lip. 'It was comforting to know she became a part of something much bigger in the end.'

Wren's mouth hangs open. 'Was there a storm?' she asks.

'Not that afternoon, but there was a *huge* one the next morning. The lightning was amazing – it felt like my own personal firework display. It wasn't scary at all. It was beautiful. Shall I show you how I'd create a lightning scene for your mum?'

'Yes please,' Wren replies, hugging her waist.

I study Sophie as she sketches, taking in the freckle on the side of her nose and the hollow at the base of her throat. The Möbius strip necklace I gave her hung below that dip. I used to kiss her there and work my way up, feeling her nails dig into my back as she arched her neck. I blink, trying to stay focused. Her long, graceful fingers make intricate swirls on the page; mine had once fitted perfectly between them.

'Here you go.' Sophie shows Wren where the panda, cakes and a storm scene will fit into the quilt.

'Oooh! It's going to be so good.' Wren rubs her hands with delight.

That's a tic she's inherited from me . . . I noticed it when her mum suggested we all went to the park to help break the ice during our first meeting.

'What do you like, Adam?'

Sophie gazes at me, her face flushed with pleasure at Wren's reaction.

I want to reply: *You! You're the most amazing girl,* woman, *I've ever met.*

'Numbers, I guess?'

'There's a surprise! Any specific ones? Or random?'

'You decide! My life's in your hands.'

Sophie scribbles furiously in her notepad. She's biting her lip so hard with concentration that a tiny dot of blood appears.

'How about this?'

She pushes the pad towards me, revealing a complex whirlwind of digits. They look as though they've been swept into the air before being sucked towards a tunnel, getting smaller and smaller.

'I'll embroider these panels, but it's a rough draft to give you an idea of how it could look. What do you both think?'

'I love it, Sophie!'

'So do I!' Wren smiles broadly.

I raise my hand for a high-five. She brushes it limply with her 'good' hand rather than slapping it, but at least she didn't leave me hanging as usual.

Finally, I'm doing something right. The quilt is slowly helping me get through to Wren. Dr Hunt's given me a short extension for my dissertation, and I didn't lose control of my year 9s yesterday – well, not for the entire lesson.

Things are looking up.

It feels like the universe is sending good luck my way.

I can't help thinking this has something to do with Sophie re-entering my life.

24

SOPHIE

SATURDAY, 22 MARCH 2025

I'm kicking myself for letting them see my drawing. Why did I keep it, let alone accidentally bring it here? That was another stroke of bad luck, along with giving Bernard a final push towards retirement. I couldn't turn down the developer's improved offer on Mum's house; I accepted it this morning and need to clear the property over Easter. Likewise, I can't refuse Adam and Wren's pleas to use my structure in their quilt. Neither will understand its deeper significance, but my failures will become permanently stitched into fabric.

A 13-sided shape: the number of people I've failed to save, including, shortly, Adam.

I try to focus on my panel sketches, but my vision blurs and my lip throbs.

'Can I use your bathroom?' I stand shakily.

'Upstairs, first on the left,' Adam replies.

I take a quick peek inside the sitting room on the way. It's surprisingly neat for Adam – his bedroom was usually a tip. Children's novels and maths textbooks lie on the table by the sofa, along with soft toys, which have their price tags attached. The mantelpiece has a row of awards, which must belong to Wren, but no family photos.

The bathroom on the first floor smells of a floral shampoo and is wet underfoot. Wren's brought the hairdryer in here even though there's no socket – the plug dangles precariously over the basin. I place it on the clothes basket, away from the dripping tap. Wren's and Adam's toothbrushes are on either side of the sink, like generals from opposing armies. I put them both in the same holder. What *is* going on with them? Wren didn't want to sit next to him when I arrived and her high-five was unenthusiastic. Was their relationship always this tricky or has Carley's death driven a wedge between them?

I dab at my bleeding lip in the mirror. Making this quilt is even more painful than I expected. I must ignore the fluttering sensation in the pit of my stomach whenever Adam smiles at me; how my heart leapt when we accidentally touched in the hall, and when he tried to hold my hand at the table. How it would have felt so natural to let him. I shake the unsettling thoughts away and walk out.

Nothing will ever happen between us. We have no future. All that matters is giving Wren and Adam happy final memories.

On the landing, Adam's bedroom door is ajar. I can't resist nipping in and immediately spot potential danger. Trip hazards (mainly abandoned clothes) are strewn across the carpet and an extension lead is overloaded with electric plugs. After switching it off at the wall, I stare at the bed, trying hard not to picture him in it with Carley. It's covered with books, a pile of Wren's clothes and toy unicorns, as if he's dumped everything in here after a tidying frenzy elsewhere. The bedside table has framed photos of Wren as a baby and toddler, but none are recent. Parenting manuals and maths journals are piled next to them. The tip of a photo is sticking out of one of the books – it's probably one of Adam and Carley.

Invading his privacy is wrong. I absolutely shouldn't look but curiosity gets the better of me. I tiptoe over and flick open the pages. My heart skips a beat. It's the selfie Lily took of the four of us on the beach after we discussed prom night. We all appear jubilant and carefree. Beneath it is the pic Tom took later that evening. I'm touching the side of Adam's face, revealing the Möbius strip he drew on my wrist. He must have been reminiscing about our school days, but that's all in the past. I snap the book firmly shut.

On the way to the stairs, I loiter outside Wren's bedroom. I feel even more guilty about spying in here, but I could get a better idea of the colours and styles she likes. It's equally untidy, with clothes scattered across the carpet. Her white bedspread is covered with green bamboo shoots and pandas. Crystals and multicoloured unicorn toys feature prominently on the shelves, which is useful to know: we can incorporate gemstones and mythical creatures into the design.

Breath catches in my throat as I spot a metal urn next to a photo of Wren with a woman who must be her mum: they share the same freckles, gappy smile and auburn hair. They're both wearing bright-pink T-shirts and standing close to a towering giraffe. Only its legs are in the shot and Carley and Wren are laughing. They were probably on a day out at Bristol Zoo. My chest squeezes: they look happy. I glance around but there's no photos of Wren with Adam, or the three of them together. Why aren't there any in the house? Has Adam put them away because they're too painful to look at?

I head downstairs and find the pair hunched over separate pads at the kitchen table, but they're sitting closer than before. Wren's sketching an animal and Adam's drawing a pointed shape.

My shape!

I inhale sharply and they both look up.

'This is such a bizarre coincidence!' Adam says, smiling. 'My dissertation is all about identifying a shape that slots across a surface without creating gaps, overlapping, or the pattern repeating. I think you may have drawn something that does just that! Do you . . . ? Would you mind if I take a photo and show it to my supervisor at Stanford?'

'Oh, I doubt he'll care. It's a meaningless scribble.'

There's no way I want *more* people to see my shortcomings.

'I'll credit you, obviously,' Adam adds. 'But this could be an important breakthrough in my research paper.'

His eyes are shining, his cheeks pink with excitement. I can't snatch away his exhilaration. I must make his last few weeks as happy as possible, encourage him to feel that anything and everything is possible before it's all over.

'Sure. If you want.' I return to my seat. 'Shall we choose the materials for the different panels and decide on a colour scheme?'

He doesn't reply and studies his drawing.

'Adam!' Wren nudges him.

'Hmmm.' He jumps and pushes the piece of paper aside. 'Sorry. Yes, let's do that.'

Wren hides her eyes with her fingers as I empty the sacks on to the table. A jumble of vivid fabrics spills out: cottons, silks and even brocade. Running my fingers over the materials, I notice deep gashes in the blouses and dresses.

'Can you use any of this?' Adam asks.

'It's not a problem to cut around these tears. I only need small pieces.'

I smile reassuringly at Wren as her fingers uncurl from her face. Neither volunteers what happened to Carley's clothes and I'm not going to ask.

'You should both choose pieces that represent your favourite stories about Carley,' I advise.

Wren buttons her lip and Adam's brow remains furrowed as he sifts through the outfits.

'Erm, in that case, I would probably say this.' He holds up a damaged red Stanford sweatshirt, his cheeks matching it. 'Because . . . well, that's where we met.'

I try not to let emotion flicker across my face, or – worse still – picture them holding hands and kissing on campus, laughing and drinking together in bars and making love in his room.

'What do *you* think, Wren?' he asks gruffly.

She shrugs. 'I don't remember. I wasn't born then!'

'True. Well, what about this top?' He finds a green blouse. 'When did she wear it? Or . . . how about this dress?' He points to cyan-blue silk.

I stare at him, surprised. Why doesn't *he* know?

'Mummy said that was her lucky blouse,' Wren explains. 'Whenever she put it on for my swimming competitions, I won! And she wore the blue dress at my Christmas show.' Wren rummages through the cottons and picks up a bright-pink T-shirt. 'We had matching tops when we visited the zoo and saw giraffes!'

I recall the photo in her bedroom. It must have been taken two or three years ago, but Adam didn't join them.

'That's a great memory. Let's put this to one side since it's so special. What else?'

Wren pokes at a mound of T-shirts. Her bottom lip wobbles and her eyes shine with tears. 'Mummy wore *everything*. I don't want to choose!'

Adam hesitates before putting his arm around her. She doesn't shrug it off, which is encouraging.

'In that case, why don't we use small pieces from *all* of this?' I suggest.

Wren manages a watery smile.

'I love the sound of this!' Adam exclaims.

He stretches his arms above his head, and I catch sight of his taut stomach as his white T-shirt rises. Something stirs in the pit of mine. He catches my eye and I look away quickly, tidying my books.

'We've made a good start, thank you.' I neatly fold the clothes, slipping them back in the sacks. 'I'll leave you to your Saturday.'

'Here, let me help.'

Adam reaches over and we both pick up the same skirt, our fingers grazing. Electricity shoots between us, and I drop it.

'Sorry!' he mumbles.

'No problem.'

'Sophie, can we . . .'

'I'm starving,' Wren says, interrupting. 'What's for lunch?'

Adam flicks a look at the clock. 'Wow! Time flies by when you're having fun . . . I mean, it's been nice . . .' He coughs. 'Would you like to stay, Sophie? I can't offer haute cuisine, but I make a mean tuna melt.'

Wren screws up her nose. 'It's not bad. But it's not good either.'

'That's an outrageous slur on my abilities as a chef!'

She giggles. 'It's the only thing he can cook without burning.'

'This is 100 per cent true. Although, I had wondered about us baking together. We could learn how to make a cake.'

'When?' Wren demands.

'I don't know . . . Soon, I guess? I'll have to buy the tins first.'

She sighs and walks over to the cupboards. 'I'll get the plates.'

'How about it, Sophie? Has my sous chef persuaded you to join us?'

I hesitate. It's tempting but my eyes are pricking; a lump is forming in the back of my throat. I shake my head, continuing to pack up my stuff. 'I should get back. Thanks for the offer though.'

'Are you sure?' Adam looks crestfallen.

No! I want to stay with you and Wren, but it's too difficult. I need to get my head straight and have a private cry.

'How about we meet tomorrow?' I suggest.

Flora won't mind if we rearrange our pub lunch with Stefan – she hasn't got round to booking a table yet.

'So soon?' His face brightens.

I blush, realising this sounds ridiculously keen. I'd never ask future clients to meet as quickly. But Adam isn't just anyone, and today isn't purely professional.

'I'll cut the strips of material and put together the colour schemes tonight. I don't want to go ahead with everything until you're both completely happy. Unless you're busy?'

'I was only planning to work on my paper. Do you want to come here?'

I remember the lack of family photos, Carley's pink T-shirt and what Walter said about building lasting memories. He sent a supportive text this morning, after I let him know I'd followed his advice and arranged to meet Adam and Wren.

Well done, Sophie! he wrote. Keep collecting those tiny joys for the three of you.

'I have a better idea,' I say slowly. 'I think you'll both love it.'

25

ADAM

Sunday, 23 March 2025

'Is it time to see the animals?' Wren hops from one foot to the other at the zoo entrance. 'I'm so excited I'm going to burst like a gigantic bubble. POP!' She claps her hands, while I attempt to tie her hair into bunches.

'Erm, not yet. Hold still for a minute . . . We need to wait for Sophie. She said to meet outside.'

We were running late and arrived at 10.10 a.m., but Sophie's also delayed. I manage to wrestle Wren's bobbles back on and take a swig of my coffee. Hopefully, I don't look as knackered as I feel after working until 2 a.m. For the first time in ages, the numbers and equations flowed easily. I made more progress in one night than I have in months. When I eventually fell into bed, I dreamed about Sophie. She ran towards me on a Devon beach, her hair flowing behind her. She threw her arms around my neck and lifted her face towards mine. Disappointingly, I woke up before our lips pressed together.

Would kissing her feel the same? Would my knees weaken and my heart feel like it's going to fly out of my chest?

'Are there any pandas?'

'Hmmm . . . what was that?'

'You're not listening! Will we see pandas?'

'I think there's a red one. Was it here when you came with your mum?'

'No. I only remember giraffes and monkeys. I can't wait to see a red panda! Is that why Sophie wants to come here?'

'Perhaps . . . You'll have to ask her!'

Wren was reeling off questions about the quilt and this trip last night. I've no idea why Sophie suggested coming here, but I'm thrilled we're having a day out. We can get to know each other all over again . . . well, try to fill in the gaps at least. I check my emails. I sent my supervisor a photo of Sophie's shape, but an out-of-office reply bounced back saying he's on vacation. I suck in my breath when I discover another reminder about the school fundraiser in three weeks' time.

'What is it?' Wren asks sharply. 'Is something wrong? Has Sophie cancelled?'

'No, it's nothing . . . Just work.'

'You get red splodges on your face when you make things up. That's how I know you're lying.'

I sigh. Wren is unusually perceptive when it comes to identifying my faults.

'Sorry. It's an email about a party at my old school. I didn't mention it because I'm not planning to go.'

'Don't you like parties?' She dances around me, eyes sparkling. 'I love them!'

'I'm busy looking after you and have loads of work to do over Easter.'

'I could come?'

'Children won't be allowed.'

'Rude!'

I laugh as she pulls a face. I scroll through Instagram and Facebook, attempting to find old school friends who might be discussing the evening. I've lost touch with my former maths and science classmates and rarely go on social media; if I'm sucked into that vortex, I'll get even less done. I click on an old Instagram notification and am hit by a blast from the past. Tom messaged me weeks ago! I lost touch with him at Stanford, but he's pasted a screenshot of the school invite along with a short message:

Hey mate. It's been forever! I came across this on Facebook. Let me know if you fancy meeting at the party? I'm back in Kingsbridge, looking after my dad for a few months. I've booked a ticket – apparently, loads of our old year group are going. It should be quite the reunion! Would be great to see you again. Let me know. T.

Tom doesn't mention Lily, Sophie, or anything about prom night. Should I say yes? God knows I need a night out. But it would mean cancelling Wren's camp and staying at Mum's over Easter. I rub my brow, debating.

'I'm thirsty,' Wren announces.

I dig into my rucksack, grateful for the diversion, and pull out her water bottle. She takes a few swigs. My fingers brush against something rigid when I put it back.

'I forgot to say I brought something for you.'

'Is it another present?' she asks vaguely. 'Can we go in the zoo?'

'No, I didn't buy it . . . and not yet.' I pull out the framed picture of Wren and Carley with the giraffes that sits on her bedroom shelf. 'I thought you might like this so you're both here together.'

I'd remembered her joy at seeing Carley's doodle but Wren's eyes shine with tears. I fear I've made a huge mistake and should have bought her a new soft toy instead, but the corners of her mouth curl into a big smile and she clutches the frame to her chest.

She butts my arm gently with her head. That's one-sixth of a way towards a hug, and 2,000 per cent more affection than she usually shows. I call that a win! My heart swells.

'She's here!' Wren cries, looking up.

Sophie pelts towards us, hair streaming behind her shoulders, the way it did in my dream. My heart quickens. She's wearing a turquoise floral dress and a pink cardigan, identical colours to Wren's outfits.

'Sorry! Bernard rang and I missed the bus.'

'It's fine. We haven't been here long, and I've been catching up on work emails.'

'Adam gets red spots when he lies,' Wren chips in. 'He was invited to a party at his old school but doesn't want to go.'

Sophie flinches. 'I saw that email. I'll be back in Modbury around then.'

Interesting.

Before I can ask Sophie about any potential plans, Wren shows her the picture of her mum.

'That's lovely.' She produces her phone, pulling up an old photo. 'This is my mum, Jude. She loved beach yoga.'

Wren stares at the pic of the petite woman balancing on one leg, and back at Sophie. 'You both have the same colour hair but hers was shorter. And you have nicer eyes.'

'Thank you. You and your mum look exactly the same.'

Wren's face shines with happiness and she studies Jude's yoga pose.

'Erm, are you going, Sophie?' I ask as we join the queue. 'I mean, to the party? It's Saturday the twelfth of April.'

I'm attempting to sound nonchalant, but my mind is racing. Anna's on holiday over Easter so we *could* go back. But can I survive a week at Mum's if Sophie says yes? Will the holiday camp refund my deposit?

'Not a chance,' she says, dashing my hopes.

Wren's brow wrinkles. 'Why not? You might get a party bag with sweets *and* cake.'

Sophie stares into the distance, her eyes misting up. 'I'm not a fan of my old school.'

She's probably remembering Lily and the crash, which was my reaction when I spotted the email. Should I mention Tom? Probably not . . . she cut ties with him too.

'School wasn't all bad,' I point out. 'I was happy . . . for a time. *Very* happy.'

It sounds like a cliché to say those were the most blissful years of my life but looking back now it's 100 per cent true.

'So was I.' Sophie coughs, her tone changing. 'But I doubt there'll be cake, Wren. And I'll be too busy. I need to empty my mum's house before the completion date.'

'You're selling it?'

'I accepted an offer yesterday from a property developer who wants a quick sale. It'll go through in the next few weeks.'

'Oh!'

I'm unable to keep the disappointment out of my voice. My ties to Sophie are loosening. Our childhood homes were five miles apart, a forty-five-minute bike ride or a fifteen-minute car trip. Once this quilt is finished, she could drift away from me forever.

'It's too expensive to keep on,' she explains. 'I need to rewire the whole house, sort out the damp and get a new roof, among other things. The buyer wants to gut it.'

'Really? It looks in good condition to me . . . well, it *did* when I last saw it. Not that I know much about houses. Or yours in particular.'

I can't admit to taking detours past her old childhood home whenever I'm back, longing to catch a glimpse of her. I always held out hope her mum's house would help us reconnect. I never imagined a dry cleaners in Clifton Village would bring us together.

Wren gives a theatrical yawn. 'Why are grown-ups so boring? I'd like to go to parties every single day. You two are party poppers.'

'Do you mean party poopers?' Sophie asks.

'Party pooper poppers. Pop, pop, pop!'

'Don't encourage her,' I say, groaning. 'She might go pop!'

Wren titters quietly.

'Can you give me a grand tour, Wren?' Sophie asks as we approach the pay booths. 'I've never visited this zoo.'

'Okey-dokey.'

Sophie insists on buying her own ticket, despite my offer to pay for us all. I pick up a map for Wren, our designated leader, and slip the photo frame into her rucksack.

'Ready to explore?' Sophie stretches out her hand as we enter.

I manage to check myself in time and not fall into old habits by taking it. Wren's fingers slot between hers, and she swings their hands happily.

'I haven't been here before either,' I admit. 'I keep meaning to bring Wren, but our weekends are usually busy with ballet and swimming lessons. We never seem to have time for anything else.'

'There's always time,' Sophie says softly.

26

SOPHIE

Sunday, 23 March 2025

'How many rocks are by that giraffe?' Wren asks, pointing into the enclosure.

'87.'

'How many leaves are in that tree?'

'10,674.'

'How many—?'

'I think that's probably enough mental arithmetic tests for one day,' Adam says, interrupting her rapid-fire questions.

'Why don't I get a picture of the two of you?' I ask, shielding my eyes from the bright sunlight.

'Not another one!' Wren groans. 'I want to see the zebras.'

'This won't take long,' I insist. 'Move a bit closer together so I can get the giraffe in the pic. Three, two, one!'

I hold up my phone, attempting to take a snap, but Wren's studying her map.

'Both of you need to look at me and smile.'

They manage to synchronise their gazes and look happy for a microsecond as I take the photo. It feels hypocritical ordering them to look cheerful when I'm feeling the exact opposite, but Wren will need these memories to look back on.

'What about a selfie of the three of us?' Adam suggests.

'Yes!' Wren whoops. 'Then we need to see the red panda again and Bear Wood.'

'Are you sure, Adam?'

'100 per cent,' he says, taking my phone.

I feel the heat of his body against mine as we move in for the photo. My stomach drops as I inhale his scent – citrus aftershave mixed with soap and his own muskiness. This is the first photo we've taken together in almost ten years, and it could be among the last. We're unlikely to return here before his death. We probably won't ever stand this close again. I want to pull him into my arms for a hug and beg him to be careful. *To live.*

'Even bigger smiles,' Adam orders. 'Smile, Sophie!'

It's hard to cling on to the joy in these small moments, as Walter suggested, when everything is collapsing around me. Bernard rang as I was leaving my flat to chat through his retirement plans. The shop will close permanently at the end of August, and he'll shut it temporarily over the Easter holidays to give me time to get everything sorted in Modbury. I'm dreading finally sorting through Mum's old belongings. To cap it all, I received another nasty email last night. I've blocked the sender – presumably Trevor – who claims I'm a phoney for making memory quilts.

'This is great!' Adam examines the photo he's taken. 'Can you forward it?'

He passes my phone back and I ping it over, stepping aside to put distance between us. Wren skips further down the path as my phone vibrates. Dread washes over me as I open the email. It's a third message sent via the website, but using a different address.

You can't get rid of me! I won't let you forget. I will NEVER forgive you. I hope your memory quilt business fails. You don't deserve success. You don't deserve to be happy!

My hand trembles. Blocking Trevor doesn't work. Should I reply? I could explain that I *am* being punished for my past mistakes. Getting close to Adam, while knowing I'm going to lose him imminently, is pure torture. But that could wind him up more. He may visit the shop. I tuck the phone into the bottom of my rucksack, vowing not to check it while we're here.

'Everything all right?' Adam asks, glancing at me.

I don't want to worry him in his final weeks or ruin today by talking about my tormentor and financial worries.

'Bernard's retiring over the summer so I'll need to find a new job.' I pause, judging my words carefully. 'And a customer's unhappy with my repair. I couldn't do better but he's angry.'

'I'm sorry. Is there anything I can do to help?'

'Rewind time?!'

'I wish! You'll find another position . . . you're brilliant at sewing. And I'm sure if you talk through what you did, your customer will understand. Confronting things head on is the best policy, or so I'm regularly told by my head of department.'

'Says the man who puts off absolutely everything,' I retort.

'Aagh!' He runs a hand through his hair. 'You're right. The king of procrastination shouldn't be lecturing anyone.'

'Sorry,' I say, touching his arm. 'I didn't mean to take my problems out on you.' I try to focus on enjoying the warmth of the sun on my face, as well as Adam's company. 'Being here makes everything feel better.'

'Ditto! I'm glad you suggested coming. It was a surprise . . . but a good one.'

'It helps with the commission,' I say hastily. 'I'll use Carley's pink T-shirt in the quilt, but I can machine-embroider an animal that Wren likes today, or we might find something in the gift shop to stitch on. That way, the three of you are incorporated into the design.'

'It's a great idea!' Adam replies. 'I think our project's helping Wren already . . . yesterday was the first time she's talked about coming here with Carley.'

Wren turns around, checking we're still with her before running up to the cheetahs' enclosure.

'Why is that?'

He frowns. 'You mean not wanting to talk about their day trips?'

'No!' I hesitate. 'I hate to pry, but you didn't come here with them, and you didn't seem to recognise Carley's clothes, or the memories Wren talked about yesterday.'

Adam shoves his hands into the pockets of his jeans.

'That's because I don't remember much about her,' he admits. 'Carley and I only dated briefly at Stanford. We met towards the end of my freshman year. We were both lonely and wanted . . . well, comfort, I guess.'

Heat rises in my neck and face. Was he haunted by that summer, like me?

'We were together less than a month when we split, amicably. Carley was in her senior year, so she came straight back to the UK when she graduated.'

I've already done the sums; Adam had another two years of his degree course to complete after Wren's birth.

'It must have been hard keeping up a relationship with your daughter while you were over there,' I murmur.

'I had no idea Wren existed! Carley told me I was a dad when she was diagnosed with stage four breast cancer in July 2023. I left Stanford without finishing my PhD and met Wren for the first time two months later. By then, I'd started my PGCE here in Bristol.'

'Wow! Your head must have been spinning.'

Mine certainly is, as I try to piece all this together.

'It was strangely clear,' he says. 'I knew I had to become a teacher so I could look after Wren if, when . . . Carley and I were hopeful she could beat the disease, but we needed a plan.'

'And that's when you started to get to know Wren? During your teacher training?'

'We didn't meet regularly,' he says stiltedly. 'Carley thought it best if I was eased into her life gradually. We both thought she had more time . . . a few more years . . . Anyway, it's been the two of us for the last seven months.' He exhales heavily. 'Some days it feels much longer, and other times it's like Carley died yesterday and I'm getting to know Wren from scratch.'

I'm reeling from his revelation but manage to keep pace with him. I'd assumed he and Carley had been together since Stanford, right up until her death.

'If it's any consolation, I think it's pretty amazing how selfless you've been – what you've given up for Wren.'

I can't help comparing his reaction at becoming a parent to my mum, who abandoned me eight months after my head injury.

'I'm her dad,' he replies, shrugging. 'Even if I'm not a very good one!'

'Of course you are. You're doing a great job.'

'Am I? I'm not so sure. You should see my dismal calendar skills.'

'I can imagine. I've heard it's the number one reason why people flunk Dad School.'

A smile flits across his face.

'But seriously, you're spending time with Wren today, aren't you?'

'Thanks to you! I would never have got round to arranging this. I'd have come up with reasons why it wasn't possible.'

'Maybe you should start saying yes to things, and see where that leads you?'

'Yes, Sophie.'

'You see? All your problems are solved.'

He laughs. 'You *do* make things better, like a superhero. You were the same when we were teenagers. I'd be stressing out, and you'd make me happy to be *me*, as if that was somehow enough. You made me feel . . .' He stops walking, his words tumbling out. 'I know you don't want to talk about that night, but I have to say this . . . I hurt you, Sophie, and I'm sorry. I've regretted the way I treated you ever since. If I could turn back time and change things, I would.'

I clench my fists, digging my nails into my palms.

'We both made mistakes. We've moved on – to here!' I clear my throat, gesturing to the enclosures. 'A few months ago, neither of us could have predicted we'd be counting giraffes *and* rocks in a zoo.'

I'm trying to lighten the mood; I'll crack if he digs deeper into old, buried feelings.

'I need to say the things I didn't that summer,' he says in a low, husky voice. 'I always wanted to tell you . . .'

'Cheetahs!' Wren races back over to us. 'Come see them!'

'In a minute—' Adam begins.

But Wren tugs at my hand, pulling us apart.

After touring the 50-acre site, we end up in the café. I'm wondering what Adam wanted to say, but it's probably best he didn't finish his sentence. Heartfelt words would have finished me off after I counted so many numbers, and not just in the animal enclosures.

Adam touched my waist twice, my arm 3 times and smiled 23 times.

I disguise my emotions by closing my eyes and taking a large forkful of carrot cake.

'What's the verdict?' Adam asks.

'It needs more cinnamon, but the frosting is pretty good,' I say, blinking. 'I'd give it a six-and-a-half out of ten.'

'Ditto. I was thinking the exact same number!'

Our gaze meets and the bustling noise in the café seems to fade into the background. A smile plays on his lips, and there's a familiar tugging sensation in my chest. Warmth swirls around my stomach. I must ignore these doomed feelings if I'm going to get through the next few weeks. I grab my phone and flick through.

'What do you think of this pic?' I pull up one of Adam and Wren laughing close to the red panda. I managed to catch them off guard; they look relaxed and happy.

'It's okay,' Wren says non-committally. 'Can I see the giraffes?'

I scroll back and push my phone across the table before picking up a paper bag.

'Talking of giraffes, I bought this in the gift shop.' I show her an animal hand puppet with distinctive dark brown patches and a creamy tan coat. 'We could use the material in the quilt, along with your mum's T-shirt? It'll remind you of the giraffes today and on your earlier visit.'

Wren nods her head vigorously. 'I like that idea.'

'This is what I've done so far.'

I open my rucksack and retrieve the panels I stitched last night, using pink, yellow and green strips.

'I'll embroider the red panda there,' I say, pointing to a square. 'And the giraffe coat could go here. What do you think?'

'I love it!' Wren reaches out and touches the material.

She and Adam rub their hands with excitement.

'It looks tricky and a lot of work,' he remarks.

This is a good time to bring up my plan to guarantee he spends more quality time with Wren. Normally, I'd only expect customers to pick out the fabrics and designs, but I need them both to become heavily involved in its construction.

'Would you both like to help me make the quilt?'

'Ooh, yes!' Wren looks hopefully at Adam before scrunching her forehead. 'But I'm not sure I'll remember how to sew. We only had one lesson at school.'

'Hmmm . . . and I probably wouldn't be much help,' Adam admits. 'I only know how to do basic mending, like reattaching buttons.'

'I can teach you both. That way, you could quilt after school.'

Wren's expression brightens again. 'Can we?'

'But there's your hand . . . and my dissertation . . .' Adam's voice trails off as he notices the excitement drain from her face. 'Your stitches are coming out on Tuesday, and I can make time. I guess we could learn together? If you'd like that?'

Wren nods enthusiastically. 'But you have to promise to sew, not just look at me doing it.'

'I promise! 100 per cent stitching, not watching.'

Adam grins at her and she beams back.

'When's our first lesson?' he asks.

'I was hoping you'd say that.' I grab my sewing kit from the bottom of my rucksack. 'I'll show you both a simple back stitch while you finish your drinks. This won't take long, and then we can go back to the giraffes.'

'*And* the red panda,' Wren stresses.

Adam laughs. 'You're not wasting any time, are you, Sophie?'

'Not a single second,' I reply firmly.

27

ADAM

Monday, 24 March 2025

'Can you see what I mean if we start with number one here?'

I point to the top centre of Sophie's quilt, which I've pinned on the classroom wall for my postponed year 9 lesson on Pascal's triangle. 'For each following row, we write "1" on both ends. The number inside is the sum of the two numbers directly above it.'

I spin around. My pupils are gazing at Sophie's creation instead of muttering to each other. Mr Cross is sitting at the back with a notepad, providing feedback for the senior leadership team. My confidence is sky high despite only learning about the spot check this morning. I feel capable of anything! I had a great day at the zoo with Sophie and Wren and made huge inroads with my dissertation last night: the end is finally in sight! I'm also having a brilliant start to the week. Wren smiled and waved back for the first time ever when I dropped her off at school and I've remembered to book a plumber to fix the tumble dryer.

My gaze rests on Khalid, who's frowning as if he's concentrating rather than daydreaming. I had a word with him about his behaviour before the lesson.

'Can you come here and work out the sequence?' I smile encouragingly at him.

Khalid drags himself up and shuffles to the front.

'If we add these numbers in row two, what does it make this?' I gesture at the fabric triangles.

'Two?'

'Yes! And below?'

'That's three, four, five.' He continues counting as I point to the descending rows.

'Exactly! Brilliant. Do you understand now?'

Khalid smiles sheepishly. 'Yeah, this makes it much clearer, sir.'

I grin at him. 'I thought so!'

Mr Cross nods approvingly from the corner.

'That's why I asked my friend if I could borrow her quilt,' I say as Khalid returns to his seat.

'Is she your *girl*friend?' he calls out.

Titters ripple across the classroom.

'No! Well, she was . . . but . . .'

Mr Cross coughs loudly.

'That's enough,' I say sternly. 'Continue with the questions on the whiteboard. If I hear chattering, I'll set more homework.'

Silence descends. I return to my seat and pretend I'm recalibrating test scores so Mr Cross doesn't think I'm skiving. When the bell rings for the end of school, my students troop out uncharacteristically quietly. Khalid slouches past and winks.

'Hope you win back your ex-girlfriend, sir,' he mutters. 'You're not *so* bad.'

I pretend I haven't heard and reshuffle my books until Mr Cross comes over.

'Well done, Adam. That's a big improvement since I last sat in. It was an inspired idea to bring along a practical object to make the class more accessible for everyone.'

'Thank you! I enjoyed the lesson.'

For once, I'm not just telling him what I think he wants to hear. Getting through to pupils like Khalid, and helping them understand maths, *is* more rewarding than I ever expected during training.

'Are you coming to the pub later?' he asks. 'We're meeting at the Old Market Tavern from five thirty. There are wild, unsubstantiated rumours Roger might buy a round.'

'I can't, sorry. Me and Wren have our first sewing lesson at six.'

'Ah, I see. Another time, perhaps.' His gaze rests on Sophie's bedspread. 'Best of luck with your quilt lady!'

At the dry cleaners, we spend twenty minutes stitching our 13-sided shapes, the way Sophie's taught us, when Wren declares she's 'starving' despite having tea at her after-school club. Sophie slips out to buy takeaway pizzas while we finish our sections. Wren's sitting next to me, concentrating on making neat stitches.

'This is fiddly diddly!' she says, shaking her wrist.

'Shall I finish yours?'

'No, I want to carry on.' She twirls her hand before pointing at the window. 'Someone's outside.'

An elderly man puts his hand against the glass and peers in. He shuffles along and tries the door handle, tapping it with his walking stick.

I shake my head and mouth: 'It's closed!'

He raps again. I head over and unlock the door, pulling it open. 'Sorry, we're—'

'May I come in?' the man asks. 'I need to give my friend, Sophie, something, and Chico could do with a bowl of water.'

'Oh . . . right. Sure. She won't be long.'

I open the door wider and he steps inside with a small white dog on a lead.

'Perfect!' He tips his hat. 'I'm Walter and this is Chico. You must be Adam, of course.'

'Erm, that's right!'

I shake his hand, wondering how they know each other. Sophie's talked about me, which must be a good sign, surely? I particularly appreciate the *of course*. These two words have potential and make me sound like a foregone conclusion, rather than a horrible mistake.

'And this is my daughter, Wren.'

'It's lovely to meet you both!'

Wren flashes a shy smile. His dog trots over and sits at her feet, staring up expectantly. He wags his tail furiously as she pets him.

'What did you say he's called?' I ask.

'Chico – after Einstein's dog, but, sadly, not as clever. He's scared of garden gnomes.'

'Why?' Wren asks.

'Who knows? Chico refuses to tell me. He's stubborn like that, but he loves you!'

'And I love dogs,' Wren states. 'But Adam won't let me have one.'

'Hmmm. I said I'd think about it . . . Perhaps at some point in the future.'

My neck feels hot. I hope Wren hasn't noticed my 'tell' . . . I can't fit in caring for an animal on top of everything else.

Walter eases himself down on to a stool. 'May I get that bowl of water for Chico and, perhaps, a cup of tea while you're there? Nice and strong. Two sugars.'

'Erm . . . sure!'

I retreat to the back and find a small kitchen. I send Sophie a WhatsApp, saying her bossy friend Walter is here. Within seconds, her reply flashes up.

What has he told you?

Her message throws me momentarily.

His dog is scared of garden gnomes?!

Yes, bizarre! On way back.

Her reaction is odd. Has she said something about me to Walter? If I grill him, will I unearth a compliment or two? I find a bowl in one of the cupboards, fill it with water, and make mugs of tea. When I return, Walter is examining Wren's sewing, while she plays with Chico.

'This is beautiful,' he says, holding the patchwork pieces. 'Wren tells me you're making the quilt together?'

'Trying to! Obviously, Sophie's amazing at quilting, and Wren's great at stitching. But I'm not sure what I bring to the table. I'll never be the most talented sewer.'

'Who cares? You're doing this as a family and will have created something remarkable and lasting at the end.'

'I hope so, if I don't manage to ruin everything!'

'You couldn't even if you tried,' he replies quietly.

I'm about to quiz him when Sophie bursts through the door, panting and clutching pizza boxes. She shoots a sharp look at Walter, her chest heaving.

'I wasn't expecting you tonight. Is everything okay?'

'It's perfect! I was passing and saw the light on.' He points to his lapel. 'You said to pop in and get this tear repaired. It's good timing. Chico has made a new friend, and the lovely Adam has given me a cuppa. Now it appears I might get a slice of pizza.'

Her shoulders relax. 'How can I possibly refuse you?'

'Never!'

'How do you two know each other?' I ask.

'We see each other on our walks and Sophie was kind enough to help me with a problem,' he replies. 'We've since become firm friends.'

She gives him a kiss on the cheek before pulling out paper plates from behind the counter.

'We have margherita, Hawaiian or pepperoni,' she announces.

'I think I'll try Hawaiian. You only live once.' Walter holds out his plate.

Sophie's hand trembles as she passes him a slice, before dishing out margheritas and pepperonis for Wren and me.

'Remember, no touching any of the clothes, otherwise Bernard will kill me!' She locks gaze with Walter. 'This needs to be our secret.'

We chat while Sophie mends Walter's coat and finishes off the shapes we've been sewing. Walter discusses Chico's daily routine, the mechanics of Clifton Suspension Bridge, and his family's love of surfing. He shows us photos of his son, daughter-in-law and grandchildren on the beach in Sydney. I'd love to stay longer, but Wren is stifling a yawn. I throw the plates and napkins into a plastic sack and collect the pizza boxes.

'I'll take the rubbish out. Then we should head home, Wren. It's school tomorrow and I have work to do.'

'Can I come to the bins with you?' she asks eagerly. 'Chico's told me he wants a walk.'

'You've learned to speak Dog already?' Walter raises an eyebrow. 'That was quick. You're obviously a natural.'

'I understand *everything*. Chico says he wants to chase a pigeon.'

Walter rolls his eyes dramatically. 'That definitely sounds like Chico.' He attaches the lead and passes it to Wren.

'He's your responsibility. Do you promise you'll look after him for me?'

'If he runs away, I'll race after him,' she says, nodding seriously.

'It's probably best to stay with your dad and *neither* of you run off.'

'Okey-dokey.'

Sophie directs us to the recycling bins and Wren follows me outside with Chico. My cheeks warm with pleasure. Even though she obviously likes Chico's company far more than mine, she's never volunteered to spend time with me before. We walk side by side along the pavement to the alleyway, instead of our usual single file.

'Have you enjoyed meeting Walter?' I ask.

'Yes! He's nice, like a grandpa. I wish I had one.'

'I know. It's a pity you never had a chance to meet yours.'

'Would I have liked him?'

'Of course!'

Red splodges spread up my neck as I throw the bags into the bins. Dad regularly said he was proud, but I can't remember him hugging or playing with me. Would he have dished out more affection to Wren? And would Dad have admired me for looking after her? Or would he consider me a failure for temporarily becoming a maths teacher? I remember what he said on his deathbed and my spirits plummet. I *know* it would be the latter.

'So can we?' Wren asks.

'Erm, what?'

'Get a dog? I've proved I can look after Chico.'

I open my mouth to reply, but she talks rapidly.

'*And* before you say you'll think about it, can we visit Grandma? I love her dogs. Looking after them would be good practice for getting one of our own.'

'Hmmm. I'm thinking about that too.'

Wren harrumphs. '*Hmmm. I'll* think about brushing my teeth and going to sleep tonight.'

'Ha ha!'

She grins back. We reach the shop and through the glass I catch a glimpse of Sophie and Walter embracing tenderly. She pulls away and looks up at him, talking earnestly. They both jump apart when I push open the door, making the bell ring.

'Is everything all right?' I ask tentatively.

Sophie's eyes glisten. 'Yes! We were discussing the coat repair.'

That's odd. I could swear she's wiping away a tear as she turns her back.

'Before I forget, I must give you these.' Walter pulls out cards from his pocket. 'I'm having a get-together this Saturday.'

He gives one to Sophie and hands me another. It's an invitation to a private all-day party at The Wave, a surfing leisure park in nearby Easter Compton.

'Oh wow!' I exclaim. 'I've always fancied visiting. The reviews look amazing.'

'In that case, there's no time like the present.' Walter fixes me with a surprisingly hard gaze. 'Will you come?'

'Me?'

'You and Wren. And Sophie, of course.'

I gape at him. It's an incredibly generous offer, particularly since we've only just met.

'Erm. I don't know . . . What do you think, Wren? Do you fancy learning how to bodyboard? We'll get your stitches out tomorrow, and your hand should be fine to get wet.'

'Ooh yes!'

She gives me another big smile. I've been collecting them today, much like the awards I used to win at school, except these make me feel far, far happier.

'Sophie? I mean . . . can you show Wren your moves?'

I look at her expectantly. We can't exactly turn up at her friend's party if she's not going.

'I haven't been surfing for a while,' she says quietly.

'Then you need to practise,' Walter insists.

Her bottom lip trembles. 'Of course I'll be there for you. I wouldn't miss it.'

I glance at Wren, who nods vigorously.

'In that case, count us in too!' I reply.

Walter claps his hands together, smiling broadly. 'Excellent.'

'Is it your birthday?' I ask. 'Should we bring anything?'

I'm racking my brains for what to buy. Whisky? Rum? I have no idea what his interests are beyond dogs and surfing.

'Oh no! That's not until December, and I don't require a sausage. The best gift will be a big party for the people I care about. After all, what else do I have to spend money on at my age?' His hand shakes as he looks down at one of his invites. 'I've hired the venue for the day and don't want it to be full of oldies like me! Bring as many friends as you want.'

'Really?'

'Whoever makes you happy,' Walter replies.

Sophie sucks in her breath. She's probably pondering who to invite.

'I have mates from my teacher training course. I'm sure they'd all love a day out . . . Our nanny and her friends would probably come if you want to get numbers up and Wren could ask her classmates.' I look at him uncertainly. 'But only if that's all right?'

'The more the merrier. We need to fill the place!'

Wren jumps up and down with joy. This could be exactly what she needs to bond with her friends and make new ones. I'll post my first ever message in the parents' WhatsApp group.

'What about your son?' Sophie interjects. 'Have you spoken to Harry? Is he coming over with his family?'

Walter looks thoughtful as he rests both hands on top of his walking stick.

'Harry and Maddy are big surfers, which is why I booked this place. We bought tickets the last time they visited, and the kids loved it. We couldn't get them out of the water and the eldest, James, said he wished we could have the place to ourselves for a day.'

Sophie blinks. 'They'll definitely be there? All of them?'

'It's tricky for Harry and Maddy to get time off work and take the older kids out of school. I arranged it last-minute this weekend on what you might call a whim.'

'Didn't you say your son lives in Sydney?' I say, laughing. 'I'd imagine that's even trickier!'

It's a big ask to expect anyone to hop on a plane and travel to the other side of the world for a party, especially with a week's notice. It isn't even a birthday, let alone a landmark one.

'But they must come!' Sophie cries. 'You *did* tell them, Walter?' She arches an eyebrow.

'It's an ongoing conversation.' He waves his hand vaguely. 'I think Harry understands. We shall see. I remain hopeful, as ever.'

'You *have* to make it happen,' she says sternly.

I look from one to the other, mystified, as something unspoken passes between them. I have absolutely no idea what's going on or why Sophie thinks this party is so important.

'Sometimes all you can do is wait and see,' Walter replies. 'You have to play all your cards and hope everything works out for the best.'

28

SOPHIE

SATURDAY, 29 MARCH 2025

I can barely keep my eyes open despite a can of Red Bull on the way here. I'm working flat out on the quilt, as well as filing Bernard's monthly takings and Flora's VAT returns. Apparently, during Flora's infamous birthday party, I also promised to look over Stefan's finances and work out his best mortgage options for buying a one-bedroom flat. If this wasn't Walter's big send-off – and Adam's day 15 – I'd spend the weekend hibernating beneath my duvet. But I can't miss the party. It's far too important.

I pull out a compact and dab concealer on the dark shadows beneath my eyes, pinch my cheeks to give them colour and run a brush through my hair. It's a good job I'll be around water since I resemble a ghostly mermaid. I spot Adam and Wren in the distance, and click the mirror shut. Wren's swinging on his arm, and he's grinning and lifting her off the ground. Now she's pirouetting around him. He's copying and almost falling over. My plan is working! They both look happy and far more relaxed in each other's company. Adam messaged to say they've been sewing together every night before a bedtime story.

He looks ridiculously handsome as he laughs and pulls faces at Wren. *When he does anything.* My stomach contracts and I shake the thought out of my head. They reach me and Wren scampers ahead, leaping up for a high-five.

'Hey, Wren. And Adam.'

I stand on tiptoes to kiss his cheek, but he moves in the wrong direction, and we collide.

'Sorry!' he cries. 'My co-ordination is off this morning.'

'Is it ever switched on?'

'Ha, true!' He scans the outside of the building. 'This looks impressive! It must be hellishly expensive to hire out. This is definitely not a pre-birthday party?'

I shake my head and change the subject. 'How was the rest of your week, Wren?'

'The best! My stitches are out, I got ten out of ten in my maths test, and Adam helped me with my sewing. Now we're here! I'm so excited I could go pop. Pop, pop, poppety pop!'

'Is that a new pop song?' Adam asks.

Wren giggles and jumps up and down. 'Are the waves this high?' She stretches her arms as high as possible.

'I think they'll be poppety-pop higher,' Adam says as his phone vibrates. 'Hold on, that might be Ollie, saying he's close by . . . He wants to meet.' He pulls it out from his rucksack. 'Oh, it's an email.'

His hand quivers as he reads the message. 'My supervisor is still on vacation, but he's looked at your shape, Sophie. Dr Hunt thinks it's "special and unique", to quote his exact words!'

My heart sinks. I was hoping he'd take longer to get back to Adam, and the whole thing would be quietly forgotten.

'I want to get on a surfboard!' Wren says, tugging his arm.

'Hold on a minute . . . Dr Hunt wants his colleagues to look over your design, if that's all right with you? He may commission further research.'

I shrug. 'Sure – if it helps.'

'It does, thank you! This may take some time, but it's a brilliant first step!'

Adam pulls me into a big hug. I momentarily sink into his chest, feeling safe and secure, the way I used to when he held me. *My anchor.*

My heart thuds painfully as I remind myself he probably won't receive an answer within the next fortnight. He'll die without ever knowing whether my shape *is* significant.

Adam lets go and steps back. 'Sorry! I got carried away. Wren and I are both having a poppety-pop fantastic week.'

They grin at me, and I try to muster a smile. It's hard to look cheerful when I know their worlds will come crashing down, exactly two weeks today.

We've spent the last hour bodyboarding with Wren and her classmates. Now she's cold and wants a hot chocolate so one of the mums offers to take the kids to the café. Adam's asked for a quick refresher surf lesson. I tell him where to position his feet on the board, and try not to think about how broad and muscular his chest looks in the wetsuit.

'You need to take a few more strokes to get ahead of the wave that's coming.'

He pushes off, glancing backwards at the 1-metre-high breaker.

'Look straight ahead and arch your head! That's it. Push up on your fingertips and bring your right knee forward. Easy does it – pull the other knee to your chest. Balance and stand.'

'I'm trying!'

'Stand. On your actual feet!'

'Aagh!'

Adam tumbles off and disappears beneath the foam. I breaststroke towards him as he pops up.

'I'm good!' He wipes his eyes, spluttering. 'Well, I'm not. I've lost a contact lens and I'm still terrible at this!'

'Some things never change.'

We're laughing, and I'm suddenly aware that our bodies are inches apart. It feels like old times. Back then, he'd have slung an arm around my waist and pulled me into a passionate kiss. I shiver at the memory.

'Are you cold? Do you want to go in?'

His eyes wrinkle with concern. I could lose myself in those gorgeous pools of blue. I want to grab *him* and press my lips against his. This could be one of our last chances to kiss if I return home next week as planned. I shake away the image. This, *us*, can never happen. I scrape my hair back, making sure the scar on my scalp isn't showing.

'I wouldn't mind catching a few more waves. I'm pretty rusty.'

'You haven't been out recently?'

'Not since I left Modbury.'

His eyes widen with surprise. 'Why not? You love . . . I mean, you used to love surfing.'

I shrug. 'I've been busy. Life gets in the way.'

'It has a habit of doing that.'

That's not the whole truth, obviously. I couldn't face returning to old haunts. It felt safer to keep a lid on everything, and avoid the things I loved – surfing, seeing Adam and visiting Lily's parents.

'Go for it!' Adam says. 'I'll see how Wren and her friends are getting on. Ollie and the rest of the guys should be here. I'll introduce you . . . they're all a good laugh.'

'Are you sure you don't want to stay in? I could give you more lessons.'

'I think we both know how that will turn out,' he says, laughing. 'I don't want to hold you back like I always used to.'

'You didn't. I never felt that way about you.'

'Ditto. In case you're wondering, which you probably aren't . . . But I need you to know that.'

Adam doesn't move away, and I can't help but feel we're talking about something completely different. He rakes his hands through his hair, and more memories stir as I catch a glimpse of his wrist tattoo.

'I've always preferred watching you surf,' he murmurs. 'I couldn't keep my eyes off you when we were teenagers.' He takes a breath. 'I still can't.'

He reaches out and brushes hair from my forehead, making butterflies skitter in the pit of my stomach. His hand hovers as if he's debating whether to place it at the back of my neck. I shiver again with anticipation as he stares at my lips. I should stop this, but I desperately want to kiss him and feel his body pressed against mine.

One last time.

'Coming through!'

A guy loses control and falls off with a shout, forcing us apart. I catch hold of his board before it whacks Adam in the face and push it towards the man. The distance between me and Adam has widened, the moment lost.

'That was close. I almost gained a matching dent.' Adam touches the other side of his nose. 'I'd have lost my boyish good looks.'

No chance! You'll always be gorgeous.

'I guess I should go . . . ?'

His eyes are filled with hope that I'll tell him to stay. I need him to leave before either of us tries to pick up where we left off.

'Yes, see you soon, Adam.'

He wades away, his hair curling at the nape of his neck. He looks back one final time.

'You keep saving me, Sophie,' he shouts. 'You're definitely my guardian angel!'

I wish.

My lucky number is 13 – that's how many waves I caught on the advanced peak in the last hour. I managed to kick out and sprint-paddle back to catch extra multiple ones from each set, even when more guests arrived and the queue lengthened. I pull myself out of the pool, completely knackered but on a high.

I'd forgotten how much I missed this!

Adrenaline and exhilaration pumps through my body, and my muscles scream with pain. Nothing beats this feeling – the elation of pushing myself to my physical limit and getting the timings exactly right.

After a hot shower, I dry my hair and change into jeans and a sweatshirt. I check my phone and discover a message from Flora, saying she's arrived.

Thanx for VAT return and invite! Heading to beginners' lesson with Stefan. FYI he's still available. You could play lifeguard and perform mouth to mouth? xx

I'll pass, thanks! I reply. Catch you both later xx

I haven't told her about Adam and Wren yet. Flora will be mad I didn't 'fess up straightaway about my ex being back on the scene. She'll demand a TED Talk about Adam, with slides and a thirty-minute Q&A session. I quickly check my emails and Instagram quilt page in case Trevor's back. He hasn't contacted me all week. It looks like he's stopped for now, thank God.

When I reach the café, it's heaving with people of all ages, from babies with their parents to pensioners. All their numbers are high. I spot Wren, wearing a party hat, at a table with six other little girls and their parents. The children are talking animatedly and laughing while eating hot dogs and burgers and chips. Wren waves happily when she sees me. I wave back and scour the room for more familiar faces.

The crowd suddenly parts and there's Adam, with his back turned, in jeans and a blue T-shirt. He's chatting to a blond guy and a woman in a flowing green dress who's carrying a baby in a sling. Two little boys play with a remote-controlled car at their feet. I recognise them from the photos Walter showed us in the shop. His son, daughter-in-law and grandchildren have come at short notice!

I walk over as Chico appears and barks furiously at the plastic truck. Walter arrives three seconds later, wearing a bright-red Hawaiian shirt and a straw hat. He warmly embraces everyone in turn with one arm as he leans on his stick. I freeze.

His digit's wrong.

It should be 8 today.

I must be mistaken. I rub my eyes, which are stinging from the water, attempting to clear them.

I blink rapidly, but I'm not imagining it.

Walter's number has changed – it's gone up to 21.

He has an extra 13 days to live.

29

SOPHIE

SATURDAY, 29 MARCH 2025

How is this possible? No one's number has ever changed before! But Walter's has risen on its own without me attempting to alter his fate. Goosebumps spring up on my arms and the back of my neck tingles. I shiver with excitement.

'Walter!'

My voice is hoarse, and he doesn't hear. I clear my throat and shout louder, waving. He takes off his hat and bows. His family and Adam turn to look. I mouth a 'hello', hoping I don't look like a total lunatic as I frantically beckon him over. I need to grill him, alone. Walter's son and daughter-in-law continue talking but Adam's gaze is unwavering.

'How are you enjoying my party?' he asks when he reaches me.

'It's the best one ever!'

I throw my arms around his thin, bony shoulders, hugging him closely.

'Whooaa!'

I steady him as he almost loses his balance. 'Sorry! I'm just so happy to see you.'

'Adam must be thinking the same.' Walter jerks his head in his direction. 'He can't stop talking about you. I knew my party was a good idea. This looks extremely promising!'

'It certainly does. What's been happening since I last saw you? Have you been back to the hospital? Or has your GP put you on new meds?'

'Oh no. I'm done with all that. Harry and his family arrived yesterday and they're staying for three weeks. I'm not wasting my final days on more medical appointments. I intend to die in my chair at home, surrounded by loved ones and Chico. But before that, we have a lot to pack in.'

I catch hold of his arm. 'Your son and daughter-in-law will need to stay longer than planned.'

He frowns. 'How do you mean? I've made arrangements for my funeral, so they don't need to bother with that. I'm treating this as a dry run but without all the dreary, weepy speeches. Thankfully, I'll be in a coffin and won't hear them.'

'No, I'm talking about your number.'

He rests both hands on the walking stick, the lines on his forehead deepening. 'Oh dear. Has it dropped further?'

'No! It's the opposite. It's gone up by 13 days. I can't explain why. It's never happened before.'

'You're sure?'

I nod. 'The number I can see today is 21. You have until the eighteenth of April – Good Friday.'

'This is fabulous news,' he says, beaming. 'Extra Easter eggs for me and the grandkids!'

'Exactly.' I smile back. 'I need to work out what you've done to make it change. It could help Adam.'

'Nothing special! I've stuck to my usual routines – walking Chico, having a pub lunch and enjoying the views from the suspension bridge.' He rubs his jaw thoughtfully. 'But Harry and his family have been on my mind. I desperately hoped they'd make it today. Now they're here. I'm looking forward to spending all my time with them.'

'They must have changed something inside your body. You must be fighting the cancer!'

He guffaws. 'I'm too tired and old to fight anything, my dear. I'm simply content. I have everything I need here in this room – my family and friends.'

I stare at Adam, and then Wren, my heart pounding with elation.

Somehow, Walter's life has been lengthened due to the joy of being reunited with his family. His love for them has boosted his mortality.

It's not by much, but it's enough to give me a tiny sliver of hope.

I must convince Adam to go back to south Devon over Easter and spend quality time with his mum and Wren.

Because if I do, there's a slim chance I might be able to extend *his* countdown.

30

ADAM

Saturday, 29 March 2025

A glitterball hangs from the ceiling and music booms out in the venue's café, which has been transformed into a dance floor. I'm watching Walter do a circuit of the packed room. He's speaking to all the guests, including our nanny, Anna, who's brought a gaggle of friends. It's incredible his son and daughter-in-law made it at short notice. Harry became teary-eyed and repeated his dad's line about the party being organised on a whim, but also admitted he's whipped the older kids out of school and his wife has taken unpaid leave. Why would they do that when it's not his birthday or another special event? And why did Sophie look as if she'd seen a ghost when she spotted Walter earlier?

They were talking earnestly away from everyone else, but by the end of their chat it looked as though a weight had lifted from her shoulders and she became more like her old carefree self. She's currently dancing with Wren and her classmates to Harry Styles' 'As It Was'. Walter joins them with Chico, his grandsons and Harry. They make a big circle, clapping their hands as each one struts their stuff in the middle. Hopefully, they don't spot me lurking on the sidelines . . . my dancing is as bad as my surfing. That could be due to my lack of co-ordination or because my limbs turn to liquid whenever I'm around Sophie.

'Why are you lurking in the shadows?' Ollie arrives, clutching drinks. 'Your dancing is legendary, and don't get me started on your karaoke skills. They deserve a wider audience.'

'Erm, I'm sitting this one out, thanks.'

'Shame. I fancied a laugh.' He passes me a can. 'The surfing was insane! Have you been in?' He clinks his lager bottle against my Diet Coke; he's calling a cab but I'm driving Wren home.

'I'm surprised you missed the spectacle. You'd have found it hilarious.'

'Remind me how you got us all in for free today? It's that old guy, right? The one dancing with the pretty girl over there?'

I nod, taking a slow sip. 'That's right.'

'What's the occasion? I'm guessing a big birthday?'

'No! Just a party that his family have flown around the world to attend with only a few days' notice.'

Ollie raises an eyebrow.

'I've no idea why and Sophie changes the subject when I ask.'

'Mysterious. But who's Sophie?'

He follows the direction of my gaze to the dance floor.

'Oooh, *her*. Wait! That name rings a bell.' He looks at me. 'Don't tell me this is childhood sweetheart Sophie, of the famously brutal Hallmark break-up? The Sophie otherwise known as she-whom-no-other-woman-can-ever-live-up-to?'

'Hmmm. I think she prefers the title Ms.'

'It is! Holy crap.' He thumps me on the arm. 'Well done, Adam! You're back together?'

'No. This is a business arrangement . . . I mean, she's making a quilt for Wren.'

Sophie looks up from dancing and gives me a dazzling smile that makes my legs turn to jelly and my heart flutter. It's the happiest I've seen her since we've been reunited, and I grin back. We don't break our gaze, electricity fizzing between us.

'Gotcha,' Ollie drawls sarcastically. 'This is totally professional and not personal *at all*. She probably looks at all her customers that way! You know, like she wants to shag their brains out on her sewing table.'

I shake my head, but I'm secretly pleased I haven't imagined the mutual spark of attraction. A girl wearing a party tiara and a tall muscly guy with spiky blond hair approach Sophie. The man's hand lingers on the small of her back as he whispers in her ear. There's an ease between them, as if they know each other intimately. I feel a sharp pang of jealousy. Is he an ex or currently on the scene?

'You have competition,' Ollie observes. 'He's a ten and probably a personal trainer, whereas you're barely scraping a six today. Did you get any sleep last night?'

'Thanks for the pep talk. It boosts my confidence.'

'Shut Up and Dance' blares out, stirring memories. Sophie played this song whenever I became stressed in the run-up to my A levels. We would dance in her bedroom, flailing our arms around and not caring how ridiculous we looked. Sophie managed to look cool and me less so, but I always felt better afterwards.

Sophie beckons me to join her. Before I can shake my head, Ollie gives me a hard shove and I fly forward, almost falling over.

'What are you waiting for, mate?' he calls after me. 'Carpe bloody diem and all that.'

I walk towards her, with what's left of my dignity. I know, with 100 per cent certainty, that none will be left after the song has finished.

'This is me,' Sophie says, staring out of the car window.

I pull over to the kerb and turn off the engine outside a block of flats close to Temple Meads station. I've given her a lift back from the party, which ended at midnight with Walter belting out Frank Sinatra's 'My Way'. Wren is fast asleep in the back seat, her head lolling against the giant panda she's decided to keep in the car for company.

I shift in my seat, facing her. 'I had the best time today.'

'Me too. Walter definitely knows how to party.'

'I feel bad we didn't bring him anything . . . apart from us!'

'That's a big enough present,' she says jokingly. 'Talking of which, I have something for you.'

'Whaaaat?' I run a hand through my hair. 'Now I feel doubly guilty.'

'It's not *that* exciting.'

She rummages in her rucksack and passes me a plastic bag. I pull out a cake tin and a pack of batteries. I stare at them, baffled.

'The batteries are for your smoke alarms, and Wren wants to make a cake with you.'

I'd completely forgotten both!

'I told you not to get your hopes up. It's only a practical gift.'

'No, it's kind and thoughtful! I wish . . .' My voice wavers. 'I should have brought something for you.'

'Can you gift-wrap a new job and put a bow on top?'

'How about I distribute your quilt flyers in the staff room?'

'That would be great.' She unclips her seat belt. 'Actually, there is something else you could do.'

'Name it!'

'I'm heading back to Modbury on Friday to sort through Mum's old stuff and finish your quilt. I'll need breaks. I'm open to walks, bike rides or surfing, if your plans change and you end up at your mum's.'

My heart thumps faster. That definitely sounds like an invitation to spend more time with her personally rather than professionally.

'Yes!' I say without hesitation.

'Really? I thought this would be a much harder sell.'

'I'll need to cancel Wren's holiday club and sort out a few things first, but I can work from Mum's house.'

I think about the message I received from Tom. I still haven't replied.

'Does this mean you've changed your mind about the school party?' I ask hopefully.

'No! I'm giving that a wide berth.'

I'm debating whether to mention Tom getting in touch when she looks over her shoulder at Wren.

'Will this earn you more Dad points? Wren sounded keen to see her grandma.'

'Yes! She'll be delighted. I've been pretty bad about arranging regular meet-ups. I must admit I've been avoiding Mum.'

'You've fallen out?'

'It's nothing as dramatic as that.'

'So not pistols at dawn?'

'Only blunt daggers.'

She stares at me quizzically.

'We've been rubbing each other up the wrong way ever since I came back from Stanford. It's easier to avoid the whole situation.'

'What are you arguing about?' she asks, getting straight to the point.

'Everything! It's not great returning as The Big Disappointment. I might put my title on a badge to stop it from being the elephant in the room.'

She's the first person I've admitted this to. It's not something I'd mention to Ollie; he'd probably turn the discussion into a joke, and we'd change the subject.

'I'm sure she doesn't think that about you. Why would she? Look at everything you've achieved.' She nods towards Wren. 'Deep down, I bet she's incredibly proud of you.'

'Hardly!' I scoff.

'Just because she hasn't said it doesn't mean she's not thinking it.'

I stare at her, surprised she's defending Mum. My parents weren't exactly her biggest fans. They worried she was a distraction from my studies and never tried to make her feel welcome.

'Hmmm.'

'Hmmm,' Sophie repeats back. 'If you don't mind me saying, no one in your family has ever been the world's best at discussing what matters.'

'I have no idea what you mean,' I say, pretending to be offended.

'Sure you do.'

She stares at me intently. I shiver, battling my rising emotions. This is my chance to tell her how I wish I'd been more open about my feelings for her, but the seconds tick by as I search for the right words.

Sophie wipes something from her cheek. 'It'll be good for Wren to spend more time with your mum if you're busy working.'

We're back to talking about my family and the opportunity to be truthful has slipped away, as it did at the zoo when Wren interrupted us.

'I must admit I felt guilty when I saw Walter with his son and grandchildren. Mum should get to know Wren better, and vice versa.' I take a deep breath, attempting to work my way up to what I want to say. 'I'd like the three of us to spend more time together . . . you, me and Wren. That's not just because you're making the most amazing, beautiful quilt but I . . .'

Despite everything I feel for her, the word jams in my throat. I touch my tattoo. I can't bring myself to say the 'L' word even though I feel it so strongly my heart might explode. Sophie only re-entered my life around two weeks ago; there's no rush to tell her. I can't risk destroying the fragile relationship we're slowly rebuilding by saying or doing the wrong thing. I've discovered how badly that can turn out with Wren.

'You make me happy. Aagh! Sorry . . . that sounds lame.'

She faces me, her lips parted. 'No, it didn't. And ditto.'

I smile as she borrows the word I quoted whenever she used to say she loved me. Does she remember its deeper meaning? Perhaps she *does* have stronger feelings for me, rather than just fond memories. The gap between us narrows. I don't know if I leaned closer first, or she did. We may have intuitively moved at the same time, our bodies totally in sync.

We spring apart guiltily as Wren wakes up with a loud yawn.

'Are we home yet?' she asks sleepily.

'No. I'm dropping Sophie off. Go back to sleep.'

'Okey-dokey. Night night, Sophie.'

'Night, Wren. Night, Panda.'

Sophie's fingers brush against mine before she opens the door and climbs out. She peers back in with a dazzling smile that makes my heart beat faster.

'Goodnight, Adam.'

'Bye, Sophie.'

I watch her run to the front entrance. She turns and waves before disappearing inside. Sophie needs to know how much she means to me, even if I haven't managed to say it properly. I pull out my phone and forward a picture Ollie took of us dancing. Within seconds, she responds with a heart emoji.

Returning home has never looked more appealing! I tap out a quick message for Mum to read in the morning.

Sorry I haven't let you know about Easter sooner! Been busy with work. Thought I could visit for a week with Wren. Is Fri, April 4 good? Or we can come later if that's not convenient?

She's awake unexpectedly late and responds within seconds.

Fantastic news! I look forward to seeing you both. Come on Friday. Let me know what Wren wants to eat and I'll stock up! xx

This will be the perfect opportunity to show Wren my old haunts *and* see more of Sophie. She was happy today, surfing and dancing. It felt more like old times. We came close to kissing in the water and just now. We *might* find our way back to each other, as long as I don't mess up everything. The reunion party is another great chance for us to spend time together, if Mum agrees to babysit. A bigger *if* is whether I can persuade Sophie to come. She's understandably reluctant but this could be good for both of us. We can try to leave the ghosts of the past behind and move on.

I'm going to say yes to things, as Sophie suggested.

Carpe bloody diem, to quote Ollie.

I retrieve the school email and RSVP before clicking on Tom's DM and telling him about my plans. He's also online and replies.

Great news! Looking forward to it. BTW are you in touch with Sophie?

I message back: Yes! We recently met after all this time!

He types: That's good to hear. Is she coming to the party? I'd love to catch up with you both.

Hopefully, I write. She's heading back to Modbury next week.

I throw my phone on the passenger seat and turn on the engine.

I have fourteen days to change Sophie's mind.

31

SOPHIE

Thursday, 3 April 2025

My sewing machine, needles, presser feet and cotton reels are neatly packed into boxes, ready to be lugged to the hire van. It's not far away; I managed to park a few doors down from the shop. I need to tidy up before meeting Flora for a drink. My phone vibrates on the table. That's probably Flora, warning me she's running late. But the familiar cold, sick feeling returns. It's an email with the strapline You're fake. I click it open.

You moved on, but I couldn't. I'll never forgive you! I hope you fail at quilting – at everything. Your whole life. You deserve NOTHING and NO ONE.

Trevor! He hasn't contacted me for almost two weeks but he's back. A flurry of notifications lands – this time from a new follower commenting on my Instagram page, beneath the recent photo I posted of my North Star-patterned quilt.

Buyer beware! Do not use this seller. She can't be trusted.

She is a charlatan. Avoid!!!

Do not buy anything from this fraud!! She will let you down. She lets everyone down.

Oh God! When will he stop? Potential customers could be scared off by these false accusations. Quickly, I delete my quilt picture and block his account, but I'm not ignoring his latest email. I tap out my reply.

You're completely wrong. I never forgot. I loved her so much. I think about her every single day. I'm sorry about everything.

I press 'send' and wait. The bell above the door rings, making me jump. I didn't remember to lock up when Bernard left. An elderly man steps inside and a dog barks.

'Walter!' I press a hand to my chest. 'You scared me.'

'Sorry. I slipped out to buy milk and saw your light was on. I thought I'd say hello.' He unclips Chico's lead. 'Unless it's a bad time?'

'It's good,' I say, breathing out heavily. 'I could do with the distraction.'

'Problems with Adam?'

'No. He's driving back to Devon with Wren tomorrow to stay at his mum's. I'm hoping that spending time with them will help increase his number.'

Walter's eyes narrow. 'And mine? Dare I ask?'

'It hasn't dropped – you have those additional days.'

'Phew. That was another reason for dropping in. I was worried the clock might have speeded up, so to speak. I have to fit in more with the grandkids this week. They have a wish list of the zoo, back to The Wave, and a trip to Bath to "see where the Romans swam naked".'

'Sounds fun!'

I jump as my phone vibrates. My hands tremble as I open the new email. It's a one-word reply: *Liar!*

'Bad news?'

'A guy from my past keeps emailing,' I admit. 'I tried to stop his mum's countdown years ago, but it went horribly wrong. He still blames me for her death.'

'Have you tried talking to him?'

'No way! Trevor's messages are bad enough. I don't want to hear his accusations on the phone or face to face.'

Walter eases himself on to a stool, and Chico lies at his feet. 'It sounds like Trevor remains in a great deal of pain. Perhaps if you explain exactly what you did, and answer the questions that keep him awake at night, it will give him closure. He might be able to move on with his life.'

'Hmmm.'

'You sound like the delightful Adam.'

My mouth curves into a smile. 'I'm *that* decisive?'

'Think about it, my dear.' He winces as he shifts position. 'As we know, life is short. We all need to tie up loose ends before it's too late and make amends.'

'Will you ever stop being wonderfully wise?'

'In sixteen days, apparently.'

'That's not funny!' I bite my lip. 'In fact, it's terribly, terribly sad.'

'It's anything but. I'm eighty-six and have enjoyed a full life. When you think about it, it's a miracle any of us are born – the stars that must align for our parents to meet, the number of cells that has to divide and multiply for us to be conceived. Most importantly of all, I've been loved by Hellie and have loved in return. I've tried to live the remainder of my life more, not less, in her honour. I'm making myself and my family happy while I can. Talking of which, I must get back for our movie night.'

He slowly stands, leaning heavily on his stick. Chico jumps up, planting his paws on Walter's leg.

'Can you see how long other species have left to live?' Walter asks, patting him.

'No, sorry. Only humans.'

He continues stroking his dog. 'No matter. I know the answer already – Chico has a long and joyful life ahead of him.'

'I'm sure he has.'

Walter straightens and kisses me on each cheek. 'Goodbye, Sophie. We've only known each other for the shortest time, but our friendship has given me the greatest pleasure.'

'I feel the same. I'll meet you—'

Tears prick my eyes. This could be the last time we see each other in person unless I return to Bristol before Friday, 18 April. But I sense Walter is saying goodbye now. It's only right he spends the remaining time with his family.

'Goodbye, Walter.' I hug him tightly. 'I'll miss you so much. Thank you for encouraging me to appreciate all the little moments with Adam and Wren.' I stumble over my words. 'And for helping me think about my numbers in a different way. You're the best.'

'I know, I know,' he says, patting my back. 'Thank *you*.'

Teary mascara was streaked down my face after Walter left and I couldn't face going to a noisy bar, so Flora's come over. She promised to help me get ready for my trip to Modbury tomorrow, but she's lying on my bedroom floor, working her way through our bottle of chilled Sauvignon Blanc.

'I'm totally obsessionable about this.' She holds up the picture of Adam and Wren at the zoo. 'And this!' She gestures to another framed photo of them near the red panda, giving an 'aww face'.

'Firstly, "obsessionable" is not a word,' I point out, nudging the Sellotape and scissors closer with my foot. 'And secondly, you're supposed to be wrapping, not obsessing.'

'But they're too cute for words,' she says, sipping her wine. 'And don't get me started on this!'

She studies the photobook I've created from the zoo, Walter's party and our sewing lessons, while I tick off items on my checklist. My cutting tools, iron, masking tape and wadding are packed. My appliqué threads aren't in my main sewing basket, but I remember the old box in my wardrobe beneath the sealed bags of quilts. Dust motes spiral when I pull off the lid; I haven't opened this in years. Inside, I find templates, braid and felt that could be useful for Wren's and Adam's panels, as well as a bag of multicoloured bouclés, metallic rayons and viscose knits.

My heart thuds as I spot a border collie print at the bottom of the box. I pull out the green-and-light-brown log cabin design. This belonged to Joan! She started making it for Trevor, featuring his dog. The strips of material Joan gave me to stitch around the panel are still pinned into place; I couldn't face completing it after her death. Walter thinks Trevor is suffering and needs closure. Could a memento of his mum be what he needs to finally come to terms with her death? I could finish sewing it after Flora's gone.

'Okay, I'm officially dead from cute overload.' Flora closes the photobook and flops on to her back. 'You're all off-the-charts adorable!'

'Enough with the cuteness and wrap the presents, please.'

'One more cute thing about the three of you,' Flora says, rolling on to her side. 'You, Wren and SSD will make a lovely family in the future.'

'SSD?'

'Sexy Single Dad.'

I laugh. 'Adam will love your abbreviation. But we're not . . . it's, well, complicated.'

Walter's right. I do sound like Adam.

'Thank you,' I add.

It's true – 3 is a wonderful number, but I mustn't get ahead of myself. All I can think about are 8 digits: 12/04/2025. I have to help Adam live beyond this date.

'And about complications, I have a teeny-tiny cute confession to make.' She sits up and takes a large gulp of wine. 'You're not going to approve so I'm going to come out with it quickly – I want to get back together with Libby. I think she does too.'

I begin to speak but she talks over me. 'I know . . . We both want different things . . . There's no future in our relationship . . . blah blah blah.'

'That wasn't what I was going to say.' I kneel beside her. 'I was wrong. I think you should go for it with Libby. Take the risk to love and be loved.'

Flora reaches over and feels my forehead. 'Are you delirious? Should I call for an ambulance?'

'Very funny! But I mean it, I swear. You should do what makes you happy – live life to the full and enjoy every minute.'

Flora lets out a small, joyful cry and hugs me.

'You deserve happiness,' I tell her. 'We both do.'

32

ADAM

Friday, 4 April 2025

'We should go back for the cake tin,' Wren mutters unhappily from the back seat of the car. 'We have enough time.'

I glance in my mirror as we speed along the fast lane of the M5. Droplets of water spatter my smeared windscreen, but it's not raining hard enough to flick on the wipers. Wren glares at me, next to Panda, who looks even more judgemental than usual.

'No, we don't. We were late leaving.'

That's the understatement of the year. I slept through the alarm after working on my dissertation until the early hours. I had to throw our stuff in a suitcase and hope for the best.

'Don't worry! Mum probably has tins.'

Does she? She didn't bake much when I was growing up, but that's hardly surprising when she worked full-time as a solicitor.

'It was a present from Sophie. But you forget everything!'

I drum my fingers on the steering wheel. Unfortunately, this is true. I suddenly realise I haven't packed Wren's swimsuit or hairbrush. I'll secretly add those to the shopping list when we reach Plymouth. Sophie messaged yesterday, suggesting we meet in the city centre for lunch instead of in Modbury as planned, as she has an errand to run.

'*And* you said we could bake together last night,' Wren continues hotly.

'I didn't forget . . . I was snowed under with work, sorry. I wanted to get as much done as possible so we can have days out next week. We have been sewing though.'

Aagh. I've forgotten to pack our pin cushion, but Sophie probably has a spare. I could buy another in the shopping centre, as well as an umbrella. The rain is picking up and it's reminded me I've left ours by the front door, along with Wren's wellies.

'Hmmm.'

'Is that a hmmm I'm forgiven or a hmmm you're still cross with me?' I ask.

My gaze flickers back to my mirror. Wren folds her arms, scowling.

'I'll make it up to you while we're at Mum's. We'll go to the beach and build sandcastles, whatever the weather.'

'Do you promise, *Adam*?'

'I poppety-pop promise.'

Wren's lips finally break into a smile. '*Pop, pop, pop.*'

Popping has become our 'thing' now. I laugh and look straight ahead – the traffic has stopped. I slam on my brakes. We're thrown forward, our seat belts straining, and skid to a halt, narrowly missing the stationary Land Rover in front.

I almost went into the back of it!

The thought barely registers when a horn blares loudly behind us. My gaze fixes on the wing mirror, horror mounting, as a lorry rumbles towards us at speed.

It's not going to brake in time.

'Jesus Christ!' I shout.

Wren lets out a high-pitched scream. At the last moment the juggernaut swerves into the middle lane. Our car shakes from the vibration. I flick on my hazard lights, gripping the wheel tightly as the vehicles behind slow.

'Are you all right?' I yank at my seat belt and turn around.

Wren is speechless, rigid with terror. I unclip my belt and reach through the gap, taking her hand. It feels small and clammy in mine. My heart pinches and I repeat the words that Sophie used to say to me.

'You are safe. This will pass. Take it one moment at a time.'

She squeezes my fingers.

'I'm here and so is Panda.' I nudge her toy closer, and she rests her head on the furry animal, not letting go of my hand. I'm in an awkward position and my neck's getting a crick, but I don't care. I'll stay like this for hours if it makes her feel better.

'My teacher says you shouldn't use "Jesus Christ" as a swear word,' she says eventually in a small voice. 'It's rude.'

'I'm sorry. It slipped out.'

Talking of which, I might have wet myself a little. One minute I was laughing with my daughter, and the next we were almost flattened by a truck.

'Mummy was ruder than you in the car,' Wren admits. 'She said "fucking hell" a lot when she was driving.'

I laugh under my breath, feeling the tension melt from my shoulders.

'You mustn't use those words . . . But your mum *did* swear like a trooper! Did you know that when she was a child, her parents made her put money in a swear box? She said it broke from the weight of the coins!'

'No!'

'That's true. I poppety-pop promise.'

Wren snorts with laughter. 'She never told me that. Naughty Mummy.'

She fumbles in her rucksack, pulling out her unicorn toy and a shiny object, which is partially hidden by her hoodie. I squint harder. It's her mum's urn. I had no idea she'd packed it. Wren catches me staring in the mirror.

'I didn't want to leave Mummy behind. She'd be lonely. She enjoyed the zoo and wanted to come to Grandma's.'

'Erm, good idea!'

'She says she's glad we're both safe.'

Wren kisses the metal container and puts it back in her bag as rain patters loudly on the windscreen. Is this a good time to bring up scattering her mum's ashes on a beach? And how it might not be the best idea during a storm? Or will it upset her? Hmmm. I'll leave it and wait to check the long-term weather forecast.

'I don't know how long we'll be stuck here . . . It must be a bad crash for all three lanes to be out of action.'

'Are people hurt?'

'Erm, I don't know. Possibly.'

'Should we check? Mummy said you should try to help people whenever you can.'

Through the blurry glass, I notice car doors opening.

'Stay here with Panda. I'll have a quick look.'

Rain slashes my face as I climb out. I hear the faint whine of an emergency vehicle further down the motorway. A few motorists are standing in between the stationary traffic.

A man suddenly lets out a cry and runs towards an unknown horror.

I smell burning tyres.

A terrible memory flickers and ignites deep inside my mind.

33

ADAM

Saturday, 11 July 2015

'Sophie . . . Stop!'

I pelted after her, catching up at the end of the golf club driveway. I grabbed her arm, but she shook me off. Her eyes glittered with fury and betrayal.

'You tricked me? You're going to Stanford? Not Cambridge?'

Her staccato words sounded like the rattle of a machine gun, making my heart pound painfully. Mum was horrified when she realised Sophie didn't know about my decision. Well, it was mainly Dad's, but I'd gone along with him, not wanting to cause friction.

Tell her right away! Mum had warned after discovering Sophie creeping out of our house. *This is going to be far worse if you keep putting it off and she finds out from someone else. You've been together a long time. She deserves better and you know it!*

Mum was right. I should have listened. But it was too late.

'I'm sorry! I never found the right time to tell you . . . I was going to . . . but I was being cowardly. I couldn't bring myself to ruin everything. *Us.*'

'There is no *us* when you've been lying to me. You've known for months!'

'I thought I could talk Dad round and go to Cambridge, but this is all he ever wanted for himself and then me . . . I didn't want to disappoint him.' I raked my hand through my hair. 'Going there didn't feel real. I tricked myself into thinking that if I didn't say it out loud . . . well, it wouldn't *be* real. I wouldn't be going. I know it sounds stupid.'

'Yeah, it does! Because you *are* abandoning me, like my mum whenever a better offer comes along. But at least she has the guts to tell me herself, rather than leave it for someone else to break the news.'

'I'm not like her,' I insisted. 'You know how I feel about you.'

'Do I? You've never even said you love me.'

Her accusation was an arrow to my chest. 'Erm, yes, I have! Lots of times.'

'No, Adam. You've never said the words back. All you ever say is ditto.'

'But you know I mean it with this!'

I reached out to touch her necklace, but she stepped aside.

'This was a gift to ease your guilty conscience. You're a typical rich boy who throws money at things to solve your problems. Problems like me!'

'That's not true!'

'Isn't it?'

I opened my mouth to tell her how I felt, but the words jammed in my throat.

Before I could think what to say, Lily lurched down the driveway, followed by Tom.

'Where are you going?' she shouted. 'The taxi's waiting!'

Sophie wiped her eyes, smearing mascara across her cheek, as they reached us.

'I'm not coming. Sorry, Lily.'

'Hey! Don't cry.'

Lily shot a fierce glare at me before hugging Sophie. Tom had obviously filled her in – he was the only person who knew my secret. He'd found out weeks ago as his mum chatted to mine whenever she had cleaning shifts at the solicitors' office.

Sophie stepped back, her gaze lowered. 'I'm fine, Lily. I don't want to ruin your night. Get the taxi with Tom. I'm going to the beach party. On my own.'

She stalked off towards the lane and was consumed by blackness within seconds.

'How could you do this to her?' Lily demanded.

She didn't wait for an answer and ran after Sophie. I switched on my phone's torchlight and followed. Tom did the same. Our beams caught glimpses of two ghost-like silhouettes through the slashes of rain.

'Come back and we'll talk!' I called after Sophie. 'You won't get a taxi out here . . . and you can't walk two miles alone in the dark.'

'Don't tell me what I can and can't do!' she yelled back.

I caught up but she pushed me away. The road was slippery; I tripped and stumbled towards the wet hedgerow. Brambles scratched my outstretched hands, but I didn't care about the pain.

'Stop following me, Adam. Leave me the hell alone!'

'Sophie!' Lily cried. 'Come back to the taxi with us. We'll drop you off at the beach if you really want to go?'

'No! The cottage is in the opposite direction. I'll be fine, honestly.'

'You're not,' Lily hiccupped. 'You're drunk. Me too.'

'Which is why this is madness,' Tom said, gripping Lily's arm. 'It's pissing down and we're getting soaked. Let's leave them to it.'

'No! We have to make her come with us.'

The thud of a distant beat-box grew louder. We pressed ourselves into the wet hedge as a car rounded the corner at speed. I shielded my eyes, dazzled by the headlights. The vehicle swerved past Sophie and mounted the grass verge. The driver's door swung open, music blaring. Vinny leaned out, his eyes glazed. His on-off girlfriend, Priti, sat in the passenger seat, her head lolling against the window.

'Anyone want a lift to the beach?' he slurred.

I reached Sophie, panting. 'No, we don't. And you shouldn't be driving!'

'Well, fuck you, ten A*s boy!'

I winced. I hadn't shaken off the nickname since my first term; someone had stuck the newspaper cutting on the sixth-form common room noticeboard.

Vinny almost fell out of the car as he yanked the door shut. He rammed the clutch into gear and stalled the engine.

'Don't speak for me,' Sophie said icily. 'I can make my own decisions, thanks. Unlike you, I don't need *Daddy* to make them for me.'

The engine started up with a roar and Vinny flicked a finger out of the open window as he pulled away.

'Well, staggering around out here, drunk, isn't your best choice,' I hit back.

Her accusation about my dad had struck a nerve.

'You're judging *me*? After what you've done?!'

'Sophie, let's—' Lily began.

'Hold up!' Sophie yelled after the car. 'I'm coming with you.'

'No, you're not!' I tried to catch her hand, but she slipped from my grasp.

She waved her arms wildly, chasing after the vehicle. Its brake lights suddenly glowed red, demon-like.

'I don't care what you think when you're fucking off to America without telling me!' she retorted over her shoulder. 'I'll do whatever the hell I want.'

'Adam's right,' Tom shouted. 'It's too risky to go with Vinny.'

His warning was a red rag to a bull, and she lunged towards the rear passenger seats. She opened the door and turned around. Her gaze radiated hatred as she ripped off her pendant.

'Have your Möbius strip back.' She tossed it in the air. 'It's meaningless. It doesn't go on forever. This ends now!'

I heard a faint tinkle as the chain hit the ground, seconds before she climbed into the car.

'Wait for me!' Lily cried.

'No!'

Tom tried to step in Lily's way, but she dodged past him. Sophie swiped for the door handle, but Lily hung on, preventing her from closing it.

Sophie leaned out, sobbing. 'I want to be on my own. Please go back with the boys.'

Lily shot a pleading look at Tom. 'I'm sorry. She needs me. I'll call you later.'

He shook his head vigorously and strode towards her. 'Don't do this! Vinny's wasted and the seat belts don't work in the back.'

'It'll be fine for a short distance. I can't leave my best friend alone on prom night. She's in a complete state.'

'This is her problem, not ours,' Tom claimed.

Lily blew him a kiss and jumped in. The car sped away before she'd managed to shut the door properly. It veered across the lane and screeched around the bend.

Tom rounded on me, jabbing a finger at my chest. 'What the fuck? You and Sophie have wrecked everything!'

'I'm sorry! Should we . . . I don't know . . . call the police? We could report Vinny for drink-driving and get him pulled over.'

'We can't, without getting the girls into trouble – Vinny's probably got drugs in the car. There won't be any police nearby anyway.'

'Oh God. If anything happens to them . . .'

The words were barely out of my mouth when a metallic booming noise rang out, followed by smashing glass. We stared at each other in horror before running blindly towards the appalling sounds.

Rain slashed my face with tiny, vicious knives. The air smelled of burning rubber.

We turned the corner and found a car ablaze. A second vehicle was a mangled mess. A body hung half out of the windscreen and the three other people inside were motionless. Then I saw the blood. So much blood. It was dripping down the passenger door.

Tom said something but his words disappeared into nothing.

Screams pierced the darkness, above the roar of the flames.

I realised they were mine.

34

SOPHIE

Friday, 4 April 2025

Music is playing at 97.5 decibels from the semi next to Trevor's house, and 6 parakeets are squawking in the 37.6-foot-tall oak tree, which has 563 branches and twigs. Taking in all the numbers is a good delaying technique – Adam's influence must be rubbing off on me.

You can do this. Joan would want you to help her son and give him closure.

This is risky, but Trevor's never threatened me physically, and he's always put his accusations in writing, usually hiding behind social media. He used to be a decent guy. Face to face, I'm pretty sure he'll back down, particularly when I give him the framed log cabin sampler. I lick my dry lips, walk up the path and rap the knocker. After 31 seconds, I hear the tap of footsteps and the door opens. A young woman with bright-red hair, and 29,564 days, appears with a toddler clamped to her hip.

'Can I help you?'

'Sorry. I thought Trevor Harding lived here?'

Her eyes narrow into slits as she dabs at a mark on her daughter's blue dress. 'And you are?'

'Sophie. I used to be friends with his mum, Joan.'

'She was my nan!' The woman kisses the top of her little girl's head. 'I'm Nadia.'

I sway slightly. Joan talked so much about her granddaughter and grandson. Will Nadia hold a grudge, as well as her dad?

'Do you want to come in? I have a few minutes before I need to head out.'

I clutch my bag to my chest as she leads me through the hall and into a tiny sitting room. Toys are scattered across the carpet and on the sofa. Family photos cover every shelf and the mantelpiece. My throat tightens with emotion as I spot a picture of Joan and Trevor, hugging each other.

'Sorry about the mess.' Nadia scoops up a stray rattle and toy rabbit. 'It's chaos as usual this morning.'

My throat is dry; I should have taken a swig of water before knocking. 'Don't worry – you should see my flat.' I cough. 'Will Trevor be back soon? I'm down from Bristol for a few days and hoped to catch him while I'm here.'

'You'd better take a seat. Would you like a drink? I can put the kettle on.'

I shake my head, perching on the edge of the sofa. She sits on a chair opposite, cradling the sleepy toddler on her lap.

'I'm sorry to have to tell you this, but Dad died six months ago from lung cancer.' She clears her throat. 'It was weeks from diagnosis to the end – a huge shock. He didn't have time to get his finances in order. Debt collectors still call round. That's why I was suspicious just now.'

My mouth falls open. Inwardly, I'm reeling. 'I'm sorry! I had no idea. I shouldn't have disturbed you.'

I'm about to stand when Nadia frowns. 'Did you say you're called Sophie? Dad used to talk about a girl with that name. Nan taught her to sew before she died.'

'That's what I wanted to discuss with him.' I steel myself for her reaction. 'You see, your dad blamed me for her death.'

Nadia nods, but her expression doesn't change. 'That's right. He said you persuaded Nan not to go out that night.'

'I was worried about her walking in the storm.' I take another breath. 'I wanted to tell your dad that I'm sorry and how much Joan still means to me. I never forgot her. She inspired my love of sewing and I make quilts in her memory.'

'Dad would have loved that.' She kisses the top of her child's head. 'You know, he regretted the way he treated you.'

'What?' I gasp.

'He was ashamed of the nasty letters he sent and the stuff he posted online back then – he told me what he did a couple of years ago. He said he was distraught but knew that wasn't an excuse. You didn't deserve it.'

I grip the side of the settee, my heart beating wildly. I can scarcely believe it.

'Dad tried to track you down to say sorry, but never managed to find you. He couldn't remember your last name, so didn't have a chance.'

Blood pounds in my ears as my mind races. Trevor forgave me. He didn't send those recent accusatory messages and it's unlikely anyone from his extended family did either.

'You look shocked,' Nadia remarks.

'I am. I thought your dad still hated me.'

She shakes her head, leaning forward. 'I'm glad I've had the chance to apologise on his behalf. He was a good dad and Joan was a lovely nan. She enjoyed cooking treats for me and Mikey and made quilts from our old clothes.'

'I know. She showed me them.'

'That was another of Dad's big regrets – everything in Nan's house was destroyed in the explosion. He couldn't pass on her wedding and engagement rings or the home-made bedspreads to me and Mikey. All he ever had were his photos and memories.'

'That's where I can help.' I pull out the sewing sampler from my bag. 'Joan had started making a new quilt for your dad, using a print of his dog in this log cabin design. She gave it me to work on the night she died. I forgot I had it.'

Nadia's eyes well up and her hand flies to her mouth.

'I came across it again yesterday. I thought it might comfort your dad.' I pass it to her. 'But it's yours now, to remember her by.'

Tears roll down her cheeks. 'This is Chester, my dad's old border collie. He'd have loved this, loved *you* for bringing it.' She hugs the frame to her chest, her bottom lip quivering. 'You have no idea how much this means to me, to Mikey, our whole family. It's the most precious thing in the world. We'll always treasure it.'

Nadia and I exchange numbers and promise to keep in touch. Afterwards, I buy a large bunch of yellow, pink and white tulips from a local shop and walk the short distance to the site of Joan's old semi. The street has barely changed; I remember the house with the bright-green front door and the large old oaks. The damaged tree that lost a branch in the storm that night has been hacked back to a stump. I stand outside number 40, which is unrecognisable. A detached, modern-looking white house now stands where my wonderful, kind friend used to live. I place Joan's favourite flowers by the gate.

'I'll never forget you,' I whisper. 'You're a part of every quilt I stitch and the fabric of my life. I'll always love and remember you. Goodbye, Joan.'

I blow her a kiss and leave, smiling to myself. I've finally done a good deed for her after she did so many for me. Nadia will treasure the heirloom, eventually passing it on to her own daughter. Hopefully, my quilt will bring long-lasting happiness to Adam and Wren too.

Walter was right about the need for closure, and Trevor had managed to find it without my help.

But who hasn't?

I stop walking and re-run in my head the list of people I tried and failed to save. Who connected to them might hold a secret grudge? Who is still in pain after all these years?

I have no idea. They're all strangers. But the person writing the emails seems to know *me*.

This definitely feels personal.

I stride away with the claws of the past clinging on firmly.

They refuse to release me.

35

ADAM

Friday, 4 April 2025

I buy ice creams in Plymouth city centre even though it's chilly and drizzling. We both need a sugar hit after our near-death experience. We sit outside the shops, eating giant whipped cones with chocolate Flakes.

'Mummy told jokes whenever we ate Mr Whippies.' Wren stares at me expectantly from further along the bench.

'Erm.' I rack my brains, which are completely frazzled.

'What do you call a dinosaur with an ice cream?' she asks.

'Hmmm. I don't know.'

'A sundae-saurus!'

'Very good! Wait . . . I've got one. What did one scoop of ice cream say to another?'

Wren's nose crinkles, and I realise mine does the same when I'm thinking.

'What?'

'You're cool!'

'That's lame.' She shakes her head with a laugh.

I break off the end of my cone, dip it in the mixture, and pass it to her. 'You've got me licked on the joke front! Here's a teeny-weeny ice cream a-pop-ology.'

She explodes into giggles and moves her rucksack, shuffling closer. I bump her arm gently. She does the same to me, but much harder, and I pretend to fall off my seat.

Ice creams finished, we buy everything I forgot to pack (I think), along with a wetsuit and trainers for Wren. Now we're making our way to a Mexican restaurant I found online. My heart leaps as Sophie WhatsApps. I stop outside a jewellery shop and call up her message.

Am running 20 mins late, sorry. See you soon! x

No problem! x

Wren peers into the window, attracted by the pile of polished semi-precious stones below a case of glittering engagement rings. My gaze rests on them before travelling down to the trays of silver and gold necklaces which feature knot designs.

I ponder our journey. Two cars had collided and ended up, mangled, on the hard shoulder – there may have been fatalities. If that lorry hadn't swerved in time, *we* wouldn't be here. Ditto when I was crossing the road outside Wren's school.

I've found Sophie after all this time, reconnecting quicker than I ever dreamed possible. Wren and I are growing closer. *Life is good.* I should seize the day, as Ollie suggested.

'Let's go in,' I tell Wren. 'We have time.'

'Sophie!'

Wren waves and stands, almost knocking over her chair. My heart pounds loudly as Sophie waves back across the restaurant.

She's a splash of colour as usual: a teal blouse and jacket that makes her pale face and reddish-blonde hair stand out.

'It's great to see you both,' she says, smiling.

'Ditto!'

I catch the scent of lilies and vanilla as she kisses the side of my face, and briefly feel her hand on the small of my back. I wish I could freeze-frame this moment and make it last longer.

'Sorry I'm late.' She breathes out slowly. 'I hope you're having fun in Devon?'

'We almost died on the motorway, and then we had ice cream,' Wren replies. 'Oh, and Adam told *very* bad jokes.'

'Oh no!' Sophie sinks into the seat opposite me. 'Are you okay? Accidentwise, rather than surviving Adam's tragic puns.'

Her foot accidentally brushes against mine beneath the table, but I don't move it away. I'm enjoying feeling her this close, teasing me like old times.

'It was a near miss, but we're fine.'

Wren holds up the semi-precious stones she bought with her pocket money at the jeweller's. They were just for decoration, but the assistant let her have two for £7 after I described our motorway ordeal. She hands the purple stone to Sophie.

'This is for you. I'm keeping the pink one.'

'It's lovely, thank you.'

Wren smiles warmly at her before looking around for the bathroom. I point to the blue door at the back, thrilled that she's bonded so quickly, and deeply, with Sophie.

'Shall I come with you? Or do you want Sophie?'

She shakes her head. 'You can talk about maths together, but don't tell her anything interesting while I'm gone!'

'Hmmm. We'll only discuss boring equations and formulae, I promise.'

Sophie watches her scoot off. 'You two seem to be getting on well.'

'I don't get on her nerves nearly as much! Only 75 per cent of the time. But seriously . . . things are much better, thanks to you. Can you work your magic on my mum too?'

'I could pray every night for a miracle if that helps?' she says, eyes twinkling.

I laugh. 'Sooo . . .'

It's tempting to make another joke, but I want to get on to the subject of 'us' before Wren returns. Reaching over the table, I try to touch her hand as she picks up her glass. Wincing, I rub my neck instead.

'Are you sure you're okay?' Sophie asks. 'It sounds like you had a nightmare journey.'

'Yeah, I'm tired from the drive. I'm looking forward to chilling out tonight.'

Why did I say that? I sound middle-aged. I want to see *her*, not spend the evening bickering with Mum, which is probably what will happen.

'Being back home does have its advantages though,' I add quickly. 'I'll have a babysitter on tap . . . if you want to go out at any point. Or not. Just so you know.'

She raises an eyebrow, a smile hovering on her lips. 'Are you asking me out on a date, Adam Bailey?'

'Would you say yes if I did, Sophie Leroux?'

'I heard rumours there may actually be decent places to eat now, not only greasy burgers and chips from snack booths by the beach.'

'*Whaaat?* Who said anything about going to a restaurant with non-plastic cutlery? I'm feeling nostalgic.'

Sophie laughs, tossing her hair over her shoulder. 'I'll go anywhere you want.' She reaches out and takes *my* hand. I can't stop smiling and glance at the bathroom door to check for Wren.

'In that case, will you come with me to the reunion party next Saturday?' I ask, my heart beating faster.

The smile disappears from her face, and she snatches her hand back. *Aagh*. I should have found a better way to bring this up instead of blundering right in.

'I know you weren't keen initially,' I explain. 'But I thought this could be a good way for us both to come to terms with what happened and find closure . . . Plus it might be fun to dress up and dance, like old times!'

'You seriously want to go?' The colour has drained from her cheeks and her voice comes out as a whisper.

'Erm . . . sorry. I *have* been feeling nostalgic lately . . . I wouldn't mind catching up with old classmates.' I take a breath. 'Including Tom. He says he's going.'

She grips the side of the table, her knuckles whitening. 'You've kept in touch with him?'

'No, we drifted apart at uni. But he contacted me out of the blue recently and asked to meet there.' I fiddle with a napkin, tearing it into pieces. 'To be honest, I've already RSVP'd . . . I'd love you to come but will 100 per cent understand if it's too big an ask.'

Sophie slumps back in her seat. 'You're *definitely* going? With Tom?'

'As long as Mum will babysit . . . I thought it was a chance to say goodbye to the past . . . Make a fresh start.'

I want to add *together* but Sophie is staring at me as if I've informed her that dead people are standing outside the window, waving at us.

Wren slides back into her seat. 'What did I miss? Have you talked about anything exciting?'

'Erm, just the latest breakthroughs in maths and science,' I tell her.

She squints hard, scouring my face. 'Liar, liar, pants on fire! You have red blotches on your neck.'

'Fine. We were discussing the school party. I've decided to go. I've asked Sophie if she wants to come.'

'Ooh, it'll be fun, like Walter's.'

Sophie shakes her head. Her face is as white as the menu she picks up. She hangs on to the laminated plastic as if it's a lifebuoy.

'I'll go if Sophie doesn't want to,' Wren chips in. 'We could pretend we don't know the rule about no children?'

'Nice try! You'd get us both kicked out. Anyway, you can have chocolate ice cream if Grandma's in a good mood.'

'I'll need to think about it,' Sophie says finally.

'Absolutely! The offer's there if you want a slightly awkward escort who might struggle to fix his bow tie . . . But there's zero pressure, I promise. I'm totally happy going alone.'

She shivers, even though we're sitting away from the door. 'I'll come – if you're absolutely set on this.'

Wren doesn't notice her apprehension and reaches across the table. 'High-five!'

Sophie's hand quivers as she gently strikes Wren's.

'Are you sure?' I say, my eyes widening with surprise. 'I don't want to force this on you . . . It's not a problem if I don't have a plus-one.'

'No, as you say, it could be good.' Her voice cracks with emotion. 'For us both.'

'Thank you!' I beam at her. 'This means a lot.'

She's prepared to put her reservations aside . . . Surely that means, deep down, she still cares about me? I'm brimming with hope this week could be the turning point for *us*. We might have a future together.

I can't wait for next Saturday!

Hopefully, I can reassure Sophie and help put the painful memories from our past behind us.

I won't let anything go wrong.

36

SOPHIE

Friday, 4 April 2025

I've only been back in south Devon for a few hours and my plans have already gone badly wrong! I had no appetite for lunch after Adam's bombshell. My throat was horribly dry, and the smell of tacos made me want to vomit. I grip the steering wheel tighter as I drive the long way to Modbury, avoiding passing Lily's parents' house.

Adam is supposed to grow closer to Wren by enjoying leisurely coastal walks together, paddling in the sea and building sandcastles. He also needs to make up with his mum to help lengthen his life. How could I have guessed he'd be unusually decisive and accept the school invitation? I don't want to see familiar faces who'll remind me of the time before I climbed inside Vinny's car, and the trauma I caused afterwards. But it's too risky to let Adam go alone. If I can't improve his relationships with Mrs B and Wren over the next 8 days, his numbers will continue to count down to the party on 12 April. Something terrible might be destined to happen there – possibly to both of us. Could our fates be linked? Am I destined to die trying to save him?

I shudder and consider another curveball: Tom unexpectedly popping up. He was understandably distraught after Lily died and repeatedly tried to get in touch, claiming he didn't blame me. I felt too guilty to see or talk to him, even staying away from Lily's funeral. That's what the recent emails could be about! Maybe he hasn't forgiven me for not going to her service or taking his calls back then. It's too much of a coincidence that he's reappeared when I'm being anonymously targeted. I'm almost relieved it's him – at least I can steer well clear. There's still time to talk Adam out of attending. We've arranged to meet tomorrow afternoon for a beach trip. I could suggest a father–daughter day next Saturday, followed by a home-cooked dinner and movie night, so we're all together in his final hours.

I pull into the village. Hardly anything has changed since I was here a few years ago to oversee fitting of the new boiler and other maintenance work. Bunting is draped across the street and flowering hanging baskets swing from the windows of the black-and-white fourteenth-century inn. I turn right off the high street up a steep, narrow road. Our terraced house is small and painted a pale dove grey. Mum inherited it from her elderly parents when I was tiny – she could never have afforded to live here on her income from yoga retreats. Pushing down painful memories that prick at the back of my mind, I park the van around the corner and walk down the hill. It takes a few trips to bring all my sewing equipment inside, and my arms ache when I finally close the front door. The cleaners aired the rooms after the last guests checked out on Monday, but the pine air freshener doesn't completely mask the damp smell.

My phone vibrates, making me jump, and I rummage for it in my bag. It's Flora.

Good luck with SSD! (and a word that rhymes with luck!) Libby sends her love. P.S. I plagiarised your 'happiness' speech and she said 'yes' to getting back together! Xx

I reply: Thanx and hurray! Much love to you both xx

I'll need all the luck I can get this week, but I doubt there will be any of the other! I leave everything in the hall and do a quick inspection. Before Mum's travels, she repainted all the rooms a clinical white, replaced most of the rickety old furniture with cheap flat-packs, and removed our personal belongings. Hardly anything is left from my childhood, apart from feelings of loneliness. Those are ingrained in the walls. It never felt much of a home, unlike Lily's house, which was filled with laughter.

Heading upstairs, I check the bathroom before stepping into my old bedroom, which has a damp patch in the corner, above the skirting board. The carpet has been removed, leaving bare floorboards, and the bed has an elaborate wrought-iron trellis and a nautical blue-and-white-striped quilt. Only the wardrobe and full-length mirror are mine. I walk over to my closet, which always needed a hard yank to open. The empty hangers rattle like skeletons, and I'm sent spiralling back to my teenage years. The bare walls are plastered with Little Mix posters once more. Lily and I are curled up on my rosebud duvet after an afternoon shopping; later, she's putting on make-up at my wonky old dressing table, which needed a magazine rammed beneath the leg. She jerks open my wardrobe, looking for something new to wear.

Inhaling deeply, I can almost smell her strawberry bubble gum and Calvin Klein perfume. Lily's reflection is in the mirror, laughing as we prepare for prom. She's putting on her gold hooped earrings as she dances to 'Black Magic' in her sexy strapless dress.

I push my thumbs into my closed eyelids but hear her tinkly laugh. It never fades.

Lily is everywhere.

I steady myself against the wall. I can't sleep in here. Mum's old bedroom will be fine this week; it contains fewer harrowing recollections.

I'd become accustomed to losing *her* long before she died.

Making amends with Joan's family was one thing, but I mustn't delve further back into my past.

If I do, I'll feel the wetness on my cheeks as I sobbed at home, alone, during Lily's funeral. I'll hear Adam banging on our front door afterwards, crying and begging to see me. I'll remember how I shrank even further away from him, Mum, Lily's parents, *myself.*

Tugging on the loose threads risks unravelling everything.

I'll fall apart.

I walk out, closing the door firmly on the memories of my best friend.

37

ADAM

Friday, 4 April 2025

Mum opens the front door with a smile. Her conker-brown bob has more whiteish streaks than usual, but she's wearing her normal dog-walking uniform: tan trousers and a navy fleece. She's joined by Bella and Max, who pad into the hall, barking shrilly.

'There you are! I'm so happy you're both here.'

She kisses me, her hair grazing my cheek. The scent reminds me of past trips to the beach during the summer. Whenever Dad was away, speaking at applied maths conferences, we'd have barbecues in one of the nearby coves together. I blink away the memory.

'It's good to see you too, Mum.'

She lingers close to Wren as she pets the dogs.

'You've got big since Christmas. You'll be taller than me before long!'

'Hello, Grandma.'

Wren hesitates before giving her a hug, making a smile creep across Mum's face. My daughter must have shot up; Mum is smaller than I remember as she kisses the top of Wren's head.

'That name makes me sound old,' she says, laughing. 'I don't feel ancient enough to be called one, despite all the grey.'

She tugs a lock of hair. I look past her at the pictures lining the staircase wall of my success in competitions from primary school onwards. They're next to Dad's framed certificates, which record a lifetime of distinguished achievements from his PhD at Cambridge to lecturing in maths at Trinity College, as well as Birmingham and Plymouth universities. A large framed photo of him stares back: a helmet of grey hair, furrowed forehead and thin, straight lips. I remember the flash of joy on his gaunt, deathly white face when I vowed to follow in his footsteps. Now, his disappointment weighs heavily on my shoulders and even the grandfather clock sounds judgemental, tutting in the background.

'You should be used to being called Grandma by now.' A brittle edge creeps into my voice.

'I would if I saw you both more often,' she replies lightly. 'It's been months!'

I frown at her. 'Erm, can I at least take off my coat before we start arguing?'

'Nonsense! No one's quarrelling today. We're all going to get on perfectly well.'

'I could call you Nan or Nana?' Wren suggests, dropping her rucksack on the floor.

'Grandma is fine. I'm just feeling my age. Come and have a drink and sit down. I've made sandwiches – you must both be starving.'

Aagh. It slipped my mind to reply to her text about lunch.

'Sorry! I forgot to say, we stopped off in Plymouth to grab something to eat.'

Mum sighs with exasperation as she leads us into the kitchen. 'Your daddy would forget his own head if it wasn't attached to his body, Wren. What else won't he remember to tell me?'

'We almost had a crash on the motorway.'

Mum glances back worriedly at me.

'There was a nasty pile-up, but we're all right,' I say.

'After that we had lunch with Sophie in a Mexican restaurant,' Wren adds helpfully. 'I had tacos and guaccy maccy.'

'She means guacamole.'

Mum stops in her tracks. 'Sophie?'

'She's Adam's old friend from school,' Wren explains. 'She's making a quilt from Mummy's old clothes.'

'You're back in touch with Sophie Leroux?' Mum gasps.

'We bumped into each other in Bristol. It was . . .'

Fate. A coincidence. A miraculous, wonderful, mathematical improbability.

I search for the right words.

'It was pure chance I popped into the dry cleaners where she works,' I say finally. 'She's creating a memory quilt for us and . . . well, it's purely professional.'

'Fancy that!'

She raises an eyebrow. Is that a disguised criticism about her job? Mum and Dad always had narrow definitions of what they considered 'acceptable professions'.

'She's a seamstress and very creative,' I say tightly. 'Her designs are incredible.'

'That's great.' She pauses. 'Have you seen much of her? Workwise, I mean?'

'Yes!' Wren pipes up before I can reply. 'She came to our house, and we've visited her at work *loads*. We went to the zoo together and Walter's party. He has a dog called Chico who's scared of garden gnomes.' She takes a breath. 'Adam's invited Sophie to *another* party next weekend. I can't go because children aren't allowed. But Adam said I can have chocolate ice cream if you're in a good mood.'

Mum's mouth almost hits the floor, and the tips of my ears burn bright red. I need to have words with my daughter about not being a snitch, but she's on a roll.

'Adam has a goofy smile and pink cheeks when he talks to Sophie, and he walks into things,' she continues. 'He's clumsy!'

'Interesting.' A smile hovers on Mum's lips. 'He was always like that around her.'

'That's not true!' I protest.

'And he gets red spots on his neck when he lies,' Wren points out.

'You're absolutely right!'

'I'm feeling ganged up on,' I say, sighing.

'Let's have a cup of tea.' Mum turns to Wren. 'Do you want to check out your bedroom before we take the dogs for a walk? There *might* be a small present on the bed.'

'Hurray!'

'It's a novel about unicorns,' she explains after Wren dashes out.

'Great. Thank you.'

I want to add she doesn't need to keep buying gifts for Wren, but that's exactly what I've been doing. She walks over to the kettle and fills it with water, while I sit down. An uncomfortable silence descends.

'Is Sophie well?' Mum asks finally.

'She is, actually. I'm planning to see her tomorrow and in the week.'

I'm waiting for a veiled barb, but she smiles. 'That's good. I always liked Sophie.'

I stare at her, stunned. 'No, you didn't. You thought she got in the way of my studies. Dad was the same.'

'We were worried about how you'd balance revision with seeing her, but you managed it. I knew she made you happy.'

She still does, I think to myself.

'It'll do you good to get some downtime when you've been tied up with teaching and looking after Wren. It must be hard to fit in your dissertation?'

I bristle inwardly. 'I *will* get my PhD . . . if that's what you mean? I should finish this final draft soon.'

'No, I was wondering how you're managing it all. You were stressed and tired over Christmas, and we haven't spoken much since.' She pours boiling water into the mugs. 'How are you feeling about Stanford now you have more distance from it?'

Aagh! I know I'm a long way from what Dad wanted for me. I don't need her to point this out. Despite all my good intentions to make an effort, irritation flares and I can't keep it in.

'Yes, I get it. I've thrown my life away. I'm a massive disappointment to you and Dad, even though I'm helping pupils in my class. Thanks for the reminder.' I check my watch. 'Exactly six minutes after I've arrived!'

'Oh, for goodness' sake, Adam!' She throws her hands in the air. 'That's not what I meant. I'm worried when you're trying to do so much single-handed. You're pale and clearly exhausted.'

'Great. I look like a train wreck. Thanks.'

'I can't seem to say anything without you taking massive offence!'

I scrape my chair back. 'Can we not do this now, please? As you said, we don't want to quarrel. I'll hurry Wren up, and we can head out for that walk.'

Mum and I call an uneasy truce and take Wren to the beach. We watch the sea tractor trundle through the incoming tide to the Burgh Island hotel, throw balls for Bella and Max and walk further along the shore towards Bantham beach, collecting seashells in a bucket. Wren finds a dead crab and insists we give it a proper burial in the sand before we head home for a supper of home-made lasagne and a chocolate cake from the local bakery. After watching

Frozen for approximately the millionth time, on my parents' faded green velvet sofa, we all head upstairs.

'Let's have a pleasant day tomorrow,' Mum says, reaching up to kiss me on the cheek.

This is her coded plea that we don't fight. I don't want to either, but I fall back into old patterns whenever I'm here.

'Can I give my granddaughter a goodnight kiss?'

Wren nods and receives hers before skipping into the bathroom. While she brushes her teeth, I unpack in my old bedroom. My duvet is the same faded navy, the wardrobe contains old T-shirts I'd forgotten I owned, and my shelves are crammed with school trophies and maths textbooks. My old tennis and track fixtures are tacked to the crumbling cork-board on the wall. Scattered between them are photos of me and Sophie. I pull one off, and stare at our happy faces. Our arms are wrapped around each other, and I can make out the chain of her Möbius strip necklace. This was taken the week before our prom party. I slip it into my back pocket and notice a row of pearly-white seashells on my bedside table. My heart squeezes. This is the treasure Wren found on the beach . . . she must have left it as a present.

I knock before entering the spare room. The wallpaper used to be a drab green pattern, but Mum painted the walls light blue and fixed fluorescent stars on the ceiling after learning she was a grandma. Wren's sitting in bed, yawning and sewing the seams of one of Sophie's shapes, cut from turquoise fabric.

'Thank you for my shells!'

'Okey-dokey,' she says, without looking up.

'Erm, why don't you do this tomorrow?'

'Grandma said we're going to the beach in the morning, and I want to get it done before we see Sophie. She needs all our shapes. I don't want to let her down.'

'You can barely keep your eyes open!'

She gives another huge yawn.

'How about I take over while you go to sleep? I'll sew mine as well and we can give them all to her.'

'Do you promise you'll finish them tonight?' She holds my gaze unwaveringly.

'Yes! I swear they'll be ready for you in the morning. Now go to sleep.'

She passes me the material and needle and thread, snuggling deeper into her bed.

'Today was fun! Almost as fun as Walter's party, except we didn't go bodyboarding.'

'We'll have more fun tomorrow *and* bodyboarding.'

'What about the sea tractor? Can we have a ride?'

'100 per cent!'

She smiles sleepily. 'Good night, Da—' She stops herself abruptly. 'Adam.'

I grin back. 'Good night, Da-Wren.'

She giggles. 'See *da* tomorrow, Da-Adam!'

'Da too!'

I turn on the night light and am about to leave when I spot the framed picture of me, Carley and Wren on the shelf. She's brought it with her and has it on show instead of burying it at the bottom of her bedroom drawer.

My heart swells with emotion as I leave the door open eight centimetres as per Carley's instructions. Back in my bedroom, I place Wren's sewing and my unfinished shapes on the desk and grab my rucksack.

As I pull out my laptop and files, my smile grows wider.

That was the closest Wren has ever got to calling me Daddy.

38

SOPHIE

Friday, 4 April 2025

I leave a bucket in the loft in case the temporary fix to the roof tiles doesn't hold during the predicted rain next week, and bring down Mum's boxes. There are fewer than I thought. Mum must have had a big clear-out before she left. I'm sorting through everything in her bedroom, helped by an expensive-looking bottle of red wine that a guest left; doing this sober is impossible. Using a penknife, I slit open one of the dusty cardboard containers and find books, ornaments, clothes and a scraggy hairbrush. Old photos of Mum at resorts around the world are stuffed into an envelope. She's smiling serenely in an array of yoga poses in front of amazing views and sunsets. I find a few pics of us next to the sea tractor on Bigbury beach when I was about fourteen or fifteen. I'm glaring at the camera, and there's a gap between us. Neither of us attempted to bridge it.

If she'd lived longer, could I have worked harder to make her love me? Been a better daughter? *Been enough?* I chug from the bottle, trying to blot out my guilt, the lost opportunities to bond. It's too late. I keep all the photos and quickly sort the remainder of her belongings into piles to chuck or take to charity before opening the remaining boxes. Emptying them on to the carpet, I fall back on my heels as clothes, books and cards spill out. They all belong to me. I only took what I could carry when I said goodbye to Mum and moved to Plymouth. I pick up a bunch of envelopes and knock back more wine before opening one. A festive robin stares back from a card, perched on a snow-covered log.

Oh God! This is from Lily's parents. They sent it that first Christmas after the accident when I was severely depressed and had crippling headaches from seeing so many numbers. I stayed in bed and refused to see or talk to anyone for weeks.

> *Dearest Sophie*
>
> *We're thinking of you at this difficult time of year. We hope you're recovering, and the migraines are becoming less frequent. Please come and visit us when you're well enough. We both miss seeing you.*
>
> *Love, Betty and Roger.*

They sent a birthday card the following March with a similar message, but it must have arrived late; I'd already moved to Plymouth.

> *We hope you manage to find happiness today, Sophie. We would love to see you and talk about our memories of Lily together.*
>
> *Much love from Betty and Roger.*

I find 'get well' cards from Tom and former classmates, and dozens of notelets and letters from Adam. I flick through, skimming over his words, and catch a few pleading sentences:

I'm so sorry.

Please forgive me. Can I see you before I leave for Stanford?

Then:

Am back for Xmas. Please, please, please can we meet?

More cards from Adam arrived throughout spring and early summer.

I still miss you, Sophie. Are you around for a drink? I'm sorry for everything that happened last year. Please forgive me.

Adam hadn't realised I'd moved out months earlier. The cleaning company had collected all the post before I eventually redirected everything.

He drew a Möbius strip at the end of every single note.

I put them to one side, knowing they'll break me. I'll study his messages properly *after* I've extended his countdown. Focusing on my old clothes is safer territory, and I begin to sift through. My breath hitches as I pick up a familiar cornflower-blue blouse. It slips through my fingers and lands next to a pink cotton sundress. Both belonged to Lily, along with the denim miniskirt and a turquoise maxi dress. She regularly borrowed from my wardrobe or Tom's and left things here. This is Tom's green T-shirt – Lily wore it when she slept over. She said she liked the smell of his Adidas aftershave next to her bare skin.

Waves of nausea wash over me as I discover the shocking-pink evening dress Lily bought in a charity shop. She was planning to wear it to the prom but changed her mind last minute and chose the strapless black number. I stuff it beneath the mound, uncovering a pale-blue T-shirt that belonged to Adam. I also kept his favourite grey hoodie.

A sob escapes from my lips as I press it to my face, smelling the scent of that summer: coconut suntan lotion, Lily's perfume and strawberry bubble gum, and Tom's and Adam's aftershave.

They all mix into one devastating formula that resulted in multiple deaths.

39

SOPHIE

Saturday, 11 July 2015

I clutched Lily's hand as the car tore away with a screech of brakes and booming music.

'I'm sorry I've ruined everything for you!' I cried.

'You haven't.'

Lily was lying, *obviously*, but I loved her for it.

'The only thing that matters is that we're together.' She squeezed my hand, before tugging at her seat belt.

I tried to put mine on, but it wouldn't click into the holder. I wrapped my arm in the strap and leaned forward, catching a strong whiff of vomit. Priti was asleep, head lolling against the window, and Vinny pounded the steering wheel with both hands.

'Can you slow down? We're not strapped in yet.'

'Soz, they're knackered.'

'That's what Tom said!' Lily flashed me a worried look.

I touched the base of my neck, but my Möbius strip pendant was gone – I'd flung it at Adam. Even in my drunken state I knew he was right – getting into Vinny's car was a terrible idea.

I clutched Lily. 'I'll hold on to you, I promise. I won't let go. We'll be there soon.'

Priti woke up with a jolt and wound down the window, sticking out her head.

'Go, go, go!' she hollered.

'Let's get to this paaaaarty!' Vinny slammed his foot on the accelerator.

Lily clutched me, her face pale. 'I'm going to be sick.'

'Hey, Vinny! Ease up.'

'Nah.'

'Okay, we've changed our minds. Pull over and we'll walk from here, thanks.'

He turned around, glaring, making the car veer. 'I'm not losing valuable drinking time. We're almost there, so why don't you shut up?'

'Keep your eyes on the road, for God's sake!' I pleaded.

The car swerved again and Lily screamed as thorny shrubs thudded against our window. I hugged her tighter.

'That's it, you lunatic,' I shouted. 'Let us out!'

'Fuck you, Sophie!' Vinny yelled back.

He rammed the accelerator harder and leaned across Priti, scrabbling with the glove-box handle as we turned the corner. I had opened my mouth to yell at him when white lights dazzled the windscreen, blinding me.

Time seemed to slow down as a car hurtled towards us. Then the seconds sped up.

The horrifying thud of impact rang out, followed by a grinding, splintering noise.

A single scream stabbed my eardrums, and fireworks detonated inside my head.

Pain ricocheted through my whole body.

Lily was ripped from my arms and flew forward.

40

ADAM

Saturday, 5 April 2025

The old photo of me hugging Sophie, along with Wren's shells and the sewing materials, lie next to my laptop as I finish typing my dissertation. It's past midnight. I only need to check a few more calculations before sending it off. Then I'll finish stitching the shapes for Wren and Sophie. I'm taking another swig of coffee when my email pings. It's Dr Hunt! He must have a sixth sense I'm working late. I click on his update.

>Dear Adam
>
>My colleagues and I have reviewed your friend's unique geometric shape and we're excited about its potential. We wish to investigate further. This will require funded postdoctoral research that could lead to a tenured position. We all agree, one person is best placed to take this forward – you!
>
>Are you interested in pursuing this after you've been awarded your PhD? If so, please email a funding proposal to me by close of play today. I can review over the weekend and present to the board on Monday afternoon. If approved, we could offer a paid

position in the department, beginning as soon as you are able to arrange your visa and return to the States.

Let me know if you are keen and we shall proceed. We also need to arrange the oral exam for your dissertation when delivered, as previously discussed.

Yours sincerely

Dr Hunt

I can't believe it! This could be the first step in making my name at Stanford and honouring my dad's memory . . . all thanks to Sophie.

I reply: Will get the proposal over to you ASAP, and the final draft of my dissertation!

I tiptoe downstairs to the kitchen and fill a vacuum flask with coffee, feeling Dad's pride radiating from the photo on the staircase. Returning to my desk, I push the shells and sewing bundle to one side, open a new Word document on my laptop and begin typing.

Four and a half hours later, I re-read my funding proposal for the fifth time and tap out the final words of my dissertation's conclusions. After attaching both documents to Dr Hunt's email, I lean back, yawning and stretching my arms above my head. My work tonight, *today*, is potentially life-changing. My eyelids droop. A troubling thought hits and I sit bolt upright, almost falling out of my chair. I've been caught up in creating the best possible pitch and haven't considered the implications *if* the board says yes. It would fulfil the promise I made to my dad, easing my guilt. But I'd have to pull Wren out of school, ripping her away from friends and her grandma. Will I quit my job that I'm finding strangely fulfilling, abandoning struggling pupils like Khalid? How will Mum react? She's on her own now Dad's gone. We're all she has left.

Then there's Sophie . . . We've only just found each other again. Do I want to rip us apart before we've had a chance to see if, well, there is an 'us'?

Hmmm.

Uncertainty grips me. My fingers hover over the keyboard.

My heartbeat quickens. I breathe out slowly, trying to calm it. There's no rush. I don't need to make up my mind now . . . I have plenty of time to weigh up my options *if* the university makes an offer. I exhale and hit the send button.

I watch the email disappear into the ether, before collapsing fully clothed on the bed. I'm asleep within seconds.

'It's morning, Da-Adam! Grandma said to come downstairs and get yummy pancakes.'

Wren bounds into the room and leaps on my bed, jumping up and down. Despite my sleep-deprived state, I manage a smile as she hurdles over me. I grope for my phone on the bedside table. It's 7.45 a.m. I've had three hours' sleep. It feels like far less.

'Tell Grandma to start without me, Da-Wren,' I say, rolling over. 'I'll be down in half an hour. I need more sleep.'

'But you have to get up now! You said we could go bodyboarding and have a ride on the sea tractor.'

I raise my head and squint blearily at the gap between the curtains. Rain spatters against the glass.

'Perhaps this afternoon or tomorrow, but the weather doesn't look good this morning.' I grab another pillow and wedge it beneath my neck.

'It looks good to meeeee!'

Wren leaps off the bed and runs to my desk. I hear a sharp intake of breath.

'Have you stubbed your toe?'

'You didn't sew any of the shapes!'

Aagh. I fell asleep before getting round to them!

I prop myself up on my elbows. 'Sorry, I had an urgent email from Stanford and it couldn't wait. I had to—'

'B-b-but you promised!' She swings around, her bottom lip wobbling. 'You said it would be ready for me.'

I sit up, swinging my legs off the bed. 'And I meant it, but unfortunately I had to do last-minute work and it meant pulling an all-nighter.'

'I b-b-believed you.' Her shoulders shake.

'I'm sorry. It won't take long . . . I can finish them off later.'

'You won't bother. You *never* keep your promises.'

'That's not true!'

'Yes, it is! In the car here, you said we'd visit the beach *whatever the weather*. And last night you said we'd *definitely* go on the sea tractor. Now you're saying this afternoon or tomorrow.'

'Because . . . you won't like getting wet on the beach.'

'Yes, I will! The sea's wet so rain doesn't matter.'

'All right. We'll go in the sea later.'

Her voice rises several pitches. 'You always say *later*, and it never happens!'

'Can you please stop shouting?'

'No!' Her eyes glitter with tears. 'You're mean. You break promises all the time! You promised Mummy you'd look after me.'

'B-b-but I am!'

I'm trying to get a grip on how rapidly our conversation is deteriorating.

'Only because she forced you! I know you don't want to.'

I stare at her, aghast. 'That's not true. What are you talking about?'

'Your friend, Ollie, came over. I went to the toilet and heard you talking downstairs. Ollie said he wouldn't want a kid, and you agreed with him. You said you didn't have any choice – that you and Mummy never had a back-up plan.'

Ice rushes through my veins as I scramble to my feet. 'I didn't mean that, I promise.'

'Your promises mean nothing!' she yells. 'You want a manual for me!'

'That was a joke. A bad one, I'm sorry.'

'*And* you promised Mummy you'd look after me in Bristol, but you told Sophie we won't be there for ever. Because you want to be in America. Stupid Stanford is all you care about, not me!'

'I swear that's not the case. You're my daughter. I do care about you!'

Guilty patches crawl up my neck. I can't admit that a return ticket to my old uni is being dangled in front of me, carrot-like.

'Liar!' she cries, pointing at the tell-tale marks.

I head over and try to put my arm around her shoulder, but she shakes me off, scrambling across the bed to put distance between us.

'You don't want me. You never did!'

'I do, Wren!'

'I want my mummy, not you. *She* loved me.'

I need to reassure her, make her understand, but my lungs constrict and I can't catch my breath. I exhale heavily and bend over, attempting to relieve the pressure mounting in my ribcage as she darts to the door.

Mum appears, blocking Wren's escape route.

'What on earth's going on?' she asks, frowning. 'Why are you both shouting?'

'Adam doesn't want me. I hate him! I wish I'd never met him!' Wren bursts into tears, dodges past Mum and runs out.

The door to the spare bedroom slams shut. I inhale deeply through my nose for a count of four.

Mum stares at me. 'Why would Wren think that?'

'She overheard something I told a friend and misinterpreted it . . . She didn't hear what else I said . . . looking after her was my decision, it wasn't foisted on me.'

'*Make* her understand, Adam. This is important – a little girl's feelings are at stake.'

I nod as my chest contracts further. I feel a panic attack coming on. I try to breathe deeply into my abdomen.

'I'll wait . . . until she's calmed down . . . then we can have a proper, grown-up conversation.'

'She's eight years old! She's not going to deal with this like an adult. She needs to hear you want and love her.'

'I know. I will.' I gulp. 'I do.'

'When? I love you dearly, Adam, but you drive me mad the way you put off everything. It's your worst trait.'

'Thanks, Mum!' My chest rises and falls rapidly. 'And yours is always piling on the pressure and criticising. Going to Stanford was the *only* definition of success for you and Dad.' I take a shallow breath. 'It's all that ever mattered . . . so Dad could live it through me . . . because he didn't get in himself. Well, you should be thrilled . . . Stanford's considering offering me a postdoc research position after I get my PhD.'

'What? You're returning?' She shakes her head. 'But I thought you were happy in Bristol? Wren too? You're beginning to get her settled in her new life.'

'Oh my God! I can't believe I'm hearing this. I can't win whatever I do. There's absolutely no pleasing you!'

I storm past her and knock on the door of the spare bedroom, holding on to the frame as my vision blurs.

'Go away!' Wren yells. 'I hate you! I want Grandma.'

Mum follows me on to the landing.

'Perhaps you're right. You should both take a moment.'

I open my mouth, but I can't speak. *Can't breathe.*

My mouth tingles, making it difficult to swallow. I lean my head against the wall as a wave of dizziness hits.

Mum touches my back gently. 'Inhale for four, hold for four and let it out for four. That's right.'

She remains at my side until the tunnel vision melts away and the discomfort in my chest lessens.

'I'll look after Wren,' she says. 'Why don't you go for a run? It might clear your head and help you figure out what you want.'

41

SOPHIE

SATURDAY, 5 APRIL 2025

I'm walking barefoot along an empty beach, the strong wind whipping rain into my face. Giant waves toss sheets of foam on to the shore. I zip up my anorak, but it doesn't keep out the damp chill. A crack of lightning reveals seagulls circling vulture-like in the damson sky.

They swoop down, and I realise they're not birds. They're numbers: 2025, 4 and 12.

They dance about, tormenting me. I sprint away, my numb feet sinking into the cold, wet sand, but the figures give chase.

I feel their presence whistling by my ears; they're not far behind. There's nowhere to hide.

In the distance, I spot a man and a child holding hands. It's Adam and Wren. I yell at them to run away, but they don't recognise the danger. They draw closer.

The numbers shuffle into place.

12, 4, 2025.

The date of Adam's looming death.

I scream louder, but the gale drowns out my cries. The numbers suddenly dive-bomb, separating Adam from Wren.

I can't reach him.

Thunder rumbles ominously.
Bang, bang, bang.

'Adam!'

I sit up in bed, panting, and stare at the bare white walls, generic Ikea furniture and reclaimed floorboards. Where am I? It takes a few seconds to remember this is Mum's old bedroom, but it's been stripped of her vibrant orange, pink and electric-blue throws and rugs from India. I roll over, ignoring the raps at the front door. I worked on the quilt until 3.30 a.m. and slept fitfully, disturbed by nightmares about Adam. Rain pelts against the window; it's not worth getting up for a walk yet. The knocking grows louder.

Dammit!

The neighbours will complain. I climb out of bed and look for the dressing gown I made from a remnant of teal silk. I'm wearing Adam's old blue T-shirt, and it barely skims my bottom. Ripping my robe from the wardrobe, I run downstairs while fastening the belt.

Bang, bang, bang.

'I'm coming!'

I throw open the front door.

'Adam!'

Wet hair is plastered to his forehead. His damp T-shirt highlights his sculpted torso, and his shorts cling to his muscular thighs. My stomach flutters. I tighten the belt on my dressing gown, acutely aware I'm almost naked.

So is he.

That thought doesn't help. I focus on his number: 8. It's still counting down, which is disappointing, but he's only been with his mum since yesterday. I can't expect miracles. His family needs longer to bond.

'Aren't we meeting this afternoon?' I rearrange my curls, making sure my scar isn't visible.

'Sorry. I went for a run to clear my head and ended up in the village . . . muscle memory must have kicked in. I couldn't leave without coming here.'

I smile, remembering the times he turned up to support me during our A levels.

He wipes his eyes with the back of his hand. They're watery, but not just from the rain.

'Is everything okay?' I ask, stepping closer.

'Not really. I'm a walking – well, *running* disaster. I've upset Wren and Mum and I've only been back less than twenty-four hours.'

Before I can ask what's happened, he splutters: 'But seeing you . . . even for a few seconds, well, it makes me feel better, makes me want to *do* better. I'll be all right now, thank you.'

He flashes a wan smile and turns to leave.

'Don't go,' I urge. 'Why don't you come in? You can dry off and have a drink of water. We can talk.'

'I should get back and make up with them . . . I'm not sure where to start.'

'You'll work it out. You're not a disaster, Adam, far from it.'

He shakes his head, absent-mindedly rubbing the tattoo on his wrist. 'I ruin everything good in my life.'

I reach out and take his hand. He startles and looks down as I gently trace my fingers over the symbol. He shivers beneath my touch, making my heart skip a beat.

'When did you get this done?' I ask quietly.

'That first Christmas without you,' he replies. 'I came home from Stanford and you didn't want to see me. But I hadn't stopped believing we'd get together. I thought it would happen at some point.'

'Because time is like a Möbius strip,' I murmur. 'It doesn't matter how long it takes, we'll eventually find our way back to each other.'

He nods. I'm still holding his wrist.

'It's been almost ten years, Sophie,' he says croakily. 'I never gave up hope, not for a minute.'

My heart beats faster. I hadn't dared to hope over the years, couldn't torture myself by holding out the possibility of an *us*. Now I know his number, I definitely shouldn't let myself give in.

But I can't hold back my feelings anymore.

I lift his hand to my mouth and kiss around the shape of the Möbius strip. I feel his pulse quicken beneath my lips. Gazing into his eyes, the longing echoes mine. The space between us disappears as an invisible thread pulls us closer.

Time seems to stand still.

All that matters is this moment.

My arms are around his neck, my lips pressing against his. A moan escapes from his throat as we kiss slowly at first, and then with growing intensity. He lifts me up, and we're inside the house, slamming the door shut and kissing hungrily against it. The jut of his hip bones pushes into mine as he kicks off his trainers. I moan with pleasure as he undoes my robe, his hands curving under my bottom. The silk slides into a puddle at our feet. Our bodies fall into old patterns, eager to create new ones. My hands thread through his hair before cupping his buttocks, pulling him into me. His lips trail down my neck and collarbone while his hands move higher, on to my breasts, teasing my nipples into hard peaks. I gasp at the hotness of his breath on my skin, the rush of desire through my thighs.

'This looks familiar.' He looks down at his old T-shirt before helping it over my head and dropping it on the floor.

'I'm a terrible kleptomaniac, sorry.'

We're both laughing as I pull off his top. I remember his teenage body, but Adam the man is exciting and new. My fingers slowly run over the contours of his chest and trace the defined lines of his abdomen.

He shudders. 'I want you, Sophie.'

I tug at his shorts as we sink to the floor. We're kissing passionately in between fits of giggles. I don't care about the coldness of the tiles beneath my back, the absurdity of what we're doing, only aware of the hotness of his breath on my skin and the desire swirling in my stomach.

'I want you too, but we don't have a condom,' I say, panting. 'We should wait.'

His chest rises and falls rapidly. 'I'm done waiting. And we don't need one for what I have in mind.'

He pushes my legs apart, and his mouth lowers, leaving a scattering of soft kisses as he slides down my body, taking his time before finally reaching my inner thighs.

I arch my back, an unquenchable fire building inside me at every touch, every flicker of his tongue.

The world outside the door fades away.

Pleasure cascades over me in giant, unstoppable waves.

We eventually make it upstairs to the bedroom, lying in each other's arms, our legs tangled together. Adam kisses the top of my head, wrapping a lock of hair around his finger. I keep my eyes shut, savouring the security of this moment. The real world outside this room is a scary, dangerous place. I can't control it. I'm sure as hell not ready for it.

'I guess we should probably discuss what happens next,' Adam says, breaking the silence.

My eyelids fly open. I have to face facts.

Adam will die a week today unless I change his countdown.

'You carry on with your run?' I say, attempting to sound light-hearted. 'You need to do another 5K.'

'Of course! Break's over.' He sits up and pretends to look for his damp running gear, before flopping down next to me.

'I mean it, Sophie. We've wasted enough time. I want to make every second count with you.'

'How can I forget? You did downstairs.'

This conversation mustn't turn into something more intense. How can we discuss beginning a serious relationship when it could end within days? I *must* create distance between us, so he devotes all his energy to getting closer to Wren and his mum. That's what could save him, not my feelings.

He stares at the ceiling, frowning. 'Seriously, though. I think we should . . . Something's come up with work and it means . . .'

'No work talk in bed, please.'

'Fine, but without sounding needy . . . How do you feel about *us*?'

'In what way?' I ask, playing for time.

'Aagh!' He runs a hand through his hair. 'You're forcing me to spell it out. Is this . . . well, a one-off for you? Or shall we try to make a go of it?'

I want to shout 'yes' to his last question at the top of my voice, but the word sticks in my throat.

'You don't want to?' He looks down, his eyes brimming with disappointment.

'It's not that, I promise.' I lace my fingers between his. 'This is sudden, and it's caught me by surprise. I haven't had a chance to catch my breath, let alone think about anything long-term.'

'True. But I'm asking you now. *Is* there any possibility, however remote, of "us" going forward?'

I shiver, trying to focus, as he runs his fingers lightly across my stomach.

'You have so much on with work and fixing things with Wren and your mum. If I'm being honest, I'm not sure where I fit into all that.'

He opens his mouth to protest but I continue talking. 'Let's take things one day at a time and see what happens this week. Agreed?'

Adam nuzzles my neck. '100 per cent. But for the record, I remember you fit perfectly.'

Picturing us having sex isn't helping my willpower, especially since we've discovered one of the last guests left an unopened box of condoms in the bedside drawer. Adam's already reaching for the packet and tearing it open.

I hate myself, but I don't argue that we should wait.

He kisses me deeply, rolling on top. 'We can go as slow or as fast as you want, Sophie. It's up to you.'

I sink into his touch and all my good intentions are washed away.

42

ADAM

Saturday, 5 April 2025

We've said goodbye, but it's tempting to join Sophie in the shower . . . I'll nuzzle her neck and make her laugh, enjoying feeling her naked body mould against mine. I won't be able to stop kissing her, making up for the time we've missed. How have I managed to get through almost ten years without her? We've arranged to take Wren to an agricultural show tomorrow instead of a beach walk later, but now I regret the change in plans. Not being able to hold Sophie in my arms for another twenty-four hours seems impossibly hard. She makes me complete, as if the Möbius strip has finished its final, most important loop.

    I hover in the doorway of the bathroom, debating whether to jump in with her, but reluctantly step back. Making things right with Wren and Mum can't wait. I pull on my T-shirt and shorts, which I'd snatched up when we retreated upstairs, and find a pen and notepad on the bedside table. I draw our symbol, add a love heart, and leave it on her pillow. I check my phone messages as I head out the door and run down the stairs. My vision's blurry after losing one contact lens while running and removing the other.

Squinting, I open a WhatsApp from Mum, miss my step and fall forward. My stomach plummets, rollercoaster-style. I grab for the rail, hanging on one-handed, as my feet leave the step. I manage to right myself in time.

Bloody hell!

The stairs are uncarpeted, and the hallway is tiled. I could have landed badly and smashed my skull. If I were a cat, I'd have used up my nine lives.

I sit on the bottom step, shakily, and check Mum's messages.

Wren's stopped crying. I've reassured her we *both* want and love her very much. She seems much happier. She's shown me photos of Chico on her phone. She also let me look at the lovely pictures of you, Sophie and her at the zoo and surfing party. Love Mum xx

It's followed with:

Gone to beach with Wren and the dogs for a walk now rain's stopped. Planning to take her out for lunch and shopping. Won't be back until later this afternoon. You'll have plenty of time to think about what to say to her.

I reply: Thanks, Mum. Sorry for everything xx

Another message from her arrives:

I'm sorry too. I'll support you whatever your decision re Stanford. I want you and Wren to be happy. Mum xx

'Is everything okay, Adam? I heard a bang!'

Sophie is standing at the top of the stairs, wrapped in a towel and frowning worriedly. Her wet hair drips down her shoulders.

'Actually, I think it is! That was my mum. She's taken Wren out for the day so there's no rush to get back.'

She raises an eyebrow, dropping her towel. 'In that case – what are you waiting for?'

Desire shoots across my stomach as she darts back to the bedroom.

This time I trip *up* the stairs in my eagerness to reach her.

We head into the village for coffee and croissants before I run home. Shyly, I reach for Sophie's hand, and her fingers lace between mine, fitting perfectly. She wants to take things slowly, and this could be a one-time thing or, technically, a three-time thing. It's too soon to think about our future, according to her, although different scenarios *are* running through my mind and they all involve us being together. I was trying to sound her out earlier, because my email to Dr Hunt weighs heavily on my mind.

What if I *am* offered the position at Stanford? I've spent years thinking and dreaming about Sophie, and fate – or rather a patchwork quilt – has reunited us. Am I prepared to walk away from this chance to restart our relationship? Would Sophie follow me to the US after such a short time? What about Mum and Wren? Mum's putting on a brave face, but she'll be gutted about seeing less of her granddaughter, and Wren will be distraught. I'll be letting down my pupils and teaching colleagues mid-term. However, if I don't go back to Stanford, I'll betray my dad's memory.

The research post might never materialise. I *could* avoid upsetting Sophie unnecessarily and wait to discover the board's verdict. But deep down, I know I mustn't put off revealing something potentially life-changing again.

I stop before we reach the high street and turn to face her. 'You asked me where you fit into my life.'

'And you made a rude comment!'

'I want you to know that when . . . *if* you decide you want us to become an item, I'll make space for you in my life with Wren . . . wherever we are.'

She frowns. 'How do you mean, *wherever you are?*'

I wait for an elderly man to pass, stepping closer to the wall.

'My supervisor was blown away by your geometric shape . . . He asked me to write a bid for a research post. If it's approved by the board on Monday, I could be offered a full-time position in the department to investigate it further on campus.'

'You're planning to go back to Stanford?' Her voice sounds strangled, and her hand slips from mine.

'No, this is early days,' I say carefully. 'They may not offer . . . I don't know whether I'll accept if they do. I have to think about Wren and my mum . . . You too.'

'That's why you wanted to know earlier where *we* stand? Because you're seriously considering this?'

'*If* they green-light the proposal, I'll have to decide. But I've changed, Sophie, I swear. I'm not holding things back the way I did when we were teenagers. I'm being 100 per cent honest and upfront about everything that's going on in my life.'

She stares at me. 'I get that it would be great for your career. But will it make *you* happy?'

I'm racked with fresh doubts. Is this what *I* want, when I've begun to enjoy teaching? And being a dad, most of all? Or am I stuck on the treadmill of academia, unable to climb off completely?

'I'd hate you to go back because you think it's what your dad would want,' she continues when I don't reply.

I run a hand through my hair. 'Aagh. It's not that simple about Dad . . . You don't understand.'

'Make me.'

I flinch. I haven't confessed this to anyone, not even my mum.

'Adam? Tell me.'

I take a deep breath, nudging a stone with my trainer. 'When Dad was dying, I flew back from the States to say goodbye before it was too late. He was flitting in and out of consciousness . . . Anyway, he managed to hold my hand and say how proud he was . . . that he could go to his grave happy, knowing I was on course to get my PhD and become a Stanford professor. He asked me to promise that I *would* get there eventually . . . I wanted to make him happy, so I gave him my word.'

Sophie's eyebrows shoot up. 'And you think you've betrayed him by leaving to look after Wren? That you need to return, at whatever cost, to fulfil your promise?'

'No.' I hesitate before deciding to tell the truth. 'It sounds crazy, but yeah.'

'Did your dad tell you he loved you before he died?' she asks bluntly.

Her question knocks the wind out of me. I turn away to hide the tear that creeps into the corner of my eye, but she catches my hand and forces me to look at her. She waits for me to speak. She's the only person I can be this vulnerable with, my most exposed. It feels like I'm back in the shallows, dripping with blood after our first surfing lesson.

'Afterwards, I whispered those three words in his ear. I waited, thinking he'd say them back, but his breathing got worse.' I rub my neck, glancing down. 'He lost the chance . . . That's if he ever wanted to tell me . . .'

'Oh, Adam! I'm sorry.' Sophie wraps her arms around me.

I cry into her shoulder, not caring that a woman stares as she gets into her car.

'I want you to be happy,' she says, her voice breaking. 'Wren too. If returning to the US is what you want, I'll support you.'

Mum sent the same message earlier and I realise my luck at having two such wonderful, strong women in my life. I close my eyes and hug Sophie closer.

'But you have to do this for the right reason,' she adds. 'It's *your* life, not your dad's. You can't keep trying to please a ghost.'

43

SOPHIE

Saturday, 5 April 2025

I cling to Adam, fighting back my own tears. The fact he has no idea he may not live long enough to return to teaching in Bristol, let alone move to America, is breaking my heart. But how can I tell him he can't pursue his dream? That it's not even remotely within reach because his life is almost over?

'I have my own confession to make.' I straighten up and meet his gaze. 'I need to tell you something about Walter's party.'

His brow wrinkles. 'Hmmm?'

'You wanted to know what it was all about – why his family flew in from Australia for a big bash that wasn't his birthday.'

'I thought it was odd, but Walter's eccentric.'

'He's dying,' I say gently. 'Walter has terminal prostate cancer. He doesn't have long – a few weeks tops. That's why it was important everyone was there, spending time with him while they could.'

'What? No!'

'Walter wanted to say goodbye in his own way, without a big fuss. He hates speeches and didn't want it to become morbid or teary. He wanted to laugh, sing and dance with his friends and family and for everyone to have a great day, surfing and bodyboarding.'

'I'm sorry. That's awful!'

'Walter would say it's the exact opposite – he's had the chance to prepare because he knows it's imminent. He's having a whale of a time with Harry, Maddy and his grandchildren. He's saying and doing the things he needs to before—'

My eyes mist up and I force myself to go on.

'Walter's preparing his family and making sure everyone's ready before he dies.'

The finality of the word tastes heavy and bitter on my tongue.

'I wish I'd had longer to get to know him,' Adam says slowly. 'Wren too. She adores him and Chico. She wants a grandfather, as well as a dog.'

'If you had spent more time together, Walter would have told you to savour the tiny joys, and the small moments – sewing and laughing with Wren, giving your mum one of your "famous" hugs, holding my hand as we walk down the street.'

'That makes sense . . . the everyday things we all take for granted.' He touches my arm. 'Why are you telling me this now? Has Walter deteriorated?'

'No, he has enough energy for day trips. But his diagnosis has made me think about the bigger picture.' I take a deep breath. 'What if this week is all either of us gets, and it's our only chance to be happy before it's all over?'

'I know being here brings back bad memories, but nothing will happen, I promise!'

'You don't know that – I could step off the kerb on the high street and be killed by a van in the next five minutes or knock myself out and drown while surfing this week.'

'Aagh! Don't say things like that. It doesn't bear thinking about.'

'Doesn't it? We both need to focus on what's important.' I grasp his hands. 'As Walter's time runs out, do you think he's worrying about what he did or didn't do in his career? Or is he thinking about his family, the people he loves?'

I gulp, battling my rising emotion. 'What I'm trying to say, Adam, is if this was *your* last week, the board's verdict on Monday wouldn't matter in the grand scheme of things. It's too late for me to mend my relationship with my mum, but it's not for you. Repairing your connection with Wren and your mum would make a huge difference. We all have to live for now and make every moment matter.'

He takes me in his arms and kisses me.

'There! I'm doing exactly that. Seizing the day before it's too late. I promise I'm not going to put off happiness. I want it to start from now . . . all of us happy from this exact minute going forward and not at some vague point in the future.'

I kiss him back.

I'm hoping with all my heart he *does* finally understand.

After coffee and croissants in a café tucked away in one of the side streets, Adam kisses me goodbye and runs home. Returning to an empty house, full of memories of this morning's lovemaking, is too painful, so I browse in the charity shop and find a gorgeous emerald silk vintage evening dress. It's too big but it'll be easy to take in at the seams. I pick up a couple of men's cotton shirts that could be useful for other quilts when I've finished Wren's.

The thought sends a sudden chill down my spine.

Have I started the chain reaction that will save Adam's life? Or will Wren be forced to use my creation as a comforter after his death?

Stepping out of the door, I spot a man with a blond ponytail and goatee on the opposite side of the street. He looks strangely familiar. Wait – is that Tom? I duck back inside as he looks this way, my heart pounding furiously. His face has filled out since we were teenagers, and he has a small paunch, but I'm sure it's him. Thank God he didn't see me.

I pretend to study the 103 dusty, torn paperbacks at the rear of the shop before re-emerging. Sticking on my sunglasses, I keep my head down and walk swiftly along the street, half jogging up the hill as soon as I turn the corner. Back home, I fetch a glass of water from the kitchen before heading upstairs. As I reach the landing, someone raps at the front door. I freeze for a couple of seconds, then pad into Mum's room. I stare down from the shuttered window, darting away when the man squints up. Tom again! Did he follow me here?

But I realise he didn't need to – he knows where I live. He was always dropping by with Lily. The letterbox rattles. I leave it another half an hour before returning downstairs. A scrappy handwritten note has landed on the mat.

Hi Sophie,

Adam said you're back and may go to the school party. I hope you do! It would be great to catch up with you both. Do you fancy a coffee before then so the two of us can chat in private? I've left my phone number and Dad's address on the back (in case you've forgotten).

BTW I bumped into Lily's mum a few weeks ago and she was asking about you – she'd love to see you while you're back if you have time to pop in. Me too.

Your old friend, Tom

Tom sounds friendly and there's no trace of malice in his words. I re-read them, attempting to recognise a similar turn of phrase from the emails. There's nothing. He *might* not have sent them. He may genuinely want to swap stories, avoiding mentioning prom night.

But if that's the case, why would he want to talk to me alone? What does Tom really want?

I screw the note into a ball in my fist. Over the last decade, I've learned to pay attention to coincidences.

Tom has got back in touch and will be at the fundraiser on Saturday, when Adam's days are destined to end – unless I can change his countdown.

I have the terrible feeling that what is doomed to happen could be linked to the three of us finally being reunited.

44

ADAM

SATURDAY, 5 APRIL 2025

The house is quiet when I let myself in. Mum and Wren must have taken the dogs with them to lunch. After a quick shower and change of clothes, I write an actual to-do list and cross off tasks as I complete them: finish sewing the shapes. *Tick.* Find Victoria sponge recipe online/check ingredients/cake tins. *Tick.* I search Mum's cupboards and the fridge before nipping out to the farm shop to buy eggs. They sell cornflowers and I pick a few bunches to make up with Mum. *Double tick.*

Back home, I put the flowers in a vase and jot a note in her kitchen pad.

> *Sorry again. Thank you for being such a great mum and grandma. I'm lucky to have you.*
>
> *Adam x*

Next, I tear off a few pages and focus on the number-one item on my list.

Dear Wren

I'm sorry for letting you down. Please forgive me. I didn't mean to hurt you. That's the last thing I'd ever want to do.

I find it hard to talk about how I feel – that's why I'm writing a letter. (I hope you can read my horrible handwriting!)

I've always wanted you, Wren. I was so excited when your mum told me I was a dad! I couldn't wait for us to get to know each other. I was also scared I wouldn't be good enough, that I'd fail because I didn't know what I was doing. I still don't, but I'm learning from you!

Every day, I'm in awe of how brave, clever and talented you are. You're thoughtful, determined and better at sewing, dancing and surfing than I'll ever be!

My dad encouraged me to excel in my education and extracurricular activities, and I thought that's what it meant to be a good parent. But that's not nearly enough. The problem is, Dad never taught me how to show I care about someone, which is the most important thing in life.

I must learn how to open up to you and other people I care deeply about. It's like my sewing and surfing – I need practice! But I promise I will do better.

I want us to spend more time doing things together. I've finished sewing the shapes and would love to make a cake with you. Come find me in my bedroom if you want to.

But if you don't, that's all right too. I'll never put pressure on you to do something just to make me happy.

Lots of love
Dad xx

I leave the letter on the counter and head upstairs. I spend the next half hour looking through next term's lesson plans, before the front door bangs open and the dogs bark loudly. I pace nervously up and down for what feels like forever. The TV turns on in the sitting room, and a *Frozen* song rings out. Wren has rejected my apology. *Rejected me.*

I've slumped on to the bed, resting my head in my hands, when there's a timid knock at the door. It's so quiet, I almost miss it. I spring to my feet and launch myself towards the handle, stumbling as I open it.

Wren stands in front of me, smiling and clutching the note. She steps inside and throws her arms around my waist.

'I forgive you, Da-Adam,' she says. 'I'm sorry too.'

Mum is in the kitchen, unloading the dishwasher after dinner. Wren's gone to bed early; she's worn out and fell asleep after one chapter of *Skandar and the Unicorn Thief*. Our Victoria sponge sits on a plate next to the coffee cups, a big wedge cut out.

Mum glances back, sensing I'm lurking in the doorway. 'This was lovely,' she says, stacking clean plates in the cupboard.

'Thanks! I thought it was overbaked, but we'll do better next time.'

'Not the cake, even though that was delicious – and a big surprise!' She turns around, her eyes misty. 'I mean having you both here for a family dinner, cooking together this afternoon, walking the dogs on the beach, me reading Wren a bedtime story. Everything!' She throws her hands in the air. 'It's wonderful to have the company. I appreciate you both coming back. I've missed Wren.' She bites her lip. 'I've missed you too, Adam.'

Sophie talked earlier about appreciating the small moments, so I walk over and pull her in for a hug. She stiffens slightly, before relaxing and embracing me back.

'You keep surprising me today,' she says gruffly. 'What was that in aid of?'

'To say sorry for not visiting more often . . . and, well, for jumping down your throat when you're trying to help.'

'I'm sorry,' she replies, grasping my arms. 'It's *my* fault you've stayed away.'

I shake my head. 'You were right . . . I'm exhausted and work's got on top of me, but I shouldn't have taken it out on you.'

'It's not just that.' She looks me straight in the eye. 'Let's be honest with each other. You think you've disappointed me. That you've somehow let me down, as well as Dad, because you've left Stanford.'

'Well, haven't I?' I blurt out. 'When you spent so much on my education? It was tens of thousands. More . . .'

My mind whirrs with the calculations. I wince at the possible six-figure final sum.

'We never begrudged it,' Mum insists. 'Dad was left a large inheritance from his parents and we both wanted to give you the best possible start in life.'

I flinch, trying to keep my emotions in check. She can hardly think what I'm doing now is 'the best'.

'That wasn't a veiled criticism,' she adds quickly. 'Neither of us is good at saying what we really mean, Adam, but please believe me when I say you're not a disappointment. I'm proud of the way you've stepped up. You're such a brilliant dad and I'm sure you're a great teacher.'

I shake my head. 'Hardly!'

'It's true. You've always been kind and compassionate. I know it's been tough, learning to put Wren's needs before your own. But I honestly think that leaving Stanford to look after her is the best decision you've ever made. Supporting Wren and all those children at your school will be the making of you.'

I watch, speechless, as she refills the water bowls for Bella and Max, who have trotted in.

'You were my miracle baby, Adam,' she explains without looking up. 'After years of miscarriages and IVF, we were told we'd never have children. We'd stopped trying, then you arrived, and we wanted to pour everything into you and give the perfect life to the perfect child. We pushed you to succeed at school, university and beyond. I tried my best to cushion you from the pressure, but I failed. I'm sorry.'

My chest contracts as I remember how she often covered for me with Dad, explaining I was checking out the local library when I had my first surfing lesson with Sophie.

'Dad wouldn't feel the same as you . . . If he could see me now, he'd be devastated that I'd . . .'

'Broken the promise you made to him about Stanford when he was dying?'

My jaw drops as she straightens, rubbing her back.

'I should have admitted this much, much sooner, but I was outside the bedroom door and overheard your last conversation with him. I was so upset I had to go downstairs.'

'Why? Had you guessed I wouldn't keep my word?'

'No! I was crying with anger. He should never have asked you to commit your life to him. I love your dad and miss him terribly, but he was in the wrong, not you.'

I draw in a sharp breath as she walks over.

'True love doesn't come with strings attached, Adam,' she says, taking my hands. 'It doesn't force you down a path you don't want to take. You have to be free to make your own choices, pursue your own dreams and love whatever and whomever you want.'

I feel a huge weight lift from my shoulders as she folds me into a hug.

'Thanks, Mum,' I say, my voice thick with emotion. 'That means a lot.'

'I love you, Adam, so very, very much. I'm sorry your dad never said those three words enough, but I don't want to make the same mistakes as him. I'll always be proud of you and Wren, whatever you do. I love you both with all my heart.'

'I love you too, Mum. I don't tell you that enough either.'

She holds me tighter. There's a scuffling noise behind us, and we break apart. Wren is grinning in the doorway.

'I thought you were asleep?' I ask, wiping my eyes.

'I woke up and was leaves dropping.'

Mum frowns. 'You were doing what?'

'Eavesdropping!' I clarify.

'Ah, I see,' Mum says, smiling. 'In that case, did you "leaves drop" what I said about you?'

'Yes!' Wren says, darting over. 'Let's have a big family hug.'

She wraps her arms around us both and my heart overflows with happiness.

45

SOPHIE

Monday, 7 April 2025

'Three, two, one, go!' Adam cries.

We're having a race after picnicking on the picturesque coastal trail and counting rabbits and seagulls. Mrs B bought Wren a bike for Christmas, and I found my rusty old one in Mum's padlocked shed at the bottom of the garden. Wren shoots ahead, pedalling furiously to the brow of the hill before lifting her feet from the pedals.

'Whoopee! Here I come.'

'Careful,' Adam calls after her. 'Not too fast!'

'I love being speedy!' she yells.

'Slowcoach,' I say, overtaking him.

'Hey! Don't leave me behind.'

'Too late!'

Hair streams down my back and the sun tickles my cheeks. Whirring numbers flash up: 57,821 leaves stretch along the hedgerow and 2,638 pebbles are scattered along the side of the lane. We reach the bottom, panting, and skid to a halt.

'I won!' Wren punches the air. 'Sophie's second, and you're last, Da-Adam.'

'I demand a rematch,' he groans. 'I'll get at least second place next time.'

'You're a sore loser!' Wren exclaims.

'Your dad's *very* competitive.' I nod in agreement, tightening my helmet.

'But he's not fast enough to catch us,' Wren declares, propelling herself forward, pedals spinning.

'I'm competitive but 100 per cent irresistible,' Adam says, leaning in for a kiss.

'This is true.'

I tilt my head and his lips draw closer before he gives a determined push with his feet and races away.

'See?' he shouts over his shoulder. 'I can definitely be number two!'

'Cheat!'

He waves and catches up with Wren before she reaches the junction with a busier road. They cycle side by side, laughing and chatting, as Adam's earlier words ring in my ears: 'Don't leave me behind.'

I'm trying my hardest to stop that from happening. Adam glows with happiness. He says he made up with Wren and Mrs B on Saturday afternoon and they're all getting on well. He hasn't mentioned today's Stanford board meeting or been distracted; he's completely in the moment, enjoying our day. Everything is going great – we took Wren to an agricultural show yesterday, and she loved the petting zoo, craft workshops and fairground rides. We all ate juicy barbecue ribs and chocolate crêpes until we almost burst. Adam and I chose artisan cheeses, freshly baked bread and cakes for today's picnic. Before we left, Adam gave me their finished shapes so I can stitch them into the quilt.

Despite all this, his number was 7 at the fair and 6 today. But that must mean his reconciliation with Wren and Mrs B needs longer to take effect. Walter's numbers changed within a week.

I still have plenty of time.

Adam turns and waves as he and Wren climb off their bikes and press into the hedgerow to let a car pass. I stick out my tongue at them. Wren leans against Adam affectionately and laughs as they both pull faces back.

'This is where I leave you, Mr Cheat,' I say breathlessly, reaching them.

They're heading straight over at the junction towards Bigbury, but I need to peel off right to cycle back to Modbury.

'Would you . . . ?' Adam begins. 'Never mind.'

'What?'

'I was thinking . . . you could come back with us . . . and maybe stay for dinner?'

'Oh, I don't think—'

'Please, Sophie!' Wren begs. 'I can show you Grandma's dogs and our cake is good. We'll make an even better one next time, won't we, Da-Adam?'

'100 per cent! You have to try it and Mum would love to see you.'

I'm not sure Mrs B *will* share their keenness. Adam said she couldn't join us today due to a book club meeting, but I can't help wondering if she's avoiding me. However, this would be a great opportunity to see if they really are all getting on well – there might be something more I can do to help nudge his number up even by a few days or weeks.

'Sure. Why not?'

'Brilliant!' Adam beams at me. 'It'll be like old times.'

Wren runs after a tortoiseshell butterfly further along the verge.

'How much like old times?' I ask playfully. 'Trying not to wake your mum while I sneak in and out of your bedroom?'

'That's a great idea!' Adam says, before seizing the chance to steal a quick kiss.

My heart beats rapidly as we wheel our bikes up the path to his childhood home. The last time I was here, Mrs B caught me leaving and was unexpectedly kind. Later, I realised she probably thought I already knew Adam's bombshell news. The front door swings open and she appears, joined by two dogs. Mrs B looks smaller than I remember, and her number is 7,455. She has another 20 years left, which means Wren will be an adult, possibly with her own family, when her grandma finally passes.

She smiles broadly. 'Sophie! I'm glad Adam persuaded you to come.'

'Thank you, Mrs B,' I murmur. 'It's good to see you again.'

'Please call me Jen.'

Adam raises an eyebrow as she steps back inside. She never suggested I use her first name when we were teenagers. Wren shoots straight in, abandoning her bike by the front step. We wheel it, along with ours, round to the back garden and prop them all against the white trestle table.

'You see?' Adam says. 'Mum's happy you're here, but not as happy as me.'

He pulls me into a long, lingering kiss against the wall. It's *exactly* like old times.

We all help make a big vegetarian chilli for supper, and Adam opens a bottle of Merlot. He's relaxed and cracking jokes with Wren, and gently teasing his mum at the dinner table. They all seem close: a happy family. After our plates are scraped clean, Mrs B – I can't get used to calling her Jen – cuts Adam and Wren's cake, putting large slices on our plates.

'What's the verdict?' Adam asks when I take my first mouthful.

'Ten out of ten.'

I'm ignoring the fact it's on the dry side – it's my rating for this evening, the whole day. Yesterday too. Wren shoots a joyful look at Adam, bursting with pride, and wolfs down her helping.

'Seconds, anyone?' Mrs B asks.

'I can't eat another thing or I'll burst.' Adam groans, leaning back in his chair.

'You said that yesterday and then you ate another two crêpes,' Wren points out. 'But you didn't go pop. Neither did I.'

'That's true. I can probably squeeze in another small slice.'

'And me! We never go poppety-pop.' Wren reaches across the table and high-fives Adam.

He cuts the cake as Mrs B gathers the plates. I follow her into the kitchen with more dishes. Barely anything has changed in the house, including in here. The large wooden clock is still fixed on the wall above the fridge, and 173 blue tiles line the splashback behind the sink. I place the crockery on the table as Mrs B runs hot water in the sink to soak a pan.

'Thank you,' she says, turning round with a smile. 'You're very kind and thoughtful.'

'It's not a problem! I can stack the dishwasher if you want?'

'That's not what I meant.' She steps closer. 'Thank you for encouraging Adam to visit. He told me that bringing Wren here for Easter was your idea. I'd been trying for weeks, months even, to get him to commit to coming but he listened to you – he always did.'

'I had to empty Mum's house and wanted company, so my motives aren't totally unselfish,' I admit.

'I can read between the lines . . . You're helping him patch up his relationship with Wren and me. It means so much to have my family here and for us all to be getting along.'

I take a breath, unsure what to say. The ticking of the clock sounds magnified as we stare at each other. Mrs B breaks the silence first.

'You had no reason to be kind to me. I wasn't as welcoming as I should have been in the past. It wasn't personal, Sophie. I liked you, but I was afraid such an intense relationship would derail Adam's A levels.' She continues before I can cut in. 'I was wrong about a lot of things. I'm happy you're back in all our lives. I want you to know you'll always be welcome here.'

She walks over and embraces me for the first time ever. I inhale the scent of salty air and sand in her hair. Sadness and regret fill my heart that we're only becoming closer now. There's a new emotion: fear.

It's raw and visceral. I'm suddenly terrified I'm going to fail and she's going to lose her only child. Within days, her heart could break into millions of pieces, together with Wren's. Mine too.

Tick, tick, tick.

I hold on to her, a woman I barely know in adulthood, feeling like I'm hanging on by a single thread above a bottomless black pit. No one will be able to help me climb out if I fall: only I know what potentially looms at the end of the week. Only I can try to stop it. I shiver. I've never felt more alone or under such monumental pressure to succeed.

'Thank you for bringing my son back to me,' she murmurs.

I screw my eyes tightly shut as the yarn snaps.

I plunge into darkness.

46

ADAM

Tuesday, 8 April 2025

Sunlight streams in through the curtains when I open my eyes. My first thoughts are about Sophie. Mum didn't mind her staying over . . . she's more relaxed about a lot of things, and Wren didn't bat an eyelid when they bumped into each other in the bathroom. In bed afterwards, Sophie told me how Wren had solemnly asked if she wanted to borrow her toothbrush. We giggled in the dark before making love for the third time. Smiling, I turn over to reach for Sophie, but her side of the bed is empty and cool.

I sit up, rubbing my eyes. Her clothes are gone from the chair and her trainers have vanished from the floor. I feel a twinge of disappointment. Fumbling for my phone on the table, I check the time: 7.02 a.m. Sophie's left before we've had a chance to chat, cuddle and make pancakes with Wren. New messages have arrived: a WhatsApp from Sophie and an email from Dr Hunt. The board's verdict! I didn't think once about the meeting yesterday . . . I was enjoying myself with Sophie and Wren.

I stare at the email strapline: it gives away no clues.

This is all I've been aiming for since I left Stanford: my potential return. But instead of being excited, a sick, heavy feeling grows in my stomach and a familiar tightness returns to my chest. The board's response feels sudden, despite the fact I'd guessed it would arrive today.

I click on Sophie's message first, which she sent at 5.33 a.m.

Woke early and couldn't get back to sleep. Snuck out of your house like old times! You looked so peaceful I didn't want to wake you. Need to crack on with quilting. Sophie xx

Meet this afternoon? I reply. Or I can ask Mum to babysit if you fancy going out for dinner. I can find somewhere with plastic cutlery and milkshakes!!! Adam xx

Two blue ticks appear, but it takes a couple of minutes before her response pops up.

Sounds tempting! But I have to finish your quilt and sort through Mum's boxes. She left more than I expected. Need to drop off at the tip and charity shop. Meet later in the week? Sophie xx

I write back: It must be tough looking at your mum's old things. Please let me help? I can check boxes, be your driver, provide carrot cake and big hugs whenever needed. Mum can take Wren to the beach for a few hours.

She answers immediately: Don't worry, am fine! Have days out with Wren and your mum. We can catch up soon. Sophie xx

I frown, rubbing my face. She's used our private language of love, but I can sense she's pushing me away. It must be tearing her apart, being reminded of her mum and Lily. Why won't she let me in? My gaze returns to the email from Stanford. Did she hear the ping and see the strapline flash up on my phone at 3.15 a.m.? She could be distancing herself because she's worried about the board's decision, and mine. She avoided mentioning the meeting yesterday. Ditto Mum. I take a deep breath and open the message.

Dear Adam
Many congratulations on your success!

Firstly, completing your dissertation is a huge achievement. It will now be reviewed in detail by faculty members ahead of your oral exam (date to be arranged).

Secondly, the board has approved our project and we have funding for a two-year research position. Ideally, we'd like you back here in the department as soon as possible to take up this post, visa applications, PhD awarding and university regulations permitting.

Please confirm you wish to proceed and we will file the appropriate paperwork from this end.

Yours sincerely

Dr Hunt

My heart pounds uncomfortably fast and my vision blurs around the edges, making the furniture appear to shift. I close my eyes and hang on to the duvet, trying to control my breathing.

This is what I've wanted for so long. Why does it feel like I'm losing, not winning? Is this the best thing for Wren and Mum? Sophie? Me?

Aagh. What should I do?

If Sophie were here, I'd hold her until my room, *the world*, stops spinning. But I need to stop expecting her to save me. I tap out a quick holding email:

Dear Dr Hunt

This is great news and very exciting! Obviously, a two-year position is a lot to consider when I have a young daughter. I'll need to discuss this with her and other family members. Please can I have a week to think about it? I'll email my decision by Tuesday, April 15.

Best wishes

Adam

My breathing calms and my vision clears after pressing 'send'. I've bought myself more time and a chance to think. I pull on my running gear and tiptoe downstairs before Mum and Wren wake up. Bella and Max sniff around my ankles but don't bark as I open the back door. Stepping outside, I inhale the crisp sea air. Gulls caw loudly from nearby roofs as I jog down the road. The knots in my chest and stomach loosen as my pace increases, and the burn in my calf muscles feels satisfying. After thirty minutes debating the pros and cons of returning to Stanford, I stop, panting, at the entrance to the churchyard. Usually, I avoid coming here when I'm back home; I'm uncomfortable around the dead.

Today, the sun casts the tombstones in a warm golden light and the air smells of freshly mown grass and flowers. Birds trill in the trees as I make my way up the snaking path to Dad's grave. As usual, guilt surges over me when I spot his black marble memorial. It's engraved with the words:

Nicholas Bailey
Loving husband and father
3 January 1947 to 15 April 2021

Mum must have paid a visit in the last few days; the pink tulips are fresh and the green glass chips are neatly raked beneath the tombstone.

'Hey Dad,' I say quietly. 'It's been a while . . . I'm sorry I haven't come to see you. I've been saying sorry a lot recently . . . To Wren, Mum and Sophie. And now to you. But here's the thing . . . I felt guilty about letting you down and lost sight of who I am. Being back here with Sophie has helped me find myself. That's why I'm not going to apologise for dropping out of Stanford. This is the best decision for me and Wren. It's made me realise how anxious I've been for years, trying to fulfil your dreams.' I lick my dry lips. 'Leaving has made me see I *can* be a good teacher. It's hard, and some days I want to give up . . . but I enjoy it. It's more fulfilling than I ever expected . . . It feels like I can make a difference now, rather than holding out for someone else's idea of success.'

I rub my watery eyes with the back of my hand. 'I wish you could meet Wren and discover how wonderful she is! And I'm sure Sophie would eventually win you over . . . the way she has with Mum. If you could see us all together, you'd know how happy we are. Now I'm a dad, it's made me realise that all I want for Wren is her happiness, and good health. I won't demand that she follows the career I pick for her . . . You won't like what I'm going to say, Dad, what I'm going to *do*, but this is my life, not yours.' I raise my chin. 'I broke my promise to you, but you should never have asked me to make it in the first place . . . All I ever wanted to hear was that you loved me. That would have been enough.'

I kiss my fingers and touch his headstone.

'I will always love *you*, but Mum and Sophie were right . . . it's time for me to make the most of living.'

47

SOPHIE

THURSDAY, 10 APRIL 2025

My phone rings with a video call as I step through the door after dropping off boxes at the charity shop. I ignore it and head to the kitchen to make a cup of coffee. It's probably Adam, suggesting we meet. I've been avoiding him ever since I woke up, excited, early on Tuesday only to discover his digit had dropped to 5 despite our day trips and the family dinner. I was still numb when he rang later that morning to tell me about Stanford's decision, and almost burst into tears when he FaceTimed yesterday, suggesting we discuss his news over a pub lunch. His number was 4, so I claimed I was busy quilting. That's true – I've worked until 3 a.m. for two nights in a row and have pinned the top, wadding, middle and backing together, ready to attach. My fingers are red and sore and I'm exhausted, but that's better than lying in bed thinking about how I've failed Adam, Wren and his mum.

He hasn't hung up yet. I grab my phone from the counter, steeling myself for seeing the inevitable number 3 when his face appears, but it's Walter, which is odd. He texts but has never FaceTimed me before. The screen spins and shrieks ring out when I accept the call.

'Walter? Are you there?'

A boy's face looms large and becomes blurry as his nose touches the screen. His brother joins him, giggling. It's Walter's grandsons, James and Luke. Chico trots up, grinning and barking.

'Hello. Is your grandad there?'

'Grandad!' James shouts. 'A ladeeee wants you on the iPad.'

The screen spins and there's scuffling noises and more barking. Eventually, Walter arrives, but I can't see him. He's pointing the device at the table. His son or daughter-in-law must be close by, and they reposition it for him. He appears, smiling, but his face is paler than usual and dark shadows encircle his eyes.

'Sophie! This is a wonderful surprise.'

I smile back, relieved his numbers haven't speeded up since I last saw him. 'Actually, your grandchildren rang *me*.'

'Ah, that was serendipitous. I was going to call you tonight to see how you and the lovely Adam are doing.'

He shifts position and the screen suddenly swerves. I catch a glimpse of his number – 9 – before the frame focuses on Chico. I don't have the energy to correct him.

'It's not great, to be honest. I'm struggling.'

'You're not enjoying yourself with Adam and Wren?'

'It *was* great,' I clarify. 'But Adam's numbers are still counting down even though he's happy and getting on well with Wren and his mum. I thought he'd get more time, the way you have, but it's not happening.'

'I'm sorry to hear that. Like you, I'd hoped things would turn out differently.'

I touch the scar beneath my hair. 'I agreed to go to a party with him on Saturday night. I thought I'd have altered his countdown by then, but now it could be when he's destined to—' I can't bring myself to say the word. 'I've messed up massively, and don't want to see him until I can figure out what I'm doing wrong.'

'Perhaps you're not doing anything wrong.'

'But I must be! His numbers are getting smaller and smaller. Nothing has changed.'

Chico tilts his head quizzically, as if pondering my statement.

'Exactly,' Walter says quietly. 'Absolutely nothing has changed since we had our first conversation about Adam on that bench in Clifton Village.'

'How do you mean?'

The silence lengthens and Walter doesn't attempt to fill it. The meaning of his words finally sinks in. Cold dread sweeps over me and I have to sit down on a stool.

'This is it?' I gasp. 'Adam *is* going to die on Saturday?'

'Possibly. Remember how we talked about final days, and making the most of these small moments, the way I'm doing now with my family?'

I brush away the tears rolling down my face.

'Dance with Adam on Saturday night, hold him in your arms and tell him you love him. Remember and cherish all these last little pleasures – the look in his eyes when he sees the quilt you've made for him and Wren, the sound of his laughter and the curve of his smile.'

I cover my eyes, sobbing. 'I can't do it. It's breaking my heart.'

'You must. Enjoy picnics, kiss on the beach, make love, knowing this could be the last chance you get to do any of it. You'll never get back those exact moments in time, however long either of you live. Don't let any of it slip away. It's too precious.'

I shake my head vigorously. 'I won't give up. I have to hold on to hope.'

'You can do that without pushing Adam away. Maybe his numbers will change for the better, maybe they won't. But don't waste these beautiful small joys, wishing for more when they must be enough.' He breaks off, coughing. 'No one is guaranteed a tomorrow. We must all live every day like it's our last. Enjoy these experiences now, instead of hoping you'll repeat them at some point in the future.'

Shouts ring out in the background and he shifts the screen, finally coming into view again with a warm, kind smile.

'I'm needed, sadly. Armageddon has broken out here – James and Luke are fighting. It's always a pleasure speaking to you, Sophie. Goodbye and God bless.' He takes a moment. 'Before I go, I want you to know that I love you, my dear. I consider you my adopted fourth grandchild.'

I stifle another cry. Walter's not just talking about ending this call.

'I love you like the grandad I never had growing up,' I reply brokenly. 'You're the best one ever. Goodbye, Walter.'

* * *

I'm in pieces when the call ends and need a lie-down. I nap fitfully for half an hour on Mum's bed, disturbed by a sharp rap at the door. Half of me wonders whether Adam's turned up. Peeking out from behind the curtains, I catch a glimpse of a man with a goatee.

Tom again!

I dart back from the window. He must have stopped emailing because he knows he'll eventually see me face to face. But it's not happening *here*. The bags in the corner of the bedroom catch my eye as I wait for him to leave. I can't face taking them to the charity shop; Lily's old clothes are among my cast-offs. Five minutes and 40 seconds later, I take the sacks downstairs. There's no note on the mat – Tom's given up for now.

I sift through everything at my makeshift sewing station in the dining room and re-read the cards from Roger and Betty. Examining Lily's turquoise maxi dress and shocking-pink evening gown, I discover Reese's Peanut Butter Cup wrappers in the pockets. Lily used to love these! I'd find the brown paper casings scattered across my bedroom floor and even inside her novels, used as bookmarks. Once, she threw up because she ate so many when we were playing her favourite childhood game, Hungry Hippos, which she'd rediscovered in her parents' loft. She loved peanut butter and anything hippopotamus related.

I hear her laughter, loud and powerful. It drowns out the piercing screech of brakes that echo around my head. Inhaling sharply, I'm winded as the truth strikes me. I've concentrated so long on the darkness, I've mistakenly blocked out all the light: the times when we danced or surfed until our legs were wobbly; walking arm in arm back from the beach and whispering confessions to each other in the dark while I lay on the camp bed in her room, sweet wrappers rustling.

Lily's stories are far too precious to lose.

I remember Nadia's joyful tears over her nan's framed log cabin sampler. Could a memory quilt comfort Roger and Betty? I lay all the fabric on the floor and sit on my heels. It won't take long to finish Adam and Wren's commission. This would be a far simpler design. I could use the boys' old clothes and mine to weave together the history of the four of us.

Me, Lily, Adam and Tom.

This could help Tom too. If I tell him what I'm making, he might finally understand I haven't forgotten Lily. Before I can start work, my phone vibrates. It's an unusually long WhatsApp from Adam.

Dear Sophie,

I promised Wren I'd be more open with people I care about, so here goes . . . I can't begin to imagine how hard it is for you being back here, processing your grief about Lily and your mum.

I've been thinking about what you said when you helped me patch up things with Mum and Wren. You told me it was too late for you to mend your relationship with your own mum. But becoming a parent means I can say this with 100 per cent certainty: it was never *your* responsibility to fix things with Jude. It was hers.

Jude was a terrible mum, but you were the best daughter, and the best friend to Lily. They were both lucky to have you. So am I. When I was a teenager, you made me feel as though I was 'enough' – but please, please know that you are billions of times more than enough.

I'm here for you no matter what. I can explain about Stanford, I promise. Please meet me for a bike ride and picnic tomorrow? I miss you so much.

Adam xx

His words of support on top of new memories of Lily finish me off. Tears roll freely down my face, but I feel overwhelming relief. I fetch the old pictures of Mum I discovered in the loft and study each one. Adam's right. I couldn't force Mum to love me or become a better parent. It had to come from within her, the way it has with Adam.

The thought of how quickly his days, hours, minutes and seconds are ticking away makes my stomach twist into painful knots.

He's my anchor, my everything.

I force myself to focus on the light: the new memories and numbers we can still make together. They won't be infinite, but they must be enough. I'll count and savour every single hug and kiss.

I tuck Mum's photos away and message Adam back.

Thank you for being you, Adam Bailey. Yes to the bike ride and picnic. Yes to everything about you. I will always love and miss you. xx

48

SOPHIE

Thursday, 23 July 2015

'Are you sure this is Lily?'

It was the first time I'd been allowed out of the neurological unit to visit my best friend, who was two floors up in intensive care. I was convinced the nurse, Erica, had led me to the wrong bed.

'I understand it's distressing to see Lily like this,' she replied. 'But our medical team is doing everything possible to support her.'

I shook my head in disbelief. I barely recognised Lily. Tubes were attached to her mouth, chest and arms, and her face was horribly swollen, cut and bruised. Her legs were heavily bandaged, and she was hooked up to a ventilator that was helping keep her alive.

Above all, I noticed Lily's number.

It was much, much smaller than the 16,425 that popped up when I saw Erica today. Her colleagues in ICU had five digits, along with the doctors on my ward. The critically ill patients in here had at least double figures, apart from Lily and the elderly man in the next bed. They shared the number 7.

I blinked rapidly, trying to bat away the floating figures, as my consultant had suggested, but they didn't disappear. Why couldn't

I get rid of them? What did they mean? Every object and person had them. When would they go?

Shit! My forehead throbbed repetitively as if with the beat of a drum.

When I came round from surgery, the first thing that hit me was the searing, fiery pain in my head. The second was that numbers were *everywhere*. Somehow, I knew the curtain was 2.53 metres long, the gap in the material was 0.56 centimetres, and the saint-like nurse who gave me more painkillers was 18,647.

I stared at Lily, willing her to recover. I had no idea why everyone had different digits, or why they got smaller each time I saw them. Mum was 383 when I first remember seeing her clearly after my op but was 373 yesterday. I had no idea if Adam had a number. I couldn't face seeing him, at least not until Lily had woken up and forgiven me.

That had to be soon, surely? Seven was supposed to be lucky and Lily was a fighter. She'd survived the initial impact that had killed Vinny, Priti and the other driver before they could be rushed to hospital, despite her lack of seat belt. My arm had been looped through the strap, preventing me from flying through the windscreen the way Priti had.

'How is Lily doing?'

'We're providing round-the-clock care and closely monitoring her responses,' Erica said quietly. 'Her vital signs remain stable, which is encouraging. That's what we always want to see.'

'She's doing well?' I pressed. 'She'll come out of the coma in the next few days?'

'It's hard to predict. Some patients wake up relatively quickly while others take much longer. But there have been small signs of improvement in the last twenty-four hours, which is positive.'

I knew it – 7 *was* Lily's lucky number!

'You can stay a while if you want?' Erica said. 'Lily's parents think it could help if she hears familiar voices and feels touch. They're encouraging her closest friends to try. Her boyfriend was here this morning.'

Thankfully, I'd missed Tom. I couldn't face seeing him after the misery I'd inflicted on everyone.

Tears stung my eyes as I kissed Lily's hand.

'I miss you,' I whispered in her ear. 'I'm sorry. *I love you.*'

I repeated those last three words over and over, praying she could hear them.

Lily's number was counting down by a digit each day, the same as everyone else in ICU.

7, 6, 5, 4, 3, 2.

The figures filled me with hope. I was visiting regularly while her parents took breaks. There were fresh signs each day that Lily was getting better. Erica said she was doing 'incredibly well, considering her injuries', and I was certain I'd felt her fingers twitch beneath mine yesterday. That's what helped me work it out – I finally knew what Lily's digit meant.

Her number was 1 this morning: she was on the verge of waking up!

The old man in the next bed, who hadn't received a single visitor since Lily was admitted, seemed to be recovering. If I was right, he should come off his ventilator shortly.

I returned to ICU that afternoon and hugged Lily's mum, Betty, but her dad, Roger, hung back, staring brokenly at the floor.

'It's going to be okay, I promise,' I told her. 'Lily will open her eyes and speak to us today. I think it's definitely going to happen.

You know how desperate she is to find out her A-level results. She'll be heading into school with me in a fortnight to collect them!'

A tear rolled down Roger's face and Betty choked back a sob.

'I hope so,' she said. 'It's awful to see her like this, particularly when Albert's died. It makes you realise how precarious everything is – the machine's keeping her alive but she's hovering between life and death.'

'Albert?' I frowned.

'The elderly gentleman in the next bed,' Roger said, his voice cracking. 'His heart gave up a short time ago. The nurses asked us to step out while the porters remove his body and take it to the morgue.'

This couldn't be right. His number was 1, like Lily's, so he should have recovered.

'What? No! I need to see her.'

'Give it a few minutes,' he replied. 'Why don't you come down to the canteen with us? We're grabbing a quick coffee and something to eat before heading back.'

'It's okay, thanks. I'll wait here.' I sat down on one of the red plastic seats.

I didn't want to be alone with Lily's parents. Their kindness and forgiveness felt more devastating than if they'd yelled or completely blanked me. Initially, after my brain surgery, they'd split their time between visiting me and Lily. They'd sat at my bedside longer than my own mum.

Betty kissed the top of my head and Roger gave me a small, sad hug. They walked away, clutching each other as if neither could stand without support. Suddenly, Betty turned around, her face etched with worry and grief.

'Tom was asking how you're doing this morning. He said you can message him any time – day or night. And Adam desperately wants to see you.'

Roger nodded, wiping his eyes. 'No one blames you, Sophie.'

The police had said the same during my interview.

But I did. I couldn't forgive myself.

Lily was critically injured because she loved *me*. She'd chosen to go with her best friend instead of Tom. I wished she'd left me to my fate.

As soon as Betty and Roger stepped into the elevator, I gave my hands a quick squirt of anti-bac and walked into the ward. The curtains were closed around the bay next to Lily's, but through the gap I saw a nurse and two men by the bed. Their numbers were 19,573, 21,412 and 10,894, respectively.

Then I caught a glimpse of Albert before a sheet was pulled over his face. His eyes were closed. His number was 0.

No!

I fell back a step, a sharp pain stabbing my chest.

This couldn't be . . . The numbers couldn't mean . . .

I stumbled towards Lily's bedside and clutched her hand. I still saw the figure 1.

'Please don't die,' I whispered. 'I love you.'

An alarm suddenly sounded from the monitor beside her. Lily's heartbeat was flatlining. Doctors and nurses ran over, pushing me aside.

'You need to leave,' Erica said firmly. 'She's gone into cardiac arrest.'

I felt the colour drain from my face as a defibrillator was pushed to her bedside and a nurse stuck pads on her chest.

I backed away, tears streaming down my cheeks.

It was too late. The electrical shocks wouldn't restart Lily's heart however many times the team tried to revive her.

The figures I'd seen weren't signalling Lily's or Albert's recovery, they'd been counting down to their deaths.

Lily's number was now 0.

49

SOPHIE

Friday, 11 April 2025

Adam's number is 2.

I'm ignoring his digit and my tiredness from sewing late into the night. I'm following Walter's advice and collecting these small moments instead: Adam laughing when Wren and I beat him in a bike race earlier, how he looks like he's melting inside when he stares at me and the feeling when he touches my arm or the small of my back, almost without thinking, as if the need to stay connected is intuitive. And his 'famous' hugs. I love these most of all.

We're sitting on a mat on Bigbury beach, sheltering against the wind in a small cove, munching cheese sandwiches and Eccles cakes that Wren and Adam made last night. Adam had suggested taking the food back to his mum's house, but I want, *need*, this: our last picnic before the heavy rain that's forecast tomorrow.

'That rock looks like Da-Adam's nose,' Wren observes, munching on her pastry. 'It's crooked and has a dent in it.'

She points to the distinctively jagged cliff face.

'Harsh, but true!' Adam remarks.

We all laugh.

'It's not *so* bad when you think about it,' he adds. 'These rocks have weathered storms for millions of years, but they're still here. They've survived against the odds.'

It takes all my strength not to flinch. Instead, I reach over and brush away the crumb from the corner of his mouth. He flashes me a smile that makes me feel like I'm the most beautiful woman in the world. I file that away in my mind too.

'Can I look for seashells?' Wren scrambles to her feet and picks up a bucket and spade, the wind buffeting her pink anorak.

'Hmmm. Sure, but don't go far,' Adam replies. 'Fasten your coat and keep in sight.'

'Okey-dokey, Da-Adam!'

She walks away, head down, her coat billowing, and snatches up her first find. I shuffle closer, leaning my head against Adam's shoulder.

'Cold?' he asks, rubbing my arms. 'I can warm you up.'

'Later,' I say teasingly.

I watch as Wren turns around, grinning, and produces another seashell for us to admire. Her expression doesn't change when she sees how close we're sitting.

'Lovely, Da-Wren!' Adam shouts. 'Find more for us.'

'Why do you call each other that? She always calls you Da-Adam.'

'It's one of our in-jokes. She started to say "Daddy" but stopped herself, changing it to "Adam". I guess she's halfway to thinking of me in that way.'

'She looks more than halfway there! Has she said she loves you back when you say it to her?'

Adam shakes his head, staring after Wren. I study him, but he avoids my gaze.

'But you've told her, haven't you? Lots of times?'

'Not as such . . . It feels like such a momentous . . . meaningful expression. It needs to be said at the right time, when everything's perfect.'

'No, it doesn't! It never has to be a grand gesture that you shout from the clifftops. It's something you tell the people you love *all the time*. Every single day.'

I shift my position to scrutinise him properly. He looks startled and I soften my tone. 'What's stopping you from telling her? What are you afraid of?'

'Erm, that she won't want to hear it . . . That I'll drive her away by not saying it right. We're in a good place and I don't want to ruin it by telling her something she doesn't want to hear.'

'Of course you won't ruin it – and she *does* want to hear it. Every daughter or son does.' I thread my fingers through the hair curling at the nape of his neck. 'You can make your relationship even better if you explain how you feel about her.'

'I will. I promise.'

He goes to kiss me, but I pull away.

'Do it soon, Adam. Don't leave it unsaid. It's too important. You're showing Wren how much you love her by everything you do, but she needs to hear it said out loud – the way you desperately wanted to hear those three words from *your* dad.'

He glances quickly at Wren, who's crouching down and digging with her spade.

'I know, and there's something I want *you* to hear while we're alone.' He takes a breath. 'It's about Stanford.'

I shake my head. 'We don't have to do this now. It doesn't matter.'

'Yes, it does! I want you to know I'm not procrastinating, as usual. I've made my decision. I can't go back to the US. It would kill me to take up the research position.'

I frown, thinking I've misheard him in the wind.

'Kill you?'

'I believed a career at Stanford was what I wanted . . . what I should want . . . but I was doing it for my dad, not myself. I've almost forgotten what it's like to be *me* because I lost myself when I lost you. Part of the loop that makes me whole was gone and nothing came together right. I never got that happiness back because . . . well, something, *someone*, important was missing from my life.'

He takes my hand and presses it to his lips. 'I've felt dead inside for so long, Sophie, but you make me feel alive. I don't want to lose that feeling by doing something that will make us all unhappy. I choose happiness. I choose life. I choose you and Wren.'

50

ADAM

Saturday, 12 April 2025

Sophie's beautiful long hair is splayed fan-like across the pillow and her lips move as if she's whispering secrets to me in her sleep. Her eyelashes quiver gently. I could study her face all day, memorising every freckle and contour. It's tempting to pull her into my arms so I can feel the warmth and weight of her on my chest, but I need to get back to Mum's. She looked after Wren while I came over here yesterday evening, and we cooked my favourite dinner: steak and chips, with a bottle of red, followed by carrot cake from the farm shop. Afterwards, we could barely get to the top of the stairs without ripping off each other's clothes. Reluctantly, I peel myself out of her bed and pad on to the landing, scooping up my boxers and jeans. I put them on and walk back into the bedroom, pulling my T-shirt over my head.

I jump at the sight of Sophie, sitting bolt upright and wide-eyed as if she's seen a ghost.

'I thought you were asleep! You almost gave me a heart attack.'

'I heard you get up,' she says. 'You scared *me*. I was worried you were leaving without saying goodbye.'

'Of course not! My parents taught me good manners.'

'They gave you post-coitum lessons on top of all your extracurricular classes?'

'Ha ha!'

She checks the clock, leaning back on her elbows. 'Come back to bed. It's only six. It's too early.'

I walk over and sit next to her, brushing a lock of hair from her face. 'This is a one-off, sorry. I thought you understood that . . . ? I mastered no-strings-attached sex in post-coitum lesson two.'

She shivers as I leave a trail of kisses across her collarbone, up her neck and, finally, on her lips. I expect her to laugh, but she looks unspeakably sad.

'Erm, you know I'm joking, right? This is a 1,000-time thing. More! I don't want to stop making love to you.'

'Then don't!' She pulls me closer, tugging at my T-shirt.

I groan. 'I'd love to, but I promised to cook pancakes for Wren and go rock pooling and sandcastle building *whatever the weather*. She wants a dad-and-daughter morning before I head into Plymouth to pick up a few things.'

'I could go with you? I don't mind browsing in a few shops.'

'No!'

She raises an eyebrow, but I can't explain why I need to go alone.

'I mean . . . I'm only planning to fly in and out, so it's hardly worth the trip. Anyway . . . I'm looking forward to the party tonight.'

She takes a sharp breath, pursing her lips. 'Let's not go. We could cook dinner here or have a movie marathon with Wren at your mum's.'

'You've changed your mind?' I'm trying to keep the disappointment out of my voice.

'I'm worried it won't go well. Neither of us will enjoy it.'

'But it's a chance to get dressed up and go out . . . something I don't get to do much anymore. I used to love the nightlife at Stanford, and Walter's party was amazing.'

'It was his last one ever,' she says sadly.

'I know. Well, I do now.' I run a hand through my hair. 'But it's not just that . . . This party could be a new beginning for both of us. Part of that is saying goodbye to Lily. I want to raise a glass to our friend and *remember* her. She'd want us to go and be happy . . . dance all night in her memory. I bet she'd be furious if we didn't.'

Sophie stares at me, speechless, as I continue.

'I need to say goodbye. Lily was my friend as well as yours, and I lost her too that night. I haven't been able to talk to anyone about her over the years . . . And I guess . . . well, I miss her.'

'I'm sorry,' she says, her voice strained. 'I shouldn't have pushed you away afterwards when you were grieving.'

'You were injured, and your life had changed forever.' I lean over and kiss the side of her scalp she touches whenever we talk about the accident. 'You're forgiven!'

She takes my hand and guides it across the raised skin beneath her hair.

'You wouldn't know the scar's there,' I tell her.

'But I do.' She shudders. 'You really need to do this tonight?'

'I feel like I must . . . For Lily's sake.'

The duvet falls away as she throws her arms around my neck. I feel the softness of her breasts through my T-shirt.

'Then we'll say goodbye to her together,' she whispers.

'You're sure?'

'I want to make you happy, Adam.'

'You do, 100 per cent! Every single day. I've never been happier.'

Her body tenses between my fingertips, and when I let go, her eyes are watery.

'I don't want that to stop,' she says, shivering. 'Don't want *us* to stop.'

I grab her dressing gown, draping it over her shoulders.

'We've found our way back to each other and nothing will get in the way of *us*. I won't let it.'

'Oh God, Adam.' Sophie presses her hands to her eyes as tears spill down her face.

'What is it?' Uncertainty grips me. 'Wait . . . you don't think we'll last?'

She takes a deep breath. I'm holding mine. It feels like she's summoning up the courage to tell me something terrible.

'W-w-what is it?' I wipe away a tear from her face. 'Tell me.'

'I've had to watch people I care about die over the years – Lily, Mum, my friend Joan. It's like I have a curse. I lose the people I love.'

'And you're worried you're going to lose me next?' I ask gently.

'I'm afraid you'll be ripped from me and we don't have anywhere near as much time together as we think.'

The pain is so intense in her eyes I can't leave yet.

'In that case,' I say, whipping off my T-shirt and throwing it across the room. 'I want to make the most of *us* while I can.'

I kick off my jeans and boxers and slide back into bed with her. She rolls towards me.

'I thought you had to burn, I mean, *make* pancakes for Wren?!'

'We don't have long . . . if this is the end, I'd better make it worth it.'

'Is that a promise?' Her lips curl upwards into a small smile, but her eyes remain tinged with sadness.

'Hold that thought!' I lean over the side and grab my jeans, searching the pockets.

'What are you doing? The condoms are here.' She points to the bedside table.

'No, I'm looking for a pen.'

She opens the drawer, pulling out a Biro. I pick up her wrist, the way I did on the beach when we were teenagers.

'May I?'

She nods and I draw a Möbius strip to match mine. I trace the outline of the shape with my lips, kissing it.

'I'm not going anywhere, I promise. I lost you once, but I won't let that happen a second time. It's taken me almost a decade to find you, but you're worth the wait.' I plant delicate kisses along her arm, moving up to her shoulders and neck. 'I love you, Sophie Leroux. I always have, from the moment we first met at the beach. I never stopped loving you when we were apart. I wish I'd told you sooner. But even if I have just years, months or weeks left to live, I won't regret a single moment if I spend that time with you and Wren. You are the first girl I ever loved and you will be the last. I love you, I love you, I love you.'

51

SOPHIE

SATURDAY, 12 APRIL 2025

This is it – Adam's last day.

I listen to the rain pattering against the window, feeling the warmth of Adam's body slowly leave the mattress. My fingertips brush against the cotton where he lay minutes ago. I press his pillow to my face and inhale his scent; I want to bottle it to keep forever. After tonight, I won't smell his aftershave on my pillowcase. We won't hug, talk in bed, have sex, make each other laugh or share a slice of carrot cake. Adam won't draw another Möbius strip on my wrist and kiss it, making goosebumps rise on my skin. He won't tell me he loves me over and over again to make up for all those missed opportunities when we were teenagers. He won't take Wren to the beach to build sandcastles or paddle in the rock pools tomorrow. They won't bake or sew together. She won't hear him say he loves her. Neither will his mum.

Unless, unless, unless.

Despite everything, I can't stop trying. My optimism has shrunk, along with his numbers, reduced to the size of a grain of sand. But it hasn't been washed away completely. I was dreading the reunion tonight, particularly having to see Tom, but maybe, just maybe, this will save Adam. The party at The Wave was pivotal for Walter. Being surrounded by faces from the past could spark something inside Adam and help prolong his life.

It's all I have left to cling on to, my last card to play.

When Adam's side of the bed is cold, I get up and shower, turning the tap to hot. My stinging skin helps distract me from the unbearable, crushing pain in my heart.

I'm towelling my hair dry, thinking about Adam and Wren going to the beach, and become light-headed with panic. I've focused on what might happen tonight and haven't considered the chances of Adam having an accident *before* the party. Wren could be swept into the sea by a freak wave, and he'll die saving her. Or his car may crash on the way to Plymouth; he narrowly missed a motorway pile-up on the journey from Bristol. Why is he even driving there today? The weather's terrible.

I dress quickly and grab my phone.

Think an agricultural show's on this afternoon. Traffic will be bad in the rain! Maybe leave Plymouth? xx

The message I fire off sounds lame, but it's the only excuse I can come up with. I can't tell Adam: *Don't do anything risky because you could die.*

My heart is beating ridiculously fast, and I flex and unflex my fingers, attempting to calm myself as I wait for his reply. It pings back after a few seconds.

Don't worry! Will drive carefully. Look forward to seeing you later. 🚗 xx

I send the same emoji and throw my phone on to the bed. I need to get a grip, otherwise I'll never make it through the day. I pack my bag and leave the house, striding down the street, away from my van and the temptation to drive over to his mum's house and shadow him all day. Walking is better; I need time to prepare myself for this visit. A plastic bag tumbles down the street before it's blown high into the sky like a shooting star and lands, tangled in a tree. Rain slices my face but it's too windy to put up an umbrella.

I plough on and half an hour later I'm standing outside Lily's parents' farmhouse, 1.1 miles west of Modbury. Crawling along the wall are 5,743 ivy leaves and 1,558 tiles stretch over the roof. The memories are countless: the movie marathons, make-up tutorials and secret drinking in Lily's bedroom before we went out for the night. I lay on her bed and confessed I'd fallen for a geeky but gorgeous boy who was joining our sixth form. I slept on a camp bed next to hers when Mum was at a yoga retreat and the loneliness had become overwhelming.

Guilt has kept me away, despite her parents' invitations. I trace Adam's symbol on my wrist with my finger before walking up to the front door and rapping the brass lion's head knocker. Lily named him Aslan from her favourite book growing up, *The Lion, The Witch and the Wardrobe*.

I hold my breath at the light tap of footsteps in the hall. The door opens and Lily's mum appears. Betty's hair is completely white, her face gaunt and deeply lined. The purple fleece swamps her thin body. Her number is 4,015: 11 years.

'Sophie!' She clutches the doorframe. 'Oh my.'

I open my mouth to explain, *apologise*, but she gathers me into her arms. 'I knew you'd come back to see us one day.'

We embrace, memories exploding between us. Finally, Betty lets go and stands back.

'Come in. This is a lovely surprise.'

'Thank you.'

I step inside, gripping my tote bag tighter as more recollections flood back. The hall was once a bright yellow, and smelt of pine freshener, but now the walls are faded, the air stale. Dust has settled into the double-stacked history books on the top-to-bottom shelves. I follow her into the sitting room: the green sofa and brown carpet are the same, but more threadbare. Framed photos of Lily smile down at me from the mantelpiece, making my heart flinch.

'I heard you were back in Modbury.' Betty slowly eases herself into a chair and gestures for me to sit on the settee opposite. 'I wanted to make contact and find out how you're doing, but I was worried that would be too difficult for you.'

Tears fill my eyes. I always found her sympathy and understanding harder to bear than anger, because I didn't feel I deserved it. I still don't.

I stare at the inside of my wrist, taking a deep breath. 'Lily left clothes in Mum's house and I wanted to—'

'Keep them!' Betty interrupts, raising her hand. 'We packed up Lily's bedroom when Roger retired. All her hippo ornaments are in boxes in the garage. We couldn't bear to throw anything out, but we didn't want to . . .' She clears her throat, straightening. 'Well, the room's become Roger's study for his local history research.'

My hands shake as I open my tote. 'I sew for a living. If I can mend a piece of clothing that is meaningful to a customer, it feels like I'm giving something back, however small. I also make patchwork quilts to help people hold on to their memories.'

I pull out the single bedspread. I finished it in a day; it's a more basic design than the one I created for Adam and Wren. But it's still stunning and meaningful, with bold blocks of pink, green and blue.

'I've made this from clothes Lily loved to wear. I've included scraps that belonged to me, Adam and Tom because we used to be a big part of her life.'

Betty covers her mouth with her hand as I point to a denim patch. 'Lily wore this miniskirt to your anniversary dinner when Roger organised karaoke and we all sang "It's Raining Men".' I touch a fragment of turquoise cotton. 'This is the dress she spilt punch down at our joint eighteenth birthday party. She couldn't bring herself to throw it out because it was her favourite colour.'

'They're such wonderful memories.' Betty's body shakes as she weeps.

'I've sewn all our stories together to show the beautiful patchwork of her life,' I say, my voice faltering. 'I wanted something permanent to show how much Lily meant, *means*, to me.' My hands shake as I hold out the quilt and repeat the mantra I said in the weeks after the accident: 'I'm sorry, so very sorry.'

Within seconds she's on the sofa, her arms wrapped around me. I breathe in a faint rose scent.

'If I could go back in time, I'd change places with Lily,' I say, through juddering sobs.

'I know, sweetheart! The same here.'

'What's going on?' a gruff voice asks. 'Why have you let *her* in?'

Roger appears in the doorway, glaring fiercely. His number is 4,020 – he'll die 5 days after his wife. I blink, momentarily stunned by his hostile tone. He was as forgiving as Betty after the crash. I rise and face him, my heart beating rapidly.

'Sophie's brought us the most beautiful present.' Betty stands in front of me, as if acting as a buffer. 'She's made a memory quilt from Lily's clothes.'

Roger's cheeks flush scarlet with anger. 'Well, she can take it with her! I don't want it. She forgot about Lily long ago.'

I stare at him, taken aback. 'That's not true! Not a single day goes by when I don't think about her or want to tell her something. I love and miss her so much. She's always here.' I touch my heart.

'I don't believe you.' Roger crosses his arms over his moss-green gilet.

Betty takes the quilt and carries it over to him. His lined face softens as he stares down at the multicoloured fabric, touching a shocking-pink patch.

'This was going to be Lily's prom dress,' he says in a strangled tone.

'That's right,' I say. 'But she changed her mind last minute and wore black.'

His face crumples and his shoulders sag.

'Oh my!' Betty points to a corner of the quilt where I've machine-embroidered Lily's favourite sweet.

'It's a half-eaten peanut butter cup!' Roger says croakily. 'God, how she loved these! I could have papered this house with the empty wrappers.'

Betty stares at the shape next to it. 'And look at this, Roger. She's stitched the face of a hippo for Lily. *For us.*'

Roger lets out a cry, his face taut with pain. 'You remember . . . the things our daughter loved the most?'

I nod. Chest heaving, he staggers to the sofa and slumps down, tears streaking down his cheeks.

Betty rushes over to comfort him. 'You see, I told you Sophie still cares.'

'I do! I love Lily. I miss her every day.'

Roger's shoulders shake harder as he weeps. Betty gestures for me to join them. We all hold on to each other and cry for the girl we loved and lost, the quilt and all our memories draped over our knees.

We look through photo albums and drink tea, swapping anecdotes about Lily before Betty gets up to make a fresh pot.

'Lily would be glad we're doing this together,' she says. 'But she'd want the two of you to make up properly.' She stares pointedly at Roger. 'You must apologise.'

'There's no need,' I protest as she heads to the kitchen. '*I'm* sorry. I should have visited you both years ago.'

Roger adjusts his gilet and sighs deeply. 'And we'd have welcomed you into our home gladly. But Betty's right. I'm sorry too.'

I frown. 'For what? You didn't do anything wrong.'

He coughs, clearing his throat. 'The messages I left on your website and Instagram page – I should never have stooped so low.'

I can hear the blood pounding in my ears. 'That was you?' I gasp.

'Betty was horrified when she found out, but not as disgusted as I was with myself.'

I shake my head, trying to make sense of everything. 'You *do* blame me for Lily getting into the car?'

'No. I came to terms long ago with the fact that Lily used free will – she chose to follow you, her best friend, that night. It wasn't your fault.'

'But what then?'

'You moved on with your life without a backward glance.' Before I can protest, he talks rapidly. 'We treated you like a second daughter, but you cut us off completely after Lily died. You never replied to our messages or came to see us. You never contacted us on the anniversaries of her death, when we'd have appreciated the support. Tom stayed in touch over the years, as did Priti's parents and the family of Margaret, the other driver. But it felt as though you left *us*, and Lily, behind without another thought.'

I touch the scar beneath my hair. 'It wasn't because I didn't care. I felt too guilty to see either of you. I blamed myself, and still do. But I never stopped thinking about Lily or the two of you. I never stopped caring. I didn't move on. I feel like I'm always trapped in that car, but in my dreams I shut the door before Lily manages to climb in.'

'I had no idea.' He rubs his bristly jaw as Betty returns to refill the biscuit plate.

'I'm not excusing what Roger did, but it was a shock for us both hearing Tom mention you after so many years,' she says. 'He came round to see us several weeks ago and admitted he'd come across your quilting business online. He said you'd started a new life in Bristol.'

My mouth falls open. 'Tom claimed I didn't care about Lily? That I'd moved on?'

'Not at all,' Betty replies. 'He was happy for you. Tom's had his own struggles, and he was glad you've managed to make something of yourself.'

'But the news triggered something dark inside me,' Roger admits.

'You lost all reason,' Betty agrees. 'I barely recognised the man you became.' She rests her hand on his shoulder.

'It's awful, I know, but I wanted to punish you for having a career, *a life*, when Lily didn't get to have one.' He squeezes his wife's hand. 'Our lovely daughter could never find her vocation, get married or have children. I wanted a *reaction* from you, anything to acknowledge that you hadn't forgotten her. I lashed out in the worst possible way and I'm extremely ashamed. Please forgive me.'

'Of course I do! I always marked the anniversaries of Lily's death privately by lighting a candle for her, but I should have reached out to you both. I will always love Lily and you and Betty. I won't be a stranger anymore, I promise.'

I *will* stay in touch, despite selling Mum's house. Even if I'm alone and have lost Adam, I'll come back and visit. I won't shut everyone out like before.

'We both want you in our life, no matter what,' Roger says firmly.

After more tea, hugs and sharing memories about Lily, they wave me off at the front door, clutching the quilt.

I pull up my hood against the rain and wind and notice the drawing on my wrist. The ink has streaked, but the symbol remains.

Adam once told me the Möbius strip proves that if you travel far enough, you'll end up where you began without even realising it.

He was right.

I mistakenly blamed Trevor and then Tom for the messages I received, but the fault lay squarely with myself: I'm the culprit.

I turned my back on the past instead of having the courage to confront it.

Everything is finally coming full circle tonight for me, Adam and Tom.

We're all going back to the beginning.

52

ADAM

Saturday, 12 April 2025

Wren uses a stick to draw a circle around the towering sandcastle. Actually... 'sandcastle' doesn't do our creation justice! It's a palace with eight turrets, an inner courtyard and roomy stables for her toy unicorns. It's taken us an hour to construct. Wren refused to leave despite the wind and rain, so we've powered on with our anorak hoods up. My glasses are dotted with drops of water and I wipe them, looking out to sea. The tide was creeping in slowly at first but now it's streaming rapidly towards our trench.

'We're running out of time!' Wren cries. 'The moat isn't ready yet.'

I use the larger spade and we dig deeper and faster, as frothing water threatens.

'It's almost here,' Wren says, hugging my waist. 'My unicorns are scared. Me too!'

'Don't be afraid!' I leap over the moat and shovel the sand into thick walls. 'This is our barricade... the first line of defence.'

Wren squeals excitedly and rescues the purple plastic toys before the flood finally arrives. Water swills against my barrier, and a crack appears. It deepens and widens, before splitting open. Within seconds, our palace is overwhelmed.

'It's time to abandon base and retreat!' I declare as the water surrounds us.

'I don't want to give up,' Wren cries.

'Neither do I, but we don't have a choice.'

I reach out my hand. She grabs it and we run up the beach, bent over against the gale. Wren's grip loosens, but I hang on tight and don't let go. We reach higher ground, panting.

'I wish Mummy could have seen it.' Wren sighs. 'And Sophie.'

'They'd have been impressed! But we can show Sophie and Grandma the photos.'

I call up the selfie I took when we'd finished digging. It's the first ever successful one of the two of us. In all my previous attempts, one of us blinked or looked away. Wren's face is pressed against mine as I hold my phone, crouching down. We're both grinning despite the weather, our palace proud and majestic in the background.

Wren presses the heel of her wellie into the sand, creating a pattern. 'Is Sophie going to be my new mummy?' she asks, without looking up.

I'm dumbstruck for a few seconds, and debate how to reply.

Perhaps? I hope so at some point?

Sophie doesn't want to think beyond this week, but I can't help visualising our future . . . the three of us happy and living together in Bristol.

'Erm, well . . . It's interesting you say that, because . . .'

'I like Sophie a lot more than Claire,' she interrupts.

My eyebrow shoots up. I never introduced her to my former course mate the few times she came over late at night.

'Claire was . . .' I begin.

'Noisy. She had an annoying laugh. And she woke me up whenever she had a nightmare and shouted for you.'

'That's true!' I say, my face reddening at the memory of Claire's loud orgasms.

'I'm glad she's stopped visiting,' Wren continues. 'But I don't want Sophie to leave. I want her to stay with us.'

'Ditto.'

Wren's candour is a way into a difficult conversation I would definitely have put off.

'The thing is, I've liked Sophie ever since we were at school.' I take her hands, which feel tiny and cold in mine. 'Carley's your mum, and nothing will ever change that. Sophie could never replace her.'

'I know,' she whispers.

'But I want Sophie to be a part of our lives going forward, if that's all right with you?'

'My unicorns say okey-dokey.' She holds up the toys and puts them to her ear. 'They told me they love her, a teeny-weeny bit.'

I kneel beside her, not caring about the knees of my jeans dampening in the wet sand.

'I love *you*, Da-Wren, but not a tiny bit . . . I love you 100 per cent. I want you to be poppety-pop happy more than anything else in the world.'

She falls into my arms. 'My unicorns are poppety-pop happy, Da . . . Da-Adam.'

I feel a prickle of disappointment she didn't call me Daddy or tell me she loved me back, but there's no rush. We have plenty of time to make our relationship even stronger.

When she finally lets go, we look for our palace in the distance but only a small mound of sand remains from one of the turrets.

Then it sinks beneath the tide and disappears, leaving no trace it ever existed.

I'm fiddling with my bow tie in front of the mirror above the fireplace, while rain pounds against the window. I'm wearing contact lenses to avoid steamed-up glasses all night.

'Let me do that for you,' Mum says, taking over. She finishes the knot and pats it. 'There. Very handsome. What do you think, Wren?'

'Hmmm?'

She's kneeling on an armchair, the top half of her body hidden behind the curtains as she stares out of the window.

'Never mind!' Mum cries. 'Have you seen any lightning yet?'

Wren ducks beneath the fabric, her eyes saucer-like. 'No! Will there be?'

'Probably. Thunder too. It'll be quite the storm.'

'Ooh!' she gasps. 'Sophie's put lightning strikes in our quilt. She sent Da . . . Da-Adam a picture. I hope we see lots later.'

I'm less excited about the crappy weather; the roads could flood. Staying in with Wren for a movie marathon probably *is* a better idea. Sophie has never been keen to go to the party and the driving conditions will be even worse later. On the way to Plymouth this afternoon, I passed an overturned caravan. It had been blown over by the high winds, hitting the car behind. My journey was without drama, but flying debris just missed me when I stepped out of the jewellery shop where Wren bought her gemstones. I pat my dinner jacket pocket for the hundredth time, feeling for the hard outline of the small boxes.

'Got everything?' Mum asks.

'Hmmm. Think so. I'm wondering if tonight . . .'

The doorbell rings, interrupting my nagging doubts.

'That must be Sophie!' Wren cries.

She scrambles off the chair and shoots out of the room. I give my bow tie one last tug in the mirror, feeling ridiculously nervous as Sophie chats to Wren in the hall. My palms are damp. My stomach swoops as Sophie appears in the doorway. I stare at her, open-mouthed. She's wearing a long green dress with a plunging neckline and has never looked more gorgeous, despite her worried expression. She's checked in regularly today, anxious about my Plymouth journey and beach trip with Wren.

I breathe out slowly. 'Wow!'

'Sophie looks like a fairy princess.' Wren nods approvingly, balancing on one leg.

'She certainly does.' Mum walks over and kisses her on the cheek. 'You look beautiful, dear.'

'Thank you!' She lifts the damp hem of her dress. 'But I'm a bedraggled princess after running from my van to the front door.'

'Was that thunder?' Wren hurdles on to the chair and peers between the curtains.

'Hopefully not.' Sophie shivers, turning to me. 'I'm glad you got to Plymouth okay. The roads are pretty bad.'

'It was fine. No problems.' I lower my voice. 'Do you want to pass on tonight? The cab should be here soon, but we could cancel if you're worried?'

'No!' Wren cries, leaning against the cushions. 'The princess must go to the ball!'

'You have exceptionally good hearing when you shouldn't be "leaves dropping".' Mum says. 'Cinderella and Prince Charming will get wet feet. Talking of which, I have to let the dogs out in the garden, and you need to stop bouncing on my chair.'

Wren slithers down but jumps back up as soon as Mum leaves the room.

I turn to Sophie, continuing Wren and Mum's ball theme. 'We might have problems finding a pumpkin to turn into a carriage if the roads flood. We could give it a miss if you'd prefer to stay in?'

Sophie frowns. 'But I thought you wanted this?'

'I did. I still do . . . but I don't need to if you're feeling apprehensive. It could be tricky getting a taxi back.'

I've given her a way out, but to my surprise she doesn't seize it.

'I'm willing to give it a shot, if you are?' she says. 'I think it's important we're both there – we talked about what we want to do.'

Toast Lily. Say goodbye. Leave the past behind us and start afresh.

'True. In that case, you can't go like that. You're missing something.' I pretend to look worried and rub my brow.

Sophie feels for her dangly earrings, checking they're in her lobes.

'What do you think she needs, Wren?' I ask.

She reappears from beneath the curtains. 'A unicorn?'

'Good point, but I was thinking this.'

Sophie's brow wrinkles with surprise as I whip out a black velvet box from my pocket.

'Adam!' she breathes. 'What are you doing?'

Wren slides down the chair and runs over. 'What is it?'

'Wait and see!' I reply.

Sophie opens the box. She lets out a small gasp as she pulls out a gold necklace with a Möbius strip symbol.

'It's to replace the one we lost,' I tell her. 'I know how much it meant to you.'

Sophie gulps, her eyes misty.

'D-d-don't you like it? I had it made specially, like before.'

'I love it,' she says. 'Can you help me?'

She lifts her hair and I fasten the catch, inhaling the scent of fresh flowers. *Lilies.* Turning around, she looks down, touching the knot. Her chest rises and falls rapidly.

'It's perfect, Adam. Thank you.'

I pull out another gift from my pocket and face Wren, hiding it behind my back.

'I have something for you. Which hand?'

She taps my right arm. 'Correct!'

I produce the box and she snaps open the lid, squealing with excitement.

'Oooh, a bracelet that matches Sophie's!'

I help put it on her wrist.

'It has the same mathematical symbol . . . a Möbius strip. Look at this.' I run my finger over the curved silver loop. 'Do you see how I'm back to where I began? It means that Mummy's love for you never ends. It goes on forever even though she's not here anymore.'

Wren's eyes fill with tears. 'I've been thinking about Mummy a lot today. I miss and love her so much.'

'I know. But she's still with you in your heart and memories.' I put my arms around her. 'And I love you too, Wren. Like the pattern in the bracelet. That won't end either.'

She lifts her chin and manages a watery smile.

'It's time for my presents,' Sophie says. 'Wait one minute.'

She leaves the room and returns with a bag, handing it to Wren. She dives in and pulls out gifts, unwrapping them in a frenzy.

'Look at this, Da-Adam. It's you and me!' Wren grins and holds up framed pictures of us from the zoo and a photobook.

'They're fantastic.' I'm about to flick through the pictures when Sophie darts into the hall.

'And now for the big one,' she says, reappearing. 'You both have to close your eyes and put your hands out. No peeping – I mean it.'

'Fine!' I put the book down and stand behind Wren, stretching my arms over her. Sophie places something soft and heavy in our palms.

'You can open them now,' she says.

I look down at the brightly coloured fabric.

'Mummy's quilt!' Wren exclaims. 'You finished it!'

I stare in amazement at the joyous shape of our lives: Carley's, Wren's and mine. Finally, I see the bigger picture: from my chaos, upheaval and confusion, Sophie found order, beauty and love. So many colourful fragments of memories make up the happy pattern.

'Here's the giraffe from the zoo,' Wren cries, pointing to the light-tan and dark-brown patches. 'And this is the pink T-shirt Mummy wore when we went there together.' Her fingers trail across the material, resting on a bluish-green patch. 'Mummy's dress! She had it on for my Christmas show, and this is her lucky green blouse that helped me win at swimming.'

Wren's excitement mounts as she discovers the embroidered panels. 'The red panda and Mummy's cupcakes! That's her thunder and lightning.'

Sophie has stitched Wren's favourite animal and represented Carley's sweet tooth in the centre of log cabin blocks. They're close to coal-black storm clouds and jagged yellow slashes, stitched in glittery gold threads. I recognise Carley's Stanford sweatshirt as well as Wren's unicorns and tiny gemstones.

My gaze rests on the tunnel that represents my love of maths. It's intricate and must have taken Sophie hours to stitch. The numbers 13, 7, 3, 24, and 112 are being sucked towards a shimmering white pinprick of light, getting smaller and smaller. At the centre of the quilt are embroidered versions of Carley's squiggles, surrounded by triangles and love hearts, and Sophie's unique geometric shapes, which Wren and I sewed together.

I touch the 13-sided outlines. I don't feel the slightest pang of regret about not taking the research forward. I'm emailing Dr Hunt with my decision first thing Monday morning and will tell Mum afterwards, out of Wren's earshot.

'What do you think?' Sophie asks.

'I'm speechless! It's amazing! Everything I want to say ends in an exclamation mark!'

'Me too!' Wren throws it over her shoulders, cape-like. 'I love, love, love it! It feels like Mummy's giving me a hug. She's here with us tonight, loving our quilt and the storm. She'll have her own giant firework display later!'

She pirouettes around the sitting room. I laugh, my heart swelling with joy. I'm expecting Sophie to be thrilled with our reactions, but she looks on the brink of tears.

'You've done a brilliant job,' I say, taking her hand. 'It goes far beyond what we were both imagining.'

Her fingers are cold and trembling, and there's a pained look in her eyes as if she's been given terrible news, not unconditional praise.

'It's perfect,' I add. 'We'll both treasure it forever.'

53

SOPHIE

Saturday, 12 April 2025

It's 7 p.m. and our driver's messaged, saying he's waiting outside. Potentially fatal scenarios play over in my mind as Wren and Mrs B walk us to the front door. Within the next five hours our cab could be crushed by a tree on the way there or swept away by a torrent as we cross the causeway on our return; a fire could ravage the golf club during the party, leaving no survivors. I try to breathe out slowly, reminding myself that Joan died after staying in her house during equally bad weather 8 years, 3 months and 26 days ago. The threat could be lurking anywhere: inside or out.

'Can I wait up for them?' Wren asks, looking at Mrs B. 'We could all watch the thunder and lightning together.'

'No, they'll be late back,' she replies. 'Everyone can catch up in the morning.'

I close my eyes briefly, praying we do, and pull on my coat.

'Remember to ask Grandma for her secret stash of best chocolate ice cream.' Adam winks at his mum. 'It's hidden at the bottom of the freezer.'

'Ooh, chocolate ice cream!'

'Love you.' Adam kisses Wren on the top of her head.

'Bye! I'm going to find the sprinkles and chocolate sauce.'

Wren darts away before I can tell her to give Adam a proper hug in case it's their last. She needs to tell him she loves him and call him Daddy, but the kitchen door bangs shut.

Mrs B stands on tiptoes, kissing Adam's cheek and then mine. 'I won't stay up. Have a lovely time, the two of you. See you both in the morning. Love you.'

''Til tomorrow!' Adam declares brightly. 'Love you too.'

I gulp, trying to force down my rising panic as he takes my hand and pulls me through the rain to the taxi.

Adam is FaceTiming Ollie, who's in the pub. Adam had protested, saying they never video call, but I claimed it would help pass the time in the car. Ollie's a good friend – he deserves to see Adam, in case it's his last chance. While they're chatting, I FaceTime Flora, who's out with Stefan. This could also be a goodbye: my numbers may be destined to end tonight too. I'll do anything to save Adam, to give him more time with Wren.

'Thanks for the mortgage advice, Sophs!' Stefan butts in, raising a beer glass.

'No problem. Good luck with your flat-hunting.'

He grins and passes the phone back to Flora, who is predictably blunt.

'I hope you and SSD shag happily ever after. Bye, Numbers Girl!'

I blow kisses back. 'Goodbye, Flora.' I clear my throat. 'Hope to see you soon. Love you!'

Adam raises an eyebrow as I hang up. 'SSD?'

'Sexy Single Dad.'

'I should get that printed on a mug next week!'

I stare out of the steamed-up window, my chest pinching with pain.

By the time our cab arrives at the golf club twenty minutes later, the wind has picked up sharply.

Adam grabs the umbrella from the seat. 'Are you ready?'

No!

Memories of our prom night here paralyse every muscle. I want to tell the driver to take us straight back to Mrs B's house, but Adam's numbers *could* increase after seeing Tom and other familiar faces. I have to give this a shot. I fumble with the seat belt, and Adam releases me, leaping out. His umbrella blows inside out as he runs around the car and opens my door. I hang on to his hand, flinching at the sight of the club's flagpole on top of the building. It's being battered furiously by the gale; the stick could fly off, javelin-like.

'Let's make a run for it,' Adam declares.

I hold my trailing skirt and we sprint for the door, avoiding the potential hazard. Inside the lobby, we brush ourselves down. While Adam takes our damp coats to the cloakroom, I study the chequerboard floor, remembering how Lily would only step on the black tiles when we arrived for prom, claiming the white ones were unlucky. I glance across at Adam's shoes, which bridge both colours. He returns, clutching pink tickets.

'My raincoat's number three and yours is thirteen, sorry. But at least it's not Friday the thirteenth today!'

I rock on my heels. Adam is my thirteenth attempt to save someone, so this feels like a sign, but I'm not sure how to interpret it. Is this good luck or bad?

'Are you sure you're all right about doing this?' he asks.

I nod, gazing at the sea of unfamiliar faces beneath the large, glittering chandelier. Nobody has a double digit, let alone a single one.

'Let's grab a drink and try to find people we recognise.'

After collecting our name badges, we head to the bar and knock back vodka shots with a few guys who were lower down our school. We reminisce about our former teachers before old classmates appear. We're joined by a woman who used to be in Adam's maths lessons, and a man he sat next to in physics. Adam is enjoying himself, but the socialising isn't affecting his number yet. It's stuck on 1.

The music rises in volume and 'Shut Up and Dance' by Walk the Moon booms out.

'Our song,' Adam cries. 'Come on! I have new moves.'

'That sounds scary. I'm guessing I won't be able to unsee this.'

Adam laughs and drags me on to the dance floor in the banqueting suite. The digital New Year clock is back but fixed on a different wall.

It's counting down to midnight, like before.

Cold dread creeps across my skin as Adam shimmies wildly – a bizarre combination of Irish dancing steps, windmill arms and hip thrusts. People nearby clap and cheer, forming a circle. He pulls me into the centre. I try to savour the pressure of his hand on the small of my back, his breath on my neck and his warm, woody citrus scent.

Adam's body presses against mine, and we mould together, becoming one.

Suddenly, he pulls away, twirling me around and around as the tempo picks up.

Nausea rises in my throat.

The whole world is spinning out of control.

I can't stop it.

54

SOPHIE

SATURDAY, 12 APRIL 2025

We've danced cheek to cheek to Ed Sheeran's 'Thinking Out Loud' – another musical blast from the past. I felt the softness of Adam's hair curling at the nape of his neck and the broadness of his shoulders beneath my fingertips, squirrelling away these moments in my mind. Adam fetches more drinks while I wait by the window, watching the dancing and hoping to spot familiar faces. We haven't met anyone else we know since the bar.

All I see are numbers. Strangers' digits swirl feverishly in the air; the countdown clock continues to descend.

There's only 3 hours, 57 minutes and 36 seconds left until midnight.

35 seconds, 34, 33.

I squeeze my eyes tightly shut, but the diminishing digits are branded beneath my lids. I can't escape from them. Numbers are everywhere.

'Sophie . . . Hello.'

My eyes fly open.

Tom.

'Hey, there!'

My attempt at jollity sounds strained, but I remind myself he has no idea I've been thinking the worst of him. Tom hesitates before giving me an awkward peck on the cheek. We stare at each other as he steps back. His blond hair is receding, pulled into a ponytail, and the starched white shirt stretches across his stomach. He tugs at the hem of his cream dinner jacket, clutching a pint glass of orange juice in his other hand.

'It's good to see you. I was hoping the weather wouldn't put you off coming.' He gazes around the dance floor, taking a sip of his drink. 'Is Adam here?'

'He's at the bar – he should be back any minute.'

We exchange polite small talk while we wait for Adam – I'm not ready to bring up prom night or Betty and Roger. The rain pitter-patters on the window as I explain how we reconnected through the quilt for his daughter. Tom confesses he's never married or had children. He worked in investment banking after leaving Durham uni, before retraining to become a paramedic five years ago.

'That's quite the career change,' I remark.

'I wanted to do something more useful than buying new sports cars and making billionaires even richer.'

I raise an eyebrow. This was his dream when we were teenagers. He only ever talked about making 'shitloads of money'. But I guess the City's long-hours culture and stress must have taken a toll. Betty mentioned he's struggled.

Tom takes a breath, his eyes moistening. 'I'd been wondering about joining the ambulance service or becoming a doctor ever since the crash.'

'Really? I had no idea.'

'Well . . . I wouldn't expect you to.'

My cheeks warm. I cut all ties with Tom and Adam, blocking them on my socials. I feel the same stab of guilt I experienced when visiting Lily's parents.

'Nothing could be done for Margaret, the other driver,' he says. 'But I always wondered if Lily, Priti and Vinny could have been saved if Adam or I had known how to perform CPR or a defibrillator had been on hand.'

I glance at him, swaying. 'Probably not. They were all so badly hurt.'

'We'll never know.' He clutches his drink closely to his chest, blinking back tears. 'I watched Vinny and Priti die while we waited for the ambulances. That stays with you. It can't help but leave a mark.'

'Of course – you and Adam were the first to arrive.'

He nods. 'We were completely alone and panicking.'

The colour rises in my face. To my shame, I've never considered how awful it must have been for them finding the four of us critically injured or dying in the mangled wreck and Margaret already dead.

'Everyone said I was Vinny's best weed client, but he was a good friend. I lost him and Lily.'

Before I can speak, he continues. 'Vinny was an irresponsible shitbag who killed the others. But he was a kid like us – eighteen – and made a dumb decision. He didn't deserve to die. No one did. I can't turn back time but at least I get to help others now. I also go into schools with colleagues to warn about the dangers of drink and drug driving.'

'I think it's great you're making a difference,' I say thickly.

'Joining the ambulance service helped *me*. I got my life back in order. It was chaotic for a long time. We all had different ways of coping: you cut everyone off, Adam threw himself into his studies and I turned to alcohol, I'm afraid.'

'I'm sorry.'

He shakes his head. 'I've been sober for six years, three months and two days.'

'Those are good numbers,' I tell him.

'Yeah. I still talk about Lily in my meetings. And you, Sophie. I've wanted to speak to you for a long time and set things straight . . .' He tugs his bow tie nervously. 'I saw you on the street last Saturday and wanted to break the ice before tonight. I'd hoped time had healed things, and we could talk, but you ducked into a shop. I called by your mum's house a few times, but you didn't come to the door.'

I attempt to speak, but he interjects.

'Please let me say this – part of my recovery is about making amends with people I've wronged. I don't blame you for wanting to sever ties with me. I just want the chance to say sorry.'

'*I'm* the one who should apologise. After the crash, I felt too guilty to see anyone. I deliberately cut myself off and that was wrong. I should have faced what happened instead of running away.'

'And now?' His eyes narrow.

'I'm ashamed to say I've been avoiding you. I thought you held a grudge over Lily's death.'

I don't mention Roger's emails, or how I believed *he* was responsible for the hurtful messages.

He shakes his head. 'I only ever blamed myself.'

'Why?' I frown hard. 'Lily followed *me* into the car.'

Before he can answer, Adam approaches, clutching champagne flutes.

'Tom!'

He looks hesitantly from him to me, before passing a glass. I smile back, and the tension dissolves from his jaw.

'How are you?' He gives Tom a hug. 'It's great to see you.'

'You too.'

'Tom's switched careers to become a paramedic,' I tell him.

'Wow! That's a huge change!'

Those were my exact thoughts, but we can't waste more time on small talk. This might be the only chance for Adam to resolve his feelings about prom night.

'I've said sorry to Tom,' I say, cutting in before he has a chance to reply. 'I was caught up in my own misery and didn't think about what either of you went through, coming across the cars that night, and how you both suffered afterwards.'

Adam flinches but remains silent.

'And I've wanted to apologise to the two of you for a long time,' Tom admits.

'There's no need. We're all good.' Adam puts an arm around my waist, pulling me closer. 'We've got back together.'

'That's fantastic!' He smiles warmly. 'I'm happy for you both.'

'What did you want to tell us, Tom?' I prompt.

'I've always felt responsible . . . If I hadn't told Sophie your Stanford news, she wouldn't have fled and got in the car. Lily wouldn't have followed. I was the catalyst.'

'No, that was me,' Adam insists. 'I should have told Sophie sooner. You weren't to know I hadn't broken the news to her.'

'But I did,' he blurts out. 'That's the point. I told Sophie on purpose. I *wanted* to cause trouble.'

'Why?' Adam stares at him, open-mouthed. 'I thought we were friends?'

'We were – *are*. But I was jealous. Everything seemed to come so easy to you.'

Adam shakes his head, placing his glass on the windowsill. 'I swear, it didn't.'

'It looked that way from the outside. Your parents were wealthy and bought everything you wanted. You had top grades, universities falling over themselves to offer you places and . . . Sophie.'

I gaze at him, aghast.

'You only ever had eyes for Adam, but he was careless with your feelings,' he continues. 'I wanted him to confront the consequences of his indecision, *punish him*. Obviously, I had no idea how it would turn out. I've been racked with guilt ever since. I'm sorry.'

Adam pulls him into his arms. 'It's behind us, mate. *We're* sorry. All three of us did things we regret. It's time we move on.'

I stifle a cry, joining in the joint hug.

'It feels good to finally get my confession off my chest,' Tom admits.

'Me too,' I say.

'Let's toast Lily.' Adam grabs his champagne flute.

'Don't forget Priti and Vinny,' I add.

Adam raises an eyebrow but doesn't comment. 'To absent friends.'

'We'll never forget any of you,' I vow. 'Or Margaret.'

'To old friends who found their way back to each other after a long time,' Tom says, as we lift our drinks. 'It's fitting the three of us are here tonight to remember the people we lost.'

We clink glasses, and I glance at the clock.

3 hours, 42 minutes and 7 seconds remaining.

Hope soars.

This must be it – the moment of forgiveness, reconciliation and redemption that alters something deep inside Adam, lengthening his life.

I turn back to him, grinning with anticipation.

But the smile vanishes from my face. Nothing has changed, except the waning minutes on the timer.

Adam's number is still 1.

55

ADAM

Saturday, 12 April 2025

Sophie stares at the countdown clock while Tom explains he's taking unpaid leave to look after his elderly dad, who has Alzheimer's. I suggest we all meet for a drink next week. Sophie agrees and asks after Tom's dad before fading away from the conversation. A melancholy expression has crept back into her eyes. I don't understand why; a minute ago she looked jubilant that we'd all reconnected to toast our lost school friends.

I pat my dinner jacket, checking for the final box that should, hopefully, lift her spirits. I need to find the perfect moment . . . probably after the last slow dance. My fingers creep back into my pocket, brushing against the solid velvet shape, as my phone vibrates.

Sophie jumps, almost spilling her drink, but I ignore the caller.

'Monday or Tuesday is good for me,' Tom says. 'Dad's carer will be there in the evenings.'

'Hmmm. Shall we say Monday? I'll give you my number.'

'Great.'

I tap the digits into his phone and pass it back.

'Thanks. Do you need to get that?' He nods at my jacket.

I pull my phone from an inner pocket, checking the screen. 'It's Mum. I should take this, sorry . . . Wren might want something.'

'No worries. I need to head off before Dad's carer clocks off. See you both on Monday.' He gives me a quick hug.

I step away, pressing my hand against my other ear to block out the music as I accept the call.

'Adam!' Mum says loudly. 'Thank God you've picked up.'

Panic flutters in my throat. 'W-w-what's wrong?'

'Wren's missing! She's not in the house. I've looked all over. She must have slipped out while I was on the phone to a friend.'

'What?' I spin around, staring at Sophie and Tom, who are embracing. 'When . . . ? How long has she been gone?'

'About fifteen minutes. I left her watching TV in the sitting room while I went upstairs. When I came down, she wasn't on the sofa. Her coat and wellies are gone from the back door.'

Sophie and Tom step closer, their eyes wide with concern. I quickly relay Mum's news.

'I don't know where to look!' Mum's voice is high-pitched with panic. 'Where would she go?'

Sophie squeezes my arm, but I can barely feel her fingers. My body has turned to ice from a mixture of fear and guilt over leaving her.

'Check her bedroom and see if Carley's urn is still there. It should be on the shelf near her bed.'

'Why? Oh no! You don't think she wants to empty it on her own?'

'Just look, please!'

Mum's breathing sounds laboured as she hurries up the stairs.

'It's not here,' she says eventually. 'But surely she wouldn't? She doesn't like the dark or loud noises.'

'It's the only thing that makes sense . . . Carley wanted her ashes to be scattered by the sea during a storm. I saw the forecast for next week and was going to suggest a day to do it together. I didn't get round to it . . . Wren must have decided to go by herself.'

'I'm heading down to the beach,' Mum says briskly. 'I'll rally the neighbours. She can't have gone far on her own. We'll find her, Adam, I promise.'

'I'll grab a cab with Sophie and meet you there. Call the police if there's no sign of her nearby . . . ring me as soon as you know anything.'

'Will do. Bye, Adam. I love you.'

'I love you too, Mum.'

She hangs up and I cling on to Sophie's hand, my lifeline.

'I could help look?' Tom suggests. 'It's Bigbury beach, near your mum's house, right?'

'Thanks, but you should get back to your dad,' I say. 'I'll message you when we find her.'

'Call if you need me,' he replies. 'You know I'll be there for you both. Good luck.'

Sophie leads me through the bodies on the dance floor and we burst into the lobby, which echoes with the pounding beat. My heart thumps in time. I fetch our coats from the cloakroom and push through the revolving doors, the wind knocking the breath from my lungs. Rain strikes my face. Sophie grasps my arm, her dress and hair rippling wildly, as we stagger on to the driveway. Panic crushes my chest; no taxis are waiting for pick-ups.

Sophie whips out her phone. 'Don't worry. I have a local cab number.'

She darts back to the porch, shielding her other ear against the screech of the gale as she makes the call. I clench and unclench my fists, trying to control my breathing.

'A car's nearby,' she says, stepping forward. 'It should be here in ten to fifteen minutes. Come under here and shelter.'

How can we wait that long? *What should I do?* Fear spirals in my throat, threatening to choke me. My chest spasms. Wren's alone in the dark. She could have wandered off a cliff or been knocked over by a car. I'm not there to save her.

'We should start walking. All the cabs from town come along the same road. We can flag one down sooner.'

'No, let's stay here. It's definitely coming.'

'I can't wait. Wren could be injured, or worse . . .' I shudder. 'We have to get to her before it's too late!'

'We will. She's not going to die, Adam. I *promise* she'll be okay.' Sophie's tone is strangely measured. She's managing to keep it together, whereas I'm unravelling.

'You don't know that for sure. I have to go!' I sprint off.

'Come back, Adam!'

I switch on my phone's torchlight as I reach the end of the driveway. Shadowy memories jump out from the hedgerows. This was me, almost ten years ago, running in a blind panic along the lane, except tonight the roles are reversed. Sophie is chasing after *me*, frantically calling my name. Her voice is tossed away, the wind smothering her shouts.

Car headlights sear the hedgerow, picking out a pair of glassy, staring eyes. A rabbit or a fox? I wave my phone, the light dancing around. The driver swerves to avoid me, hammering on the horn.

'Adam!' Sophie yells.

I jump on the narrow grass verge, waiting for her to catch up.

'You have to stop!' she says, gasping. 'You're not thinking straight. You'll get yourself killed. We should go back and wait at the club.'

I shiver, rain dripping down my face. She's right, I know she is, but I can't stop. Something visceral is driving me forward, overriding my rational thoughts. I realise this must be what it means to *really* love your child: you're prepared to risk everything, including your own life, to protect them from harm.

'Please,' she says, tugging my sleeve. 'You'll be knocked over, and that won't help Wren!'

Another set of headlights illuminate the foliage, seconds before a car appears. I ignore her warning and leap off the wet grass, waving my arms. Sophie screams as the vehicle slams on its brakes, sliding to a halt just metres away. Result! It has a private hire sign on the roof. I run over and hammer on the driver's window. He unwinds it, glaring furiously.

'What the hell? That's a good way to get yourself killed.'

'Sorry! Can you take us somewhere?'

'Nah. I'm off shift. You'll need to ring the office, but I doubt you'll have much luck. Not many cars out tonight. The boss has pulled rides – it's not safe on the back roads.'

I slam my hand down as he tries to wind up his window. 'Please! I'll pay £50 cash to get to Bigbury beach ASAP.'

He shakes his head. 'No one's getting anywhere ASAP.'

I push two £50 notes through the gap. 'Whatever you can do to get us there quickly.'

He looks at me, debating, and shrugs. 'The missus will kill *me*. But get in.'

I throw open the door and turn to Sophie. Her chest is heaving, her breathing shallow.

'No, Adam!' She catches my hand. 'Please don't.'

'What's wrong? He said he'll take us.'

'But it's not the cab we booked.'

'There's no point waiting for ours. It'll probably be cancelled. This could be our only chance to get there!'

She hangs on to my sleeve as I attempt to climb inside.

'This is a bad idea.' She takes a deep breath. 'I'm afraid he'll crash and you'll be injured or worse.'

'What? Why? Wren's at risk, not me!'

Sophie shakes her head. She must be having a flashback to prom night. Unsurprising, given the circumstances: a last-minute decision to flag down a ride during a storm.

'Tonight is different.' I put my arm around her damp shoulders. She's shaking, almost uncontrollably, and still grasping my coat. 'He's a professional driver who knows these roads, not a drunk, speeding teenager. He'll take me to Wren. I'm not going to die, I promise. Do you want to wait at the club . . . ? I'll understand if this is too hard for you.'

Sophie studies my face before loosening her grip on my sleeve. 'No! We'll find her together. I'm not leaving you.'

She climbs into the cab first and I jump in, leaning through the gap in the seats. 'Go, go, go!'

Before we've managed to strap in, a car looms, veering on to our side of the road.

White light dazzles.

Sophie screams.

I fly out of the seat, an unstoppable missile.

56

SOPHIE

Saturday, 12 April 2025

I grab Adam's arm as he propels forward, my other hand looped through the seat belt, and hang on. He doesn't slip through my grasp the way Lily did. He slumps back into the seat. Brambles bang against the windows as our driver pulls closer to the hedgerow, hammering on the horn. The other motorist swerves out of the way just in time.

'Sorry.' The driver – Bob, according to his badge by the dashboard – flicks a glance in his rear-view mirror. 'Idiots are out on the roads tonight.'

The wipers flap frantically, but not fast enough to wash away the deluge of water hitting the windscreen. I fumble with my seat belt as the sky growls ominously; my fingers are trembling too badly to click it into the holder.

'Let me.' Adam takes over, strapping us both in, before placing his hand over mine. 'We're safe. You're all right.'

I can't reply. It's not *me* I'm frightened for. I jump at the crackle of lightning in the distance. We're heading towards the centre of the storm.

'Is this . . .' He shuffles in his seat. 'Are you having a flashback?'

'I'm mega stressed, like you.' I dig my nails into my palms. 'You should tell your mum we're on our way. See if she has any news.'

Adam calls up her number, jamming the phone against his ear.

'I can't get a connection . . . What if she hasn't found Wren?'

It's *my* turn to reassure *him*.

'Then she'll keep looking until the police arrive.'

He takes my hand. 'You're right. We have to stay positive. Everything will turn out all right, I'm sure.'

I'm certain this journey will lead to Adam's death and, possibly, mine. I force myself to nod while squeezing his fingers.

There's nothing else I can do except hold on.

Nineteen minutes later, Adam's anxiety is mounting. Mine too. It's 9.50 p.m. and time is running out. Bob's been forced to reverse back to the intersection due to flooding near the estuary and he's taking another, more long-winded route. I peer out of the window at the dark shapes looming either side of the car.

'These trees are dangerous in high winds,' I warn. 'One of the old oaks came down in a storm a few years ago and killed a motorist.'

I remember the news story when I came back to oversee repairs at Mum's house. Bob eases his foot off the accelerator.

'You're right,' he says. 'The council's supposed to fit braces to tree trunks along here. We should turn back before it's too late. The road could be blocked if large branches have fallen.'

'A little further, *please*!' Adam cries. 'We need to be dropped as close to the beach as possible. My daughter's only eight and she's out there, alone, in this!'

On cue, thunder booms and the sky lights up with bright slashes of electric white.

'Fine.' Bob clutches the steering wheel tighter.

We turn the corner, and I hold my breath at the sight of more huge, dark silhouettes. The trees lean towards the car, as if attempting to catch a glimpse of our worried faces.

'Dammit!' Bob exclaims.

He ploughs through a deep puddle and takes his eyes off the windscreen, attempting to change gear. Up ahead, I watch an overhanging bough bend by 2 degrees, and then another 3. At this rate, it will fall in 5 seconds, 4, 3 . . .

'Brake!' I scream.

Bob slams his foot on the pedal, and our belts strain as we grind to a halt. A terrific cracking sound rings out above the sound of the engine and howling wind. A dark shape crashes on to the road, just missing our bonnet.

Bob turns, rubbing his grey, stubbly chin. 'Are you a psychic?'

Adam hangs on to the door handle, his mouth open in an O shape.

'It was a lucky guess,' I say.

Bob turns off the engine. 'Do you want to give me a hand shifting it? We might manage it between the three of us.'

'No.' Adam's voice wavers. 'Reverse and turn around in the opening we passed. We'll make our own way from here.'

'Are you sure?'

'Yes! You've done enough, thank you. It'll only take us five minutes by foot.'

Adam flings open his door, making the newspaper on the front seat flutter.

'Wait!' Bob opens his glove box and pulls out a torch. 'Take this. Good luck finding your daughter.'

'Thank you!' Adam ducks out of the car.

I follow, and the door is ripped from my grasp. I catch hold of it, slamming it shut. Adam pulls up his collar and I attempt to fasten my coat, but we're both soaked within seconds. The car reverses up the lane, headlights flickering before they're swallowed by darkness. We're completely alone.

'Ready?' I ask, kicking off my heels.

Adam turns on the torch. A strange expression flickers across his face – a mixture of fear and bewilderment.

Before I can ask if he's okay, he clasps my hand and we run into the heart of the storm.

57

ADAM

Saturday, 12 April 2025

'Ready?' Sophie asks.

Am I? My mind is whirring. Sophie was certain we'd be involved in an accident before we got into the cab . . . We've narrowly avoided one. Was that a hunch due to the bad weather? Or did her prediction have something to do with her mathematical skills? She could have calculated the probability of a crash happening in these conditions.

I bat away the questions and take Sophie's hand. We run silently to the end of the lane, almost bent over double against the wind. I check my phone as we reach the car park. It's empty except for an abandoned camper van that's being rocked by the gale. Litter is whipped out of the bin and catapulted into the air.

'Still nothing from Mum! What if . . . what if she's deliberately avoiding my calls?'

'Of course she isn't! Why would she?' Sophie's voice catches with pain as she hobbles barefoot.

'Because she has terrible news. She's waiting to tell me in person that Wren is . . .' My throat dries. I can't utter the word.

'Wren *isn't* dead. We're going to find her. She's going to be okay, I promise.'

That's the second time she's said this. Sophie has 100 per cent certainty that Wren is alive, whereas my conviction is dipping well below 50 per cent. Anything could have happened to her! Sophie's trying to make me feel better because she's kind and thoughtful. But she doesn't *know* my daughter is safe and well. No one does.

We head across the slippery, wet concrete, dodging a traffic cone that twirls past, and reach the footpath. The torch illuminates an uneven sandy trail with jagged stones. Brambles sway on either side. I go first and Sophie follows, touching my back to steady herself. Questions multiply in my head as we make our way down to the beach.

'How did you know that tree bough was about to fall?' I ask. 'You warned the driver right before it hit the road.'

I'm about to repeat the question when she replies.

'I saw the minuscule changes in the angle of the branch as it was giving way.'

'That's amazing!' I frown, remembering her terror when I flagged down the taxi. 'But what numbers did you see before we got into the cab?'

'How do you mean?' she asks.

'You thought the car was going to crash and I could be injured.'

'I figured there was a high chance we'd be involved in an accident in this weather.'

My brows knot together deeper. Sophie had sounded petrified when she attempted to stop me from taking the ride. But she was worried for me, not herself, and was specific about Bob's car.

'You worked it out like a risk assessor . . . the likelihood of a crash in a storm? And you knew the diverted route we took would be extra hazardous?'

'Exactly! The wind is blowing at 70 miles per hour, and those trees are unstable and more than two hundred years old. There was a 98.8 per cent chance one of them would come down tonight.'

I throw a quick glance over my shoulder. The gale buffets us forward, and it's hard to stay upright.

'Have you done a calculation for Wren?' I call back to her. 'Is that why you think she's all right?'

'Sort of.'

'How?' I prompt when she doesn't elaborate.

'I told you I see numbers for people – their exact heights, number of freckles on their cheeks, and so on.'

'Erm . . . how does that help you work out the level of risk they face?'

'I'll explain later. Look, that must be the search party.'

She points down at the beach, where lights dance like fireflies. We quicken our pace and after a couple of minutes the ground softens into sand underfoot. We repeatedly shout Wren's name, but our voices are tossed away by the wind. I hold on to Sophie and plough on towards the beams, sand whipping our legs.

'Mum!'

Torchlights swing wildly as we draw nearer. Mum breaks away from two dark figures and staggers towards us.

'Adam! Thank God! I've tried calling but couldn't get through.'

'Anything?' Panic claws at my throat.

'Nothing,' she gasps. 'The police are on their way. They asked if we're sure this is where she'd come?'

'It's the only stretch of sand she'd be able to find in the dark. It's the closest to your house. She wouldn't know where else to go. She *must* be here somewhere.'

Fear flits through Mum's eyes as she gazes out at the huge, towering waves crashing on to the shore.

'The police have alerted the coastguard . . . just in case.'

Pain rips through my chest as though a tiny, invisible hand has reached inside my ribcage and squeezed my heart.

'W-w-what if she's been swept out?'

'Wren would never have gone in the sea on her own,' Sophie says firmly.

'But the tide's coming in!' I exclaim. 'She could have been knocked over by a wave while she was paddling. We should look for clothing . . . or the urn at the shoreline.'

'That's a waste of time,' Sophie insists. 'She's somewhere along the beach. We need to split up.' She turns to Mum. 'Why don't you go to the rock pools? We'll head towards Bantham. Turn your torches off and on three times if you find her and we'll do the same.'

'All right. Good luck, both of you!' Mum returns to her huddle.

Sophie walks away, but I don't move. I can't rip my gaze from the seven-foot-high breakers. Wren could be tossed around helplessly before sinking beneath the surface. I could have drowned as a teenager if Sophie hadn't dragged me up. What chance does an eight-year-old have in a swell like this?

I kick off my shoes and roll up my trousers.

'No, Adam!' Sophie doubles back. 'She wouldn't still be alive if she'd gone in the water, but I *know* she is.'

'How is that possible, mathematically?' I shout above the wind. 'What numbers are you using? I don't understand your calculations . . . Why are you 100 per cent certain?'

'*Please* believe me, Adam.'

'I want to! But you need to give me more, otherwise I'm going in.'

My torchlight picks out the panic in her eyes.

'Tell me!'

'This is going to sound impossible, but I swear it's true.' Her voice wobbles as she steps closer, holding my gaze. 'I can see how many days Wren has left to live.'

'W-w-what?' I gape at her. 'How?'

'It just happens, like all the other numbers I can see.'

'You know when my daughter will die,' I say numbly.

'Yes.' She breathes out slowly. 'Wren will live to have her own children, if that's what she chooses, and grandchildren. She'll be an old woman when she takes her last breath.'

I fall back a step, reeling. 'What you see . . . Is it only for Wren?'

'No. I see *everyone's* numbers counting down. That's how I knew about Walter's prognosis.'

I stare at her, the enormity of what she's confessed gradually sinking in. She's right . . . it does sound impossible, but Sophie would never exaggerate or lie about something so serious. This explains why she desperately wanted Walter's family to fly over for the party at The Wave! She knew he had little time left. Had she told him? Is that why they were close? Walter claimed she'd helped him with a problem.

More questions swirl around my brain:

When will I lose Mum?

Will it be in the next ten years? Sooner?

What are my numbers?

'I know it's a lot to take in,' she says quietly. 'That's why I don't usually tell anyone. It's too much for most people to understand.'

'I'm sorry,' I say, taking her in my arms.

She frowns. 'What for?'

'Keeping those secrets, alone. It must be lonely.'

She holds on to my lapels, pressing her head into my coat. 'It is. But now you know Wren survives tonight.' She looks up, blinking away tears. 'Do you think she could be where we picnicked yesterday? She might be sheltering near that funny-shaped rock.'

I bite the inside of my mouth, trying not to picture Wren lying somewhere badly injured. She can't be in a life-threatening condition, according to Sophie's prediction, but she *could* have hurt herself. She's alone and must be terrified.

'Good idea!'

We run, shouting Wren's name until our throats are hoarse, struggling to keep upright in the wind. Sophie's revelation continues to play on a loop in my mind as thunder growls louder.

She knows when every single person will die.

Including me.

Scary thoughts creep into my brain. I remember Sophie's horror-stricken face in the café window when we met to discuss the quilt. She fled, distraught, and threw up. She claimed she was ill but looked horribly shocked. What did she see that day? Why did she tell me about Walter's prognosis and the need to make the most of life? She said this could be our last week and the Stanford's board decision wouldn't matter in the grand scheme of things. And why was she jumpy about me driving to Plymouth, and during our cab journey?

Lightning streaks across the sky, picking out the cove.

'We're almost there!' Sophie cries, overtaking me. 'It's around these rocks.'

'What can you see when you look at me?' I shout after her.

She reduces her pace but doesn't reply.

'What's *my* number?' Fear catches in my throat. 'How many days do I have left to live?'

She stops walking. 'Don't do this, Adam. Please! Let's keep going.'

My heart thuds painfully and I raise my voice. 'How much time do I have left to spend with you and Wren?'

Whatever figure she says, I know it will never be enough.

Slowly, she turns to face me. Her bottom lip quivers and her face is taut with pain. Icy-cold dread grips my heart; I can hardly breathe.

My voice is a faint whisper. 'How long?'

She looks at me with pleading eyes, begging me to stop. But I can't.

'How long?' I repeat. 'I have to know.'

'I'm sorry, Adam,' she says, weeping softly. 'This is it. Your numbers will run out tonight.'

58

ADAM

Saturday, 12 April 2025

This is it . . .

Three words, my death sentence, swim around my head. I stumble towards Sophie, my foot tangling in a swathe of seaweed. She catches hold of my sleeve, steadying me, and I collapse into her arms. It can't be true. I feel fine, apart from the stabbing pains in my chest. But that's stress and shock. I'm young and healthy! I haven't hit thirty! Even when my life is apparently about to end, I still use too many exclamation marks!

'I'm really going to die tonight?' I ask, my voice breaking.

I'm hoping I've misunderstood her or she's playing a macabre prank, but this is Sophie, the love of my life. She'd never willingly cause me pain. The anguish etched across her face, and her jittery behaviour today, tell me this is real.

'I'm sorry, Adam,' she repeats.

'H-h-how?' My tongue feels too big for my mouth.

'I don't know. I only ever see the numbers counting down.'

I shake my head, unable to speak.

'After the accident, I saw Lily's digit getting lower and lower in ICU. I thought she was going to wake up, but she didn't – that's how I learned what the numbers meant. It's why Mum went travelling and never came back – I'd told her how much time she had left. And it's why I didn't want to see you again, Adam. It wasn't because I blamed you for not telling me about Stanford or for me and Lily getting into the car. It was because I loved you so much. I couldn't face discovering your number and watching it drop day by day. It would have been too much to bear.'

Intense pain shoots through my chest. I wonder if I'm about to suffer a fatal cardiac arrest due to an undiagnosed heart condition.

'You still loved me . . . ? All the time we were apart?'

'Of course I did! I've never stopped loving you. Not for a minute.'

'That's why you didn't want to meet when I emailed you about the quilt . . . but I persuaded you. And you ran away when you saw I had, what, three weeks to live?'

'Your number was a shock. I never expected it would be—'

'So low,' I finish her sentence. 'If I'd known . . .'

I glance sideways, flicking my torchlight towards Sophie before scanning the side of the cliffs for the unusually shaped rock. Somehow, I manage to keep moving forwards, with Sophie at my side.

'What would you have done differently if I'd told you sooner?'

I ponder her question.

'You'd never have taken off like my mum. Wouldn't you have chosen to stay and become closer to Wren and your own mum?'

Tears prick my eyes. I don't have a big bucket list of places or experiences to tick off. I don't need to walk the Inca Trail, scale Mount Everest, visit the Taj Mahal or see the northern lights in Iceland (although I have always fancied doing this). Everything I need and love is here in south Devon.

'You gave me back my family,' I say, my voice thick with emotion.

'You had it all along, Adam. I couldn't alter your numbers, but I could help you enjoy every single moment with them before it was too late.'

I let the tears slip down my face in the darkness.

'I wouldn't have changed any of the days I've spent with you and Wren this last week.' I let out a hollow laugh, wiping my eyes with the back of my hand. 'I'm being greedy. I wish I had more time! I wish I'd found you sooner and learned how to be a better dad quicker.'

'I wish *I* could rewind time,' she replies. 'I'd go back to that night and stop the car crash. I'd save Lily and the others. I wouldn't have this condition, but you'd still have gone to Stanford and probably met Carley and had a daughter.' She touches the Möbius strip necklace, which peeps out from beneath her coat. 'We could have ended up here, at this exact moment in time, looking for Wren together.'

I lift my chin. 'I love you, Sophie. I need to tell Wren I love her too, make sure she knows that . . . She *remembers*.'

'You will. Let's go.'

We run towards the cliff edge, the torch picking out the distinctive rock formation.

'Wren! It's Daddy. Are you here?'

The pain in my chest worsens, as if a heavy weight is crushing my ribcage. My arms tingle with pins and needles.

Is this it? I can't die before I find her. I have to say goodbye!

I ignore the cramping sensation, scrambling over stones. Thunder rumbles loudly and lightning slashes the sky. A small, dark figure appears from a gap in the cliff, a pale light flickering.

'Over there!' Sophie shouts, pointing.

The sky erupts and Wren appears, apparition-like in her anorak and wellies. She's clutching her mum's urn and a torch.

'Wren!' I holler.

I stagger closer and fall to my knees, wrapping her into my arms as the ache intensifies in my ribcage.

'I was scared I wouldn't get here in time, terrified I wouldn't find you!'

She clings to me, weeping against my chest.

'S-s-sorry. W-w-wanted to do this for Mummy. She loved storms, but I d-d-don't. The thunder scared me. I hid.'

I take the urn from her, placing it on the sand. 'We're here now and you're safe. I love you so much, Wren. I haven't said it nearly enough times, but I do.'

'I love you too, Daddy. 100 per cent.'

My heart contracts. This is the first time I've ever heard her say these precious words – and it'll possibly be the last. I hug her tighter, feeling her shudder beneath my fingertips at the clap of thunder.

'Why don't you both empty the urn while I let your mum know we've found her?' Sophie suggests.

She takes my phone and the torch, moving away a little. She attempts to get a connection, before flashing a signal to the search party further down the beach. I take the lid off the urn and crouch next to Wren.

'Shall we do it right here? I think your mum would have liked this spot.'

'Okey-dokey!'

Carefully, I position Wren with her back to the wind. 'Are you ready?'

'I think so.'

We turn the container upside down and step back. The wind scoops up the ashes, twirling them high into the sky. The particles shimmer as lightning strikes again.

'It's beautiful,' Wren gasps.

'Goodbye, Carley. We'll always remember you.'

'Goodbye, Mummy! I love you.'

Wren leans against my legs, shivering, as she stares up at the darkness. 'It's just us now, Daddy.'

My heart feels like it's breaking into a million pieces. I rub her back briskly, attempting to warm her. 'This is one of my "famous" hugs and it comes with a 100 per cent guarantee to make you feel better.'

'It does, Daddy.'

I'm fighting back tears as Sophie returns, holding my phone.

'Your mum says the police have radioed for an ambulance to get Wren checked for hypothermia, but it could take at least twenty minutes. They're inundated with emergency calls and some of the roads to the beach are blocked.'

The phone rings and Sophie passes it to Wren.

'Grandma got cut off. She wants a quick word.'

Wren sits on a rock, pressing the phone to her ear. I seize the chance to speak to Sophie alone.

'Has my number changed at all today?' I ask hopefully. 'That tree bough didn't hit our cab . . . we didn't crash.'

She shakes her head, gesturing for us to step further away.

'It's not possible to change what's destined to happen?' I flick a look at my watch. 'Within the next hour and a half?'

'I tried many, many times to save people, and nothing ever worked until recently.'

'What happened?' My heart leaps.

'Walter's numbers increased after Harry and his family flew over from Australia for the party. Being around them lengthened his life. That's why I wanted you to come back here this week and spend time with Wren and your mum.'

'So it *is* possible . . . we can beat this!'

'It was only a small change, Adam. And it's the only time I've ever seen it happen.'

'But there's hope! I can't give up.'

Wren walks over, passing the phone. She picks up the empty urn. 'Can we go home? I'm cold and Grandma says she'll make hot chocolate.'

'That sounds great, Da-Wren! Let's go.'

'Okay, Da-Daddy!'

I scoop her into my arms and we retrace our steps across the sand. A few minutes later, thunder erupts and another bolt of lightning streaks across the sky, illuminating the whole stretch of beach.

'Grandma!' Wren cries, pointing at the figures in the distance.

She slithers down, clutching the urn and her torch, and runs towards them. Sophie follows. I stop as I feel the solid velvet shape in my pocket. This is it . . . The only moment I'll ever have. I flick it open with my thumb.

'Sophie!'

She turns around and gasps as I get down on one knee, producing the open box.

'W-w-what are you doing?'

'I've been waiting all evening for the right moment, but you've shown me there's no such thing as the perfect time.'

I hold up the diamond engagement ring I designed, along with Sophie's necklace and Wren's bracelet, at the Plymouth boutique. It's a solitaire with a Möbius strip engraved on the inside of the gold band, along with our entwined initials.

'I love you with all my heart, Sophie Leroux. It began with you, and it will end with you. You are the love of my life, my forever. Will you do me the honour of agreeing to be my wife? I can't promise to grow old with you and have children or grandchildren. We have no future, only this . . . the here and now. But I promise I will love you passionately until my dying breath, whether that's in minutes or seconds. I want to spend every single one of those numbers with you. I'll treasure them.'

'I will!' Sophie struggles to hold back her tears. 'You'll always be the love of my life, Adam. However long *I* have left on this earth, I want to be with you.'

She stretches out her hand and I slide the ring into place. It's too big and slips down her finger. It needs to be altered, but I won't live long enough to see that happen. I'll never turn around at the altar and see her walking towards me in a beautiful dress, with Wren as our bridesmaid. I'll never have more children or celebrate my daughter's birthdays. We'll never enjoy a family Christmas together . . . The realisation is agonising.

'Let's go, Mrs Bailey,' I gasp, barely able to breathe.

'I love the sound of that, Mr Bailey!'

She helps me to my feet. We kiss, briefly, desperately, before running after Wren, hand in hand.

'Wait for us!' I shout.

Wren turns around and holds the urn up as thunder explodes overhead.

'Look, Mummy. I'm not scared of the big bangs anymore and the pretty lightning is for you!'

We've almost reached her when there's a devastatingly loud crack and a flash of pure white.

'No!' Sophie cries.

She launches herself at Wren, but I get there first, throwing my arms over them both. Pain sears through my body like molten lava, setting every nerve ending on fire.

Sophie screams and drops first.

My knees buckle. I hit cold, wet sand yet I'm plunging deeper and deeper into a furnace, the skin flayed from my body.

Cries ring out but are smothered with hot ash.

Blackness descends in a heavy, smothering veil.

Something swirls feverishly beneath my eyelids.

A tunnel appears, stretching far ahead, filled with dazzling, dancing numbers.

They spin around in infinite combinations and incomprehensible patterns, as if attempting to be solved.

I'm sucked towards the swirling, luminous figures.

I can't find their correct order. I'm losing my own number.

I'm becoming smaller and smaller.

I fade into zero.

59

ADAM

Saturday, 12 April 2025

I'm back!

Blackness explodes into a brilliant frosty white. My numbers have run out, but I haven't disappeared completely. I'm hovering below the storm clouds, watching the people on the beach. Sophie is lying next to my motionless, stricken body. She's not moving either.

Sophie!

I cry out, but my voice doesn't travel far enough.

Wren's head is thrown back, as if she's searching for me in the sky. Her mouth is open wide into a scream. The sound is a gentle murmur by the time it reaches me, but it cuts like a knife.

I'm here, Wren. Don't cry!

But she can't hear me either. I can't swoop down to comfort her or Sophie. I watch, helplessly, as figures run towards them. *Mum and the search party. Two police officers.* A woman crouches next to Sophie. Mum throws herself on to her knees and pulls off my bow tie, undoing my top buttons. A policeman checks the pulse in my neck. Now he's compressing the centre of my chest, too hard. I hear a gentle crack as a rib breaks, but don't feel a thing.

Sophie's moving. *She's* alive!

Mum's neighbour eases Sophie into a sitting position. Her hand covers her right eye. Wren falls into her arms for a hug, before attempting to throw herself at me.

'Daddy! Wake up.'

A policewoman catches her arm, pulling her back, as her colleague continues to pump my chest.

'Let's wait for your daddy over here.'

Wren cries as she's gently led away. Sophie crawls closer to my body and reaches for Mum's hand. They cling on to each other.

'How long for the ambulance?' Mum asks.

'It was diverted to a three-vehicle crash,' the policeman replies. 'It'll be another fifteen minutes.'

'That's too long!' Mum cries.

The policeman listens to my chest and feels my neck and wrist before glancing at his partner. 'Radio for help again.'

'Adam!' Mum cries.

'Breathe for us,' Sophie says, sobbing.

I'm trying! I want to live! I'm still using too many exclamation marks!

I feel the intense pain in Sophie's right eye, down the side of her face and in her heart, even though I'm no longer inside my skin. I absorb the pain in Wren's chest and Mum's.

I'm the first to notice a man running along the beach towards them, clutching a bag. As he draws closer, I recognise him.

Tom!

The group looks up as he shouts and waves.

'You came!' Sophie exclaims, clutching her eye.

'I found a taxi after you left.' He kneels next to the policeman, who is compressing my empty chest. 'I'm an off-duty paramedic. Can you tell me his status?'

'A twenty-eight-year-old male is in cardiac arrest after taking a direct lightning strike. I've performed CPR for one minute but there's no pulse. A female patient also suffered burns to her eye and face.'

Tom glances at Sophie. 'I'll check you over after I've stabilised Adam.' He nods at the officer. 'Keep going while I get this ready.'

He opens his bag and pulls out a black box, sitting back on his heels.

'You brought a defibrillator to the golf club?' Sophie gasps.

He rips open my shirt, making a button pop off. 'I always take my emergency kit to parties, just in case.'

'Because of the car crash,' she states. 'You want to be able to help.'

'That's right.'

He pulls two pads out of a packet, placing the electrodes on my bare torso. An electronic voice from the device announces it is evaluating heart rhythm and preparing to shock.

'Everyone stand clear, please,' Tom orders.

Mum and the policeman help Sophie scramble to her feet.

Do not touch the patient. Delivering shock.

Red-hot pain rips through my chest, tearing veins and arteries and squeezing and cracking bones corset-like.

My heart flutters.

Oxygen rushes in a flood through my body, extinguishing raging fires, but it trickles away. I'm still floating above them as Tom continues CPR for two minutes.

'Please don't stop trying!' *Sophie.*

'Daddy!'

The device issues another command to shock.

'Stand clear!' Tom warns.

Pain surges and subsides. Lights flash on and off, burning brightly like a dying star before being smothered by darkness.

I'm drifting higher and higher into the storm clouds, yet it feels as though I'm sinking . . . I'm surrounded by a mass of whirling whiteness as if I'm back beneath the wave that knocked me off my surfboard as a teenager.

The bubbles transform into numbers, and the tunnel returns. An invisible current drags me towards it. I thought these mathematical sequences were impossible to solve, but I realise the answer is obvious.

It's 3.

Me, Wren and Sophie.

It's the only number that ever mattered: the secret formula for my happiness. No other patterns are as important or meaningful as the ones I've formed with them. They will be everlasting . . .

I feel the figures that form my body, the trillions of blood cells, molecules and atoms, split and reduce in size, getting smaller and smaller.

But I refuse to give up on our beautiful patchwork of experiences, our wonderful future life.

I'm battling my way back towards their voices, away from the powerful, piercing light. I won't quit this life. Not yet. Not ever.

'Stay with us, Adam,' Sophie begs. 'We love you!'

I love both of you. Very much.

'Please, Daddy, stay!'

I want nothing more than to be with the two of you! You've both changed my life for the better! I'll always be with you! I love you both with all my failing heart!

I hold on to this moment for as long as possible.

The three of us together.

Then I'm forced to let go.

60

SOPHIE

SATURDAY, 12 APRIL 2025

Searing heat pours down the side of my face with the sting of a million bees. The lightning struck us both for one-thousandth of a second, with a force of more than 10 million volts and a current of 106,000 amperes. The electrical current stopped Adam's heart, before scorching my cheek and eye. Dressings cover the wounds and the odour of burned flesh fills my nostrils. The devastating sounds from the beach reverberate in my ears: Wren screaming, Mrs B crying and Tom calmly issuing commands and taking over chest compressions. Adam regained a weak, fluttery pulse as the on-duty paramedics arrived. He's being lifted into the ambulance, the urgency in the crew's voices loud and distinct. I'm lying on a gurney in a separate emergency vehicle, Adam's catastrophic number sequence scorched into my mind: 0, and then 1 again when Tom brought him back to life.

Around 3 metres separate us. I can't reach Adam to say goodbye; I try to sit up, but my head feels like it's about to explode.

'Hold still,' a woman says. 'I'm administering morphine. It'll make you feel more comfortable.'

I feel the sharp prick of a needle in my hand and hear the door of Adam's vehicle slam shut. Sirens blare and fade. A child's wail grows louder.

Wren.

Mrs B is comforting her quietly. Now her voice is louder and closer.

'Sophie. It's Jen. We're heading to the hospital. My neighbour's driving me, Wren and Tom. She'll follow the ambulance. I'll come find you when we get there, I promise. I'll see you soon.'

'No,' I whisper. 'Stay with Adam. He needs you.'

Did she hear? I have no idea how much time has passed, how many hours or minutes Adam has left. Whether his heart has failed again and he's gone for good.

'What time is it?'

Mrs B doesn't reply. She must have left.

A door closes; the paramedic speaks but I can't make out her words. The ambulance is moving.

The pain blunts and softens around the edges, slowing my thoughts and making my eyelids heavy. As I slide into a warm, comforting drowsiness, I throw a silent plea out into the universe, 93 billion light years away.

Take me, not Adam.

I send another appeal much closer to home, to the paramedics in Adam's ambulance, which is 650 metres ahead: please don't stop trying to save him.

Don't give up. Don't let him die.

When I open my eyes, the world is sparkling white with hazy grey borders. Everything is shifting. I tilt my head and pain explodes and recedes. The blurriness expands and contracts into oceans of blue.

'Don't panic,' a voice says. 'It will take time for the vision in your left eye to adjust.'

I exhale slowly, gripped by rising nausea.

'I'm Dr Choudhury, an emergency consultant,' the man continues. 'You've suffered second-degree burns to your face and retinal damage in your right eye. There might be minor injury to your left. We're monitoring you and optical surgery isn't ruled out.'

I lift my hand to my face and feel soft wadding.

'Your right eye needs to stay covered, and there's a large dressing on your cheek. We can give you another dose of morphine if you're in discomfort?'

'Not yet.'

I need to stay lucid and awake. My left eye comes into focus, and a man with a black goatee beard and a stretched earlobe piercing gradually appears. He's wearing a dark blue uniform. It takes longer to see his number: 14,010.

'Where's Adam? Is he alive?'

'Your boyfriend's in ICU,' he explains. 'He's in a critical but stable condition.'

Oh God! For how much longer?

'What's the time?'

'Let me check . . . It's 11.21.'

Adam has 39 minutes left.

Paper rustles as Dr Choudhury flicks through his notes. 'I know this is hard to hear, but Adam's been placed into an induced coma to give his body the best possible chance to recover. His mum and daughter are currently with him.'

'I need to be there too.'

I sit up and Dr Choudhury appears to break into two and whirl around my bed.

'That won't be possible yet, sorry. You need to rest while we carry out more tests.'

'No! I have to see Adam. His heart stopped on the beach. He was dead, but our friend, Tom, brought him back.' My voice sounds strangled. 'I'm worried his heart is fatally damaged from the lightning strike. I don't think he's going to make it.'

'My colleagues will do absolutely everything they can to provide—'

'I need to see him before it's too late,' I cut in. 'I'm begging you. This could be my last chance.'

He hesitates. 'Let me see what I can do.'

'Please hurry! I'm scared he doesn't have much time.'

I hold my breath as minutes tick by. I count them silently. Three minutes and 20 seconds later, Dr Choudhury returns with a grey-haired porter pushing a wheelchair.

'Ron will take you to ICU. But this can only be a brief visit, and you must come straight back.'

'Thank you, I will. I need to get there as soon as possible.'

Ron helps me into the seat. 'I'm on it!'

Numbers swirl as we fly through corridors, passing patients, their families and doctors. The digits are faint and fuzzy grey. We take the lift to the fourth floor and I see three figures in the distance: two adults with a child. I screw up my eyes.

Mrs B, Tom and Wren.

'I'm surprised they let you up here so soon!' Tom exclaims as we draw closer.

I squint, taking in their body language: no one is distraught with grief. Adam must be alive!

'I used my famous powers of persuasion.'

He smiles as Ron steps away to give us privacy. I hold out my hands and Wren grabs them, climbing silently on to my lap. I wrap my arms around her.

'Hey, Wren.'

'I've been in to see Adam and was about to come downstairs and look for you,' Mrs B says. 'How are you doing?'

'I'll be okay.' I peer at her. 'What about Adam?'

It takes me a few seconds to realise her eyes are red from crying.

'Daddy's still asleep,' Wren whispers. 'He won't wake up.'

'But he's going to be fine,' Mrs B replies briskly. 'Absolutely fine.'

Tom stares at the floor. Nobody wants to let their guard down in front of her.

'I've asked Wren if she wants to see her daddy, but she's reluctant, which is understandable,' Mrs B says. 'Hospitals are scary places for children. I can bring her tomorrow when she's had time to come to terms with what happened tonight.'

'No!' I say vehemently. 'I mean, it might be more comforting if she can see how well the doctors are caring for him.'

Wren *has* to say goodbye to Adam. This will be her last chance.

I climb out of the wheelchair, turning to Ron. 'I'll be good from here, thanks. I'll get someone to bring me down.' I pause. 'Do you have the time? Just so I know when to be back.'

He hesitates, before removing the walkie-talkie from his belt as it beeps. 'It's 11.36. Make sure you do, otherwise I'll be in trouble.'

I nod, trying to keep my composure as he leaves.

'Why don't we go in together, Wren?' I'm fighting to keep the fear and desperation out of my voice.

'That's a great idea!' Mrs B says. 'What do you think? The nurse says your daddy can have family visitors, one or two at a time.'

Wren's bottom lip trembles and she edges away.

Tom crouches beside her. 'You could talk to your dad. Say hello. It could help him feel better.'

'But he's asleep! He won't hear me.'

'He's not sleeping, he's in a coma, which is different,' he explains. 'Doctors believe people can still hear and feel comforted even though they can't move or reply. Hearing the voices of loved ones can help their recovery.'

'You mean they can wake up?'

Tom nods his head. 'Yes, that can happen. In some cases, certainly.'

His voice is riddled with doubt. Has he realised that Adam won't recover?

'What do you think?' I ask.

'Maybe. I don't know.' Wren stares down at the grey tiles, nudging an abandoned sweet wrapper with the tip of her wellie.

Mrs B's phone rings. 'It's my sister. I need to give her an update. You should take Wren in if she changes her mind. I'll be back in a few minutes.'

She hurries further along the corridor. Wren throws herself on to one of the plastic chairs, swinging her feet.

'I need to make a few calls, then I'll stay with Mrs B,' Tom says.

'What about your dad?'

'I rang his carer from the golf club and he agreed to stay overnight. I can be here as long as you need me.'

'Thank you! If you hadn't arranged to meet Adam at the party and brought the defibrillator . . .' I stumble over my words. 'He wouldn't still be with us.'

'He's not out of the woods yet.' Tom lowers his voice. 'Adam's heart suffered considerable damage from the electrical current. He was placed in an induced coma to protect his organs. The extent of his injuries is severe, Sophie.'

I dig my nails into my palms. He's trying to break it to me gently that Adam's unlikely to pull through.

'I understand,' I say thickly. 'Whatever happens, I'll always be grateful. You couldn't help Lily and the others that night, but you saved Adam on the beach. Thank you for giving us more time, however long that might be. Thank you for everything.'

We hug each other.

'That's what old friends are for,' he replies sadly.

61

SOPHIE

Saturday, 12 April 2025

Tom and Mrs B are further down the corridor on their phones. I have just minutes to convince Wren to see Adam and kiss him goodbye.

I sit next to her. 'Why don't we pop in and see your dad quickly? You can tell him you love him. It will be two minutes tops.'

She shakes her head vigorously. 'I can't. I'm scared!'

'I'll be with you, I promise. It won't be frightening. The nurses and doctors are kind and they're trying to help him.'

'They can't! He won't get better because of me. I did this to him.' She bursts into tears, covering her face.

'No!' I pull her towards me. 'This was an accident. You mustn't blame yourself.'

'If I hadn't gone to the beach, this wouldn't have happened!'

I push a stray tendril of hair from her face. 'Your dad could have been hit by lightning when we left the party or outside your grandma's house. This isn't your fault, I promise.'

'Yes, it is!' she splutters. 'I killed Mummy and now I've killed Daddy.'

I stare at her, confused. 'That's not true, Wren. Why would you think that?'

Thick tears spill down her cheeks. 'I can't tell you. You'll hate me.'

'Never! You can tell me anything.'

'Do you promise on my Moby dip?'

She holds up her wrist, pointing to the bracelet. Memories swirl around my head. Lily called the Möbius strip a Moby-Dick that day on the beach.

'Daddy said this squiggly shape means something is never over, like his and Mummy's love for me. But I think I broke their circles.' Her voice shakes.

'You haven't,' I say quietly, picking up my own pendant. 'I swear on this Möbius strip that I won't hate you. I couldn't – that's a mathematical impossibility.'

She smiles through her tears. 'That's the sort of thing Daddy would say!'

'Tell me,' I urge, lacing my fingers between hers.

Her chest heaves. 'When Mummy was poorly, I got cross because she couldn't go to the park or swimming lessons. She couldn't walk me to school or come to play dates and read me stories at bedtime.' She takes another breath. 'I didn't see her because she spent so much time in bed and that made me sad and angry.'

I nod, squeezing her hand. 'It was a big change in your life, and it was hard to cope with. You wanted everything to go back to normal and for her to be well.'

'But I was mean! I lost my temper when she was too tired to take me to a birthday party. I told her I hated her and wished she was dead already.' Her voice rises in volume as she wipes her face with the cuff of her sweatshirt. 'I never meant it, I swear! I said sorry straightaway, and Mummy kissed me. She said it was okay, but it wasn't.'

'Your mum knew you didn't mean it. She forgave you because she loved you, *always*, like the pattern in your bracelet and my necklace.'

'But I couldn't take it back! She died because of me, because of my bad wish.'

'No,' I whisper into her hair, as her body is racked with more juddering sobs. 'It had nothing to do with what you said.'

'Are you sure?'

'I'm 100 per cent positive.'

'That's another Daddy phrase!'

'I know. I learned it from him.'

'I did another bad thing,' she whispers. 'I was angry at Daddy. I thought he'd forgotten Mummy and didn't care that I want to remember her. I told him I wished he was dead instead of her. I didn't mean that either.'

'He forgave you.'

'Are you sure?'

'He loves you unconditionally – that means his feelings for you don't change even when you fall out.'

She gives me a shy smile. 'Is that how you love Daddy?'

'Yes,' I admit. 'I've always loved him, ever since we were at school.'

'Daddy said the same.' Wren points to the engagement ring that's slipping down my finger. 'Did he give you that?'

'You're observant! Yes, he asked me to marry him shortly before the accident.' I hesitate. 'How do you feel about that?'

'I like it, like *you*.'

'I like you too, Wren. Very much.' My voice wavers with emotion. 'I'll always be here for you, no matter what. Nothing will change that. Ever. I promise.'

I want to be a part of Wren's future even without Adam – if Mrs B will let me. She throws her arms around my waist, hugging me. I kiss the top of her head and squeeze my eyes shut to prevent tears from falling.

'How about we both tell your dad we love him?'

She slides off the seat. 'Okey-dokey. But I'm going to stop making wishes because they give me a tummy ache.'

'Good idea.'

'I'm going to start believing in maths, the way Daddy does. He says it explains everything in the world.'

I clear the lump in my throat. 'He'll be proud of you.'

She flashes me a small smile and takes my hand. After washing our hands with sanitiser, I press the button and push open the door to ICU. It's frighteningly familiar. Hazy figures spring up: there are 10 beds, and 7 members of staff. More appear. I clasp Wren's hand tighter as my heart beats faster and faster.

A nurse approaches and I explain Wren urgently needs to see her dad. She leads us to Adam's bed. He's bare-chested and pale-faced, and has tubes coming out of his head, mouth and chest. His number is still 1.

I stare at the clock, squinting to read the time. It's 11.51 p.m.

'What's that?' Wren asks, pointing at the equipment.

'This monitor is checking your daddy's heart is pumping normally,' the nurse explains. 'Can you see the numbers? It's a good pattern. Don't be afraid. You can talk to him and hold his hand if you want.'

Wren walks up to his bedside and kisses his cheek.

'I love you, Daddy. Sophie loves you too. We're going to be a family. I'm so excited I could go pop, pop, pop!'

She strokes his face and whispers in his ear.

'Is there any change in his condition?' I quietly ask the nurse.

'He's stable for now – he's incredibly lucky a defibrillator was close at hand. We'll continue to do everything we can for him, but the next twenty-four hours will be crucial. Just a couple more minutes, okay?'

I nod, trying to read the clock face. 'Do you have the time?'

'It's 11.53. I need to check on another patient, but I'll be back soon.'

I return to Wren's side.

'Is Daddy going to wake up? Did telling him we love him work?' Her voice is full of hope.

'Let's see.'

I take Adam's hand, praying for a miracle. It's warm, soft and has 34 muscles, 27 bones and millions of capillaries. My fingers lightly brush against his tattoo before landing on his pulse. I'm counting the beats, attempting to ignore the erratic rhythm.

I imagine an infinite number of cells within his body, which are constantly increasing and growing stronger instead of slowly withering and dying. They want to form new patterns, refusing to give up hope. They're desperate to curve into a strip that bends to meet its opposite end, going on forever.

'He's fighting his hardest to come back to us,' I say honestly. 'He wants to open his eyes and talk. He wants to say he loves us both.'

'How can you tell?'

'Feel here.' I take her hand and press her fingers on his wrist. 'I'm counting the number of beats in fifteen seconds and multiplying by four.'

I blink as his heart rate soars above 100 beats per minute, then 120, 125. The monitor beeps in warning accordingly.

The nurse returns. 'Can I show you out, please?'

This is it. Adam is dying and no one can save him, least of all me.

Wren can't be here for his final minutes. I need her to hang on to this memory of her dad, looking as if he's sleeping peacefully.

'We have to say goodbye, Wren.'

She leans over and whispers in his ear. 'I love you, Da-Daddy. See you pop, pop-popping soon!'

Wren mustn't stay for this, but I can't let Adam die alone.

'Go out to Grandma and I'll be right behind you,' I tell her, my voice cracking. 'I need another minute or two.'

'No longer,' the nurse says.

I nod and Wren takes one long final look before being led away. When the door closes behind them, I kiss Adam on the forehead. Then I bring his wrist to my lips, gently kissing his Möbius strip tattoo.

'I'm here,' I tell him as the clock counts down. 'Wren's gone and it's just you and me. I thought I could save you, Adam, but you saved me. You don't have to hold on any longer. Wren has your mum and me. I promise I'll help look after her. You can stop being in pain. You can be at peace.' My final words almost break me. 'It's okay to let go.'

I cover his hand with mine, my head resting next to his on the pillow. His heart rate surges.

An alarm screeches from the monitor and the crash team runs towards his bed.

I squeeze my eyes shut.

I don't want to see his number return to 0.

'I'll love you until the day I die,' I whisper. 'This will never be the end. We'll see each other again one day. We'll always find our way back to each other, however long it takes.'

62

SOPHIE

Friday, 2 May 2025

My patchwork quilt drapes over the coffin in a joyous burst of colour.

I cried when I stitched it, permanently uniting the materials and memories from his family and friends who miss him. All our love and shared histories have slotted into place. Orange, turquoise, light blue and green cottons and cerulean linens unite with yellow satin, shocking-pink tulle, brown plaid and purple organza to pay a dazzling final tribute to an incredible man.

Walking past the casket, I dig my nails into my palms to hold back the tears. I must stay strong for Wren's sake. Her stare sears my face as I step in front of the microphone. Gazing across the cremation chapel, I wait for my eyes to focus. Everything remains foggy around the margins and the mourners form a giant, united mass of bright hues instead of black, because this is supposed to be a happy celebration of life, not a sad memorial. The blurriness clears and the shapes of 211 people appear. Their numbers loom shortly afterwards, but I ignore them and focus on the good: how the threads of this remarkable person's existence touched so many men, women and children, weaving them together in different, wonderful ways.

My vision improves further, and I recognise familiar figures in the closest rows: Wren is being comforted by Mrs B, Tom and her nanny, Anna. Flora's here with Stefan and Libby – they're planning to start a family soon. Bernard has come for moral support, along with Ollie and the rest of Adam's teacher-training friends.

I rub the stone of my engagement ring to give me the strength to carry on. I only recently got it back from the jeweller's after having it sized down.

'I'm incredibly touched and grateful to be allowed to say a few words about such an incredible man who left us all too soon,' I begin. 'He touched my life and changed it forever. He didn't want to let go and fought to stay with his loved ones for as long as possible.'

I blink back the moistness from my eyes, smoothing the skirt of my sea-foam-green silk dress. 'Thanks to him, I'll remember to savour the tiny joys and small moments: the rainbow colours that everyone's dressed in today, the scent from these beautiful flowers, the opportunity to meet more of his friends, and the chance to tell the people closest to me that I love them. Someone here calls me the Numbers Girl because I'm good at maths, but I can't calculate the amount of love in the air. It's impossible to put a figure on.' I bow my head, blowing a kiss at the coffin. 'Thank you for sharing a small part of your life with me and opening my eyes to all the joy in mine. We all love and miss you. Goodbye.'

Somehow, I manage to return to my seat without breaking down. Anna and Tom shuffle along and I squeeze past Adam's mum to sit next to Wren. A middle-aged man approaches the microphone for the final reading: 'The Chariot' by Emily Dickinson. Wren lets out a small sob. Mrs B takes one hand and I hold the other.

'I'm here for you, Wren, like I promised. Your grandma is too.'

Mrs B – I don't think I'll ever get used to calling her Jen – flashes a small, sad smile over her head. She thought Wren was too young to come to the service. We were both worried she'd be traumatised all over again after seeing the lightning strike down Adam, but Wren insisted she had to say goodbye. She helped me stitch three of the panels for the memory quilt. We wanted today's send-off to be perfect.

'Let's get some fresh air,' Mrs B suggests, as Wren's cries grow louder.

We've already agreed to slip out before the curtains close around the coffin; the finality of the act would be too upsetting. Mrs B shuffles out of her seat and we tiptoe to the back, opening the door.

Sunlight dazzles as we step outside. I hold my hand up to my face, momentarily blinded as my vision swims. My left eye is virtually back to normal, but I don't know if the sight in the right will improve; I've been referred to an ophthalmologist for further retina tests.

Wren suddenly breaks free and runs down the path towards a fuzzy shape.

'Wait for us!' Mrs B cries.

I steady myself against the side of the building, waiting for my pupils to become accustomed to the bright light.

The greyish-black blob transforms into a person with a walking stick, holding the lead of a scruffy white dog. Wren throws her arms around the man's waist.

'Careful, Wren,' Mrs B calls. 'You'll knock your dad over!'

'I'm stronger than you think,' Adam says, smiling.

He kisses the top of Wren's head. She hugs him before erupting into giggles as he tickles her. Chico barks loudly and runs around them in circles.

'Stop it, Daddy!' Wren cries.

'I'm chasing away your tears. Walter wouldn't want you to be sad. He asked for everyone to celebrate his life today, not mourn him.'

'I know!' Wren replies. 'People told jokes and laughed. Sophie gave a speech that everyone liked, but it made me cry.'

Adam lifts his gaze and our eyes lock. A grin breaks out across his face. My heart flutters and my stomach lurches, the way my body always reacts when he looks at me. *His* heart stopped on the beach and again in ICU, but the doctors managed to resuscitate him for a second time. He came out of his coma three days later.

Our lucky number is definitely 3!

Adam is rebuilding his balance and mobility with the help of regular physiotherapy. He's determined to walk unaided soon and return to teaching. He volunteered to take a few circuits outside the chapel during the service – Chico was terrified of the clay ornaments Walter's grandchildren had placed by the coffin and wouldn't stop barking.

I see his number clearer as I walk closer: 0.

It remains stuck on this single digit; it hasn't moved during the weeks of his recovery. I kiss him on the lips before petting Chico. Walter drew up a list of last wishes, which included us adopting his dog and giving him a happy home. Other final requests were me giving a short speech, for none of the readings to 'drone on forever or pretend he was a saint', and for everyone to promise to live their lives more, not less. Afterwards, each guest must bring loved ones and friends for another huge party at The Wave.

'How was it?' Adam asks.

'Sad but happy,' I reply. 'Wherever Walter is, I'm sure he'll be reunited with Hellie, and they'll surf a big wave together.'

'I think so too,' Mrs B says, smiling.

She's offered to babysit tomorrow while we go out for dinner for the first time since the accident. She's visiting regularly and is excited for our winter wedding in Modbury at Christmas. Tom and Ollie will be best men and Flora will finally get her wish to be my bridesmaid, along with Wren, who is desperate for snow even before we honeymoon in Iceland.

Chico yaps and pulls on the lead, almost making Adam lose his balance. Mrs B takes the leash from him.

'Why don't we have another quick walk before we drive over to the party, Wren?'

'Okey-dokey, Grandma.'

I wrap my arms around Adam as they walk away. In my peripheral vision, I catch flashes of vivid hues as mourners stream out of the chapel. Tom's wearing bright orange. He waves at us, and chats to Bernard, who's dusted off his favourite cherry-coloured suit. Ollie, Stefan, Flora and Libby follow behind in shades of citrus yellow, shocking pink and lime. Last to leave are Walter's family, Harry and Maddy, and their children, Matilda, James and Luke, who are all dressed in cobalt blue.

'How's your wrist?' Adam asks, nodding at the cuff of my jade-green cardigan.

I peel back the bandage and peep at my Möbius strip tattoo.

'Still a bit sore, but it's healing,' I reply.

'Ditto!'

He lifts my hand to his lips and kisses the ink. I'll never know how many years, months, days, hours or minutes we have left. The final tally will always be a mystery, but every extra second we're together is a gift. Thanks to Walter, I'll savour these small moments we almost lost: Adam's smile as he holds his wrist against mine to make our tattoos meet and become one, the warmth of our skin touching, the sun kissing our foreheads and our eyes lighting up with love for each other.

I'm planning to make the most of everything, including taking over Bernard's dry cleaners. I've used money from the sale of Mum's house to put down a deposit on the rent. I'm turning the premises into a quilting and dressmaking shop and already have orders. Stefan wants a memory quilt for his nan and Joan's granddaughter, Nadia, has commissioned a patchwork bedspread for her brother, Mikey. I'm in regular touch with Nadia, as well as Lily's parents, Betty and Roger. They're all coming to our wedding.

Most of all, I'm looking forward to spending time with my new family.

I see 9,078 shimmering leaves in the old oak tree we're standing beneath, and endless fresh possibilities stretching ahead.

I'll create new, surprising sequences and patterns, with Adam, Wren, his mum and Chico.

Adam's fingers slip between mine and we follow Walter's family and friends to the car park.

'A new café's opened in the countryside close to Bristol, which apparently sells the best carrot cake in the whole world,' he says. 'It's off the beaten track . . . How do you fancy a taxi ride into the unknown tomorrow to try to find it with Wren?'

'The unknown sounds amazing,' I tell him, smiling. 'I can't wait.'

The Times

Friday, 20 February 2026

Dressmaker invents new maths shape – The Lily-Joan – that 'disrupts order'

Sophie Leroux, a keen seamstress, has solved a long-standing maths problem through her love of quilting.

The 28-year-old has invented a new 13-sided shape that can be arranged in an orderly tile formation across an infinite area but will never form a repeating grid.

Mathematicians believe this is significant because it breaks usual patterns, without leaving gaps or overlaps, and may help physicists understand the structure and behaviour of atoms.

Ms Leroux's discovery is all the more amazing because she has no mathematical training and admits to only achieving a D in her maths GCSE.

However, she views the world 'differently' after suffering a brain injury aged 18 and finds sewing a pleasurable way to express the geometric shapes and numbers she sees in daily life.

She included the new shape in a memory quilt she made for her stepdaughter, Wren Ellis-Bailey, nine, following the death of her mother, Carley Ellis, from breast cancer in 2024.

Ms Leroux, who is five months pregnant, has christened the shape 'The Lily-Joan' in memory of a former best friend, Lily, and her old mentor, Joan, who inspired her love of sewing.

Her husband, Dr Adam Bailey, 29, who was awarded a Doctor of Philosophy (PhD) in Mathematics from Stanford University after writing his dissertation on geometric shapes, had recognised the significance of the pattern and sent a photo to his former supervisor, Professor Robert Hunt.

Professor Hunt commissioned further research from a fellow mathematician at Stanford and a group of computer scientists.

Ms Leroux, who owns a dressmaking and quilting shop in Clifton Village, Bristol, said: 'I used to be afraid of all the numbers I could see, but Adam has shown me the beauty in maths.'

Dr Bailey, a maths teacher at Bristol City Academy, said: 'Sophie and I first met as teenagers and fell in love, but we parted under traumatic circumstances.

'However, as a keen mathematician, I always believed in the Möbius strip theory – that even if we travelled in different directions, we would eventually loop back to each other, however long it took.

'That's because true love, like maths, will always find a way.'

ACKNOWLEDGEMENTS

A big thank-you to my brilliant editors, Victoria Pepe and Victoria Oundjian, for their enthusiasm for my book and support. Both loved *Counting Down To You* from the start and helped me craft it into the best possible version. Thank you to the rest of the Lake Union team including copy-editor Jenni Davis, proofreader Sarah Day, and Emma Rogers for the gorgeous cover.

As always, thank you to agent extraordinaire Alice Lutyens, for being a sounding board early on and supporting me throughout.

All the characters and concepts in the book such as the Lily-Joan shape are figments of my imagination and not based on real people or happenings. A new 13-sided geometric shape was actually discovered in 2023 by David Smith, a retired British print technician. His hat-shaped tile, known as the 'Einstein' shape, took the mathematical world by storm.

I'm interested in maths and the workings of the brain – I researched the impact of head injuries online. I'm also fascinated by neurological conditions such as synaesthesia, which I researched for my debut novel, *The Colour of Bee Larkham's Murder*. There is a form of synaesthesia whereby people can visualise numbers spatially around them. However, Sophie's condition is extreme and purely from my imagination.

Sewing is another interest, although I'm yet to make a patchwork quilt. I visited a Kaffe Fassett quilt exhibition at the Victoria Art Gallery in Bath as part of my research, and watched quilting videos on YouTube. A big thank you to the Ealing Quilters for allowing me to come to one of your meetings – particular shout-outs to Carol Wilkes and Rekha Wadhwani. I enjoyed my evening and learned a lot! I also found the book *The Quilter's Bible* by Linda Clements extremely useful.

I chatted with student Matilda Drewett about life at Stanford University, thanks to an introduction from Melody Moppett, and trainee doctor Harry Crook answered my medical queries.

Thanks to my lovely writer friend Sarah Govett, who was an early reader and gave invaluable feedback on my first draft – you're always spot on!

Thank you as ever to my husband, Darren, for helping me with the mathematical aspects of this book, and for your unwavering support.

Thank you to all my family – my mum (an early reader as usual), dad, sons James and Luke, sister, Rachel and mother-in-law, Maureen.

Finally, a big thank-you to my readers for coming on this incredible journey with me.

If you enjoyed *Counting Down to You*, why not read *Meet Me on the Bridge*, also by Sarah J. Harris?

PROLOGUE
MARIANNE HOCKNEY
Sunday, May 9, 2004

'We're late! You're not going to make it, Marianne.'

Mum's voice is tinged with worry, and criticism, as we scan the destination board on the busy concourse at Euston station. A woman streaks past, pulling a large bulky suitcase. I swing Julia out of the way to avoid a collision, but she deliberately makes her knees jelly like and won't stand when I try to put her down. I scoop her up and plant her on my hip.

'Is there a later train you can catch?' Mum asks.

'No! I've told you already – I've booked the tickets and they're non-refundable.'

'Oh dear. You should have set off earlier.'

I stifle a sigh. Mum's rising anxiety – together with her talent for always stating the bloody obvious – isn't helping my own nerves. I'd slept through my alarm clock after yet another disturbed night, punctuated by terrifying dreams. Julia catches hold of a lock of my hair and plays with it, the way she did when she was tiny. She's been clingy ever since I told her I was going away.

Mum squints at the board. 'Glasgow Central is platform one! I don't think you have enough time. The train's already boarding.'

She takes a deep breath. 'Perhaps you should ring and say you can't make it, love? It's not the best timing with everything that's going on.'

'No, Mum! I can't let everyone down at the last minute.'

I need this catering gig. It's cash in hand and could lead to more work at other music festivals and events across the country. A tiny part of me is also desperate to get away. I'm dying to let my hair down and have some fun. I feel like I turned forty-five two months ago, not twenty-five. I'm still processing everything Mum told me; it's a hell of a lot to take in. I should probably book another appointment with the psychiatrist to help get my head straight, as well as the sleep specialist. Maybe persuade my GP to refer me for another brain scan; the hospital *may* have missed a tumour during that battery of tests. I've never felt so unwell. But for the next couple of days, I can forget it all – a music festival on a remote site, miles from civilisation, in the southern uplands of Scotland, where no one knows me, has never sounded more appealing. I feel a small twinge of guilt at leaving Julia, but she'll be happy with Mum.

'I can make it if I run. The ticket barrier's only over there.' I point in the direction of the turnstile, which is blocked by dozens of commuters and tourists.

Mum bites her lip. 'We'll only hold you up. Go ahead, and we'll follow.'

I try to put Julia down again, but she plunges her hands deeper into my hair and holds on tightly.

'Can you let go, Pickle? Pretty please?'

'No!'

'Julia!' Mum tries to prise her fingers free from my tangles. 'Mummy can't miss her train.'

She buries her head into my chest. I pat my necklace, checking she hasn't accidentally pulled it off.

'It's okay. I can carry her if you take the suitcase?'

Mum nods, grabbing the handle. I lead the way through the crowd, my arm aching beneath Julia's weight – she turned five last week and is growing up fast. It feels like only yesterday when I could tuck her into the sling and take her everywhere with me. I jiggle her onto my other hip so I can grab the ticket from my pocket.

'I guess, this is where we'll have to leave you,' Mum says flatly as we reach the gate.

I feel Julia tense beneath my fingertips. I glance at the attendant standing on the opposite side of the barrier.

'Please can they come onto the platform to see me off?'

The fifty-something woman smiles and swipes them through. We lurch towards the platform. The train is only fifty metres away, but it may as well be miles. I'm exhausted despite nodding off twice at the breakfast table and again on the tube here. Luckily, Mum scooped Julia onto her lap; I was out of it for twenty minutes. I'll need another nap on this train. Shortly before my birthday, Mum had explained that the sleep attacks were a genetic condition and they would worsen, but I didn't think they would be *this* bad.

We're both out of breath by the time we reach the correct carriage. Most of the seats are taken; thank God I booked one, otherwise I'd be napping outside the toilet cubicle.

'It's time, Julia,' Mum says, gently. '*Now,* you have to let your mummy go.'

She sighs deeply and slithers down my long, turquoise dress. I'm tempted to snatch her up, turn around and go home with Mum. But haven't I earned some 'me' time?

'You've got everything?' Mum asks briskly. 'You didn't forget to pack your stimulants and other medication in the rush to get here?'

'Of course I didn't!'

She flinches.

'Sorry, Mum,' I say, softening my tone. 'Please don't worry about me. I just need . . . *this.*'

She nods. 'I can't help worrying. You and Julia are all I have now.' Her eyes moisten as she adjusts the belt on her favourite camel coat.

I feel another stab of guilt – Dad's death from cancer three years ago was bad enough, but her only sibling, Rose, was killed in a car crash last November, devastating her further. The pressure that comes with being an only child has never felt so intense.

'Let's talk more when you get back,' Mum continues. 'But please remember what I said and don't do anything silly. You need to look after your health.'

I'm about to hit back with a snarky remark when the announcer says the train is ready to leave. I heave my suitcase into the carriage and turn around.

'Time to go.' I pull Julia towards me, but she resists. 'Do you promise to be a good girl for Grandma?'

'No!' She folds her arms, glowering. She's still furious I'm not letting her come.

'Can I get a goodbye kiss?'

She shakes her head.

I bend down and point to my chest. 'What if I let you play with my necklace as an extra special treat?'

Julia's eyes light up.

'For goodness' sake, Marianne!' Mum looks daggers at me.

'What's the problem?' I say, glaring back. 'It's just a lullaby and she loves it.'

I ignore her and sing: '*Spin the stone and make a change. Transform the world and rearrange.*'

Mum harrumphs disapprovingly as Julia reaches out and taps the gem, making it twirl around, gleaming red and black.

'See? You changed the stone's colour. You're making everyone in the world happy. Can I get a kiss now?'

She darts behind Mum and clings to her skirt.

'Never mind. Bye, Pickle. I love you.'

My heart shrinks a little when she doesn't reply. No doubt Mum will tell me I deserve that snub. Instead, she envelops me in her arms.

'Take no notice. You know she loves you more than anything in the world. Me too.'

I inhale her familiar rose scent. Tears prick my eyes; this is the closest I've felt to her in months after all our heated arguments.

'I love you, Mum.'

'Promise me, you won't keep running away. And you won't stay too long. You'll come back.'

I let go of her abruptly. 'Of course I'll come back. It's only a week!'

I manage to swallow the 'for fuck's sake' I'm longing to add and climb inside, shifting my suitcase further along.

'Remember, Marianne—'

I slam the door shut, cutting off Mum mid-lecture. It feels like a small victory until I attempt to pull down the window and it jams. I can't remind my daughter I love her. Mum puts her arms around Julia and pulls her closer. *Away from me.* They smile warmly at each other. We're separated by glass and something far, far bigger than I can ever begin to describe. The barrier feels solid, *permanent,* preventing me from reaching them.

I grab the handrail to steady myself as I'm hit by a wall of tiredness.

My vision shifts and softens. Mum and Julia are blurry like ghosts, but maybe it's me that doesn't exist anymore. I blink. My eyes fill with tears, obliterating them completely.

Who am I? What kind of mother and daughter can I ever be?

A rubbish one! I'm cracking up and failing them both.

I touch my pendant. I don't want it; *I don't want any of this*. I whip it off and immediately feel lighter, as though a weight has been lifted from my shoulders. I yank hard at the window, pulling it down far enough to dangle out the chain.

'Take it!'

Mum's face brightens as she springs forward. I drop the necklace into her cupped palms.

'Thank you!' she says, sighing with relief. She stuffs it into her pocket. 'Ring me as soon as you arrive, otherwise I'll worry.'

I nod. That's a given – I'll never hear the end of it if I don't call.

'Love you!' I mouth at Julia, but she's deliberately staring further down the platform.

I wave as the train pulls away. Suddenly, Julia breaks free from Mum and runs alongside the glass.

'Stop! I want to kiss you goodbye.'

Tiny daggers puncture my heart.

'Come back, Mummy!'

It's too late. Julia's cries become fainter.

Then she disappears.

1

JULIA

Thursday, May 9, 2024

'She's back!'

My eyes fly open. Where am I? Bright lights. The scent of garlic and tomato. A vibrating, loud noise. *Applause?* It ripples around the table, punctuated by laughter. More sounds: the tinkle of cutlery, the pop of a champagne cork, a woman's voice rising at the end of a sentence. Is she asking me a question? I straighten in my seat. Too late. I'm slipping away. My head nods forward.

'Julia!'

'Oh no! We've lost her again.'

Sounds and lights shrink, becoming a distant pinprick in a never-ending tunnel. I'm swamped by crashing waves of grey nothingness before plunging into ice-cold water. Splashing. Something's dragging me down. I'm sinking beneath the ripples, deeper and deeper. Now, I'm being pulled up and away from danger. An invisible thread draws me towards a handsome man with bluish-green eyes and curly brown hair. He's in soft focus, as if I'm staring at him through a blurred camera lens. Butterflies dance across my stomach as he smiles and reaches out his hand.

Instinctively, I sense I'll be safe. I'm trying to reach him, but the background shimmers. Faint voices pierce the film-like bubble.

'Is she okay?'

The strangers' voices become louder. More insistent.

'Is she always like this? It must be difficult for you.'

Pain stabs my arm. Repeatedly. Red-hot pincers.

'Julia, for God's sake, wake up!'

I'm fighting my way to Ed's voice. My eyelids flicker open briefly. Sharp colours fade fast. Sounds drift from my grasp. I blink and blink.

Stay awake.

I gasp for air. A familiar hot, shameful heat creeps across my cheeks for falling asleep *and* imagining that man who isn't my boyfriend. I have no idea who he is or why he's been making fleeting appearances in my dreams recently, but I'm not complaining. It's far better than my usual nightmares. My lids droop. I widen my eyes, saucer like, trying to resist the invisible invader that wants to drag me to foreign shores. It's hovering on the edges of my brain. Waiting to claim me again. I can't let it. Tonight is important. I can't remember why.

Think.

I check the edges of my mouth for drool and attempt to concentrate. My eyes refocus on a sea of unfamiliar faces. A middle-aged man with black-rimmed glasses glances away. Two twenty-something women are talking behind their hands at the end of the table. They freeze.

Who are these people? What am I doing here?

My brain restarts. I'm in an Italian restaurant in Clapham with Ed's work colleagues and boss, Tony, a classic car enthusiast. I'd been talking to his wife, Sabrina, who was far less passionate about his hobby. Before we'd set off from White City, Ed admitted he'd researched famous old cars to impress Tony, ahead of next week's pay appraisal. He'd begged me to chat to members of the marketing company and their partners.

Unspoken words had lingered between us:

Please make a good impression.

Don't embarrass me.

Oh God. That ship has long sailed.

'I'm so sorry,' I blurt out. 'I can't help it. I have no control over when it happens. The tiredness just hits me.'

No one speaks. Someone a few seats down clears their throat. An uncomfortable silence lengthens. I wait for Ed to leap to my defence, the way he used to when we first got together, but his mouth is a tight, straight line. His hands grip the sides of the chair, his shoulders rigid.

'How long was I out for this time?' I whisper, leaning closer.

'About ten minutes *and* you were snoring,' he hisses. 'I couldn't wake you.'

'Sorry.'

That's a word I've used a lot recently. I feel for his hand under the table, but it's out of reach.

'Don't worry,' Tony says. 'My wife sends me to sleep with some of her stories. Don't get her onto the subject of her sewing group. You'll definitely nod off!'

Sabrina rolls her eyes dramatically. '*I* do that when you talk about restoring Jaguar E-Types!'

She flashes me a sympathetic smile but I'm dying inside. I'd asked Ed to explain my narcolepsy to everyone before we came tonight in case I had an attack, but it must have slipped his mind. Now I feel like the evening's circus act.

'It's not that, I promise. My brain can't regulate sleeping and waking properly. I fall asleep at inappropriate times.'

'*Very* inappropriate times,' Ed says, laughing loudly. 'Like at your birthday party last week when you fell off the chair! It was incredibly dramatic – worthy of an Oscar.'

I take a swig of Diet Coke; my throat is horribly dry. 'Thank you! Florence Pugh had better watch out. I'm after all her roles.'

I'm playing along, but my cheeks burn hotter. I shoot him a look – he could have picked a million better ways to lighten the mood.

Miranda, the firm's latest recruit, giggles, making her dangly star earrings shimmer delicately. 'Omigod. That's terrible!'

Ed has previously described her as annoying and loud, but he obviously forgot to mention she's also flirty and attractive. She tosses her long, blonde mane and nudges his arm. 'What happened? Spill the beans!'

I stare harder at Ed, silently begging him to stop, but he's on a roll and had too much to drink.

'The waiter almost tripped over her, but never spilt a drop from the beer glasses on his tray. He was a total pro!'

Miranda snorts with laughter, her hair brushing against his suit sleeve. 'God, I can't even begin to imagine what that must have been like.'

No, you can't.

'It was a shock.' Ed takes a large gulp of wine. 'Luckily, Julia wasn't hurt.'

I catch hold of his hand as it returns to the table and squeeze it gently. He knows I hate discussing my episodes with strangers, and my birthday party is an evening I want to erase from my memory *forever.*

'Yeah, but—'

I apply more pressure. He finally gets the message and gives me a brief, apologetic smile as the waitress returns to our table. He loosens his old Harrovian tie and takes off his jacket, slinging it over the back of the seat.

'How are we doing for drinks?' the young woman asks. 'Can I get anyone a coffee or a liqueur?'

Tony bangs the table with his fist, making his wife wince. 'I fancy a port. What about anyone else?'

I grab my handbag, seizing the chance to escape. 'I'll be back in five.'

'Sure thing,' Ed mumbles.

Miranda swishes her hair as I pass her chair. 'Will she be okay on her own?'

I don't hear Ed's reply. He reaches for another bottle of red and tops up their glasses. They clink them together. I want to tell Ed to slow down before he blurts out something he'll regret in front of Tony. But I can hardly lecture him when I've created a spectacle. I weave my way through the closely positioned tables to the bathroom and lock myself inside a cubicle. Tears slide down my cheeks.

Why is this happening to me?

I already know the answer. In some rare cases like mine, narcolepsy runs in families due to an inherited genetic fault. I'll thank Mum for the permanent leaving present if she ever bothers to get in touch with me or Gran again. The bathroom door creaks open as I tear off a piece of tissue and dab beneath my eyes. I hear footsteps, a tap turning on and water splashing into a basin. I breathe out slowly. I need to go back to the GP; the stimulants she prescribed aren't working. If anything, I'm getting worse. The episodes have been happening up to a dozen times a day since my twenty-fifth birthday. Ed is probably describing in graphic detail how I ruined my party last Friday. When I came round on the restaurant floor, I couldn't stop crying about Mum. It felt like she'd abandoned me yesterday, not twenty years ago.

I unlock the cubicle, praying one of the cold-eyed girls from the end of the table, or worse still, Miranda, hasn't followed me in.

Thankfully, the elderly woman rummaging in her handbag by the sinks isn't from our party. I peer in the mirror. Jesus. I resemble Dracula's bride. My short-sleeved black blouse emphasises the ghostly pallor of my face. My eyes are bloodshot from crying and mascara is streaked beneath them for added gruesome effect. The humidity in the restaurant has curled my hair into tight, red corkscrews; it never stays straightened for long. I pull out my brush and make-up bag, searching for powder to fix my shiny nose before moving on to the rest of my 'raised from the dead' appearance.

'You have beautiful hair,' the lady remarks, dabbing at her face from a powder compact. 'Such a lovely colour and texture.'

She looks older than Gran – mid to late eighties – and has deep wrinkles engrained on her forehead and cheeks, but her blue eyes sparkle brightly, and her white hair is cut into a fashionable bob.

'That's kind of you, but *this* is the bane of my life.' I hold up an unruly tendril. 'Sometimes I think I should cut it all off.'

'No, you must make the most of everything while you can.'

Her voice is tinged with sadness. Her liver-spotted hands shake as she grips the side of the basin to steady herself. She's frailer than I first thought.

'Are you okay? *You* look fantastic by the way.'

'When you get to my age . . .' She coughs, clearing her throat. 'It hurts to remember things you took for granted in your youth. Your looks, career, friends . . . You don't realise how quickly everything can be taken away.'

She smiles but it doesn't reach her eyes. They've moistened.

'I'm sorry.'

She forces a brittle laugh and applies lip balm. 'Ignore me. I'm being maudlin. Don't let a tired, old woman ruin your night.'

'It's already ruined.' I sigh as I dab at the dark streaks beneath my eyes with a tissue.

'Boyfriend trouble?' She snaps her compact shut.

'Possibly.'

'I've had some bad boyfriends in my time too. You should dump him.'

My mouth falls open as I stare at her in the mirror. God, she's blunt, like Gran was – still is when she has brief moments of lucidity. They both come from an era when you could apparently say whatever the hell you wanted to people, including total strangers. Or, maybe, when you get to a certain age you don't care anymore and tell it straight.

I give my hair a quick brush and throw everything into my bag. 'My boyfriend's great. He'll be wondering where I am. It was nice meeting you . . .'

She hesitates. 'Patricia.'

I feel a tiny shiver down my spine as she stares at my arm. I glance down. Small crimson bruises have sprung up across my pale skin, the same as last week.

She sniffs. 'That's what your generation calls "a red flag", I believe.'

I gasp, remembering the shooting pain while I was asleep. Was Ed pinching my arm to wake me?

'Honestly, it's not what you think . . .'

'That someone gripped your arm tightly and left fingermarks?'

I open my mouth to argue.

'It can be scary to make the break,' she continues. 'But believe me, you're far better off on your own than stuck in a relationship with someone who doesn't respect you. I hate to . . .' She stops herself, shuddering. 'I can't bear to see a young woman treated badly.'

Omigod! This is embarrassing. She's completely misunderstood the situation.

'It's fine, honestly. Ed hasn't hurt me. Well, he didn't mean to. You see . . .' My voice trails off. I can't face explaining my condition again tonight. No one ever truly understands. 'Please don't worry about me. Ed's a good man. We're happy.' I pause. '*I'm* happy.'

Her eyebrows raise. 'You don't look happy. Good men don't make their girlfriends cry or give them bruises. Why don't you leave him? What are you afraid of?'

I glare at her. *How dare she?* I shouldn't have to defend our relationship to an interfering old woman. She's grasped the wrong end of the stick. She doesn't know anything about me or Ed, but she's judging us both. And she's crossed *way* over the line.

I grit my teeth, resisting the urge to tell her to mind her own business.

'Goodbye, Patricia,' I say, marching away. 'Enjoy the rest of your night.'

'Goodbye . . .'

The door swings shut.

Before it closes completely, I spin round. I swear I heard a single word drift out.

Julia.

ABOUT THE AUTHOR

Sarah J. Harris is an award-winning author and freelance education journalist who regularly writes for national newspapers. *Meet Me on the Bridge*, published by Lake Union, was an Amazon ebook bestseller in the UK and US.

Sarah grew up in Sutton Coldfield, West Midlands, and studied English at Nottingham University before gaining a postgraduate diploma in journalism at Cardiff University.

Her debut novel, *The Colour of Bee Larkham's Murder*, won the Breakthrough Author award from Books Are My Bag and was a Richard and Judy pick.

Sarah is a black belt in karate and a green belt in kickboxing. She lives in London with her husband and two sons.

Follow the Author on Amazon

If you enjoyed this book, follow Sarah J. Harris on Amazon to be notified when the author releases a new book!
To do this, please follow these instructions:

Desktop:

1) Search for the author's name on Amazon or in the Amazon App.
2) Click on the author's name to arrive on their Amazon page.
3) Click the 'Follow' button.

Mobile and Tablet:

1) Search for the author's name on Amazon or in the Amazon App.
2) Click on one of the author's books.
3) Click on the author's name to arrive on their Amazon page.
4) Click the 'Follow' button.

Kindle eReader and Kindle App:

If you enjoyed this book on a Kindle eReader or in the Kindle App, you will find the author 'Follow' button after the last page.